SLEEPSPELL

There, in the blackness of her mother's little rose garden, Kyra wrought her spells. She called up the Circles of Light, and Earth, and Air. Then she built the house within her mind. Room by room she touched it, every surface, every angle and smell, down to the pattern of her mother's comforter and the jumble of her father's shaving things.

Sleep, she thought.

Sleep fill this house.

Sleep fill this house . . .

Then, finally, she settled back on her heels. To her inner perception of magic, her spell felt hard and smooth, like blown glass cooled perfectly to its final shape. She listened to the sounds of deep breathing and of slumber.

It was, she realized, the first great magic she had ever done.

Completely illegal, of course . . .

By Barbara Hambly
Published by Ballantine Books:

DRAGONSBANE

Sun Wolf and Starhawk
THE LADIES OF MANDRIGYN
THE WITCHES OF WENSHAR
THE DARK HAND OF MAGIC

The Windrose Chronicles
THE SILENT TOWER
THE SILICON MAGE
DOG WIZARD

The Darwath Trilogy
THE TIME OF THE DARK
THE WALLS OF AIR
THE ARMIES OF DAYLIGHT

Sun-Cross
RAINBOW ABYSS
THE MAGICIANS OF NIGHT

STRANGER AT THE WEDDING

THOSE WHO HUNT THE NIGHT

SEARCH THE SEVEN HILLS

STRANGER AT THE WEDDING

Barbara Hambly

A Del Rey Book
BALLANTINE BOOKS • NEW YORK

A Del Rey Book
Published by Ballantine Books

Library of Congress Catalog Card Number: 93–90862

ISBN 0–345–38097–5

Manufactured in the United States of America

First Edition: April 1994

10 9 8 7 6 5 4 3 2 1

For George Alec Effinger

Special thanks goes to Janus Daniels for his workshop on neurolinguistic programming, "Thinking Like a Writer," for the inception of the seed of this idea, and to Kathleen Woodbury and her Salt Lake City Writer's Workshop.

Although this story takes place in the Empire of Ferryth, neither Antryg Windrose nor Joanna Sheraton is part of it.

PROLOGUE

"IT TURNED TO BLOOD. THE WATER TURNED TO BLOOD."

Kyra the Red's fingers shook as she picked up the bronze candlestick she had knocked over and summoned fire back to the burnt stump of the wick. Wavery light broadened in the darkness of the Summer Hall, picking out the twisted shadows of the monsters, flowers, and birds carved on the ceiling beams. The maple tree growing up through the floor—and out again through the thatch of the roof—had put out clusters of new leaves that the candle's glow turned into tiny, trembling hands.

Kyra's mentor and teacher, the Lady Rosamund Kentacre, leaned forward, frowning not in disbelief but in puzzlement. Her fingers brushed the translucent porcelain bowl on the table's marble top. The water within was as clear as it had been fifteen minutes previously, when, with proper incantations, Kyra had dipped it from the fountain in the court outside.

"Water sometimes turns colors during a scrying or a divination," the Lady said, angling the bowl a little so

1

that the small, clear reflection of the candle flame danced on the surface, and secondary glints flickered in her jade-green eyes.

At forty-one, after twelve years of teaching novices here in the Citadel of Wizards, Rosamund still retained the breathtaking beauty for which she was famous, though her coal-black hair had begun, last spring, to gray. "In some ways water is the easiest medium in which to see things far away, certainly the easiest to see across time. But water is frequently a liar. What were you seeking to see?"

"It was just practice," Kyra insisted, and leaned her bony elbows on the table. Her voice was steady and matter-of-fact; it was a curious voice, husky, like cinders and honey, like an old woman's, though she was only twenty-four. Amber splinters of candlelight threaded her coarse hair with copper as she moved her head; her level, dark brows flexed with distress. "I'd heard there was to be a dancing over in the town of Lastower, with the fur traders coming in. I thought I'd practice on that; I have exams next month. And then ..."

The helpless gesture of her hands nearly overset the candle again.

"Seeing the color blue in the water during divination can mean that another wizard is seeking you," the Lady said thoughtfully. "Sometimes when one sees a green aura, it means—"

"This wasn't the *color* red, Rosamund." The mended old chair creaked as Kyra leaned forward, her strong fingers catching the older woman's slender wrist, willing her to believe. "This was *blood*. It looked like it, it ... it *smelled*." Despite her outer calm, Kyra's mind flinched from the shock of the memory, the sudden flooding of ruby-dark viscosity that had wiped away the drenched indigo darkness, the gay torchlight and bright skirts she'd seen in the scrying-bowl, the horrible sweetish stench that had stabbed her nostrils. Just for an instant she had the hideous sense that if she'd put her finger into the bowl, the liquid would have been warm.

She could barely bring herself to look at the fragile old vessel, its cracked green glaze the color of cabbage against the pitted white of the table's surface. But water was clearly all it now contained.

Rosamund leaned down to sniff it, then dipped her fingers and tasted. "Curious," she said. "Most odd."

"Damn it, it's the fourth time!" Kyra paused in her pacing, turning helplessly to face the assembled master-wizards in the Senior Parlor. Along the room's north wall diamond-paned windows looked out over the Citadel battlements to the endless flat wastes of spruce forest and snow-fringed bog: the Sykerst, swallowed in cold spring darkness, utterly without sight of any dwelling's lights as far as human eye could see.

In this, one of the older sections of the Citadel, tiled fireplaces had not been replaced by more efficient stoves. The cheery flicker of burning pine boughs vied with the softer, brighter light of half a dozen glowing balls of witchlight that floated like errant bubbles among the rafters. On the opposite side of the wide hearth from Lady Rosamund, the mage called Daurannon the Handsome stared contemplatively into the blaze; on the floor beside him, gray-haired Issay Bel-Caire, known as the Silent, sat trailing twigs for the edification of three Citadel cats.

From where he stood with his shoulder against the rough brick chimney breast, Nandiharrow the Nine-Fingered said, "That spread you saw in the cards yesterday could have meant anything, Kyra. Cards are even more unreliable than water-scrying."

"The Death card turning up in ten out of twelve practice spreads?" Kyra's eyebrows levitated, and she shook back the auburn masses of her hair. "And always in the same position? No matter what question I asked? That sounds reliable to me."

"The Death card doesn't necessarily mean death." Issay would occasionally go for a year or two, or five, without speaking, with no explanation—but the period since March had been relatively talkative.

"Well . . ." Bentick, the Steward of the Citadel, looked up from his cribbage game and waved one immaculate hand dismissively. *"Cards . . ."*

"It still doesn't explain the Summonings." Daurannon's hazel eyes went from Rosamund to the others and then returned to the gray-robed, gawky junior on the intricate red and blue rug. He explained, "She's been working on Summonings all week. You know she had trouble with it on the last exam. Two days ago we were out on the hills, summoning clouds. But instead we got winds from all corners under heaven, winds so violent for a few moments that they forced the birds down out of the sky. I was with her. I know she had the words, the runes, the Limitations, absolutely correct."

Rosamund stirred uneasily in her chair. The Summoning of clouds—in fact all weather working—was such a basic form of magic that there was no possibility of Daurannon mistaking what Kyra had done.

"Last night I was in the gardens, summoning moths," Kyra added slowly. "I just need practice in the basic Circles and Limitations for my exam. And again, though no one was with me, I'm certain I performed the spells right. I don't make mistakes like that." She looked from one to the other of her teachers. "You know I don't. I haven't since I was a novice."

Nobody said anything. In the silence, threads of music could be heard from the Junior Parlor a floor below, where Zake Brighthand was playing the lyre. The sound of Bentick's coffee cup against his green porcelain saucer was like a sword blade falling on a stone floor.

"What came were flies," said Kyra. "Flies, at night." She looked nervously down at her hands, her stomach curling a little in on itself with the memory of the disproportionate horror she had felt at the whining drone of the insects' wings. It seemed to her that they had come from everywhere, crawling on her face, blundering into her ears and hair—it seemed to her, just for an instant, that she had felt hot within her robe and that her nostrils had been filled with the stench of garbage and human sweat. But of that she could not even speak.

All the mages were silent. The True Name of moths, by which such creatures could be summoned, was *phasle*; for flies, *dzim*. There was little room there for a mistake.

"It may be that you're simply tired," Nandiharrow said at length. "It happens, you know. Your examinations are coming up, and I know how hard you've been working. The concentration . . . warps."

"I am *not* tired!" Kyra began indignantly.

"Or it may be," Issay said in a voice like wind in weeds, "that there is some other . . . influence . . . skewing your magic. Something over which you have no control—something about which you may never learn. The conjunction of stars under which you were born— some power of your own that is affected by the migration of certain birds. Such things are not unknown, and in time—and usually not very much time—the effects simply pass off."

Kyra flung up her hands. "Well, that's gratifying to hear," she sighed. "I'm supposed to test for the next level in three weeks. Now you're telling me my only recourse is herb tea and bed rest."

"Well." Daurannon looked like a rueful cherub when he smiled. "I would have said 'patience,' but I suppose that comes to the same thing."

Someone scratched at the door. Bentick glanced at the gold watch around his neck and said, "Come," and one of the sasenna—the soldier-servants of the Citadel—entered, carrying the day's mail, a sheaf of letters, two or three western scientific journals, a newspaper from Angelshand for Otaro the Singer, and a small package that he handed to Phormion Starmistress, who was quietly sorting through her cribbage hand during

the discussion. As the others took various missives—
wizards as a rule corresponded widely—her ladyship
rose from her chair and walked over to Kyra, who, in
stepping politely out of the group, had managed to snag
her sleeve on a small armillary sphere on the table beside her and barely managed to rescue it from falling.

"The examination can be put off, you know, if there
are still ... strange effects ... connected with your
working of certain magics."

"I appreciate that—and thank you very much." Kyra
set the spiky network of concentric rings back on the table and tried to conceal her dissatisfaction with this so-
lution to the problem. "But I'd feel a great deal better
if I knew why this was happening so I can take it into
account if I need to work a spell or something in an
emergency. It's bad enough having to alter spell-
weaving in time to the phases of the moon."

"Yes," Rosamund sighed ruefully. "If it's any comfort to you, I am *not* looking forward to relearning half
my own magic in ten years when my own moon cycles
cease ..."

"Kyra Peldyrin?"

The guard was standing at her elbow, a last letter in
his hand. "I looked for you down in the Junior Parlor.
Cylin said you might be up here."

Kyra noted automatically that the letter was written
on rose-pink paper, folded in thirds, and sealed. It took
her a moment to recognize the handwriting. Graceful as
a garland of flowers, it was very similar to her own.
The last time she'd seen it, it had not been nearly so
well formed.

Excusing herself, she retreated to one of the tall-
backed, old-fashioned chairs that surrounded the long
parlor table and broke the seal.

Angelshand, March 1

Dearest Kyra,
This is to let you know that Father has finally ar-

*ranged a marriage for me, a truly splendid match. I
am to wed Blore Spenson, the new President of the
Guild of Merchant Adventurers and one of the
wealthiest men in Angelshand.*

*We're to be married on the first of May, in the strict
form and with great ceremony. I'm writing because I
want your good wishes to be with me, and I'm not
even sure Father will send you an announcement. You
know how he is.*

*Still, I wanted you to know. On the first of May, look
in your magic mirror and you'll be able to see me
standing up before the Bishop of Angelshand in all
the splendor Father can possibly buy. Please wish me
well and know that, in spite of everything, I will always remain,*

Your loving sister,
Alix

Kyra smiled ruefully and slipped the folded papers
into the pocket of her gray wool robe. Yes, she thought.
She knew how her father was. She would get no
announcement—much less an invitation—from him.
For the first two years of her studies—until her mother
had written—she hadn't even been sure he knew where
she was.

It was just as well, she supposed with a sigh. Alix
had always been the pretty one. It had been a long time,
Kyra realized, since she'd even sought the images of
her family in her scrying-crystal. At first the pain had
been too sharp; later there had seemed to be no point.
But she knew that her younger sister had grown from
fairylike charm into truly striking beauty. The sight of
her coquetting among the sons of the wealthy merchants
and bankers of Angelshand—with perhaps the odd
scion of Court nobility here and there, the ones whose
parents had instructed them to marry heiresses—would
probably have been more than Kyra could have taken
with a straight face. Even if she, the older and decidedly

unmarriageable daughter, hadn't entered the College of
Wizards—even if she'd remained at home with a private tutor and become a dog wizard, outside the Council's jurisdiction—her own acid comments wouldn't
have improved the situation with her father.

If she knew Gordam Peldyrin, president of the Bakers' Guild and leading corn broker of the city of
Angelshand, for the past six years he'd been working
like a squirrel in a cold autumn to get the other merchants of the capital to forget that the elder of his
daughters had so disgraced herself as to have been born
with the powers of wizardry. Possibly to forget that he'd
ever had more than one daughter at all.

Kyra shut her eyes, her wide mouth just a little wry.
President of the Merchant Adventurers . . . quite a coup.
Better than her dull and fussy cousin Wyrdlees, at any
rate. She remembered old man Spenson—dessicated,
dyspeptic, iron-willed, and wealthier than most of the
nobility. He'd probably be Mayor of Angelshand by
now, with her father bowing to him deeper than ever.

But with a double portion for Alix's dowry—her own
and Kyra's—the match was hardly a surprise. Garlands
of hothouse gardenias and gold-threaded veils and sufficient rose petals to carpet the streets from Baynorth
Square to the Old Bridge and a traditional crimson wedding gown fit to make the daughters of the courtiers
look like washerwomen. And Alix, beautiful as she,
Kyra, had never been beautiful . . .

Kyra wondered if the Church's tame wizards still
routinely set spells of scry-ward on sacred buildings—it
was a practice that had fallen into abeyance in many cities. Just like Alix not to know. Of course she might
very well scry in the crystal to see the procession. If the
marriage was to be celebrated by the elaborate ceremo-
nials prescribed by the Holy Texts, that alone should be
something to behold.

Or water—water-scrying sometimes worked even
against spell-wards . . .

She shuddered suddenly as the memory flooded back of water darkening to crimson, of the hot feral stink.

She shook her head, sickened. No, she thought, not water.

Just as well that she had her examinations to study for and this curious skew in her magic to occupy her attention. It would give her something to think about other than the hurt of an exile it had taken her six years to forget.

Around the fire the seniors, the master-wizards, were talking quietly, sharing journals and correspondence and old jests among themselves. Her teachers, her colleagues to be. Not perfect—last spring's upheavals with renegade magic had left their mark on the faces of Phormion and Otaro, and at the moment Bentick was fussing about the iniquity of the village contractors hired to rebuild one of the Citadel's covered bridges that had been wrecked in the confusion—but closer to her in some ways than her family had ever been.

There wasn't one of them, she reflected, whose family would be comfortable about admitting a connection. They had chosen one another, passing through this pain she now felt to the serenity of their chosen path.

As would she, one day.

Herb tea and patience, indeed!

CHAPTER I

"OH, MY GOD."

In the nearly twenty years Kyra had known Barklin Briory, she had never seen her father's butler shaken from the magisterial calm imposed by her office. But by the look on Briory's round, stern face when she opened the door and saw what waited for her on the tall brick porch in the misty twilight, it was clearly touch and go.

"Miss . . ." Briory swallowed hard. "Miss Kyra."

"In the flesh." Kyra pushed back the black woolen hood from her hair, picked up the battered tapestry satchel that had been her only luggage when she had left Angelshand six years before, and breezed past the stunned servant and on into the hall. "I take it I haven't missed the wedding. Is my father at home?"

The great central hall of the house hadn't changed. Above the honeycomb pattern of faded yellow sandstone tiles it rose to the full height of the building, galleried at the second and third stories where doors opened into the living and sleeping quarters of the family. The rafters, forty feet above her head, had been freshly painted, their carved flowers touched up with crimson and cobalt and their edges freshly gilt, and the gilding around the house shrine of the Holy Widow Wortle had been renewed as well. A new hanging of plum-colored velvet covered the niche where the family's ancestral masks were kept. Lilacs, tuberoses, and towering sprays of stock brightened the hall's corners like multicolored bonfires, though the cold of the room deadened their scent. Outside, the house didn't have much in the way of facade—none of the fortresslike mansions that fronted onto Baynorth Square did, their owners being far more interested in cherishing their goods indoors than in display for the undeserving hoi polloi in the streets—but its porch and steps had been set with urns of thick-fleshed gardenias, and chains of smilax and ivy swagged above the massive front doors. Personally, Kyra thought the effect rather like that of a lace cap on a bull, but she knew hothouse gardenias were very expensive this time of year, and as far as her father was concerned, that was the point.

"Yes, miss." Briory's blue eyes bulged somewhat as she surveyed the tapestry satchel and its implications sank into her appalled consciousness. "That is . . . I will inquire. If you would care to wait in the book room . . ."

She curtseyed just slightly as Kyra strode past her toward the carved door at the foot of the stairs. The curtsey, Kyra guessed, had cost the butler some inner debate, but she knew Briory could conduct such debates with the speed and efficiency of the weaving machines in the new steam-run factories down by the river. To have curtsied as to a member of the family would, of course, have been to disregard Master Gordam Peldyrin's formal disavowal of his eldest child; to omit all mark of recognition would have been to relegate a member of the family to the status of a tradesman. There were those—the butler almost certainly among them—who would say that Kyra had sunk herself far

below even that status, but Briory thought too much of
the rest of the household to admit it.

"Thank you." Kyra caught herself with practiced ease
on the book-room door jamb as she tripped on the marble threshold; Briory closed her eyes briefly. In some
unacknowledged corner of her mind, she'd clearly been
hoping this was all a nightmare. But no nightmare
would have included Miss Kyra tripping over her own
feet.

In a moment the butler followed her in, carrying the
tapestry satchel as if it contained snakes and poison.

The first hurdle cleared, Kyra thought. For days
she'd lived with the fear that she wouldn't even be admitted to the house.

She reached out with her mind to kindle the lamps on
her father's desk, more for Briory's sake than for her
own. As a wizard, she could see clearly in the dark. The
butler started almost imperceptibly as, within their
glassy chimneys, the wicks sprang into flame, immediately followed by the lights of the seven-branched porcelain candelabra on the room's long table. At the
Citadel Kyra had forgotten the effect such things had on
those who weren't used to being around the mageborn.
The rosy amber glow broadened over the shelves of her
father's ledgers, year after year of corn bought and sold,
of sea coal and wood for the five bakeries operating in
various corners of the city, of purchase orders for the
great charity hospitals and barracks, of investments in
merchant ships, tenements in Southwall, farms. A
twinge of guilt plucked at her like sharpened tweezers
at the sight of the abacus and wax calculating tablets on
the table, the pens and blotters grouped like sleeping
pets around the candelabra's base. *Who helps him in
here now?*

Not Alix, that was certain.

A fire still flickered low in the grate, its warmth, after
the chill of the hall, welcoming. When Briory left her,
Kyra walked to the shelves and ran her hand gently

along the backs of those prosaic brown books. At one time she had known every page of them. There were dozens exclusively in her handwriting: the dull earth from which flourished the gay colors of the Peldyrin family's wealth.

Those colors lay in great rolls immediately beneath the bookshelves, bannerets and pennoncels and hangings to decorate the house for the wedding feast. All new, she saw, the purple and yellow of the Peldyrins fresh and unfaded. Among them she discerned the softer buff and blue of Lord Earthwygg, her father's noble patron at the Emperor's Court. She bent to examine the big hangings more closely and smiled. They were embroidered and appliquéd rather than painted, of course.

She rose, smiling, and dusted off her hands. "Trust Father," she said aloud, "to have nothing but the best."

"You mean trust Father to let everyone know how much we can afford."

Kyra spun around with such suddenness that she knocked over the nearest pennon staff and, in scrambling to catch it, overset three more. The beautiful nymph who had been framed in the book room doorway laughed and ran to her side, helping her prop the long bundles against the wall again.

"Good heavens, Alix!" Kyra stepped back in surprise, and her sister caught her in a delighted embrace. It was strange to feel the younger girl's chin on her collarbone, those delicate shoulders high enough for her to put her arms around them.

"Are you surprised I've grown?"

"Certainly not. You'd have looked tremendously silly if you'd remained four feet, seven inches tall all your life." Stepping clear to look at her, Kyra was a little breathtaken nevertheless, although she'd known even six years before that Alix would be beautiful. Even *this* beautiful.

Alix was, in fact, everything that her older sister was not or was slightly too much of: tall enough to set off the hooped skirts of her lettuce-green silk gown without Kyra's gawkiness, with enough amber in her eyes to lighten their brown to brightness without those disconcerting tawny glints. The dark rust of her older sister's hair survived only as a burnishing flame in the masses of golden curls, and while the red hair was coarse textured to frizziness on wet days like this one, the blond was only luxuriantly thick. Framed in those corn-silk ringlets, with clusters of pink rosebuds and sprays of forget-me-nots, Alix's face was a delicate oval, while the sharpness of Kyra's cheekbones and jaw turned her face nearly square; also, Alix's voice was a low, pleasing alto, well above the drawling huskiness of the other's tones.

Alix was laughing. "It might have been better if I had. You know, I'm only an inch shorter than Master Spenson. Tellie—you remember Tellie Wishrom? Neb Wishrom's daughter next door?—says her father's been negotiating to have her marry Mole Prouvet, and Mole's *inches* shorter than she is, though I think he's *perfectly* sweet in spite of having his nose buried in a book all the time. It's so wonderful to see you! I didn't think you'd come!"

"Quite obviously neither did Briory."

"Poor Briory! The house has been in chaos—they have to put up the banners, and the big garlands for the banisters and the pillars on the porch tonight, as soon as Master Spenson and the other guests leave. Master Spenson and the Bishop and Lord Earthwygg are all coming for dinner, you know."

"Well," Kyra purred ruefully, "Father *will* be thrilled to see me. Hence the gown . . ." Her gesture took in her sister's embroidered petticoat with its cream-colored lace and bunches of silk flowers, while her somewhat harsh features melted into a smile. "In which you look beautiful, by the way."

"Oh . . ." Alix blushed a little and shook her head.

"It's just the dress. This shade of green was always my color."

"Dress forsooth. You were always twenty times prettier than I, though I suppose the same statement could as accurately be made about Mother's lapdogs."

It had taken Kyra some years to become reconciled to that fact.

Alix's eyes twinkled. "Now, you shouldn't make comparisons like that! Those lapdogs are specially bred to be beautiful. But yes, Papa's gone into one of his fusses to get everything ready. I think if the Emperor's Regent showed up for dinner, Papa would fly into a frenzy about having to lay an extra plate. Ever since the wedding date was moved up—"

"Moved up?" In the soft lamplight Kyra felt herself blanch. "Moved up to when?"

Alix blinked at her with those soft brown eyes. "Tomorrow."

"Tomorrow!" Kyra was still getting her breath back against the cold shock those words had brought her when the door of the book room opened again and Briory said colorlessly, "Master Peldyrin."

Alix swung around, smiling with her usual sunny welcome—in this case, Kyra knew, assumed.

Kyra herself stepped briskly forward past her and held out her hand. "Father," she said.

Gordam Peldyrin's sharp eyes, topaz like her own and like hers rather heavy-lidded, cut to Alix with a glint of suspicion and more than a little anger. "I thought I told you—"

"She didn't invite me, if that's what you think," Kyra said as Alix's face turned pale under its smile, rice powder, and rouge. "She merely sent me an announcement, something you can scarcely fault her for, considering you had my tutor make me write out a list of all the members of my family to the fifth degree a hundred times in punishment for not sending Cousin Plennin in Mellidane a note when I was presented at the Guildmaster's Ball when I was fifteen. And a wedding ranks a good deal higher than a Guildmaster's Ball."

There was brief silence in which the spicy fragrance of the carnations bound to the newel post near the still-open door seemed almost palpable in the waxy air.

"Cousin Plennin isn't a witch."

"Of course he isn't," Kyra agreed equably. "It would be difficult to state exactly what he *is*—the man has so little personality that he verges on the invisible. I hope he's outgrown his tendency to blend into the wallpaper or his valet will have to hunt him every morning. Has he, do you know, Alix?"

Alix had pressed her hands briefly to her mouth with shock and distress at her father's words but managed to stammer, "Yes, I . . . I think so . . ."

"If I were his valet, I'd make him wear a bell, myself," Kyra mused, turning back to her speechless parent. "And a sister, even a disowned one, ranks more highly than semivisible cousins from Mellidane. To be exact, Alix sent me an announcement of the date so that I might watch through a scrying-crystal, but since there are spells of scry-ward on so many churches, I thought I'd come. My decision was my own."

"I won't have you making a scandal!"

Alix flinched visibly; Kyra's eyebrows rose. "I assure you I'll devote my best efforts to avoiding one."

"If avoiding scandal was your aim, you'd have stayed where you were, away from this city!" her father snapped harshly. "You may attend the wedding if you feel it's your right, but I won't have you riding in the procession to the Church . . . And I won't have you dressing like some Old Believer rag peddler, either." The jerk of his hand indicated the faded black robe that all wizards, from novice to Archmage, wore when abroad from the Citadel. "Blore Spenson has just been elected the President of the Guild of Merchant Adventurers now that his father is Lord Mayor of Angelshand. I've put a year and a half into negotiating this contract and more than that into getting people to forget the last scandal you caused. . . ."

The muscle in Kyra's jaw jumped as if someone had laid a birch rod across the backs of her legs, but she said nothing.

". . . so I'll thank you to keep a civil tongue in your head while you're under my roof. Thank God it won't be for more than a day. And I won't have you upsetting your mother, either."

"Well, that's something beyond my guaranteeing, since Mother is capable of upsetting herself over a collapsed soufflé at the best of times . . ."

"None of your pertness, miss. And you'll stay clear of your sister, and I mean *well* clear. Do I make myself understood?"

"With the clarity of trumpets." Her hazel eyes narrowed dangerously.

"Papa . . ."

"And you, missy." Gordam swung sharply around on the younger girl. Briory had tactfully vanished—Kyra knew the butler had far better manners than to be listening outside the book-room door. Alix had sunk back onto one of the sturdy oak chairs, her eyes wide with anxiety and distress in the swimming amber lamplight. "I won't have you sneaking into your sister's room in the middle of the night for secret talks, understand?"

She almost whispered, "Yes, Papa."

He turned back to Kyra, his long face with its high cheekbones and square jaw—even the fading reddish hair beneath his black velvet cap—an echo of hers. "As her sister, you have the right to come to Alix's wedding," he acknowledged grimly. "But as a householder, as your father, I suppose I have some rights, too. Or was that another of the things you swore away when you joined up with the wizards?"

"I wasn't the one who locked the door," Kyra said, her head coming up and her golden eyes cold. "I wasn't the one who instructed the servants to tell me that you

had left town and wouldn't be back." She looked away
and stood for a moment studying the banners she had
set awkwardly up against the wall. The design into
which the staff of the Merchant Adventurers and the
loaves of the Bakers' Guild had been worked had not
been well thought out—it would probably provide a
certain amount of amusement to the younger appren-
tices who'd be in the crowd.

"You can't have it both ways, you know," she went
on after a moment with her old ironic lightness, turning
back to meet his furious glare. "Either I am your daughter and owe you the obedience of a daughter, and as
your daughter have the right to attend the wedding *and*
to ride in the procession if I should wish, or I am not
your daughter and owe you no obedience, and shall attend the wedding as and how I might."

"Don't chop logic with me, miss!" His brows, as
straight and thick as hers, plunged down over his eyes,
and his wide mouth tightened. "I'll have Merrivale pre-
pare the yellow guest room for you and send you up
something decent to wear to supper, and you'll wear it,
you understand? Lord Mayor Spenson and his son will
be here in an hour, and the Bishop Woolmat—"

"You got Old Wooley to officiate?" Kyra asked inter-
estedly. "The choir at St. Cyr must have been in desperate need of new robes. If you want me to wear
something fashionable, you'll need to parole Alix long
enough into my presence to lace me."

"Cannady will lace you," her parent snapped. "Alix,
send someone to the kitchen to see how Joblin and that
apprentice of his are coming on the dinner and tell
Briory to lay an extra plate. Don't you go yourself,
mind! I won't have it said that any daughter of mine
spends her time with servants! And tell her to find those
damned musicians we hired for the wedding and make
sure they're sober enough to play for our guests at supper. I'm told the Spensons have their own house musicians who play for them every night, and I won't have

them thinking we're marrying into their family for the money. How I'll get through the next twenty-four hours I don't know."

He strode from the book room, his elder daughter picking up her tapestry satchel to follow, his younger gathering her pastel skirts and hurrying across the hall to the big double doors that led into the service wing. At the foot of the long flight of stairs he halted, turning to glare at Kyra. "I don't understand why you came back for this wedding at all!"

"Don't you?" Kyra asked softly as her father, not waiting for a reply, left her and headed across the hall likewise, the plush skirts of his old-fashioned coat sweeping behind him like clumsy, rust-colored wings. She sighed and started up the stairs to the first of the galleries above. In an even quieter voice she added, "I'm afraid that makes two of us."

CHAPTER II

TOMORROW! PANIC RACED IN KYRA'S PULSE AS SHE DEscended the tight, square turns of the second-floor stairs, the heavy taffeta of her skirts rustling over the polished oak steps. *Tomorrow, good God!*

Alix's note had said the first of May. It was only the third week of April. She had thought she'd have more time.

Wizards did not travel as a rule by the public stage line, which ran from Lastower through the endless rolling hills, the rude villages and sprawling, muddy trading towns of the Sykerst; it was felt that more good would be derived from walking, improving one's acquaintance with the grasses, stones, and sky. The morning after her receipt of Alix's note, however, Kyra had driven into Lastower with Bentick, Steward of the Citadel, and Pothatch the cook and used the money she had begged from Lady Rosamund to purchase a stage ticket, praying it would get her to Angelshand before it was too late.

Her heart hammered thickly under the stiff whalebone of her bodice. *Tomorrow.*

Damn it, she thought, irritation flashing through her dread. *People should make up their minds to a plan and stick to it!*

Below her in the hall she could hear the voices of the arriving guests.

"Lord Earthwygg, I cannot tell you how honored I am to welcome you into my home. My lady . . ." The high ceiling of the hall, designed for the unbearable muggy heat of Angelshand summers, picked up sound like a well; two stories above them Kyra could hear her father's voice as if he were standing in the next room. "And my dear Lady Esmin! You grow more beautiful every time I see you . . ."

For all his stiffness, Gordam Peldyrin knew how to make himself gracious when he chose, and Lord Earthwygg, though a fairly minor viscount in the Emperor's court, was his patron, his channel both to Imperial contracts and to the higher social position that he had craved as long as Kyra had been conscious of a world outside the walls of the house. From the rail of the gallery she could see them, below the bright glazes and floating lights of the porcelain chandelier. Footmen were divesting Lord Earthwygg, his wife, and his daughter Esmin of their wraps while Briory stood and supervised with a mien considerably haughtier than that of her employer.

Caldyx Prethness, Lord Earthwygg, she recognized from her childhood and teenage years. Small and slender, he looked as if he'd wasted still further, a delicate little shadow of a man in gray satin whose diamonds flung a refracted galaxy of chandelier light. Without the thick cosmetics affected by the Court, he would have been as invisible as her cousin Plennin. The fair, luxuriant hair Kyra judged to be a wig—his had been thinning six years ago, and no human hair was ever *that* copious. His wife's, on the other hand, was undoubtedly real, coiffed and flowered and looped with jewels, the gray and black of storm clouds setting off a stern, handsome face as her rose-colored gown set off the snow mountains of her breasts. She was saying something exceedingly gracious to Kyra's mother, a plump little woman from whom Alix had gotten both her golden hair and her endless warm loquacity. The condescension in her ladyship's tone, Kyra realized with a smile, had gone straight over her mother's head.

Most things did, of course.

"Well, one doesn't want to appear cheap, but frequently, at this time of year, what's in season in the markets *is* the tastiest, and it would hardly make sense to pay half a crown apiece for apples that are mealy or pears that *look* as if they'd come a hundred and fifty miles on horseback. . . . My dear Esmin, *such* a beautiful dress . . ."

Esmin Earthwygg had been ten when Kyra had left her parents' walls, a skinny, overdressed child who always reminded Kyra of a ferret. As Kyra came to the head of the last, single long flight of stairs down into the hall, she could see that like Lord Earthwygg, Esmin would always be thin and small. Under her pearl-ornamented fair curls, her face had acquired a kind of pixie prettiness, assisted by some well-paid genius with the makeup brushes, but her eyes still looked as if they should be investigating underbrush for mice.

"Hylette made that, didn't she?" Alix asked, coming over to greet Esmin with a warm embrace and naming the most expensive dressmaker on the Imperial Prospect.

"Oh, Hylette makes everything *I* wear."

"I can always tell the way she cuts a bodice. I have to tell you, I was in her shop yesterday for the final fitting on the wedding gown . . . don't you wish brides could get married in *something* other than red? It absolutely turns me into cheese."

It was a lie, of course, Kyra reflected—Alix looked as spectacular in the crimson and gold dictated for brides as she looked in any other color—but Esmin,

flaxen like her father, *would* go ghastly when it came
her turn to proceed up an aisle under the saffron veils
the strict-form ceremony required, and it was kind of
Alix to put herself in the category of those whom bridal
red would not suit. Kyra recognized that sort of generosity these days, though she had never had it herself. In
her own years of going to Guildmasters' balls and the
dancibles given by the other merchants of the city, she
had been a source of both scandalized amusement and
dread to those her own age as a result of her scathing
and witty observations on the shortcomings of others.

Alix, she thought, her belly going cold again. *Alix is
marrying tomorrow* ... What on earth could she do?

Briory announced, "His Honor, Mayor Brune
Spenson—Master Blore Spenson."

She stepped back, severe in her dark blue suit, to admit the Mayor of Angelshand—looking even more like
a steel mummy than he had six years ago—and his son,
the newly made President of the Guild of Merchant Adventurers and Alix's long-negotiated-for groom.

He was another one, Kyra reflected dispassionately,
who ought never to be allowed to wear red.

In a nuptial mood, however, he had donned a court
suit of it—satin, too, always a bad choice on a stocky
man—and with his powerful shoulders, broad-boned
face, and short, sandy hair, he bore an unfortunate re-
semblance to a very large apple.

Not that he was fat, she thought, watching him as he
kissed Alix's hand with rigid formality and Alix flung
her bright and all-encompassing carpet of small talk
over him like a bird catcher's net. He just couldn't wear
red without *looking* fat. He stood mumchance, his
whole body radiating stiff discomfort, though whether
that was because of the strait fit of his suit or because
of Alix's nonstop babble, Kyra couldn't determine. His
neck cloth looked as if it had been tied by a particularly
unskilled dog.

"You remember my daughter, Esmin, don't you,

Master Spenson? Of course, you met at the ball here when you returned from the spice islands."

Kyra, lazily beginning her descent of the long marble stair, observed how close to that stocky form Esmin insinuated herself and how his hand first lingered on, then quickly dropped hers. Even at that distance Kyra saw the rise of blood to his face.

". . . going to be taking over the Presidency of the Merchants' Guild now, aren't you, Master Spenson?" Alix chirruped. Always talkative, she was positively blithering this evening. "How exciting for you! It must be quite a change to be living in a house and not a ship's cabin—though it isn't really fair to add to your burdens with all those upholsterers and carpenters . . . Do you know, Esmin, he's having the master's suite redecorated in their house on Prandhauer Street? With the most enchanting painted wallpapers, a sort of shell-pink, hand-painted silk . . . Not to mention all the things that have to be done for the wedding and getting his trading fleet ready to sail . . ."

"Oh, Master Spenson . . ." Esmin moved a little closer to him and raised black shoe-button eyes to his. "You aren't leaving us again so soon for the high seas? I thought Father said you had done with journeying." Her hand stole to his lapel, and Master Spenson turned a color that went most unbecomingly with his satin suit.

Kyra strode forward from the foot of the stairs, her hand extended. "Master Spenson," she said in her deep voice, "I'm Kyra Peldyrin."

He looked quickly away from Esmin as if Kyra's words had broken some kind of spell, and his eyes widened at the sight of her. *Probably,* she thought, *it's the dress.* Merrivale, the housekeeper, had brought one of Alix's gowns up to the yellow guest room, a soft powder-blue silk that would have enchantingly set off the girl's radiant fairness and would have made Kyra look like a week-old corpse. Instead of putting it on, she had gone up to the attic and found hanging in an armoire all her old gowns, gowns that had been the talk of her own set for their flamboyant disregard of current fashion. Centuries out of date in pattern and cut, some of them, they had been made to her instructions in colors darker and bolder than anything that had been worn for seventy-five years. Against the frail rose and ivory of Esmin's costume and the lettuce greens of Alix's, Kyra's black and yellow stripes and face-framing collar of point lace stood out like an orchid among daisies.

Nevertheless, Spenson reached out to grasp her hand, and at that moment Kyra, who had not worn a formal gown or anything resembling one for six years, stepped on the hem of one of her petticoats and went sprawling into his arms.

His reflexes were quick. She found herself caught with a surprisingly light strength and set back on her feet, and for a moment she stood looking at very close range into a pair of twinkling blue eyes on a level with her own.

"I'm so sorry," she said, stepping back a little and shaking straight her voluminous skirts. "I'm always doing that ... You're taller than I thought you'd be. And that color doesn't suit you."

"I thought Father's tailor carried on a little too much about how well it did." Master Spenson ruefully considered one satin sleeve. "And I'm taller than *I* thought I'd be, once upon a time."

"Master Spenson ..." Gordam Peldyrin appeared, almost impossibly, in the small space between them, caught the arm of his prospective son-in-law, and steered him hastily away. "Lord Earthwygg wanted to ask you about the cargoes you're shipping this week."

Esmin looked up at Kyra, who was standing now beside her. "Is it true you're a witch?" she asked, her black eyes greedy.

"Witch?" Lord Mayor Spenson grumbled, glancing around from the crystal glass of muscat the liveried footman was handing him on a tray. He squinted at her belligerently. Kyra met his gaze calmly, knowing what he was going to say and knowing there was no way of stopping him or anyone else. "Aye ... You *were* that old hoodoo's pupil, weren't you? The one they burned ..."

"His Grace Dromus Woolmat," Briory intoned from the door, "Bishop of Angelshand."

"My dear, I'm *so* glad you returned for your sister's wedding, and I'm *so* glad to see you again," Binnie Peldyrin murmured into her elder daughter's ear as they turned the corner from the ascending stair and passed along the wide gallery toward the formal dining hall. "But I hope you don't mind being crowded. Your turning up just now threw my table completely off. If we'd had even a day's notice, we could have invited Mole Prouvet—Tellie Wishrom's intended, you know, and a *very* dear boy even though the Prouvets *do* own that factory—or your cousin Wyrdlees or somebody to balance it."

Entering the dining room, Kyra could see her mother's point. In six years of quiet in the remote Citadel she'd forgotten about the intricacies of properly balancing a dining table.

She ended up seated between Master Spenson and Esmin Earthwygg, since that was virtually the only place they *could* put her. Certainly her father would not have risked seating her next to Bishop Woolmat, who had regarded her with a kind of startled outrage the moment he'd entered the downstairs hall and thereafter had refused to speak to or go near her. Nor could she have been seated next to either Lord Mayor Spenson or Lord Earthwygg, which would have placed her opposite the indignant prelate. As it was, she had Esmin between her and his grace, which was just fine with them both, though Esmin didn't look particularly pleased about the arrangement.

"It should be the finest wedding this city has seen for

years," Gordam Peldyrin predicted proudly from the head of the table, nodding and reaching over to pat his younger daughter's hand. "And a great credit to this little minx of mine."

"I believe it's the first wedding in your family to be performed in the strict form," Lady Earthwygg purred, glancing along the table at him with eyes as black as— but far more intelligent than—her daughter's.

"Well ..." Binnie Peldyrin began deprecatingly, and her husband said, "Oh, no, far from it, far from it," which Kyra knew was a lie. As a rule, strict-form weddings were performed only among the nobility and the very rich. There was a kind of social cachet to them, but the complications of getting an episcopal dispensation, coupled with the sheer expense of the materials prescribed by the ancient Texts, discouraged even the wealthy merchant classes from going to the trouble when marriage by signature would serve just as well. "Why, my parents were married in the strict form down in Parchasten ..."

The two footmen, very stiff in their purple and yellow livery, bore in the fish course; at the far end of the long dining room the musicians played some airy piece of nonsense, like a fill of starlight that softened the clinking of tableware and the small slurps and crunches of eating. The musicians, Kyra had been informed by the maid who'd laced her, had been hired by her father to play for the wedding procession, the wedding itself, and the feast afterward, and were among the best in the city. The flute player was currently making sheeps' eyes at Tellie Wishrom, Alix's closest friend and, with Esmin Earthwygg, her maiden of honor for tomorrow's ceremony. On the other side of the Bishop, Kyra could see Lady Earthwygg eyeing the young man, too.

"Personally, I can't imagine why any woman would want to be married in the strict form," Kyra drawled, just barely stopping herself from spearing one of the honeyed quails. She let the footman—she knew he'd been with the family before her departure, but she never could remember servants' names—put it on her plate for her. Even before she'd spent six years waiting on herself in the Citadel, her family had not had the servants put the food on the plates for them. This, like the musicians and the tale of strict-form weddings in Parchasten, had been rehearsed to show the Spensons and the Earthwyggs how grandly the Peldyrins lived.

"Oh, but it's tradition," Alix said a little too quickly, and Tellie sighed, her large blue eyes brimming with sentiment. The Wishrom grandparents, Kyra suspected, had gotten married by jumping over a broom, and in that household signature marriage was undoubtedly considered the apex of respectability.

"Tradition to get up at the crack of dawn for a ritual bath and spend hours in the church breathing incense that smells like carrion . . . ? Whyever did the prophets choose civet as the proper incense for the rite, your grace?" She leaned around Esmin to address the Bishop, who was sitting rigidly between Lady Earthwygg and her daughter. "And then afterward one has to put up with *being married* in the strict form . . ."

"The strict—or true—form of marriage is not a matter for disparagement," the Bishop said in the golden-voiced baritone that every week had the congregation of St. Cyr Cathedral sighing and weeping like some delicately played wind instrument to the rhythm of his sermons. "Its form—and its symbolic materials—were all specifically laid down in ancient times and recorded in the Texts—"

"Aye, and damned wealthy those old-timers must have been," Lord Earthwygg jested in his thin, drawling voice. He raised a quizzing glass to one heavily painted eye. "Just watching poor Peldyrin here buying the incense, and the jewels, and the golden vessels, and the proper music . . . the horses drawing the bride have to be white mares and twenty ells of saffron silk to make the bridal tent ... Makes me think I'll invest in a good broomstick when time comes for my Esmin to wed."

"Oh, what a japester you are, my lord," his lady laughed, with a glare that could have fleshed a deerhide.

"Well, I can easily understand how people started marrying by signature as a place holder to promise the Church that a real ceremonial would take place as soon as everyone could afford it," Kyra remarked. "Which, of course, then nobody ever did."

"Kyra!" her mother said, shocked.

"And once the women found out how much more convenient it was *not* to be legally their husband's chattel—"

"A woman shall enter into a man's house and become as his daughter," the Bishop quoted sententiously. He patted the corners of his mouth with his napkin with great care not to upset either his makeup or the black velvet beauty patch glued just beside his lips—a silly place for a patch, Kyra thought, if one was going to dinner. *"He shall be a father unto her, and she shall come into his home with bowed head and contrite heart ..."*

He leaned forward as he said it, to see around Esmin to Kyra, so Kyra was aware of Lady Earthwygg reaching behind his gray velvet episcopal back to hand something to her daughter.

"I think that's ... that's very touching," Tellie Wishrom said hesitantly. "I mean, to be taken care of as a daughter ..."

The Bishop beamed paternally.

"Well, that's all very well if your father keeps his accounts straight and doesn't drink," Kyra remarked, ladling applesauce onto a fragment of ham.

"Accounts!" Lord Mayor Spenson raised his wrinkled visage from his plate for the first time during the meal. The same dog, Kyra thought, must have tied *his* neck cloth as well—beside him, his son sat stolidly consuming baby peas and fricasseed goose, radiating consciousness of Esmin Earthwygg like heat from a stove.

"Just taking the time for this wedding is putting our accounts out of balance!" the old man went on, jabbing with his oyster fork in Kyra's direction. "Our ships should have set sail two days ago when the first of the easterlies began to blow—and a week early they are—and old man Nyven's fleet is already on the sea. Ours would be, too, but for this wedding, for there isn't a trader in the fleet up to Spens for getting his cargoes past the islands and away! No, nor for avoiding pirates in the Jingu Straits, either!"

His hand trembled with a slight, continuous quiver of palsy, but his eyes were pinpoints of blued steel. It wasn't difficult to see how this man had built the old banking house's modest family fortune into a staggering trade empire on will and stubbornness and bulldog strength.

"Pirates!" Esmin gasped, clutching her hands—and whatever her mother had passed her—to her bosom. "It sounds thrilling!"

"When a boy's young, I suppose it is," he allowed dourly. "But a man can't keep at it forever, and time comes when he must settle and tend his nursery." He cast that steel-hard eye on his only son and then past him to the flowerlike beauty of his daughter to be. "Though what with the clothing for him for this precious rite, and horses of this color and that color, and all those candies and trinkets that need to be flung out, and hiring maskers and learning dances and meantime the corn factors are cheating us out of our eyeteeth every chance they get and two ships down this autumn ... *Two ships!* There's witchery in it, I tell you ..."

"Nonsense," Kyra said, while her father—who was a corn factor—only glared.

"You say nonsense, girl," the mayor snapped testily, while Lady Earthwygg signaled a footman for more wine for her daughter. "But you can't tell me it's coincidence that two of my ships went down and none of Dutton Droon's did, any more than you can tell me that great storm two winters ago that wrecked the entire fleet wasn't cooked up by dog wizards in the pay of those whose ships survived! Not to mention all that talk of ruin and abominable things just a year ago! And you should know more about that, miss, than anyone at this table!"

"Father, there's no proof—"

"You stay out of this, Spens!"

Master Spenson looked as if he would say something else, but his father had already turned away.

Gordam Peldyrin, red-faced with mortification, glared at Kyra as if by his will he could make her disappear, and Lady Earthwygg turned to Binnie Peldyrin with some piece of gossip from the Court to distract her from the powder that Esmin was rather clumsily dropping into the wineglass she held.

"*If* I know anything about it," Kyra said calmly, "it's only as a matter of academics. Real wizards—those trained by the Council, as I am—take a vow not to meddle in human concerns, and most dog wizards don't have the training to call enough power to sink a ship. You might ask his grace. The Church has wizards working for it."

"The Magic Office is strictly advisory," the Bishop grated.

"Well, why does it need to be?" she asked. "Why can't each guild have its own wizard as a consultant in matters such as this?"

"They shouldn't have it at all!" the Lord Mayor stormed. "Nor that worthless Inquisition, paid a fortune for doing nothing but poke and pry! Waste of public money, I call it!"

"Oh!" Esmin made an exaggerated grimace over her wine. "What a strange taste."

"Perhaps," the Bishop majestically—and politically —said, ignoring both Esmin and the Lord Mayor, "because the guilds are formed under the aegis of the Church and its saints. Wizards, having been born without souls, as agents of illusion and evil—"

"Really, you can't believe that if you follow the advice of your own wizards."

"You keep a civil tongue in your head, girl!"

"Would you try this, Master Spenson, and tell me if you think it's all right?"

Esmin started to hand her blown-glass goblet of wine to Spenson behind Kyra's back. Kyra had only to jerk her elbow back to knock it spinning from the girl's grip, shattering it in an explosion of shards and Chablis.

"Oh, dear!" she said, springing to her feet. "How terribly clumsy of me. You—er . . ." She still couldn't recall the footman's name. "We need a towel here."

The fast, despairing glance Esmin threw to her mother wasn't lost on Kyra, but Lady Earthwygg had gone back to her quail without a blink.

Alix looked as if she was about to cry with mortification and stress. As the meal progressed, Kyra became increasingly aware of the nervousness that underlay her sister's flood of talk. Not that Alix wasn't a chatterbox under the best of circumstances—Kyra had almost forgotten her capacity for nonstop discourse on fashion, Court events, and the lives of the people around her. But the speed of her words, the restless fussing of her hands, spelled a subtext of unhappiness readable only by the woman who had grown up in the same room with her, sleeping in the same bed.

Unhappiness at seeing how Spenson kept glancing over at Esmin Earthwygg? Kyra wondered. Or unhappiness with the idea of marriage at all? Particularly, she thought, to a blocky merchant nearly twice her age whose red suit and lace neck cloth made him look like a bull in hair ribbons.

"And now I've gotten wine on my dress." Kyra straightened up. "No, I'll be all right," she added as Alix showed signs of getting up to help her.

Their father, suspicion gleaming in his eye, added gruffly, "Keep your seat, miss; your sister will do well enough. That's why we've servants."

Kyra's curtsy took in the entire table. "If you will excuse me, Mother, Father, Master Spenson . . ."

The elder Spenson and the Bishop were too deep in their increasingly heated discussion of the cost of the strict-form wedding ceremony and the possible dark dealings between the Prophets and traders in silk and gems to take note of her departure. Spenson, who in her opinion hardly resembled the fearless adventurer his father fondly painted, bowed to her as she left.

Once out of the dining room, Kyra did not ascend the stairs to the bedrooms. Instead, and with the silent swiftness they all learned in the Citadel of Wizards, she gathered her black and primrose skirts in her hands and hurried down the long flight into the lamplit well of the hall.

As she passed through the hall toward the inconspicuous archway beneath the gallery at its rear, she deepened her concentration, probing with the hyperacute senses of wizardry at the voices beyond the closed door of the kitchen wing. She heard Imper Joblin, the cook, shouting instructions to the scullions about preparing the delicate creams and fruit tarts to be served at tomorrow's feast: "Algeron, I've told you a dozen times the sugar roses on top of the cake are to be pink!" The voices of the footmen came dimly from the drying room, where they and the housemaids had all been pressed into service frenziedly weaving festal garlands, waiting for the last guests to leave so they could bring in the gardenias for the night and hang the new banners on the walls and galleries to impress tomorrow's guests. She heard Merrivale the housekeeper's soft Mellidane drawl and the muted *thump-thump* as a laundry maid ironed one of Alix's fine linen chemises.

Tomorrow, she thought again, and the dread she had

felt earlier congealed once more behind her breastbone. The wedding would be tomorrow.

From her newly gilt shrine on the wall, the Holy Widow Wortle seemed to frown disapprovingly at her, as if that virtuous champion of the status quo knew exactly what she was up to. Kyra breathed the words that would wrap about herself a gauze of illusion, words that would cause a chance maidservant, if encountered in the rear hall, to mistake her for another maid, or to have her mind on something else, or simply to assume that whatever movement she saw out of the corner of her eye must be one of the kitchen cats. Earlier that evening, up in the yellow guest room, Kyra had wrought the necessary weather-spells while waiting for the maid to come in and lace her. Now, when she opened the door at the end of the passage that led out to her mother's garden, she smiled to see that an unseasonably thick fog, like a spilled basketful of dirty wool, had risen from the River Glidden to shroud the city.

The narrow garden passage was where the footmen hung visitors' cloaks. Kyra caught one at random from its peg, throwing it around her shoulders as she stepped outside.

Though her years in the Sykerst had inured her to cold, the damp rawness of the fog took her by the throat, the smell of turned earth in the garden mingling with the ghastly harshness of the coal smoke that hung forever over the city. She had forgotten, in her years in the Citadel's isolation, the stench of Angelshand: the sewery stink of its river and streets, the smells of wet stone, of cooking, of all the humanity packed cheek by jowl in these few square miles of territory. The salt smell of the harbor, less than a mile away, which carried startlingly on the fog, vied with the fragile scents of her mother's sweet peas and the overpowering perfume of lilac. Wizards might be able to see in the dark, but fog was another matter; Kyra stuck close to the rear wall of the house, following it around to the arm's-width gap between the main house and the stables, where she turned the corner to the long, cobbled yard.

Squares of raveled apricot light showed where the kitchen windows were nearly obscured by steam heat within. Behind her, another glowing rectangle marked the tack room, where the Earthwygg and Spenson coachmen were drinking smoke-flavored tea laced with rum and trading horse talk and gossip with old Sam while he shined up his boots to drive Alix's carriage to the wedding tomorrow. Kyra knew from a glance at her father's daybooks that he'd rented the requisite team of white mares that had to pull the carriage of a strict-form bride. With the Spenson and Earthwygg teams—the carriages loomed like ships run aground in the fog of the cobbled yard—the stables must be crowded to capacity tonight.

Her cloak held close around her, taking great care not to trip on the round, slippery stones, she moved along the house wall toward the wide gate in front.

Her breath was coming fast. Weather-magic was low-level—even if they were looking for her, listening for her, the Council of Wizards would never know that she had summoned fog. The small illusions that cloaked her were likewise undetectable at a great distance, though face to face another wizard could have seen her through them.

I swear by the power within my veins, I swear by the heart of my spirit, that I will never use the powers of magic to meddle in the affairs of humankind, neither for ill nor for that which seems to me to be good.

As she had told Lord Mayor Spenson, she had spoken those vows six years ago, upon entering the Citadel of Wizards. If she was detected at this, the Council might very well repudiate her.

She paused for a moment near the wide carriage gates, closing her eyes and trying forcibly to eject from her mind the thought of not being able to return to the Citadel to finish her education. Not being allowed to learn any more of the secrets the Council mages had in their keeping. Not being allowed to taste the great powers of which, in six years, she had only begun to sip.

Angelshand was full of dog wizards, self-taught freelance mages who had refused to take the Council vows. Some of them, like the renowned Magister Magus, made a fair living from such members of the Court as were willing to risk disgrace by consulting them about love affairs and gambling talismans. Most, she knew too well, occupied small shops or cheap lodgings and eked out their livings peddling passion potions and abortifacients, luck charms and cut-rate horoscopes, half-educated, frustrated, dodging by turns their creditors and the Inquisition, from whom the Council would do nothing to protect them.

Kyra shivered and hurried on through the gate. *I just can't let myself be caught, that's all,* she thought as she slipped out onto the flagway that circled Baynorth Square.

Shrouded by fog, the great square lay quiet before her. From over the wall that separated the kitchen yard from that of the Wishroms' nearly identical granite mansion, she heard a serving girl's shrill laugh and smelled stewing meat and coffee as someone there opened a door. Out of sight in the misty darkness, a man's voice chanted, "Meat pies, meat pies, jolly, jolly meat pies . . ." and, farther off, came the iron-wheeled clatter of a cab going somewhere fast. Unseen in the gloom, the bronze fountain trickled a mournful music, and from far off the droning of a hurdy-gurdy drifted like a spiral of colored smoke in the dark.

Kyra took a deep breath. The fog was very thick now.

Before her the high porch of the house loomed like a trading ship's stern castle, the scents of tubbed gardenias and field lilies thick as music in the air around it. Gathering her heavy skirts, she climbed the tall steps, wet now and slippery with the moisture in the air. Her mind laid a little spell toward the house—Briory, on her way to the front door to summon the Bishop's sedan chair, stopped by the entry of the kitchen wing to chide the laundry maid, and the chair carriers, on their way through the dense fog from the other side of the square, thought they saw the glint of a coin on the pavement and put down their chair to go back and look.

The signs Kyra drew on the front steps with her forefinger shone briefly against the scrubbed marble, then settled into the fabric of the stone and brick, sinking out of sight like glowing ribbons laid on still water. It took less than five minutes, counting the faint haze of protective wards Kyra set up that would serve to keep lower-level wizards from noticing that anything had been done there.

Then Kyra gathered her borrowed cloak about her and hurried down the steps so quickly that she tripped at the bottom and, under her voluminous petticoats, skinned her knees. Cursing, she scrambled to her feet and hurried on. Her hands were shaking.

Supper, she thought, should be over. She paused by the yard gate and cast her mageborn senses into the house and, sure enough, heard voices in the book room. "Surely you aren't going to let her ride with the family to the Church?" Woolmat demanded, scandalized, and Kyra knew they were speaking of her.

"Good God, no!" her father answered. "If that's why she showed up here . . ."

"Why *has* she shown up here?"

"The saints only know."

Muffled by fog as by a damp blanket, the chimes of St. Farinox Church struck their treble note. Ten o'clock—Kyra mentally recalculated to the older style of hours that the wizards used. The fourth hour of the night, or just about, given the difference between daylight hours and dark at this time of the year. Some duke, out of gratitude for a forgotten favor, had paid for a clock tower to be built at the Citadel of Wizards, complete with a handsome horologe to which most mages paid scant attention. It was correct, Daurannon the Handsome had once remarked, exactly twice a day, at noon and midnight, but its sound served to remind city-bred juniors of the rhythms of their homes.

Elsewhere in the house she heard Lady Earthwygg's voice and her mother's, somewhat laboriously discussing the laying out of formal gardens. Esmin's sweet little mew reached her—"Oh, Master Spenson, I did so wish to have a word with you ..."—and a servant's: "Gyvinna, get on with them shifts; we need a hand on these festerin' flowers!"

Ahead of her, over the wet stone and horse smells of the yard, daffodil light stained the fog and threw slick yellow gleams on the cobbles as the kitchen door was opened. A fragrance of sugared comfits, cakes, and fancy breads breathed forth. Dimly, Kyra discerned a dark, slim form hurrying across the narrow width of the cobbles toward the little doorway into the Wishroms' kitchen yard. Alix's voice called out softly, "Watch out for the puddles, Tellie! I'll see you at dawn."

The sound of a closing door. Kyra started forward, hoping to duck around the corner of the house and back through the garden before the stablemen began hitching the Earthwyggs' carriage team.

She had advanced a dozen strides along the house wall when she smelled on the fog the fragile scent of lilies of the valley, whose dried petals made the pomanders scenting Alix's clothes. She stopped, her heart lurching, and, squinting through the roils of mist, saw that Alix still stood on the kitchen porch, her arms wrapped about herself for warmth.

With her was a man.

Young, Kyra thought, though she was too far and the mist was too thick to make out his face clearly. The springy movement of his shoulders and back in their white blur of shirt said youth to her as he folded his arms about Alix from behind. Alix leaned her head back against his shoulder, a gesture of absolute weari-

ness and grief, and from the concealing darkness Kyra
saw the man bend his head down over her, fair hair
catching the kitchen window's suffused light. Silk petticoats rustled; then Alix made a noise in her throat, an
unarticulated breath like that of an injured child who
had learned that no one would pay attention to its pain.

She whispered, "I don't know how I could stand this
without you."

"Alix ..." The name was barely to be heard against
the flesh of her shoulder.

Alix ... Kyra's whole spirit was one jab of grief as
she watched her sister turn in the man's arms and cling
to him in a desperate embrace. *Oh, Alix* ...

"Don't leave me."

The mouths of the lovers met for one second. Then,
from the direction of the front porch, came a horrible
clatter and a spongy thud, followed at once by Briory's
cry, "Your grace!" and the crash as the Bishop's chair
men dropped their burden and went scrambling toward
the steps.

Inside the house everybody suddenly seemed to be
shouting at once.

Alix and her lover jerked apart, spun, and threw open
the kitchen door, and Kyra took that opportunity to flee
past the outflung bar of light and run with caught-up
skirts and billowing cloak for the garden and its way
into the house.

The Bishop, descending to his waiting sedan chair,
had slipped on the high front steps and broken his
ankle.

CHAPTER III

THE DOCTOR HAD SCARCELY DEPARTED—IN THE WAKE OF his grace himself, borne back to the episcopal palace on Angel's Island and cursing his chair men with each jostle on the cobbled street—when every footman in the house went out with messages: The wedding of Blore Spenson and Miss Alix Peldyrin would not take place in the coming morning but on the one following.

And Kyra breathed a shaky sigh of relief.

While the doctor was with his patient in the book room, setting the broken bones and winding the swollen flesh in cold compresses brought posthaste from the kitchen, Kyra, wrapped once more in the borrowed cloak—Master Spenson's, she determined by its materials and lack of perfume—went out to the front steps to ritually disperse the invisible signs she had drawn there. A mage with sufficient power and training by the Council could call them back, but it was the consensus among her teachers that the Church's Magic Office had few genuinely high-powered wizards since the death of old Garm Ravenkin. This was fortunate, she thought, as

she made her way once more through the foggy kitchen
yard and around to the garden door, her slippers wet
through now and her thick petticoats held up out of the
way of her feet. A good mage could recognize the personality of a spell-mark's maker the way most people
could recognize faces.

She replaced Master Spenson's cloak and passed
soundlessly along the little hallway, making for the
kitchen quarters and the back stairs. Too many people
were gathered in the hall, their voices echoing off the
enormously tall ceiling. Her mother, with water dribbled
all down the front of the linen apron tied incongruously
over her expensive gown, was saying, "Oh, no, of
course everything will keep until the day after tomorrow, dearest. All we need to do is carry it down to the
ice cellar . . ."

"Nonsense. Maybe people like the Brecksnifts and
the Prouvets won't notice if the flans are a little crusty
or the icing's stiff on the cake, but men who've been
raised in the correct way of doing things will know.
Merchants like Fyster Nyven will know. The members
of great banking families like the Milpotts will know.
Master Spenson will know."

"Really, Master Spenson is going to have other
things on his mind on his wedding day than how fresh
the cake is!"

"I'm talking about *Mayor* Spenson."

"I can assure you, Master Peldyrin," came the voice of
Joblin the cook, "Mistress Binnie is quite correct. If everything is taken down to the ice room immediately . . .
Algeron!" he bellowed, turning, and, framed in the amber lamplight at the end of the passage, Kyra saw the
young man who had been on the kitchen steps with Alix.
His white shirt, daubed here and there with triple-refined
flour and stains of vanilla and milk, was unmistakable, as
was his fair, shoulder-length hair. Seen clearly now, he
had the appearance of a youthful angel, the more so because his gentle, dreamy face completely lacked aware-

ness of its own beauty. He nodded obediently to the cook's blustered commands, now and then making a suggestion, such as that the garlands of blossoms that had been in preparation all evening in the drying room ought to be moved down to the ice cellar as well.

"Good heavens, who's to do all this?" Gordam demanded furiously. "Bill, Lerp, and Paskus are going to be out all night taking messages to everyone we've invited ... Sam and Trobe, too, once they've done getting his lordship's horses put to—"

"I'm sure Neb Wishrom will send over Heckson and Fairbody," his wife said, always practical, naming, Kyra presumed, two of their neighbor's footmen, and Master Peldyrin threw up his hands in annoyance at all these small machinations. The gesture affected Kyra curiously, for she knew it from her tiniest childhood—knew, too, that it was her father's way of surrendering to her mother's judgment without admitting that she was better able to cope with domestic matters than he.

Beyond him, in the lighted body of the hallway, Kyra could see the little knot of departing guests: Esmin Earthwygg pouting under her mother's irritated glare, Master Spenson helping his father into his cloak and making awkward small talk with Alix. Alix was nodding and rattling on in her usual magpie fashion, but Kyra could see her eyes follow Algeron's straight shoulders as he crossed to the kitchen quarters.

"You could at least have *tried* to catch him alone!" Lady Earthwygg snapped in an undervoice to her daughter as Briory conducted them to the outer door. "Good heavens, girl, I spent fifty crowns on that potion." There was a stir of farewells, and Kyra, seeing her chance, slipped through to the kitchen and heard no more of what went on.

Surrounded by Who-Me? spells, she crossed the corner of the kitchen between the door and the narrow entrance to the back stairs. The three chambermaids—blond, brunet, and redhead—who'd been sitting at the

big table helping the musicians finish off dinner leftovers were too busy clamoring with protest at Algeron's
news to notice Kyra. "All those tartlets and roulades to
the ice cellar? It'll take us all night!" "You mean the
wedding's been put off?" asked the laundry maid, a
thin, colorless woman with her arms full of folded shifts
and petticoats—undoubtedly, Kyra thought as she
ghosted around the door and into the steep well of the
back stairs, the elaborately lace-trimmed garments
suited to Alix's crimson wedding gown.

Quietly, she ascended the stair.

The second floor was deserted, shrouded in shadow
now that the footmen had cleared the supper dishes and
the maids had laid tomorrow's fires in the drawing-
room hearth and the porcelain stoves in the library,
study, and breakfast room. On her way into the dining
room Kyra looked through the breakfast-room doorway
to see the elaborate tub of enamel and gold, with its
canopy frame taken down and its prescribed pennons
rolled neatly into corners, in which Alix would take her
ritual bath before being gowned for her wedding. The
air—warmer in these smaller upstairs room—was sweet
with cinnamon and lilies, as the Texts ruled it must be.
Cinnamon for this world and lilies for the next, Kyra remembered from her distant religious training, and shook
her head again over the mysteries of people, like Tellie
Wishrom, who wanted to be married in the strict form.
Reaching the third floor again, she made her way along
the ill-lit gallery to the yellow guest room, which was
tucked like a poor relation between the girls' old
schoolroom and the suite reserved for more notable
company.

There she removed her wet slippers and settled down
to wait. As she listened for Alix's step on the main
stairs, she debated putting on dry stockings—the damp
had soaked straight through to her skin—but realized
that what could be done unthinkingly when clothed in
her loose gray robe was less easy in a bodice boned to

within an inch of its wearer's life. She contented herself with pulling up her skirts and sitting with her feet close to the small coal stove that filled the room with such comforting warmth. Her petticoats would cover the bruises the pavement had left on her knees, and Alix, although she was more observant than she appeared, would have other things on her mind.

In time she heard voices: her mother and Alix. Closing her eyes, Kyra extended her senses down the hall. But as she'd suspected, the topic of conversation was where things would go in the ice cellar and whether everyone who had been invited to the wedding had been sent a message of postponement. Like her mother's, Alix's mind ran very much to the practical, despite a romantic streak the width and depth of the River Glidden.

"We're not going to need *another* before-wedding banquet, are we?" she asked above the soft rustle of petticoats. From the sinuous slither of silk and the pauses of the voices, Kyra guessed that having set all the maids to carrying creams and garlands to the cellar, her mother had come up to unlace Alix before going down to assist in the portage herself.

"Oh, I hardly think so."

"Oh, thank heavens! I don't think I could *stand* another evening at the same table with Esmin Earthwygg."

"Now, darling, you know her father got your father the contracts of the charity hospital and the Prince Dittony Barracks."

"What, didn't you see how sweet I was being to her?" There was a kind of rueful brightness in Alix's voice. "Truly, I'll be like a sister to her—I will, really—at the bath and through the wedding and the feast, but honestly, it will be a relief not to have her around all the time, asking how much my jewels cost and insinuating that since Tellie's father owns a factory Tellie must eat with her hands, and poking into boxes and drawers to see what's there." There was a moment's silence. Then, more softly, "It will be a relief not to have . . . all this hanging over my head."

In the awkward pause Kyra wondered about the expression in her mother's eyes, for the next instant Alix said, with all her old vivacity, "There! Now you run along and keep Papa from fretting himself into a frenzy."

More silken rustlings as Binnie Peldyrin, plump and featherheaded as a little golden partridge, left her daughter's room and descended the stairs.

Soundless as a cloud in her damp stockings, Kyra moved along the corridor to her sister's room.

"Kye—" Alix turned, the expression of exhaustion and strain that had added ten years to her face dropping away so suddenly, Kyra was not certain she had seen it; her sister's hand flicked with suspicious casualness across her eyes. A silver-backed hairbrush was in Alix's other hand, but she was not sitting in the fuzzy halo of candlelight that surrounded her dressing table. She stood, rather, before her wedding gown on its wicker frame in the corner.

Against the white of Alix's nightgown and robe the wedding costume blazed like blood sprinkled in flame. The crimson silk of the bodice sparkled with rocaille and bullion, the stiff gold patterns of the lace repeated on the golden petticoat revealed beneath the swagged folds of the skirt. Above all that color, Kyra thought, Alix's sloping white shoulders and fragile stem of neck would lift like alabaster and honey, glittering with the traditional gems—jasper, beryl, topaz, and tourmaline—covered with the saffron veil like a sheet of fire.

But in her mind all Kyra heard was that little broken sigh, the whisper, *Don't leave me . . .*

"Are you all right?"

Alix twinkled like the mischievous girl Kyra had known. "As soon as I get over my palpitations of concern for his grace's health."

In spite of herself, Kyra giggled. It seemed impossible that they hadn't parted just last week.

"Here, turn around," Alix went on. "Have you been trapped in that thing since you left the table? You poor darling—not that it isn't absolutely beautiful. I always loved the way you dressed ... You could have got Lily to get you out of it; all she's done all evening is flirt with that flute player ... although he *is* the most gorgeous thing in nature. Did you get the stain out of your hem? Soda and salt in cold water should soak it out, or lemon juice ... Oh, but you're a wizard, aren't you? You can just make it disappear."

"According to the other wizards in the Citadel, the best spells involve soda and salt."

Alix laughed again. Her small, deft hands flew along the lacings. "I shouldn't joke. I'm truly sorry his grace was hurt, but really, he's been so *odious* about giving Papa the dispensation for the ceremony. You'd think he had a personal patent on the strict form or something."

She looked as if she were going to say something else, some other bit of trivial persiflage, but looking up, she met Kyra's eyes in the mirror, watching her with narrowed concern. Quiet fell, and in the mirror the two sisters stood for a moment, Kyra in her white chemise with her chestnut hair about her shoulders, Alix white-robed and cloaked with amber glory, the angular face and the delicate oval in some way curiously alike.

Then Alix put her arm around Kyra's waist and said, "It's so good to see you. I've missed you."

Kyra sighed and turned, scratching her sides beneath the linen with relief to be free of the whalebone sheath of the bodice. "I didn't realize how much," she said.

"I know you probably didn't think of me much ..." Alix hesitated, toying with the lace of her robe, then smiled ruefully. "I mean, I was twelve—just a little girl, really. So I must seem like somebody else entirely to you now. But you were—well, my older sister." She shook back the corn-silk mantle of her hair, which was crinkled and curled from its coiffure. The dressing table was heaped with combs, pins, forget-me-nots aromatically wilting in the candles' heat; the air was soft with beeswax and lily of the valley. In the yard on the other side of the house a groom crooned endearments; a horse snuffled in reply, and there was the clink of harness buckles.

"Are you happy in the Citadel of Wizards? Is it all you wanted it to be?"

Kyra said after long thought, "It's all I would have wanted it to be if I'd had the courage and selfishness to want that much."

She remembered her first sight of the Citadel. Very small it had seemed against the endless, cold sky of the Sykerst, the black pelt of the spruce forest. A green hill rising above a river like brown glass, shaggy with trees through which jumbled towers and roofs could be discerned: strange mirages, things of air and mist rather than stone.

She and Rosamund had been walking for more than a month through the vast, deserted steppes of the Sykerst. The previous night had been spent in the muddy, plank-built trading town of Lastower. At first exhausted by the unaccustomed effort of travel afoot, Kyra had felt her spirits gradually rising in the days of quiet, of unhurried companionship, and the sight of the magic hill with its glimmering towers had been like the fulfillment of some heart-shaking dream of peace. Larks had risen, singing, from the knee-deep grasses of the roadsides. From far off, the wind had borne her the random notes of chimes.

"Courage and selfishness." Something in Alix's voice made Kyra look sharply at the lovely oval face in the honeyed glow. But Alix moved away—rather quickly, Kyra thought—and fetched her a dressing gown from the armoire, soft and clinging and pink, as unlike as possible the gowns Kyra had once worn here.

"So magic isn't what the Bishop says? And the

wizards—are they anything like old Tibbeth? I mean, the way old Tibbeth seemed . . ." Alix had gone over to the dressing table to prick up the wick of a candle that had been burning too long, so she did not see how still Kyra had become, holding the pink robe before her.

"You know," Alix went on as she tweezed the wick straight, "I really did like old Tibbeth. It must have been awful for you to have to testify at his trial." A small line appeared between the perfect brows as she clipped the charred wick off short, the flame outlining her fingers in fragile threads of glowing rose. "And Papa couldn't have made it easier. He was terribly hurt when you told him."

Kyra frowned. "Told him what?"

"That you were going to join the real wizards—I mean, that you were going to take the Council vows. I mean, as a dog wizard like Tibbeth, at least you could have stayed with the family, and there wouldn't have been a scandal."

"Is that what he told you?"

Alix raised her head, looking at her in surprise. "He said you'd told him you were going to leave and become a wizard. That's when he packed us all up and we left for Aunt Sethwit in Mellidane." The brown eyes regarded her, wide and troubled, puzzled by the down-turned corner of Kyra's square-lipped mouth.

"Ah," Kyra said softly, and swung the robe around her, stepping clear of the jet and jonquil heap of satin around her feet. "Drat those skirts," she added, remembering how she had been precipitated into her prospective brother-in-law's arms. "No wonder the first thing nouveaux riches do is get their daughters dancing lessons. You need to be a dancer not to break your neck." She went over to give Alix a reassuring hug. "To answer your question, some of the wizards are a bit like Tibbeth in that they're terribly untidy, and they all keep things—rocks and crystals and books and pressed flowers. And speaking of Tibbeth," she added as Alix, with a relieved smile, settled herself on the edge of the great, white-curtained bed, "have you ever been into the old schoolroom where he and I worked? Or did Father have that cleared out?"

"Father just locked it up," Alix said. "I've never been in it since ... er ... since you left. I don't think anybody has." She looked worriedly up at her sister while Kyra gathered up the black and yellow dress, shook free the petticoats from their skirts, and draped them over the end of the bed the two girls had once shared. "Kyra, you weren't ... you weren't implicated or anything by testifying at Tibbeth's trial, were you? *That* isn't why you had to join the Council wizards, is it? Just so they'd protect you from the Inquisition? I mean, Papa would have ..."

Kyra was silent a moment, remembering Tibbeth's voice, startlingly small and gentle coming out of that big, bulky body, that mobile pink face. The smell of wood smoke and incense came back to her, of herbs drying, linked forever to the soft deftness of his huge hands, showing her the passes to make, the signs to draw, to call light from darkness, to make a pebble look and smell and feel like a rose in her palm.

She remembered, too, the blast of the fire's heat against her face, its greedy roaring and the horrible stink of charring flesh, the thick buzzing of the flies in the garbage underfoot. The stench of the crowd. The sound of screaming.

"No," she said hollowly. "No, I wasn't implicated. That wasn't why I ... sought out the Council." She tied the pink robe more closely about her, interested to note that despite her more fragile appearance, Alix had grown to precisely her own size through the rib cage, breasts, and shoulders.

There was silence once more. Through the open door Kyra could hear the voices of the maids complaining as they carried flowers and refreshments, now and then punctuated by the laundrywoman's tired whines and the mild, comforting tones of the young man Algeron.

"Kyra." Alix spoke after a long time. Her hands—small like their mother's and left oddly unformed by a lifetime of tasks no more exacting than the cutting of pens and the embroidery of silk—turned nervously around a single shining curl. "As a wizard, can you . . . can you make a love-spell?"

The blunt, unhandsome face of her sister's middle-aged groom returned to her mind. The way his eyes had followed Esmin Earthwygg. The uncomfortable silences—the hard set of the lips. If the youth Algeron weren't a servant, her father might see the matter differently. Or maybe not. "I *can*," Kyra said gently, "in that we're taught how. But as I said, the first thing we do at the Citadel is take a vow never to use magic to interfere in any way with the lives of other people."

The dampness of her stockings, the bruises on her knees, stung her with a momentary rebuke, but she went on. "Those are the only conditions under which they'll teach us true power. That's why people like . . . like Tibbeth—" Her voice still stuck a little on his name. "—never get proper teaching and stay dog wizards. Because they won't take the vow. That means fortune-telling, or love-spells, or—"

"*Kyra!*" Her father's voice cut like an ax across her words. She had been too preoccupied with what might lie behind Alix's question to hear him coming up the stairs from his study below.

She swung around, startled, clutching the pink wrapper close. He still wore the lush rust-colored suit he'd had on at dinner, his gold-flowered waistcoat mottled with water from the doctor's compresses. The lines from his nostrils to the corners of his mouth seemed deeper, and behind the anger in his eyes was a glitter of tiredness and the expression of a man who thought something was about to be put over on him.

"I told you I wouldn't have you speaking to your sis-

ter! God knows she's had enough to do, getting ready
for the wedding, without you putting your heathen ideas
into her head and bringing up things best forgotten!"

"You mean telling her my side of the story?" Kyra
inquired calmly.

"Papa, Kyra only came in to say good night, so that
I could unlace her—"

"Let her call one of the maids! She may have forced
her way back into this house to see you wed, but that
doesn't mean I have to let her make of you what she's
chosen to be!"

"You mean a woman who knows her own mind?"
Kyra asked. "Or merely a happy one?" She turned to
Alix. "I don't suppose we'll be permitted to meet tomorrow, but I'll certainly see you at the bath ceremony
the following morning. The Texts do say," she added as
her father opened his mouth in furious protest, "that
*mother and sisters shall attend her, and cousins to the
second degree.* If you're putting out six crowns the
ounce to stink up St. Farinox Church with civet incense,
you can scarcely get away with that silly business of
temporary adoption when you have a perfectly legiti-
mate sister to hold the towels. Good night."

She would have made a queenly exit on that line had
she not caught her foot on the collapsed pool of her discarded petticoats. As it was, her father had to catch her,
and they stood for a moment, hands and arms gripped,
topaz eyes looking into topaz, before she broke away
and strode serenely down the hall, leaving the gown
across the foot of the bed, to be picked up by the maids.

In the yellow guest room Kyra closed the door,
opened the window—Briory had obviously prepared the
room for her—and reached under the bed to find her
tapestry satchel. The spells she'd left on it told her that
the butler had tried to open it—although her dignity
would never permit her to listen at doorways, the
woman was an unconscionable snoop—but that she'd

been turned aside from doing so by the other spells of ward and guard, the spells that would cause her to suddenly recall that there were other, urgent things to be done elsewhere in the house *that minute*.

Not that it mattered terribly, Kyra reflected. Opening the bag, she pulled out hairbrush, toothbrush, and the plain cotton nightgown she preferred to the tucked and ruffled gauze one—obviously Alix's—that lay across the foot of the bed. The other things she had brought with her—red chalk made of wax and ground silver, vials of powdered silver and elkhorn, a few books and some markers wrought of bone and feathers—were scarcely incriminating, and her Council vows should be sufficient to protect her from the Inquisition even if her family wouldn't.

Provided that no one found out about the runes she'd drawn on the front step.

She shivered a little at the thought and felt cold in the pit of her stomach.

She had only managed to buy a little time.

Outside, the gallery was quiet. She closed her eyes, listening more deeply, but no sound came from the rooms farther along: the big chamber her parents shared, the little parlor and the dressing room, the bedroom where she and Alix had slept in that same big, white-curtained bed where Alix would now be lying alone, watched by the crimson gown that stood like a specter of familial duty in the corner. Her mother, she guessed, was still down supervising things in the kitchens. Her father, who pretended to find his wife's mundane preoccupations exasperating compared with his larger schemes of social advancement, would be in his study, for he hated retiring alone to sleep.

Very quietly, Kyra opened the bedroom door again.

An echoey murmur rose from the hall below, and ember-colored light reflected upward, as from a glowing well. Silent as a ghost now in her chemise and fluffy pink robe, she moved to the next door along the gallery and pressed her hands to the silver mounting of its keyhole. *Father just locked it up* ... Alix had said.

Just as Nandiharrow had taught her they would, the tiny mechanisms of the lock ticked over in response to her whispered words. Gently, Kyra pushed open the door.

The smell of dust overwhelmed her, of air too long uncirculated, of mold. Someone had in fact been through here, probably before the room was shut up for good. The little terra-cotta jars that had lined the two shelves above the narrow pine worktable were gone. So were the books. Kyra felt a flash of anger at the stripped shelves on the opposite wall, remembering how diligently she'd searched for those thirty or so volumes of astrological, herbal, and theurgic lore through the barrows of the secondhand dealers along the riverfront and in every bookshop from Butter Hill to the city's southern gates.

Her father had burned them. She knew it. There had been nothing there that wasn't available in the libraries of the Citadel, but those books had been *hers*. . . .

Memory sliced at her again with the recollection of how the Inquisitor's headsman had kindled the pyre in St. Cyr Square with Tibbeth's books. There had been hundreds of them, and she remembered very clearly how the heat had carried burning pages aloft like huge yellow leaves swirling in a gale.

The thought made her clench her teeth until her jaw ached.

It did not take her long to search the room.

She hadn't really expected to find anything there, since Tibbeth had left the household before the scandal had broken. But she knew that the kind of mark she sought, though made in a room locked up for years, would not have lost its strength. This room, however, was singularly clear of magic. Even the old echoes of the spells Tibbeth had taught her here had been worn away by time, by the friction of stirring currents of life, by the changing seasons and the far-off turning of the stars.

The implements he had taught her to use—the divining-bowl, the mirror, the crystals, wax, chalks—had gone the way of the herbs and books, the spell-treated parchments for talismanic work, the bits of copper, silver, and gold. Here and there, in the corners, she came upon bits of her own old magic, like whiffs of perfume clinging to the folds of old garments: childish cantrips and piseog, laborious illusions, the clumsy echoes of attempts to imbue sigils and seals.

Of Tibbeth himself there was not even that.

She got out quickly, knowing how easy it would be to open the windows and look down at the familiar view over the garden, visible to her mageborn eyes in the darkness now that the fog would be dispersing. How easy to reminisce about the girl who spent so many hours in that room, intoxicatedly pursuing a dream that had been all that she could then comprehend of the greater dream of knowledge and power. How easy to shed cheap tears, when what she really needed to do was sleep, and plan, and figure out what to do next.

In her own room again, she opened her satchel once more and took out Alix's note. *This is to let you know that Father has finally arranged a marriage for me, a truly splendid match.*

With a pug-faced merchant almost twice her age who had no better sense than to wear red satin.

Kyra shook her head, running the fine, stiff parchment over and over through her fingers.

Through the half-open window, the lingering rawness of the fog drifted, the pong of the river, of wet stone, soot, and sewage, the lowering, crowded smells of too many human beings living too close together. Cramped dreams, sordid secrets, desperate strivings for the most minimal of gains, petty greeds and confused issues, mixed feelings and information that read both ways, and small victories of love blossoming like flowers on a dung heap. The Citadel was not free of its greeds and griefs and private secrets, but they were for the most part troubles whose nature she understood, whose meaning stemmed from the magic that was the common heart of them all. Even those she disliked or distrusted there had goals that were her goals and experiences that paralleled her own.

She lay back on the bed, looking up at the painted ceiling, an architectural perspective of the kind that had been popular fifty years ago, garlanded with painted flowers. The room was too small for it, and the artist hadn't been particularly good; there was something disconcerting about the way those trompe l'oeil archways seemed to lean on one another against the perpetually sunny sky.

On the dressing table the candles were smoking from the draft. Kyra waved an impatient hand, and all the flames snuffed to simultaneous lifelessness, four thin scarves of smoke curling ceilingward from the amber eyes of the coals amid thready scents of smoke and wax.

Her other hand continued to turn, over and over, Alix's letter.

Water changing to blood in the scrying-bowl. Winds that rushed down when she summoned slow clouds. The guttural hum of flies in the astringent darkness of the Citadel gardens.

And the sheer horror of jolting from sleep eleven nights ago, her pulse pounding and tears on her face and the knowledge in her heart, deeper than dreams or fears or guesswork: the knowledge that her sister Alix was going to die on her wedding night.

CHAPTER IV

It was impossible at this distance for Kyra to remember the first time she saw Tibbeth of Hale.

His shop had always been there, halfway down a seedy alley off Potticary Court, in the district of Angelshand that lay halfway between the fashionable town houses and shops of the north and east and the downright slums along the riverfront. The houses there, though tall and narrow and crowded elbow to elbow along the cramped streets as they were elsewhere in the city, lacked the architectural handsomeness and the uniformity of the newer districts. With their projecting upper stories, their bow windows, their random turrets, penthouses, and balconies, they had the appearance of having grown organically from the round, moss-furred cobblestones, fighting like insalubrious plants for a share of the sunlight. In the long, stifling summer afternoons when lessons were done and on into the endless glimmer of twilights that lingered until ten, Kyra would lead her band of schoolfellows on expeditions through the mazes of court and lane east of Baynorth Square,

56

and they'd invariably pass down Little Potticary Lane on the opposite side from the house of painted bricks, with its round turret above the blue-painted door. "A witch lives there," Dann Brecksnift had said.

Kyra did remember the first time she'd gone inside.

Alix had come down with a fever—as a child Alix had been susceptible to chills and colds—and their father had gone to Respin Phylgard's shop in Potticary Court one rainy afternoon to get some of Phylgard's tisanes for her. Phylgard was the premier apothecary in the city, head of the Apothecaries' Guild and consultant to innumerable members of the Court. Thus, a visit to his shop, with its lines of shining glass bottles, its mysterious cabinets of tiny drawers, its smooth marble counter and mosaic marble floor, was always an adventure. Even at ten Kyra was already her father's pet and was beginning to grow into her role as his secretary, her sharpness with mathematics and her shrewd observations of the business of corn factoring winning not only his approval but confidences he never gave to his largely uncomprehending wife. As a result, she was much indulged and was given the books she demanded and the extra tutoring she asked for when she discovered the mathematics master at her school couldn't tell a sine from a tangent and was allowed to dress in richer colors and more dramatic styles than were considered proper for little girls.

She couldn't recall why she'd grown bored in Phylgard's shop. Most likely, she thought, looking back, her father had been involved in some interguild politics and had gotten into a close discussion of the matter with the great apothecary, something she was not able to follow without explanations the men had no time to give. She'd gone out into the court, which was dark and nearly deserted under the pregnant, charcoal-colored sky of autumn, and had stood for a few moments with her hands deep in the silk-soft squirrel fur of her muff. The chair menders, the hurdy-gurdy man, the vendors of steamed buns, flowers, and scarves who usually inhabited the flagways had all been driven indoors by an earlier rain squall. A few streets away a woman was singing, "Oranges and limes! Golden sunshine from the south!" but Kyra wasn't sure in which direction the vendor lay, and she knew the streets were so tangled around here that she would probably have trouble locating her.

So she'd tucked up her brilliant red and purple skirts and picked her way among the puddles of Little Potticary Lane to visit the shop of the witch.

She'd seen Tibbeth outside his shop on enough occasions, tending the flowers that grew in pots on his tiny doorstep or bringing back pails of water from the fountain in the square, to know him by sight, and so she felt no fear of the tall, plump, handsome man with his lined face and deep-set eyes. He wore a long and very old-fashioned gown or robe, like an apothecary or a physician, but without those dignitaries' stiff, ruffled collars. On the day she first came into his shop, he was wearing a fraying velvet cap with ear flaps such as her father sometimes wore when it was cold, and from beneath it, fine, silky sandy-gray hair hung to his shoulders.

He was reading in the kitchen behind the shop, where the light came in through the wide window's score of tiny panes, but there was a bell above the shop door that rang when Kyra opened it. She saw him put his book aside and rise—tall, taller than any man she had known up to that time—and come into the shop to bow.

"Mistress Kyra Peldyrin, I believe."

She looked around the shop. Dann Brecksnift and she used to dare each other to go up and touch the iron door handle of the "witch's house" or look through the front window into the shop, but inside it wasn't so formidable, just gloomy, with the light cut off by the buildings across the street, and filled with strange jars and cabinets, like Phylgard's, only more varied and shabbier. A mummified crocodile hung from the low rafters overhead; a skull stared lugubriously from a niche; on a shelf behind the counter were stacked innumerable paper boxes, each tied up with string.

She asked, "If you're a witch, why do you need the bell to tell you someone's in the shop?"

Tibbeth smiled. "If you're in the back garden and feel thirsty, do you call a maid and ask her to get you some lemonade from the kitchen?"

Kyra shook her head. "I go get it myself. It's easier."

"Even so. I'd rather give my full attention to the book I'm reading than put part of it into a spell to let me know something a bell could let me know just as easily."

Kyra had thought about that, looking around at the shop, at the dark, intricate shapes of orreries and celestial globes that stood on the sideboard, at the big sphere of flawless crystal and the strange mirrors of gold and mercury that flashed duskily from the walls, smelling for the first time the thick, characteristic odor compounded of dust, ancient paper, herbs, candle wax, and incense. Strings of dried henbane and borage dangled everywhere from the rafters, their desiccated scents frail yet pungent; one section of shelf held soft pieces of leather of various kinds; another, bottles of what appeared to be water and honey.

"Papa says that you aren't a witch at all, that there's really no such thing as witches. That it's all done by conjuring tricks to make people believe you have power."

"Your papa's a very wise man, Kyra," Tibbeth said gently. "Making people believe things *is* power, and it's one power wizards use. If people truly didn't believe that I have some kind of power—that I could be dangerous to them because of this power—they wouldn't be afraid of me, you know."

Her eyes narrowed. "*Do* you have power?"

"Not very much. Your father has far more, because he's a rich man, and people respect him and want to please him. You have power because your father loves you and trusts you—and because you're a rich man's daughter. I'm just a poor apothecary that some people think is a wizard."

"*Are* you a wizard?"

He shook his head. "The real wizards live in the Citadel of Wizards in the north," he said. "They don't use their power at all, and they only teach those who promise to obey them and be like them. The rest of us are just dogs to them—dog wizards, they call us." And for a moment something glinted in the back of those deep, sky-blue eyes.

Kyra looked around again, at the shop, at the herbs, at the line of blown-out eggshells on the windowsill, the myriad of crystals ranged along the edge of the sideboard, the prisms, star charts, miniature crocks of seeds. The surge of curiosity and delight she had always felt in Phylgard's shop, in the moldy library downtown where half the books were so old, they weren't even printed but handwritten—in the naturalist's shop near the river where her father had gone to buy her Aunt Sethwit a stuffed toucan when such things were a fad—returned to her with a painful insistence, a terrible sense of seeing things pass her by.

"All this isn't for casting spells, then?"

"No, my child," Tibbeth said. "It is for learning. Because that's what wizards do."

That's what wizards do. Kyra remembered the words as she pushed open the heavy gates of the kitchen yard and stepped into Baynorth Square.

By daylight, with the white mists thinning to nothing, the square stood revealed as a broad expanse of wet gray cobblestones in whose center a fountain gurgled softly within its thick-pillared house. A bronze statue of Lord Baynorth surmounted the little building's arched roof, the lord whose private city palace had been torn down to provide his heirs with thousands of royals a year in ground rent for the merchants who built their houses on the sprawling site of its gardens. Most of the noble families had moved out to the Watermeadow precinct of the city between the Imperial Gate and the walls of the Emperor's palace, pretending they would rather live there than in the still more exclusive neighborhoods around Imperial Square and Queen's Square.

Even through the urgency of her dread, Kyra slowed her hurrying steps as she passed the fountain house and smiled a little. There was an Earthwygg Square somewhere in the packed, cabbage-scented streets just this side of Prince Dittony Circle; she wasn't sure how much of that land the Earthwyggs still owned, but in any case, in that district they wouldn't be getting much from it. Then she pulled her dark cloak closer around the plain servant's dress she'd pilfered from Merrivale's mending basket and hastened on.

Shadow still lay over Baynorth Square, the morning cold penetrating her shabby clothes. On the western side of the square, the gate in the old city wall had been opened; sunlight sparkled on the gilded bronze luck gods of its turrets above the line of the eastern houses' shadows, and through it she could glimpse the sparkle of glass, the gaudy unrepentant reds and greens of the saints and birds and flowers painted on lower-class houses, the stir of movement as the merchants of Salt Hill unshuttered their windows and prepared for the day. From the streets on all sides came the jangle of bells, the tooth-jarring rattle of clappers, and the voices of the street vendors: "Hot pies! Hot pies! Meat-apple-pear-mince—*hot* pies!" "Clams and mussels! Clams and mussels!" "Fresh lovely violets! New from the country!" "Buy my milk! Who'll buy my milk?" As she approached the corner where Upper Tollam Street ran out of the square, amidst the ammonia of horse droppings and the pungency of garbage in the gutters, Kyra walked through a cloud of steamed sweetness where an old woman was selling buns from a cart. Hunger flicked at her like an elf's whip, but her sense of haste, of time running out, kept her moving. Alix's life was at stake, and besides, it would not do to let anyone recall that a tall woman wrapped in a cloak had passed that way.

The time was past when the first crowds had come into the street in the misty darkness of predawn: clerks on their way to the countinghouses; men, women, and children trudging down the dripping lanes to the factories and mills along the river. Now and then a shop girl hurried past her, or a bleary-eyed student headed for the university quarter, or servants on their way to do early marketing. Merchants like her father, if they had any pretensions to gentility—though they might have been awake since before daylight working on their accounts—did not reach their countinghouses until nine.

She started to step off the high stone curb to cross to Fennel Street but paused to let a cab rattle past. Only, to her annoyance, it didn't. It drew up directly in her path, the door opening to let out a couple of stocky men in the kind of rough clothes laborers wore. Her mind still worrying at the problem of Alix, of this morning's secret errand, she started to circle around the back of the cab when it occurred to her to wonder how a couple of laborers had been able to afford a hack's prices. By then it was too late.

Rough hands grabbed her from behind. Someone threw a shawl or blanket over her head; someone else flung a loop of something that felt like braided rope around her arms, though she knew an instant later that it was spell-cord. Cold sickness quenched the magic within her at its touch. She was so startled—so shocked—that she didn't even begin to react until the man behind her started to lift her off her feet.

But at five foot ten, Kyra was not all that easy to lift. Lashing behind herself with one foot, she entangled her assailant's leg and jerked it forward, at the same time throwing her weight back into him. Her impact with the flagstones was considerably softened by the shielding of his body—his, she supposed, was much less so, to judge by the noises he made.

She rolled, twisting, jabbing with elbows and knees as someone else bore down on top of her. She could hear the cab horse whinnying, smell its sweat and the stink of the blanket over her head. The second man was trying to lift her off her feet, and she felt the first one rolling about under her; furious, she began to scream at the top of her lungs. Folds of the blanket got in her mouth, linty and smelling like cats.

Running footsteps. She was shoved sprawling forward onto the pavement, bruising her knees again and skinning the palms she threw out to catch herself. She heard the thump of blows landing, the crack of a whip, the rattle of hooves and harness. Then someone pulled the blanket and the spell-cord away from her.

She looked up to see Blore Spenson standing over her with the articles of her kidnapping in one hand and a stout walking stick in the other.

"Miss Kyra!"

She scrambled to her feet, trod on her hem, and stumbled again, cursing as she banged her knees once more. Spenson dropped the blanket and cord and extended a hand to her. She shook free, furious at herself for reacting so slowly, for not realizing more quickly that she might be in danger in the first place . . . in fact, for not expecting something of the kind. "Thank you, I'm quite all right."

Her tone of assurance was somewhat marred by the need to pick flecks of dirt and cat fur out of her mouth. She pushed at her hair; it had come loose from its pins and hung like a crazy woman's down over her shoulders and around her face. A couple of chair carriers and a match vendor were running toward them but halted, uncertain, when they saw she was unhurt. She heard a woman loudly proclaiming that she was going directly to the local magistrate—why, they might all be murdered in their beds! So much, Kyra thought dourly, for the secrecy of her errand.

"Did they hurt you?"

"Do you wish they had so it could have been a more impressive rescue?" Her sister's haggard eyes still prickled in her mind, the question about a love-spell. Then she saw the chagrined look on his face and added, "No, I'm sorry. Thank you for coming the way you did. I don't expect I was in any genuine danger, you know, though you probably spared me a couple of days in uncomfortable quarters." She brushed the dirt from her skirt and examined her skinned palms. "She'd want me out of the way, but she would hardly assassinate me."

"Who?" Spenson asked, baffled.

Kyra pulled a hairpin free, looped up what was left of a braid, and pinned it back into place. "Lady Earthwygg, of course." Past him, a few yards down the road, she saw a two-wheeled gig standing, drawn by a beautiful liver-bay mare. Judging by the way Master Spenson was dressed, in a dark-green broadcloth suit, he had been on his way to call on Alix, though his cat-skin waistcoat looked like something a tout would wear and he had obviously tied his own neck cloth again.

"At least I assume it was Lady Earthwygg. Spell-cord that thick—and that powerful, for it's quite high-quality—" She gingerly nudged with one toe the finger-fat silk braid lying like a crimson snake on the blanket at their feet. "—isn't cheap, and if it was the Inquisition who wanted me, they'd have come to the house and talked to Father."

"Well," she added with a conciliating smile, "at least you aren't wearing that dreadful red suit anymore."

He was still looking at her as if she were speaking Old High Trebin.

"Why on earth," he asked, "would Lady Earthwygg want to have you kidnapped?" Automatically he bent and picked up the cord and blanket. He looked the kind of man, Kyra thought dispassionately, who'd pick up coins from the flagway, too.

"Oh, because of you and her daughter."

He froze in midmovement, and slowly his whole blunt countenance flushed a furious red. "There is nothing between—" He couldn't even manage Esmin's name. "—between her daughter and me."

"Oh, I didn't think there was, but I'm sure it's not for want of her trying." Kyra replaced another hairpin. "That was quite a strong passion powder Esmin tried to get you to drink last night. I wasn't sure I could have counterspelled it just in passing, so I had to knock it out of her hand, which was a terrible shame, because there were only twelve goblets in that set and the glassblower who made them has long ago retired."

"Are you telling me," Spenson said in a strangled voice, his color deepening alarmingly, "that Esmin Earthwygg was trying to . . . to give me love-potions?"

Kyra shrugged. "Well, as Father keeps pointing out, you *are* a splendid match, and the Earthwyggs have been outrunning the constable for *years*. At least they were doing so six years ago when I last heard, and that isn't a habit one changes overnight. Don't tell me that comes as a surprise. It's hardly like Lady Earthwygg to start proceedings so late in the day."

She looked up from straightening her skirt to see his blue eyes bulging at her like those of an enraged bull.

"That's the most immodest, outrageous thing I've ever—"

"Don't look at me," she protested calmly. "*I'm* not the one who's been sending you dreams about the girl." His eyes widened with a fury that told her she'd hit square on the mark. "If you wish me to, I can give you a comprehensive counterspell—"

"You'll do nothing of the sort!" Spenson shouted, causing a couple of nuns hurrying down the other side of the street with market baskets in their hands to stop and turn, eyes wide with surprise behind their veils.

"Keep your arts to yourself, my girl, if you know what's good for you!"

Turning heel, he stormed back to the gig, caught up the reins—without, Kyra noted, jagging the mare's mouth, as another man in that much of a temper might have done—and rattled away with such abruptness as to almost collide with a poulterer's wicker cart that had come dashing around the corner from the other direction. She heard Spenson curse mightily as he swerved to avoid it, and he was still cursing as he vanished down the lane, shawl and spell-cord flapping about the wheels.

"Well!" Kyra shoved a final pin into her hair and pulled her cloak about her once more. Across the street, the two nuns were whispering to one another and two servant girls and the yardman from the big house on the opposite side of the lane were staring at her as if she were a tattooed lady in a raree show. "Some people have no tolerance."

She continued her progress via a more circuitous route and stayed as much as was possible to the well-traveled streets.

The Church of St. Farinox was a relatively new one, built fifty years earlier, when all the great mansions that lined the city wall between Salt Hill and Parsley Hill had been pulled down to accommodate the rising guildsmen and new-rich factory owners in their demand for spacious city residences. The old banking families, whose wealth antedated theirs by three generations, were already firmly ensconced around Governor's Square on the other side of the most fashionable district. The owners of the factories that were making Angelshand one of the wealthiest cities of the Empire wanted, and were willing to pay for, something equally grand.

Like nearly everything else in Angelshand, the church was constructed of granite, so darkened with factory soot that even its handsome proportions and pillared portico couldn't make it appear light; it loomed above its small forecourt like an iron ox, head bowed, ready to charge. Kyra approached it casually through the colonnade that ran around its court, where shop-keepers had just begun to open the boutiques of fashionable lingerie, perfumes, and chocolate; she wove about herself again the spells of disvisibility, slipping the eyes of passersby away from her like quicksilver.

On the great bronze doors of the church a notice was affixed, informing all and sundry that the marriage between Master Blore Spenson and Miss Alixenia Peldyrin would take place on the following day. No garlands had been woven on the porch pillars yet. As she'd come downstairs that morning, Kyra had overheard the footmen complaining—as they moved the tubbed gardenias back out onto the steps—that they'd have to do so this afternoon.

Quietly she made her way around the church, through a tiny garden—only the older churches down near the river had churchyards anymore, tradition being satisfied with minute handkerchiefs of grass and flowers in the expensive urban properties. The side door was also bolted. A hand pressed to the carved oak panels, a murmured word of power. The sliding whisper of steel against steel, the vibration of the moving latch.

She pushed the door open and stepped inside.

The smell of smilax, roses, and lilac here was overwhelming, drowning the mustiness of the last sabbath's incense and the faint, fusty amalgam of dust and altar cloths. The golden sun canopy over the altar of the Sole God had been garlanded already, probably yesterday; the blossoms were drooping a little but still looked in fairly good shape. Along the wall by the door through which she had just come, Kyra saw the poles of the bridal canopy: cedar, cypress, oak, and ash, as the rite demanded, with their fittings and finials of silver. In ancient houses the fittings were handed down from generation to generation. Her father had purchased these new.

The poles themselves would be burned on the wedding night, after the banquet, when the bride and groom had been put to bed.

The bride and groom.

Alix and Blore Spenson, who, in spite of the awful neck cloth and red suit, now seemed a bit more like the pirate fighter and commander of men her father had described.

If Alix lived that long.

She shook away the thought of Blore Spenson, her anxiety flooding back. With hands that trembled slightly, Kyra bolted the door behind her, threw back her cloak, and dug in her pocket for the few things she had brought with her: chalk, a vial of mixed staghorn and powdered silver, and, wrapped in greased kitchen paper, a few bits of cheese.

"I can understand swearing not to use one's magic for ill," she'd said that first night in the Citadel of Wizards, sitting before the fire in the Junior Parlor with the woman who would be her teacher, her mentor, her sponsor during the long and tedious days to come. "And it isn't fair, of course, to use it for one's own amusement on the innocent, though I suspect that a touch of magic would liven up their days, poor things . . . But not to use it for good? What is magic for, then?"

"What magic is for is a question that no one has ever succeeded in answering." The Lady Rosamund Kentacre leaned back against the chimney breast, folding her beautiful hands in her lap. There was nothing about the Lady that was not beautiful: her alabaster skin, her absinthe-colored eyes, her low, clear voice. Like Alix, she was just tall enough to be striking, without Kyra's height; her hair so black that it was almost purple, massed in springy, sensuous curls. She was, at the time of Kyra's arrival, in her midthirties, the daughter, they said, of the Earl Maritime, ejected by him from the household when she had refused to use her powers for the betterment of the family. Perhaps this was the source of the sympathy and kindness Kyra had detected in the older woman's aloof green eyes.

"I suppose," the Lady went on after a moment, "one could ask, 'What is good?' What is the good that you would use your magic for?"

"To heal the sick," Kyra said.

"Then why did you not become a doctor? Many who are mageborn do. What else?"

"Well," Kyra said diffidently, "there are a lot of extremely poor people in the cities, people who can't feed their children, people who struggle, and die, just to put wood in the stoves through the winter. Surely one could lay words of good fortune on them, words of luck that would bring them money—or use one's magic to . . . to compel the rich to open their hearts and their purses a little more than they do."

"Thus taking from them whatever merit they might win from God—or fate—or whatever it is that controls the lives of ordinary men—from their own free choice to help? Taking from them, in fact, their free will?"

"Well . . ." Kyra said.

"You know as well as I do, Kyra, that magic cannot make something from nothing. The money that a word of good fortune could bring one man is money that is taken from another. And just because you are a good judge of which man or woman is deserving of help doesn't mean that another wizard, with equal ability, wouldn't be deceived by a plausible scoundrel's charm or tempted by an offer to split the takings of whatever that 'good-luck word' would bring."

Kyra was silent, aware that she was being argued around but for the first time in her life not certain enough of her ground to argue back. She had worked, and hungered, and given up so much to be in this place, with this woman and the others she had met during that first day, and this checked her unthinking assumption of her own correctness.

At length she said, "You know what I mean."

"I know what you mean," Lady Rosamund said softly. "But what is permissible for one must be permissible for all, you see, where magic is concerned. Else self-righteousness, and corruption, and narrow-mindedness would spread down the generations, and we would have war among the wizards, who must stand together against those who fear magic because it is a power over them that they cannot understand.

"For centuries, Kyra, every man who could afford to hire a wizard or keep one as his courtier could gain ascendancy over other men by unfair means. Thus wizardry came to be hated by all, even though there were good wizards, mages who refused to do evil for pay—or what they perceived to be evil. But many of those who did evil did so believing to their deaths that they had done good."

Rosamund sighed and, leaning forward, took a poker and made up the fire again with the neat competence of a kitchen maid. "It is not a condition," she added, "exclusive to the mageborn." The renewed light showed her beautiful face sad and gleamed in the gold pins that held back the delicate braids of her hair.

"With the coming of machines, and mills, and factories—with the coming of guns, and stronger governments, and armies, and colonies, and intricate politics of money and trade and industry—few issues are clear anymore. You know that. Your father is in business; you've kept his books. It takes very little magic to damage a machine or blow up a gun, and there were wizards who believed themselves to be doing great good in upsetting factories, destroying machines, not realizing that the factories were only a part of the changes taking place. All it left was families starving and jobless, for they could not return to the farms. And then they had to defend what they had done against armies, against politicians, who themselves had wizards who believed themselves in the right. At last, all we *could* do was withdraw. Just because we can command the natural world doesn't mean that we can command our own passions or understand what is truly right, truly best, for all concerned. It is too easy for someone to believe that what he or she greatly desires is right."

Kyra was silent at that, but she felt her own memories bleed. She found she had to look away from the fire.

Beside her, the Lady Rosamund finished gently. "That is why the vows. That is why, if any mage be found breaking his or her vows to the Council by meddling in human affairs *in any fashion whatsoever*, that mage shall be hunted down and punished, no matter who he or she is, to the limit of the Council's strength." Her green eyes grew cold and hard as diamonds. "No matter who they are, and how firmly they believed themselves to be in the right."

Standing in the silence of the church, Kyra smelled again the bite of the wood smoke and heard the Lady's voice. Rosamund had warned her before her departure against using her magic for any purpose but to scry out the source of the danger to her sister, something she probably could have done in the week or more she thought she would have between her arrival and the wedding.

Discovery of what she had done last night—of what she had come here to do—would in all probability result in her expulsion from the Citadel, the end of the education in the greater magic that had become her life. At the very best, she could look forward only to becoming a dog wizard, begging what learning she could from other dog wizards . . . like Tibbeth.

She closed her eyes.

And felt again the terror, the knowledge, that had come to her in her dream.

It was, she reasoned, opening her eyes once more, only a very small spell, undetectable by the Council and completely harmless in itself. And in fact, there was no violation of human free will involved.

Taking a deep breath, she moved quickly, her footfalls making barely an echo, past the altar rails and up to the narthex of the church.

CHAPTER V

"MICE!" GORDAM PELDYRIN'S HARSH-VOICED OUTRAGE carried quite clearly up to his elder daughter in the third-floor gallery that circled the hall.

Kyra paused and smiled with an emotion utterly unworthy of an academically trained mage. She focused her mind, letting her perceptions reach down through the lofty spaces of the hall, though in this case it was scarcely necessary. The door of his study, which opened onto the gallery below, stood ajar, and like Kyra's, his deep voice had considerable carrying power.

"You're telling me that the priest of St. Farinox is refusing to hold the wedding there tomorrow because of *mice*?"

"It's ... it's the most extraordinary thing we've ever seen, sir," stammered a young woman's voice, presumably the messenger from St. Farinox. "We've sent for the rat catcher, but the church is alive with them."

"This is ridiculous!"

Kyra's brows quirked upward. As she'd been changing out of her borrowed servant's dress and into the brilliant gown of emerald green she now wore—chosen because it was one of the several she'd designed to be put on without the assistance of a maid—she'd heard the chimes of St. Farinox and the slightly dimmer echo of St. Creel over on Great Cheevy Street speak eleven. The spell she'd laid that morning had worked with gratifying quickness.

Her plum-colored petticoats rustling, she sought her sister's chamber.

In spite of her fear for Alix, which gnawed like a rat at her nerves, she had taken her time returning home, detouring by a bookshop she'd once patronized in Ditch Street and stopping to assuage her hunger on steamed noodles from a cart in front of the Bremenntine Convent. Though everything within her screamed to be doing something, *anything*, she knew absolutely that Alix wouldn't be ready to leave her room until almost noon. Even at age twelve Alix had never been on time for lessons, dancing class, or dinner; putting herself together for the children's parties at the houses of her father's friends or sitting with her mother when she was "at home" to callers had involved hours of curling irons, lacing and unlacing, and consultations over the relative merits of baby's breath and forget-me-nots for her hair. There was no reason to think she had changed.

As she had suspected, Kyra heard her sister's silvery voice through the shut door of the bedroom and the light, quick tread that had to be Merrivale.

". . . only Tellie, after all," Alix was saying. "And everything for the wedding has been *done* or else can't be started on until later tonight, like moving the garlands up out of the ice cellar—did that keep you up horribly late last night, Merry? I wanted to help, but Mother insisted that I go to bed . . . not that I slept a wink."

"It all went fine," came Merrivale's deep voice with its flattened Mellidane vowels. For as long as Kyra could remember, Merrivale had been her mother's personal maid, combining that unexacting task with the job of housekeeper. Given Binnie Peldyrin's own abilities in menu planning and household accounting, Merrivale's chores consisted mainly of acting as corps-commander of the three chambermaids and whatever laundrywoman was currently in the household's employ, a position that frequently put her in covert conflict with Briory, who commanded the footmen and took ill any orders given to them that did not come from her. It had been worse, Kyra recalled, when there had been nurses, governesses, and tutors involved in the power struggle as well.

"So there's really no reason for me to stay here all afternoon," Alix went on, to the accompaniment of a soft creak of chair joints and the thick rustle of petticoats as she stood. "And they didn't have much of that shell-pink toile left at Brussat's. After the wedding it will be weeks before I can get out again, what with settling into the new house and getting things arranged as they should be, though thank goodness I won't have to find servants or anything—I mean, it will all just be Master Spenson's house. But I'll need to be there and learn to know everyone and how things are done. And I'm dying to make up that new gown I designed—I *know* it will be more beautiful than anything I've seen in Hylette's shop, or any of the shops, for that matter."

Good, Kyra thought. *She'll be out of the house entirely.*

Merrivale laughed softly. "And you'll have every lady of your acquaintance wondering who your dressmaker is."

Alix giggled. "And I won't breathe a word. It's funny—Mother doesn't see what difference it would make if I were to mention to Tellie or Frittilaire, not to mention that horrid Esmin Earthwygg, that I make my own dresses ... It's Papa who told me that it 'isn't done.' "

Kyra violently suppressed her urge to pound on the

wall and scream, *Would you get* out *of here, you twitter-ing numbskull, and let me get on with saving your life?*

Down in the hall she heard the opening of the main doors and muffled voices; a moment later, glancing over the carved railing, she saw Blore Spenson in his bottle-green coat ascending the stair in the wake of Briory and a darting footman who outdistanced them both, clearly bound for the third-floor gallery where she stood. Quietly, Kyra opened the door to the parlor next to Alix's room and stepped inside.

Muffled voices, Alix's small, nearly silent "Oh . . ." And then, bright as a new silver coin, "Oh, yes, of course . . ." and the foamy music of her skirts, the click of her heels descending while Merrivale and the panting footman made their way down the gallery to the back stairs.

Alix's room was empty.

At last! Kyra thought.

In times past the parlor, which opened not only to the gallery but also into both the girls' bedroom and their parents', had been used as a schoolroom where Kyra had studied her mathematics and languages, and Alix her embroidery, poetry, and harp. With both girls grown, the broad oak table beneath the wide windows had disappeared, along with the bookcases and globe. Pale yellow paper block-printed with sprays of black and white flowers had appeared on the walls, and fash-ionable bowlegged chairs with straw-colored cushions had made their debut. At the moment Babycake, the fatter of Binnie Peldyrin's lapdogs, was snoring sterto-rously on the seat nearest the white and blue-tiled stove.

Kyra waited until she heard the door to the back stairs close and felt the soft pressure of footsteps de-scending; then she flung herself into the room she had once shared with Alix.

She halted, looking around her.

Unlike the schoolroom, this had changed little. A small religious painting had replaced Kyra's lurid Uki-

Jen scroll of the serpent eating the heart of the world. A coverlet of white embroidered with wildflowers in yellow and blue—certainly Alix's masterly work—had replaced Kyra's adolescent choice of green and scarlet satin. The bed hangings were still white, as were the curtains on the two long windows.

Kyra walked slowly to the one nearer the bed and pushed the curtain aside. Below her, the garden was a jeweled geometry of pansy and alyssum, irises and lilies between crowding cinder-colored walls, the lilac trees so thick with bloom as to hide nearly all their branches. Water sparkled like quicksilver in the moss-rimmed fountain. Between pillars of soot-darkened brown brick the gateway at the far side seemed even now thick with shadow.

She turned quickly away. From its corner by the armoire, the crimson wedding dress glittered gently in the diffuse white light.

If I knew what I was looking for, Kyra reflected grimly, *this would be a good deal easier.* She only prayed she'd find what she sought in this room or the one adjoining. It was logical, of course, that it would be here.

A book of romances lying on top of the highboy yielded pressed flowers: violets, hyacinth, and a winter rose. Touching the desiccated petals, Kyra called forth the faces of the men who had given them. Young men, and all of them very handsome, two of them wearing the laces and face paint of wealthy, probably noble families. The third . . . Yes, one of the musicians had given her the violets. A giggle, a kiss, a flirtation on the dark gallery—the mandolin player whom Kyra had glimpsed only that morning as she'd slipped out on her errand; he'd been smuggling one of Neb Wishrom's tousle-haired chambermaids down the back stairs in her shift.

From none of the flowers could Kyra feel any depth of passion either in the giver or in the receiver, though all of them were touched with the kitten joy of pleasant memories.

Kyra paused, the winter rose in her hand.

Well-kept soft fingers brushing the hair aside from her cheek. The half-possessive, half-protective hand in the small of her back, guiding her to a chair. A twinkle in someone's eye. Too many men vying for a dance.

The crimson wedding gown that would fit her as well as it would Alix.

Her jaw hurt with the sudden clench of the muscles there, and she pushed the image from herself with the violence of contempt. *Really,* she thought disgustedly, *are you sorry you had better things to do than play silly games with those callow boys who only asked you to dance when their parents ordered them to? Are you really sorry no one ever treated you like a brood mare with a dowry?*

"Yes," whispered the tall girl who had always sat alone, chin high and eyes sarcastically defiant, watching her friends through too many quandriles, minuets, waltzes.

Yes.

Ninny.

In any case, here was no passion that did murder. Changing her perception, she stroked the flowers but saw nothing of magic, nothing of poison, nothing of ill will.

". . . honestly, Gyvinna, she had the nerve to say to me, 'You ought to better yourself and not stay a drudge for the rich.' "

Kyra made a bolt for the sitting-room door, barely making it as the red-haired chambermaid entered with the laundrywoman behind her, their arms filled with newly pressed linens. Kyra readied herself to retreat farther into her mother's rooms and so out into the gallery if necessary should the two young women enter the parlor, but there was no need. Her hooped skirts nearly dragged over an occasional table in her haste to return to the bedroom in the maids' departing wake.

So much to search, and there had to be something, some clue . . .

The top drawer of the dresser contained poems.

There were seven or eight of them. One was about one of her mother's lapdogs, which made her smile; one was about the vendors' cries in the street before the coming of full light.

The rest were about Alix.

They were written on cream-colored paper at two pennies the packet, the sort of thing on which plumbers' sons wrote love letters to shop girls. The best that very little money could buy.

If my love be a song, then you are the harpist's strings,
Were I a purling brook, they would find you at the springs.
If your name be the south wind, I am but the clouds which run,
As one flower in the meadow, I turn but to your sun . . .

They were tear-spotted, and the scent of passion, of yearning, of heart-tearing joy rose off them like the musky benison of perfume.

Her fingers brushed forth the face of the sender from the dry crinkle of the page.

Lamplight on fair hair, a white sleeve seen through fog. The whispered sigh of a child who knew she could never have that which she truly wanted.

Kyra whispered, "Oh, dear . . . beautiful as daylight and a poet to boot."

The rest of the dresser drawers yielded nothing. The pomanders, sweetgrass and lily of the valley, were simply pomanders, innocent of the spells she had read of in the books of ill, and she found no talismans of darkness concealed in the headboard of the bed, the favored place for such magics. She passed her hands with light swiftness over the paneled walls, the frames and thresholds of the doors, finding nothing. She was just beginning a systematic search of the floor for loose tiles of the parquetry when her mageborn hearing picked up footsteps in the hall.

Catching up her skirts, she took temporary refuge in the armoire, listening with her wizard's skills through the wall to the quick clip of a woman's feet in the parlor next door, then, a moment later, that of a man.

A whispered giggle, a little squeak: "What if Miss Alix should come back?" The red-haired maid again.

A man's voice—the harpsichord player, Kyra thought—slurred as if he were speaking around some soft obstruction. "I just saw her down the drawin' room with old Moneybritches."

Kyra seriously considered thumping on the wall and demanding, *Can't you two do that in the attic like everybody else did last night?* But her own position was as chancy as theirs. In disgust, she wrapped about her more closely the spells of diverted attention, of Look-over-There and Who-Me?, and with great care stepped out of the wardrobe, holding her skirts to keep them from rustling as she glided out the bedroom door—*not*, she guessed by the sound of it, *that I need trouble myself much over being heard.*

Back in her room again, Kyra dug in her satchel for the chunk of smoky white quartz she had brought from the Citadel, as long as two knuckles of her fingers and twice as thick. Sitting on the edge of the bed, she angled the crystal's central facet so that it caught the light of the window, gazing down into the light and through it into the lattices of the crystal's heart. For a brief time she was more acutely conscious than ever of the room around her, the smells of patchouli and candle wax and the cedar in the folds of her gown, conscious of the voices of the laundrymaid and Merrivale in the drying room far below, of Alix's light, airy chatter in the drawing room, of the tune Sam the coachman was whistling as he swept the cobbled yard far beneath her window . . .

Then colors swam in the crystal, spiraling down to gray . . .

The blur of a very old scry-ward, eroded to nothing with long neglect, momentarily darkened the stone, then crumbled away.

And she was in the Church of St. Farinox.

She almost laughed out loud with triumph and delight.

Her Summoning not only had taken effect quickly, it had succeeded with a wild thoroughness beyond her hopes.

The golden canopy over the Sole God's altar scuttered and threshed with tiny scramblings; small, nervous shapes darted wildly across the steps of the altar, up and down the canopy's garlanded golden pillars, around and over the edges of the waist-high carven pew rails. There were three men in laborers' clothes beside a harried-looking priest and some black-clothed member of the minor clergy—a young woman with red hair, probably the one who'd brought the message here—and half a dozen terriers such as professional rat catchers owned. The dogs were pelting here and there like lizards on hot glass, not knowing what to go after first; the two clergy were nervously holding the hems of their robes up off the floor. Kyra remembered getting a mouse up her skirts when she was twelve. Though she didn't have the disproportionate, morbid horror about it that so many women did, the brouhaha of having two friends lift, shake, and fumble through her four petticoats, hoops, overskirt, underskirt, and train in quest of the errant rodent was an experience she didn't care to repeat.

There was absolutely going to be no wedding taking place in that church tomorrow morning.

Kyra breathed a shaky prayer of relief. Another day.

She was starting to fold her hand around the crystal to obliterate the image when glowing indigo darkness clouded the stone's depths. A moment later she saw in it, as if reflected from some great distance away, the face of Lady Rosamund Kentacre.

"Kyra?" the wizard said, and Kyra felt a sudden wash of relief sweep over her, as if she had stepped from the chill of a stone room out into a windless, sun-flooded summer garden. After less than twenty-four hours of her mother's twittering, of bustle and servants and petticoats and worrying about what her father was going to say to her, the sight of her teacher's face was like silence after the nagging whine of a crying child.

"Rosamund!" she cried. "Oh, Rosamund . . ."

"Are you all right?"

"God, yes . . . that is . . ."

"We've been worried about you here," the mage said. "Worried about how you're faring in Angelshand and what you may have learned about your sister. Is she well? Have you found aught amiss there?"

"No!" Kyra cupped the crystal in her hands. "That is—well, as unamiss as one can get, in my father's house, with a wedding going on that neither the bride nor the groom seems to want and my father looking at me like he's waiting for me to leave so he can fumigate the furniture."

"I see," Rosamund said quietly. Kyra, remembering Rosamund's family, knew that she did in fact see. "But no sign yet of a death-spell? Remember, Nandiharrow did say that the . . . the things that happened might have been the effect of exhaustion, of too much study."

"Or they might have been a premonition." Kyra shivered, remembering the dream, remembering the cold evil she had felt, the image of Alix lying with shut eyes in her crimson wedding gown, the saffron veils sheathing her like flame among the white asphodels that mourners scattered over the dead. "Rosamund, could there be any chance that I would have a premonition over—over a death that wasn't being caused by magic? That Alix might be in danger from someone, or something, natural?"

"Such as?"

"Could I have had premonitions like that if she was in danger from a disappointed suitor, for instance?"

Rosamund was quiet for a moment, deep in thought. Behind her, Kyra could see the wide arches of her balcony and, beyond them, the overgrown wilderness of the Citadel's garden, with its peach trees, its dry rock walls, its myriad cats dozing in the afternoon sun.

"A crime of passion, you mean? Or jealousy?"

Kyra nodded. Spenson's angry face flashed across her mind, furious with embarrassment that he had been duped. Like a counterpoint melody she recalled the desperate love that warmed the very paper of the poems.

"Maybe," the older woman said slowly. "Maybe. You were very close to her, and we don't really understand much about premonitions. But it's far likelier that an Eye of Evil, a mark of ill, has been written somewhere in the house. It could have been placed weeks ago—months ago—to be activated by the marriage. And it could be anywhere." Rosamund leaned forward earnestly, the sunlight through the lattices of her distant windows flashing on the antique work of the pins that held her hair. "Will the wedding be soon? Will you have time to make a thorough search?"

"The first of May," Kyra lied, not wanting to mention that the ceremony had been put forward, only to be delayed by means best not gone into before a member of the Council. "Not long. I don't know if I can do it in time."

"You will, Kyra," the Lady said, and her green eyes held all the embrace that she would have given had she been in the room. "Trust God and keep working. If a dog wizard has been paid to set such a spell, you can go to the Inquisition; in a matter this serious, there will be no blame to you. Our good wishes will be with you."

The crystal faded. Kyra's hand closed around it, the sharp edges biting into her palm, and for a time she sat, fighting the deeper bite of longing that the sight of her friend, the glimpse through those far-off windows of the familiar herb garden, had brought.

The place that was her home.

She looked around her, her panic ebbing for a time, a strange ache filling her at the realization that this house where she had grown up was not her home, had not been so for a long time. It was like something she had read about in a book years earlier, researching and studying the life of a girl named Kyra Peldyrin who had been good with mathematics, brilliant in languages, accounting, the buying and selling of corn. Who had had a father who had loved her and, later, a teacher in magic named Tibbeth of Hale.

The colors of the walls of the yellow guest room seemed different; the perspectives along the gallery and from the bedroom window where she and Alix had slept were not quite the same.

She shook her head again. "The mark could be anywhere," she repeated softly, standing up and shaking out her skirts. The old rhyme echoed in her head, *Upstairs, downstairs, in my lady's chamber* . . .

There were plenty of merchants in town who had marriageable daughters, who wanted to ally their houses with the Spenson fortune, plenty more who would want to scupper the alliance on general principles. The grandson who, Kyra knew, was the object of the match as far as her father was concerned would wield enormous power with the union of the two houses.

There were even her cousins—such as the penny-counting but otherwise undistinguished Wyrdlees—who might feel that if they couldn't marry into the family business, they would at least take steps to see that they'd inherit it. There were dog wizards in the town who would sell a death-mark for a price, beyond a doubt.

The only way to know who would be to find the mark itself.

But the tear stains on the cheap yellow parchment returned to her, the desperation imbued there like the echo of stifled sobs. *Don't leave me ...*

"If a mark is what I'm looking for."

Kyra tripped over the threshold, caught herself on the gallery rail, and resolutely descended the stairs.

As she passed the door of the drawing room on the floor below, Kyra saw that Alix had been joined not only by Tellie Wishrom from next door but by her other two close friends, Frittilaire Nysett and Cira Prouvet, the daughters of other men high up in the councils of the guilds. Tellie, slender and black-haired and with a Senterwinger's fair skin and blue eyes, as usual had little to say, but Frittilaire, a buxom, sandy blonde, and Cira, a vivacious brunette, were more than making up for this, with the result that they had quite clearly driven Master Spenson from the room. He was leaning, in fact, in the doorway of the study, listening to her father.

"... know yourself what this delay is costing us! All the business I'd put off till tomorrow for the wedding I'll now have to put off another day. With ships to be inventoried and gotten under way, God knows what it's costing you!"

Kyra studied Spenson's square face and firm mouth, feeling a little ashamed of her brusque arrogance earlier that day in Upper Tollam Street. She had been angry at herself for walking into the attack and preoccupied with dread over Alix ... Still, she knew she had retreated into the old loftiness that had been her armor all her life.

Considering him now, she recalled his flash of rage, but even in the heat of it he'd been careful of his horse's mouth. In an odd way, the neat violence with which he'd dispatched her attackers had not been the act of a man who let passion dictate his acts. And in any case, even had she not defused his desire for Esmin Earthwygg by telling him he'd been a dupe, the most that desire would have provoked would have been a lawsuit for breach of contract, not a murder.

"Not to mention the rental on the white carriage mares and those dratted musicians who are turning the attic into a tavern and a bawdy house."

"Maybe Miss Kyra can help us." Spenson turned, leaning his broad shoulders against the door frame, his blue eyes glinting with teasing malice as he looked across at her. It was the first time she had seen him at ease. His temper seemed to be like her own, of the gunpowder variety, quick-burning and as quickly gone. His burly body had a compact quality of strength in repose, like a big, muscular tomcat. She wondered suddenly if he danced.

"I don't think there's sufficient magic in the world to reform that flute player," she remarked.

"No, but maybe you could convince our furry little friends at St. Farinox to breed elsewhere."

"No!" Her father's voice was like the slapping of a leather strap onto wood. "I forbid it!" Framed in the mauve velvet flaps of the cap he wore when he was indoors, his face was pale with anger. His velvet robe, like an old-fashioned scholar's, billowed around him as he strode forward, his hand raised as though he would strike her.

"You've caused enough trouble to this house with your wretched hoodoo and your stinking spells! You've brought scandal and unhappiness, and I won't have witchery under this roof, do you hear!"

Kyra's chin came up, and her hazel eyes flashed into the hazel glare that faced her. "Admirably—as do Alix's friends down the hall, I should imagine," she said coolly. "In any case, interference in human concerns is against the ethics of true wizardry, so I'm afraid it would be impossible for me to comply."

She gave them her best curtsy and made her regal way to the head of the stairs, a progress marred by turning the high, purple-lacquered heel of her shoe and nearly breaking her ankle. Master Spenson covered the two strides' distance between them in time to steady her, his big, rough hands surprisingly light on her fingers and waist.

He must dance, she thought as she disengaged herself and descended the stair toward the kitchen, where, with any luck, she'd locate the man who had written those poems.

CHAPTER VI

"MADAME, WE WORKED THE NIGHT THROUGH ON THIS cake!" Joblin the cook's square, heavy hand, with its inevitable ladle, gestured toward the rococo mountain of garlands, scallops, marzipan trees, and tiny gingerbread palaces, a gesture strangely balletic for a man who looked as if he should be heaving gravel in a quarry somewhere. His dark eyes under their jutting brows were pleading. "It is perhaps the finest confection wrought in Angelshand, certainly the finest in many years. Fifteen eggs went into it! *Fifteen!* And as for the sugar and the butter . . ."

"Well," Kyra remarked, plucking a shell of pink icing from the base, "in two days it won't matter if you'd used thirty eggs. It's definitely forming a crust."

"I'm afraid that's true," her mother sighed, folding her hands over the waistband of her huge linen apron. "And even after one day, I know how the flavor of a white cake begins to go off."

The cook made a noise in his throat suggestive of a man being brave about having his toes severed.

88

"We could prolong it by having it carried down to the ice cellar for a day, but you know how things sweat down there, and it would almost certainly make the gingerbread soggy. Kyra, darling, what a shame your father would never tolerate your using just a *little* spell to keep the cake fresh, with all the work Joblin's put into it ..."

"Mother ..."

"I'm not sure what Master Gordam plans to do about the mice in the church, though for the life of me I can't understand what can have drawn them there. I know he inspected the church quite thoroughly when he negotiated with the Bishop to have the ceremony there. What a shame your father's so set on the strict form, because of course if we were doing this by signature, it could all be done in our parlor. In any case, we've worshiped at St. Farinox for *years*, and never have we seen so much as a mouse *hole* ... For, of course, you know, Kyra darling, that I'd *never* attend a church that was at all mousy, and St. Farinox was always so respectable. Brentius—that's the priest there, you know, Brentius Byfillian—is related to Lord March, and was raised in the strictest propriety, and knows how all these things are done. Even if we do have a pew and aren't obliged to kneel on cushions, which I used to do as a girl because down in Mellidane they don't *have* pews, and even the *Emperor* has to kneel ... But in any case," she went on, returning to the main thread of the discourse with her usual wide-eyed aplomb, "it will certainly not be tomorrow."

"Oh, what a shame." Kyra helped herself to another buttery swirl. Anything Joblin made, from a twelve-course dinner to a poached egg, was always and invariably *the best in many years*—complete with documentation and extensive examples from the cook's wide knowledge of other households' banquets and breakfasts—but he was undeniably one of the finest cooks in the city. Though it was only midafternoon, the exertions of the day were beginning to catch up with Kyra—the long walk to St. Farinox and the struggle in Fennel Street—and the use of her magic always engendered in her a desperate hunger for sweets.

"But what are we to *do* with the cake?"

"*We'll* eat it," the harpsichord player offered cheerfully, pushing his round-lensed spectacles up onto the bridge of his nose. He and the viol player had been loitering in the kitchen in the hopes of mooching some jam. At the other end of the room the redheaded chambermaid was doing up sachets of dried verbena, looking sleek.

"He may be right," Binnie sighed regretfully. "The family can't possibly eat it. It would be bad luck to eat the cake before the wedding. You shouldn't even have taken that taste, Kyra dear. Goodness knows what sort of ill luck that will bring."

"I'm so sorry," Kyra apologized blithely, trying to keep herself from stealing another morsel of icing and failing miserably.

"On the other hand," her mother continued, "it would probably be a good idea to go down to the market and bespeak fresh eggs, because when things *are* decided, we may not be able to get as much as we need. It's so *difficult* to get large numbers of eggs at short notice. Oh, and Algeron, dearest," she added as the handsome young assistant began untying his apron preparatory to making the expedition, "could you go past the fruit market and get some oranges? There are usually some up from the south, and I was thinking of having orange-peel duck tomorrow evening. Since we do have this extra day, I've invited Cousin Wrydlees and my sister and brother-in-law—Sethwit is staying with Master Gordam's brother, you know. Orange duck is Master Gordam's favorite, and with things as upset as they are, I'm sure he needs a little extra looking after."

Her voice sustained a light, fluty babble as Algeron found his jacket—rough tweed and very worn at the elbows—and waited while Joblin fetched a silver crown and a few silver bits from one of the blue and yellow porcelain crocks on the shelf above the bin table. Kyra, unashamedly plundering the cake's rear slopes of their chantilly swags, watched him from the corner of her eye. He was very slender, almost delicate-looking, with his long, narrow face and grave gray eyes. He didn't look capable of violence, but then, Joblin, who looked like an unshaven bandit with his massive biceps and hulking shoulders, was the gentlest man she knew.

Kyra had learned once about men who seemed harmless. She would not trust her judgment again.

She stayed in the kitchen for some minutes after the young man's departure, trying not to make her own exit too closely in his wake. Like Alix, Binnie Peldyrin was capable of strewing the air with commentary for hours on end, the mechanics of the household serving as anchors to embroidered digressions about the habits and personalities of her sister and brothers-in-law, their relative position in the wedding procession and their problems with their servants, the gossip of the Court, which she followed through official gazettes and unofficial broadsides and scandal sheets, and utterly unfounded speculations on why this or that commodity—from attar of roses to chamomile tea—was more or less expensive. Kyra recalled it of old and supposed that six years ago she had only thought nothing of it because she knew no different.

Now, after years of the studious quiet of the Citadel—after years of dealing with people who studied their arts and concentrated on something other than who would be coming for dinner or how to finagle some future business transaction—she wondered how she could have stood her mother's relentless prattle and her father's single-minded pursuit of power in the councils of the town.

With a certain amount of difficulty she extricated herself from her mother's persistent account of the logistics of dealing with the Spenson family—Lord Mayor

Spenson having certain dietary restrictions that required special menus and a good deal of tact—and, wrapping herself once more in her faded black wool cloak, stepped into the kitchen yard. She could see the flute player standing in the shadow of the postern that communicated with the kitchen yard of the Wishroms' house, his dark head bent, deep in conversation with someone.

Kyra shook her head. She had slept poorly the previous night, waking often to the clatter of market carts in nearby Upper Tollam Street, the tapping of watchmen's staves, the rattle of iron-tired coach wheels, and the occasional riotous voices of those bands of Court rakes who, having exhausted the possibilities of the gambling hells of Prynnak Street and the bawdy houses of the Algoswive district, would rove the city till dawn in quest of mischief. Like her mother's chatter, it was a sound she had lost the habit of not hearing. Before sleeping, she had let her awareness move through the darkness of the house, listening to the breathing of the sleepers beneath her father's roof. Once she had heard, not far from her own room, the sound of weeping. Invariably from the attic had floated the clink of tankards, the shuffle and slap of cards, stifled feminine giggles, and now and then voices lifted in soft harmonies whose beauty had twisted her heart as she lay in the darkness.

> *Rain in the night, the sound of chimes,*
> *Thinking of you . . .*
> *An empty pillow, the empty hope*
> *That your bed is empty, too . . .*

Her mind went back to the poems she'd found in Alix's dresser, slipped beneath the handkerchiefs and the stockings of pink and lilac silk.

> *. . . But the sun break sweeps the buttercups*
> *And the last of my winter's despair*

Melts to song in the light of your smile,
and the sunlight on your hair.

She shook her head, quickened her pace a little, and pushed open the heavy carriage gate.

The aspect of the square had changed considerably since her expedition that morning. Servants—or the clerks of the merchants who had their countinghouses nearby, which amounted to nearly the same thing—hurried here and there on errands. A nursemaid hustled her overdressed charges on a rapid constitutional around the encircling flagway, her starched white cap wings vibrating and her veil flapping with every step she took. Kyra tried to guess whose she might be, but the children were young, and after six years she had no way to guess. Another nurse, her pink dress announcing the sex of her absent charge, stood gossiping with the day watchman in charge of the square, while a passing cabman pulled briefly up beside a woman selling sausages to buy himself lunch on the move. The blue of the cabman's long coat, the red of the watchman's, the bright dresses of the pair of women taking a stroll, showed up like flowers against the heavy gray of the buildings; the sausage woman was singing about steam and grease and sugar, and somewhere someone was again playing a hurdy-gurdy, the sound of it muted by distance and air into something less like the caterwauling of a dying beast and more like music. Some movement caught the corner of Kyra's eye as she started to cross the square, and she stopped, looking quickly around, remembering the two men in the cab that morning.

But there was no one near her.

Frowning, she hurried on.

It was slightly less than two miles to the great central market of the city, a distance Kyra had been used to walking two or three times daily, even as a child. A rapid and businesslike walker at need, she soon came in sight of Algeron Brackett making his way along the streets of narrow-fronted brown-brick houses that constituted the Springwell district. Small cafés and fashionable rooming houses created bright spots amid erratic turnings and tiny courtyards of crumbling flats, with laundry flapping overhead and squads of shrieking children playing in the gutters. Eastward, past the Imperial Guards' barracks, the aspect of the town seemed to improve, an occasional house front gaudy with paint or bright with window-box daffodils, until they crossed through Prince Dittony Circle under the bronze prince's benevolent agate eyes. Kyra picked her way on Algeron's heels amid the usual tangle of cabs, sedan chairs, private carriages, scarf sellers' barrows, and the inevitable religious procession, and so through the intensely fashionable colonnade on the other side of the square, half a block of silk shops and merchants in expensive liqueurs, and thence, like diving into a murky swamp, into the densely packed, winding, and odoriferous lanes of the market district beyond.

Algeron was easy to follow. Though he did not dawdle, he stopped frequently to admire the dark-purple hyacinths an old man was selling from a wheelbarrow, to see the way the sunlight turned the gilded windows of the Woolmarket Hall to a wall of flame, to watch a thin, tired-looking man and a young woman in a scholar's robe leave sesame candy at the feet of a leaden saint in a street-corner shrine. He seemed oblivious to the smell of putrefying vegetable parings under his feet and the prostitutes who whistled invitingly from the gloom of every doorway. Even on his errand, Kyra realized, he was captivated by the strange, bewildering beauty of the city—to the extent that, as he crossed the Guildhall Square, he was nearly run over by a costermonger's barrow while staring dreamily at a little girl feeding doves.

Kyra's mouth twisted in a wry smile. Hardly the man, she thought, to do murder in a fit of thwarted passion— his poems had contained nothing but doglike adoration.

She wondered if she was wasting her time following him this way. But the whisper of stronger emotions had clung to the paper, deep and biting as triple-strong *khala* liquor, and she lengthened her stride as he stood wiping from his breeches' knees the mud the barrow had thrown up on him and called out his name.

"Miss Kyra!" He nearly jumped out of his shoes; clearly he had been deep in his own meditations. But immediately he smiled and swept off his cap to her. The expression in his gray eyes seemed open, clean, and kind. "You shouldn't have come all the way down here. I was coming to bespeak the eggs. You could have told me what you wanted."

From the tail of her eye Kyra had again the brief, nagging sensation that there was something behind her that she ought to see. But when she turned her head, only the gay confusion of the Guildhall Square met her eyes, rainbow movement in which it would have been impossible to distinguish a single element as threatening even if she had known what she was looking for. Still . . .

"What I wanted," Kyra said, tucking her hand into the crook of his arm, "was to speak to you."

His eyes widened nervously, and he flinched a little, as if to pull away, then caught himself when he realized how rude that would be. "Uh . . . Oh?"

"Yes." She turned their steps across the square. Though originally intended as an ornament to offset by its spaciousness the intricate statuary that covered the Guildhall in a fashion regrettably reminiscent of her sister's wedding cake, the square had become over the years a choked and clamorous marketplace of dealers in used clothing and vendors of secondhand household goods. "I came across one of the poems you wrote about Alix. It's very good."

She said it to see what color he would turn—a very becoming carnation, as it happened. Much prettier than Spenson's blotchy vermilion.

But he only said, "You didn't show it . . . Your father hasn't seen it, has he?"

"Well, he may have taken to searching her dresser, but I'm quite sure if he had, we'd all have heard about it by this time. How is it that, with a talent for poetry such as you obviously have, you're still whipping meringues and grating orange rinds for Imper Joblin?"

"A man has to live," Algeron said after a moment. A lock of his hair, the bleached color of sun-dried onion tops, fell forward over one cheek as he bowed his head. *A man really has no business with eyelashes like that,* Kyra thought dispassionately, viewing his face in profile. "Father was a journeyman baker, and it was my right to enter the guild. Alix . . ." He paused on the name, and his face flushed again. "Alix did try to get me a post as personal secretary to Janson Milpott, the banker, one of your father's friends. But, well . . ."

He turned his eyes upon her pleadingly. "You see, I'm really no good at all with dates and figures and keeping things in order. After the third time I lost something—I think it was a letter from some merchant . . . And I really did know more or less where it was! Well . . ." His free hand, the one not occupied by his rush shopping basket and her arm upon his sleeve, gestured helplessly. As a cook's should be, it was clean and surprisingly muscular from stirring batters and sauces for hours on end. He smelled of soap and gingerbread.

"And the thing is," he went on, "I am quite good at making comfits and candying fruit. The gingerbread houses on the cake are mine, and they're better than anything Joblin could have made, in spite of what he says. But I won't be eligible for seniority in the guild in Angelshand until next year. And poetry . . ."

He paused, his eyes following a sudden flight of startled pigeons that wheeled in unison around the market's bronze clock tower, their wings catching the afternoon sunlight in a single flash.

"Poetry isn't something one can do, really, unless one is born wealthy. I was well educated—Mother used to be a governess—but unless one has a patron ..." He shook his head, his twilight-soft eyes sad. "I know Alix must marry that ... that merchant, and I won't speak ill of your father, Miss Kyra, but ... Well." He turned away, and they crossed to the great open arches of the huge stone market hall, echoing with voices like the maw of some pungent hell.

"I couldn't keep silent." He paused within the archways' blue shadow. "The poems came out of me like flowers pushing out of the ground, before I could stop myself. Please understand."

She tilted her head to one side. "Are you lovers?"

He went every color of the rainbow but could not find tongue to answer.

"No," Kyra said after a moment. "No, I suppose if you were, you would have written a poem about it."

Like a man suffocating, he managed to say, "I would never have ... have the presumption to touch the tips of her fingers with anything less than reverence."

Or to kill her, Kyra thought, *were she to wed another man?*

Looking up into that handsome face, like alabaster stained with attar of roses, she felt a pang of unexpected pity for the beautiful young poet who had such a talent with comfits and icings and no way to raise sufficient funds to even begin to support a bride. Certainly not a bride whose father expected to strengthen his dynasty with merchant capital. Her face softened, and she tugged gently on his arm.

"Well, unless Father takes to ransacking her room, he won't learn of it," she said in what she hoped was a comforting tone. "Let's go look for some eggs, and we'll say no more about it."

"I wish it would just ... get on with it."

Alix folded her arms around herself, though the bed-chamber's tiled stove warmed the big room pleasantly, and walked to the window with a restlessness that wasn't like her. Though, Kyra reminded herself, watching from the doorway, she didn't know exactly what *was* like Alix anymore. For all the ease with which they had resumed their friendship, her memories were of a twelve-year-old girl—trusting, bubbly, softhearted, mischievous but checking herself almost automatically to think whether her pranks and jokes would hurt anyone before she pulled them, affectionate with an unthinking warmth. She'd always been holding hands with someone, Kyra remembered; their father, Briory, Sam the coachman, one or another of her little girlfriends.

Six years was a long time.

"Was it so very awful?" Kyra asked. "Having everyone descend on you this afternoon and demand to be told all about it when all you wanted to do was get out of here?"

Alix looked around with a quick, rueful smile and shook her head. It was difficult to tell whether she meant it completely, for even as a very small child Alix had tried hard to like everyone, or at least to convince them that she liked them whether she truly did nor not. It wasn't hypocrisy so much as an anxiousness to make others happy. Kyra, elegant in her adult dresses, with her mouth full of barbed, literary double entendre, had seldom troubled to completely conceal her likes and dislikes of relatives or their father's business associates. Alix, she recalled, had never appeared less than wholeheartedly glad to see even such conversational horrors as Uncle Murdwym, with his loudmouthed advice on all and any topics, or their stuck-up and dirty-minded Cousin Leppice.

"Oh, it was really very good of Frittilaire and Cira to come over and see if I was all right," Alix said. "I mean, it's the sort of story—the mice in the church, I mean—that gets put around if there's something else really wrong."

"Nonsense," Kyra said briskly. "They came to gossip, and you know it."

The dimple beside Alix's mouth flickered into existence, and her brown eyes lost their tiredness for an instant in a sparkle of mischief. "Well ... I can't pretend I wouldn't do the same."

But the brightness faded as quickly as it had appeared, and the drawn expression of exhaustion returned as Alix looked away once again.

"I suppose it's just stage fright," she went on after a moment with a self-deprecation that to anyone but her sister would have sounded completely genuine. "I mean, we're getting ready for this *colossal* ceremony, with processions and jewels and white mares to draw the carriage and special music and the petals of this particular type of flower have to strew a carpet of this particular color up to the altar, and memorizing the words and the steps of the dances afterward, and worrying I'll forget or step forward with the wrong foot or trip over my train, and *everyone* we know going to be there ... And having that thing—" She gestured toward the vivid bridal gown upon its stand. "—standing there *watching* me as I go to bed every night, as if it's saying, 'Don't you dare gain any weight!' And then have everything just *stall*."

Her hand fidgeted with the fringe of her shawl for a moment, then was still. She used to pick at her cuticles when she was unhappy, Kyra remembered. Their mother had drilled the habit out of her by threatening to make her wear purple sticking plaster on her fingers to dancing classes, but Kyra was interested to see that the angry pink abrasions had returned to the corners of her sister's nails.

She considered for a moment whether Spenson would risk murder to avert a scandal, but even on the shortest of acquaintances with him, the idea was absurd. He had a temper, certainly, and a touchy pride, but the match itself was the choice of a businessman, not a lover. There were plenty of equally wealthy young ladies in the town for him to choose. His father might kill or order killed—he had the ruthlessness that brooked no refusal—but all *he* had to do to prevent the match was to speak.

Outside the wide windows daylight was dimming. Alix had already kindled the lamps on her dressing table to illuminate her work on the ivory-colored satin sleeve that lay amid a disembodied profusion of green ribbon and lace on the corner of the bed. In the garden below Kyra could just glimpse the stable hand who doubled as gardener—whatever his name was— finishing up weeding the lush beds of her mother's early-blooming roses. Shadows clustered thickly around the little gate, and Kyra wondered, with a hot flicker of anger behind her breastbone, whether that was being watched, too.

Coming away from the market with Algeron, she had felt that there was something she was missing, some element in the streets around them she wasn't seeing. She was nearly back to Baynorth Square when she realized what it had to be.

Someone was using a spell, or a talisman, of Look-over-There on her.

And when she knew that and concentrated on seeing through illusion, she easily glimpsed the sloppy-looking lounger in a brown coat whom—now that she thought of it—she had seen in the square earlier that afternoon, when she'd left to follow the cook's handsome assistant to market.

She had stayed close to Algeron the rest of the way back.

"Alix," she said now, gently, as her sister turned away to gaze, like her, over the steeply mansarded roofs and clustering chimney pots toward the ash-colored eastern sky. "I have to know about Algeron."

Alix flinched just a little, the silken fringe of the shawl picking up the vibration like a ripple of water, then for a moment she was still. Her hand went up to her hidden face, quickly touched the feathery curls at her temples, a manufactured excuse, for her eyes were still perilously bright as she looked back.

"He's such a dear," she said with a tinny falseness to her voice and her smile. "He's been my mainstay through all this, like a brother to me."

"Are you in love with him?"

The pink mouth trembled, then she made herself laugh. "How could anyone not fall *madly* in love with someone who has eyelashes like that? Aren't you?"

Kyra said nothing, just continued to look at her, and Alix's gaze fell. She averted her head quickly, to stare out the window again, her fingers in the flower garden of the shawl tearing at themselves while the wedding gown watched like an ironic maiden aunt. Lamplight caught the glisten of a tear.

After a time she drew a shaky breath. "I forgot," she said. "You were always . . . impervious. Too sensible." She met her sister's eyes with a warm little smile, even in her wretchedness concerned to take the sting out of the unsaid words: *You never loved. You were never loved.* "Even back when I was eleven and *desperately* in love with Gwillim—you remember that *gorgeous* footman we had?—and I thought I was going to die of it, I remember thinking how nice it would be to be cool, like you. It's nothing." She shook her head. "I really should have outgrown things like this."

"If you truly don't want to marry Master Spenson . . ." Kyra began, not certain how to proceed and not even sure where she wanted to proceed. The pain in her sister's voice, the evident grief written so clearly on her face, were foreign territory to her. Gorgeous Algeron certainly was and, besides that, a thoroughly nice young man, but nothing to invoke the chasm of misery into which she found herself looking.

"Of course I . . . I want to marry Master Spenson," Alix made herself say. She drew her breath again and sounded more natural. "He's a dear, sweet man, and I know that marrying him is going to be the best thing for me."

"Don't be silly," Kyra said acerbically. "Spenson is tactless, he has a temper like flashpaper, and he dresses like a fishmonger, and it's quite obvious—"

She bit down on the next words, realizing that telling her sister that her prospective husband quite obviously hadn't two words to say to her—the way Alix babbled, scarcely a surprise—was no kindness. Alix was crying now, tears running down her cheeks, and Kyra felt, in addition to a growing apprehension, a flash of annoyance.

Watching those tears, that utter wretchedness, she found herself wondering suddenly if the death she foresaw would come to her sister, in her despair, by Alix's own hand.

For LOVE? she thought in disgust. If Algeron had gotten her with child, maybe, though according to Algeron that wasn't the case. If Algeron had been telling the truth . . .

She wanted to cry, *Don't be a ninny, Alix!* but decided that the words would only elicit more tears. Upon further thought she realized that they were probably unkind as well. She reached out awkwardly to touch her but had no experience of giving comfort; at the touch of Kyra's hand upon her shoulder, Alix only shook her head, folding her arms again within her shawl and seeming to huddle closer against the window's cold glass. Kyra was left standing helplessly, wondering how she could tactfully ask if her sister was pregnant and thinking uneasily of cases she had known . . .

Girls of eighteen *did* commit suicide over lovers without being pregnant, though she herself couldn't imagine why. One of the Nysetts' maids had done so when Kyra was sixteen. Their parents, and Briory, had pretended to know nothing about it, but Merrivale had talked about it in the kitchen. And, she recalled,

Merrivale had said that a cousin of hers had done so not many years before.

"I'll be all right," Alix whispered finally. "It's good of you to be concerned, Kyra, but ... I'll be all right. Now would you please ... I'd just like a little time by myself."

Dear God, Kyra thought as she backed irresolutely from the room. *How on earth could I prevent her ... ?* She didn't even phrase it to herself. The thought that Alix would cut her wrists over that fair-haired, poetic pastry fluffer was inconceivable, eyelashes or no eyelashes.

But not so inconceivable that it didn't lodge in her heart like a fragment of broken glass as she hastened down the stairs.

Chapter VII

Alix was still in her room at dinnertime.

"I thought I told you to stay away from your sister," her father snapped as soon as Briory and her attendant footman had served the soup and borne the lobster-shaped crimson tureen from the room, leaving the family momentarily alone in the smaller of the two dining rooms, which overlooked the garden through intricate panes of beveled glass. "Until you appeared, she was perfectly happy, looking forward to marrying one of the finest men in Angelshand."

"Well, certainly one of the richest," Kyra drawled, dabbing at the small dollop of soured cream in the midst of the green lake of peas and sherry. She had forgotten the maddening leisureliness of family meals, and the necessity of sitting still and waiting it through itched like insect venom in her veins.

Small red blotches darkened the thin skin of Gordam Peldyrin's cheekbones. "After all the trouble I've gone to in arranging this match . . . After all the maneuvering I've undertaken to have people forget what happened,

I'm not going to have you stirring matters up now! Bad enough—"

The doors to the little warming room opened again, and he fell quickly silent. Briory and the footman—Lerp or Paskus, Kyra could never tell which was which—reentered, bearing scarlet platters of ham, green goose, jellied quail, and carrots in dill sauce. While they circulated the dishes and then laid them on the sideboard, there was no sound in the dining room save the graceful airs of the musicians, softened and altered to accommodate the smaller room and more modest setting.

Kyra recognized the tune, though it had been shifted from a minor to a major key and had been changed in modality to render it different, innocuous, free of the yearning grief it had held the previous night.

> *... An empty pillow, the empty hope*
> *that your bed is empty, too ...*

The light of the hanging lamps flashed in the harpsichord player's spectacles, glimmered like threads of vibrant gold in the mandolin's strings, and traced the lines of gilt flowers up the milk-white porcelain of the flute. Sensitized by Alix's desperation, Kyra had watched the maids—and Neb Wishrom's maids, who were more and more finding excuses to hang about the Peldyrin kitchen—as they dealt with these young men: tussles in the hayloft, last night's midnight scamperings up and down the back stairs. No wonder her father was irked.

Would this meal never end?

"Bad enough I'm going to have to repurchase every garland and wreath and bushel of rose petals the Texts demand," her father continued the moment the doors had shut behind Briory's plump blue back. "*And* the food for the feast, and a hundred twenty pounds of ice for the ices, and you know what ice costs this time of year, and thank God it isn't June! But it's never going to hold until the day after tomorrow."

"Will the mice be gone the day after tomorrow, dearest?" Binnie Peldyrin inquired anxiously.

Kyra brought up her napkin to disguise a smile. She'd scryed the church again after speaking to Alix and had seen her father and Spenson both there, uneasily shifting from foot to foot and keeping a sharp eye on the floor in their immediate vicinity while they argued in dumb show with the priest.

"They can stay in St. Farinox until midsummer if it suits them," her husband retorted, jabbing at the squab on his plate as if he were not only eating it but killing it also.

"Oh, don't say that, darling," his wife pleaded. "Even though Alix will be worshiping down at Holy Slippers in Fennel Street, I simply *couldn't* abide a church where I even *suspected* there might be mice, and poor Tellie Wishrom is positively *terrified* of them."

"I've spoken to Nissom Elfridge at St. Creel," Master Peldyrin went on, cutting in over his wife's chatter with the determination of long experience. "It cost me close to a hundred crowns, even with Bishop Woolmat's word added to mine, but arrangements are made to hold the wedding there the morning after tomorrow. I'll have the invitations sent out tonight."

"How lovely!" Binnie smiled radiantly.

"It's not in the best part of town, but Elfridge is of decent family, and Fyster Nyven worships there," he said. "And it was the best that could be had on short notice, since neither Holy Slippers nor Holy Sun is available for any money, though I expect if I were related to a member of the Court, they'd agree quickly enough."

He glanced sharply across at his elder daughter, who was meticulously dissecting a morsel of quail on her plate as a means of stilling the questions still racing in her mind. All the meal yet to go, she thought, and then the wait while Merrivale supervised the cleanup—she'd never find out in time. Never track down what she needed to know.

His voice was carefully controlled but steely with anger.

"Briory tells me the Inquisition is watching the house."

"Ah," Kyra said, not looking up from her task. "So that's who the young man in the brown coat is working for."

"I won't have it!"

"I suggest you speak to your friend the Bishop, then. Another hundred crowns or so should—"

"Be silent!"

Kyra raised her eyes languidly to meet his, schooling her face to the armor of unconcern. Despite having had no lunch and only noodles for breakfast, she found she had lost all interest in food.

His wide, square mouth, so like hers, grew taut; Binnie whispered, "Gordam, please."

"I don't know why you came back to this house. God knows you had little enough use for us when you left." The china rang softly with the tremor of his fork against it. "You've brought nothing but trouble in your wake, and I won't have you undoing all the care I've taken to guarantee an heir for my business, all the pains I've taken to increase our family's credit and to establish your sister as she deserves. She's going to have everything that a woman could ask for."

"Ah, but the question is, *Did* she ask for it?" Kyra ate another mouthful of quail just to demonstrate that he hadn't upset her, then set down her knife and fork with a crisp *clink*.

Bitterly, he said, "I gave you what you asked for, girl, and it nearly cost me everything I had."

Well, Kyra admitted to herself back in the yellow guest room later, *I can't argue with him there.*

She had been thirteen when first she had begun to dream of magic.

... pushing out of me like flowers from the ground, Algeron had said of his poems, of his love for Alix.

Kyra turned her scrying-crystal over in her fingers, letting the images she'd been seeking in it scatter in the flash of the candlelight. *The Inquisition must have equipped its spies with talismans of scry-ward as well as spells of Who-Me? ... They couldn't possibly be using the few mages they have for routine surveillance of a wizard new to the town.* It was unlikely they'd detected any jiggery-pokery with the front steps; if they had, they'd have moved on her at once. Still, their presence—their nosiness—irked her.

She let the anger pass.

Pushing out like flowers from the ground.

Not flowers, she thought. Chicks within the egg, when their life quickened and they knew they must break the shell or die.

She sighed and moved a little closer to the stove. She hoped that the man in the brown coat and anyone else observing the house were shivering miserably in their places of concealment. The night was cold for spring. She was aware of a malicious desire to summon rain or sleet but let that also pass.

Even now she could remember that first dream so clearly.

Kyra had never dreamed much as a child. When she did, her dreams were completely prosaic: sewing sleeves on a dress, embroidering a cuff and having to pick the stitches out ... She'd never been the expert seamstress Alix was even at the age of seven. Once she dreamed of adding up the month's ledgers and neglected to do it the following day out of a bone-deep conviction that she'd already accomplished the task. Working trigonometric proofs. That particular night she dreamed that she'd been driven home late from one of the dancibles given by the banker Janson Milpott: an accurate recollection, down to the color of the dress she was wearing—the outlandish ocher yellow with a spreading linen collar like an antique fop's—and her sense of nagging depression at having spent most of the evening among her girlfriends, keeping them in gales of laughter with her sarcasm but unwanted by any of the boys.

But in the dream she had been alone in the carriage, and when she had arrived at the house, it had been to find the place dark. She had thought, even dreaming, that she must have been a good deal later than she supposed. The front door opened under her hand, but no Briory, no footman, no parent came to meet her in the great front hall in a comforting blaze of yellow candlelight. The vast room stretched before her, black and echoing as a cavern a thousand feet below the ground. The silence frightened her.

So she had held out her right hand and summoned a ball of glowing white light to her palm, its rays shimmering to every corner of the hall, driving back the darkness and the fear.

Waking, she had sat up in her bed for a long time, staring into the moonless darkness beyond the bedposts and listening to Alix's breathing, soft among the clouds of linen and goose down at her side.

She hadn't told anyone about that dream. The next one didn't come to her until nearly six months later, when she dreamed that she'd lost Alix in the crowds along the river quays. Losing Alix was a fairly common dream for her in those days, for she often took the little girl with her when she went trawling through the secondhand book barrows, and the silly child *wouldn't* stay where she was told.

But after the usual growing anxiety, the usual horrible desperation of the dream search that always before had ended with Kyra waking herself up in a queasy sweat with a sense of disaster narrowly averted, she had gone to the nearest junk dealer's stall and purchased a mirror—she even remembered what she paid for it in the dream and recalled thinking what a bargain it was at three coppers. And passing her hand across its face, she had called Alix's image to it and had seen her sister trying to feed vegetable parings out of the gutter to the caged rabbits of a meat dealer with a red canopy over his stall.

The red canopy had been clearly visible above the crowds. Kyra had gone over to it, mirror still in hand, and there, for the first time in any losing-Alix dream, she had found her sister.

She had waked again in the darkness, knowing that the dream had been a true one.

Sliding out from under the light cotton sheets that were all they could bear in the sticky Angelshand summers, Kyra had ducked from beneath the mosquito bar and tiptoed across the room in the darkness to the dressing table. Picking up her mirror, she passed her hand across it as she had done in the dream and tried to will to it the images of her parents, who were sleeping several rooms away.

When she had seen in it the pale gray shape of the window in their room, outlined in the darkness but unmistakable by its scrolled fanlight, she had put the mirror down quickly and gone back to bed. For another three months she'd managed to make herself believe that this sequel had actually been part of the dream.

But the dreams hadn't gone away. After she started menstruating, they increased in frequency and concreteness, nagging at her with a certainty that she did her best to bury beneath her studies of mathematics and the sciences. She had long been used to the idea that she was, at fourteen, regarded as a bluestocking and therefore would never be one of the beautiful girls, the courted girls, the laughing beribboned flirts whose beaux begged for the flowers from their hair. She expected that her father would find some man for her to marry who wouldn't get in her way too much and she'd go on pretty much as she was, helping her father run the five bakeries he owned and learning to be a corn broker herself.

The idea that she was a witch had never entered her calculations.

By law, there were strict limitations on the amount of property the mageborn could hold. By law, the mageborn could not enter any business that involved the employment of others, nor would any contract they signed be legal. By law, those born with the powers of magic could not marry.

She had seen witches. Lying awake in bed, night after night while Alix slept, she would remember how her girlfriends whispered when Marin Corbina, the flamboyant and disreputable soothsayer who lived in the St. Creel district, walked by in her gypsy shawls and jangling jewelry; remember the strange, somber black figures of the reclusive Council wizards, glimpsed from a carriage window as she had been driven once past the place in the Old Quarter called the Mages' Yard; remember the dirty sense of tumbledown poverty that seemed to hang about Tibbeth of Hale's shop on Little Potticary Lane. Obviously none of them had any money. They dressed poorly and looked as if they lived on bread and herb tea, and people got out of their way as they passed.

Her father would kill her.

The thought of losing his love, of having him explode into one of his tempers, was a terror before which all her customary lemon-ice sangfroid melted to nothing.

She couldn't tell him. Fourteen years old, the underpinnings of her life crumbling away like broken pilings in a flooding river, she sat awake and sweating in the darkness, listening to the silent sleep of the house all around her and the slow, chiming progress of the St. Farinox church clock.

* * *

"Miss Kyra?"

She raised her head, startled. In the half-open door stood the red-haired maid, glancing back over her shoulder as if fearing to be interrupted or overheard. The small noises of the footmen clearing up after dinner had long since ceased. Through the half-open window casements, the air smelled of river fog.

Kyra pressed her hands to her temples, which had begun to ache, too tired to be angry with herself for letting the time drift away as she had. Merrivale should be finished with her more pressing duties by this time. She'd be able to question her unobserved.

"There's a man to see you, down the kitchen door," the maid said softly. "A toff, he is; he says not to let no one know."

"Thank you . . ." She searched her mind and remembered the harpsichord player's voice gasping "Lily" through the wall of the parlor. "Thank you, Lily." She hoped that was correct.

The maid got quickly out of her way and disappeared through the door that led to the back stairs; Kyra caught the nervous look in her eye. One of the stock sources of tales about wizards, of course, was their former servants. By the time she was fourteen, Kyra had heard them all. She sighed as she followed the same way the girl had gone, down the pitch-dark back stairs to the kitchens.

The curious servant who opened the forbidden door and found assorted body parts, sometimes, but not always, including those of wife, children, or acquaintances.

The dishonest servant who stole some trifle that later came alive to engulf him or her in a dreadful retribution. (*That should teach the little pest to steal from his betters.*)

The servant whose mind and will were taken away by the sorcerer's smokes and perfumes and who assisted in unspeakable—but nevertheless exhaustively described—atrocities.

The servant who was hired with promises of riches and later was sacrificed or almost sacrificed to demons.

Kyra wondered whether, when those stories were whispered in the servants hall these days—as she was absolutely certain they were—Briory and Merrivale and the others who had known her from girlhood spoke in her defense or simply produced even more chilling anecdotes of their own.

The man waited for her near the gate, far from the misty yellow glow of the kitchen doorway and the flickerings of candle- and lanternlight around the pit of the cellar doors. She need not, she noted with relief, have worried about whether Merrivale would still be awake at this hour. Late as it was, the housekeeper and Briory were supervising the disposition of the 120 pounds of cake ice that had arrived while the family was at dinner. The cobbles of the yard gleamed with puddles, and a drippy trail led between the pile of ice blocks and the cellar, embroidered in friezes of straw and sand.

Kyra approached her visitor cautiously. She had pilfered her father's heaviest stick from the rear hallway on her way through and held it half-hidden behind her back. If she had time to scream, she supposed that Briory and the others would come hotfoot to her assistance, but there was no telling how many might be waiting outside the gate. The one she saw clung close to its shadows.

Darkness had never presented Kyra with a problem, but the fog blurred his outline until she was close to him, and she kept warily beyond the reach of his arm. He was masked and wore a hooded black cloak, but his chin and lips were young, so young, she noted automatically, that they still boasted a pimple or two. The lock of hair straggling from under his hood was mousebrown and of the telltale wispy consistency that hinted of a premature retreat. The wool of his cape was high-grade worsted at six crowns a yard. The perfume that imbued his gloves was nearly a royal an ounce, sandalwood and cloves, with a touch of musk. The gloves themselves were stamped with gold.

Not the Inquisition, she thought, and relaxed just slightly. The sheer cost of his apparel definitely set him apart from the man in the sloppy brown coat who'd trailed her to the market and back—had it only been this afternoon? Certainly he was no colleague of the two roughs in the cab.

"Mistress Kyra Peldyrin?"

Kyra glanced back over each of her shoulders in turn. "I hardly think that, having been paid half a crown for her trouble, Lily would have made a mistake about who she brought."

The young man looked severely taken aback, though Kyra knew that half a crown was considered an extravagant but acceptable tip. The next largest single coin was a crown, and Lily would have been even more awed if he had tipped her that much. It would have been a copper if the errand had been respectable.

The young man stammered, "Is it—it is true you are a witch, isn't it?"

Irritation flashed in her like a skin rash, wrought of keyed-up uncertainty and the frustration of being, at day's end, no closer to knowing what was afoot than she had been when she had set forth that morning. She leaned on the stick and raised her brows ironically. "You certainly wouldn't have chosen a damp milieu like this one for a meeting if you didn't believe that already." Definitely not the Inquisition, unless it was an effort to entrap her. But if it was, it was incredibly clumsy.

He hesitated, nonplussed. He was expecting her to ask, *What can I do for you?* so she didn't, merely regarded him with acerbic amber eyes and waited for him to speak. It was mildly entertaining to watch him try to come in without an opening.

"Mistress Kyra, I'll be brief."

"Please do. It's chilly, and I have things to do."

A pale tongue stole out and wet the Cupid's-bow lips. "How much ... I have with me a purse of a hundred royals. It's yours, if you'll weave a love-spell upon ... upon your sister, causing her to forsake Blore Spenson and love me."

Kyra tipped her head a little to one side. "Does she know you?"

He blushed. He didn't do it nearly as attractively as Algeron Brackett. "I have known her—that is, I have worshiped her for years."

"And you didn't mention it to our father?"

"No—yes—my heart is breaking ..."

"You don't sound as if your heart were breaking," Kyra remarked calmly, and scratched at a fleck of dirt on the stick's brass horse-hoof handle. "You sound rather nervous and incompletely rehearsed. I assume that without theurgic assistance, neither Alix nor Father thinks much of your suit."

"A hundred fifty royals," he persisted, somewhat single-mindedly, Kyra thought.

"Oh, do you have a holdout purse in case I run the price up?"

"Don't toy with a man whose ... whose soul is perishing of grief, Mistress Kyra."

"I think the line is 'from grief.' It's from *The Inflexible Uncle*, isn't it?"

"No! A hundred fifty royals now and another hundred after the wedding—that's all I can give you, truly."

"The other hundred presumably to come out of my sister's dowry?" Kyra finished her examination of the stick's handle. "That's rather crass. I take it the dowry—and the connections with my father's brokerage—are what prompted this investment in the cause of unrequited love in the first place. No, *please* don't offer me a draft on your bank. Think how embarrassing it would be if I were to blackmail you later on the strength of the signature, not to mention the fact that at a guess there are insufficient funds to cover it."

"Then what do you want?" the young man demanded, losing his temper and every trace of loverlike demeanor. The lower lip pushed out unbecomingly under the pathetic attempt at a mustache. "I know that for a woman like you a spell to make a girl love a man is nothing, a bagatelle. And it isn't as if I'll treat her badly or that she'll live in poverty—all it will take is her father's connections, and her dowry, to recoup our fortunes. And I'm certainly more to a girl's liking than some fat elderly pen pusher."

"If you think Blore Spenson is fat, elderly, or a mere smatterer in other people's money," Kyra retorted with a sudden surge of anger that completely erased her own earlier reservations about Master Spenson, "you clearly are too inattentive or too prejudiced to recoup any family's fortunes. Now, I suggest, if your family fortunes are in need of recouping, you take your hundred fifty royals and invest it in one of Master Spenson's spice ships, and that will pay you considerably better in the long run than marrying my sister. Or was that borrowed, too?"

He flushed again. "Very well," he said with an attempt to recover some of his dignity. "If you won't oblige me, I'll find someone who will."

And he melted away into the fog. A few minutes later Kyra heard the clatter of a gig's iron wheels in the street beyond the wall of the narrow yard. She wondered if he'd actually find a dog wizard foolhardy enough to risk her father's prosecution and shook her head.

Six years wasn't such a long time. Every dog wizard in the city would remember.

But the thought troubled her as she swung the stick over her shoulder like a shotgun and turned back to the house. She felt exhausted at the triviality of the incident and a hundred years old.

"Oh, that's nothing," she heard the dark-haired maid, whatever her name was, saying as she approached the rear steps. "My sister knew this woman who was hired as a maidservant by a wizard in Parchasten, and he forbade her ever to go into this one chamber up at the top of his house, but she used to hear noises coming out of it—"

Abrupt silence fell as Kyra entered the kitchen once again. The girl nearly dropped the goblet she was drying—the last of the supper dishes—and covered her mouth with her hand; the harpsichord player hastily took his feet off the kitchen table and the maid Lily off his lap. Algeron, who was cleaning the last bits of straw and sand from the rear steps, tried to look as if he hadn't been listening to such things.

"Oh, don't mind me," Kyra said blithely as she walked through, cane over her shoulder, in a thick rustle of stiff green and purple skirts. "Do go on."

In the drying room next door Merrivale was writing wedding announcements to be sent out in the morning while the faded, tired-looking laundrywoman ironed sheets. The room was hazed with the smell of steam and linen and soap and thick with heat from the stove where the irons ranged. Briory had gone to bed, leaving a list of directions behind; the half-darkened room was filled with an air of finishing up, of small details that had been put aside in the midst of larger concerns.

There was little more, Kyra thought bitterly, that *could* be done today. And all her searches, all her questions, had wasted her time as surely as that silly suitor in the fog had.

"Don't mind them, Miss Kyra," Merrivale said quietly, nodding back in the direction of the kitchen, where extremely hushed voices had taken up some other piece of gossip entirely. "Ignorant, that's what they are, and you and I know as how there's wicked wizards as well as—"

"It's nothing." Kyra shrugged and came over to sit on

the edge of the big oak table next to the gray-haired housekeeper. She slid her erstwhile weapon down the length of the table out of her way; Merrivale raised her eyebrows a little at the sight of it but didn't ask. "It gives them something to talk about besides their betters." As spare as her colleague Briory was round, Merrivale had been the housekeeper as long as Briory had been butler. As children, Kyra and Alix had speculated whether the two were actually sisters, despite the fact that they looked nothing alike and Merrivale's soft Mellidane drawl was miles removed from Briory's upper-class Angelshand tones. But that, Kyra had said at the time, might simply be deliberate camouflage.

She lowered her voice. "I wanted to ask you, Merry: Were there any who were angry or hurt when Father had the banns read for Miss Alix and Master Spenson?"

The housekeeper ducked her head a little, her brown eyes sad. "You mean other than Algeron Brackett?"

There was momentary silence. "Yes," Kyra said softly. "Other than Algeron."

Merrivale sighed. "I'm sorry, Miss Kyra. Maybe I shouldn't bring it up, with all else that's gone on—I'm fairly distracted, with all the flans and tarts to do again and the garlands still to be bought and woven up, and the price they want for them, too . . . But it breaks my heart, watching the pair of them. And what would be the harm of it, except that it's not what your father wants for her? The boy's as capable of fathering an heir for the business as Master Spenson, and if not . . . Well, there's always your cousin Wyrdlees, mooching about wiping his hands and asking what's in a dish before he eats it. *He'd* step into your father's shoes quick enough."

"Yes," Kyra agreed. "If Father could stand being around him."

"It's still no reason for your poor sister to be made miserable," the housekeeper said doughtily. "The merest tithe of her dowry would set up as fine a shop for making gowns as any in this city. You know how she sews, and her sense of style—she's better than that Hylette woman everyone makes such a fuss about and doesn't put on airs, neither. And once that sweet young man passes his guild examinations, he could start a pastry shop, which she'd run for him, him being no more suited to do his own bookkeeping than your mother's lapdogs."

"Is Alix?" Kyra asked, curious.

"Fit to run a shop? She's her father's daughter and her mother's, too—and your sister, miss. She may prattle on like a finch in a cage, but she knows what silk costs and where to get it cheaper and how to make a copper do the work of a crown. If she wasn't a fit seamstress, she certainly wouldn't be making her own gowns." She shook her head and pushed back her linen mobcap from her thin, fading hair. "Well, that's neither here nor there."

"No," Kyra mused. "Not with Father hungry for a grandson who'll have connections to all the big merchant bankers in the city." She felt a twinge of guilt, knowing that it was her decision to become a wizard—to put herself beyond the dealings of business and marriage partnerships and dynastic alliances—that had made Alix the sole focus of all her father's hopes.

"I know Cousin Wyrdlees offered marriage to me—not that I'd have touched him with a barge pole. Did he do so with Alix?"

Merrivale chuckled. "If he did, it came to naught. Though for all he says about your cousin, I think your father's just holding it against him that Wyrdlees' mother married a mill owner rather than a broker or a merchant. The man's a good businessman when all's said. Besides, your father had his eye on Spens for a fair long time."

Kyra settled back and clasped her hands around her updrawn knee. "Was Wyrdlees angry at being cut out?"

Merrivale finished another line of beautiful penman-

ship requesting the honor of the receiver's company at
the Church of St. Creel in Great Cheevy Street and replaced the quill in the plain brass standish. "Well, he's
known all his life your father didn't much care for the
thought of making him his heir . . . as *you* know, miss.
My thought is that's why he's got himself betrothed to
Belissa Millpott. And as for others being angry . . ." She
shrugged.

"Well, of course there were any number of your father's friends, aye, and competitors, too: merchants and
brokers who'd hoped to put together a match with her
with sons of theirs. Aye, and not just because she's your
father's heiress, either. She's a taking girl is Miss
Alixenia. There was a spark or two from Court, either
hanging out for an heiress or who just fancied her. The
Viscount March had a *tendre* for her—used to send her
nosegays after the dances at the Guildhall—and of
course the Viscount Frayne tried his best to make her
think it was her he loved and not her dowry."

"Young man with spots on his chin and a receding
hairline?"

"That's the one."

Kyra sniffed. "And no line of conversation, either.
No wonder Alix would have nothing to do with him."

She was silent for a time, thinking. From the kitchen
came a burst of laughter at one of the harpsichord player's jokes and Lily squeaking, "Aye, well, it's no wonder the four of you got run out of Senterwing." The
laundrywoman replaced one iron on the stove's central
grill and hooked the handle into another, and the soft
thump of her work resumed with a monotonous regular-
ity, like the slowly-beating heart of a dying man.

"And none of those competitors—those merchants
and brokers—have done anything to try to . . . to scupper the match? To prevent the alliance of our house
with that of the Spensons?"

"Good heavens!" Merrivale looked up at her in genuine surprise. Then, considering it, "Well, it's some-

thing your father would be likelier to know than I, miss.
I know Fyster Nyven suspects that everything Lord
Mayor Spenson does is aimed at putting him in the
poorhouse, and vice versa, and of course the Brecksnifts
did their best to get their daughter married to Spens—
Master Spenson, that is—and were killed with outrage
when the match was announced, but they aren't the only
ones who wanted that alliance." Her fair, sparse brows
tweaked down over her eyes. "Why ask all this, miss?"

"No reason," Kyra said. Then, after an artistic hesita-
tion, "Well, it's just that I saw someone lurking in the
street outside the house this morning," she said truth-
fully. "He had the air of someone watching the place. It
may have had nothing at all to do with Alix's wedding."

"Belike," Merrivale murmured, frowning. "On the
other hand, the way business is run in this town, you
may be right to think there's some as would try to disrupt the match. And even if he's not, with the house
nearly empty on the morn of the wedding, it's always a
temptation for thieves. I'll have Trobe take a look
around."

Almost as good as sleet, Kyra thought. The groom, if
he was the one she was thinking of, was very large.

"And Algeron himself?" she asked a little awkwardly. "He wouldn't . . . try to stop the match himself,
would he?"

Merrivale's brown eyes grew both sad and just a little
amused. "Well, he loves her. But he'd be more like to
do himself an injury, sinking into a decline and writing
sonnets about it. She's the one I worry about the more."

"Do you?" Kyra's voice grew suddenly sharp, and
she lowered it again to exclude the laundrywoman.

"Poor thing." The older woman shook her head and
dipped her pen again. "Well, there's many that come to
love after their first child's born, and she'll not do him
wrong. And why wouldn't a man who's just returned
from years of taking ships to heathen parts welcome
quiet and wealth and running the guild, and a lovely

new wife in the bargain? He's thirty-seven, after all, and the only heir to his father's affairs. High time he came back and settled down."

She paused in her writing and patted Kyra's hand comfortingly. "There, now. She's a sensible girl is Alix. She'll come through it all fine. She's always been one as to control her feelings."

Control them? Kyra thought, remembering the glitter of tears in candlelight. *Or hide them from herself as well as from others?*

The housekeeper sighed and drew another sheet of finely-pressed vellum paper to her, glancing at the scribbled formula of the announcement. "Myself, I'll just be glad when this is all over."

"That will be two of us." Kyra sighed and, gathering her skirts in hand, returned to the back stairs and started the long ascent to the yellow guest chamber once again. It had been an extremely tiring day.

CHAPTER VIII

KYRA LEFT THE HOUSE WELL BEFORE FIRST LIGHT, AFTER A night of anxious dreams. In her worn cloak and the maid's plain blue frock, she blended into the shadowy ranks of men, women, and children in rags who made up the sluggish stream flowing southward toward the factories on the river's banks, people about whom, before she became a mage, Kyra had seldom troubled to think at all.

They had been driven off the farmlands by landlords who'd gone over to sheep rearing or large-field tillage or were the children of those who had; they worked for a few coppers a day and slept three and four families to a room in the slums of St. Cyr and Seven Ways. They shivered in their rags, though Kyra, used to the bitter cold of the Sykerst, was far from uncomfortable. White, undernourished faces swam up around Kyra through the soot-laden fog, troubling her like unanswered questions, for she was well aware that without the factories, no maidservant in Angelshand would have been able to have two gowns, one to be worn while the other was mended or washed or pilfered by her master's daughter for incognito excursions to questionable portions of the town.

At the Citadel such questions never arose.

No wonder, she thought, coughing as the raw smoke in the air filed at her throat and lungs, *the mages chose to retreat, to declare themselves incapable of judging right and wrong.* Perhaps these days right and wrong *didn't* exist, in politics and money, anyway.

And it was certainly no business of the Inquisition's to judge.

The subject of the Inquisition still rankled, for it had cost her some trouble to slip past the Witchfinders who, she was certain, still watched the house.

Fortunately, as she fretted through last night's endless hours, her mind and senses had roved through the darkened house between her bouts of dreams, and whispered conversations had come down to her from the attic. "Aye, he's gone over to the house next door," she heard the mandolin player tell someone in his drawling voice, and the sight of the flute player standing in the postern to Neb Wishrom's kitchen yard returned to her. The Wishroms' scullery door, she recalled, opened not into their yard but into the alley behind. Whoever the flute player had trysted with at the Wishroms' had locked the cellar door behind him when he left, but an hour and a half later Kyra had no trouble slipping the latch and moving like a trail of smoke through the Wishroms' drying room and storage pantry through to their scullery and thence up the slippery stone steps of the areaway, looking for all the world like a servant sent to do early marketing.

Her anxiety driving her on, she took a circuitous route first, fearing to use any magic to summon the fog more thickly about her or to veil herself from watching eyes. It was her pursuer's spell of Look-over-There, she remembered, that had flagged her attention the previous day. After six years absence she had to negotiate carefully through the narrow alleys that she'd pelted along so blindly as a child: Faggot Court, Upper Little Pinnikin Alley, Songbird Lane. Difficult, too, even with mageborn senses, to sort the breathing and footfalls of the silent, ragged ghosts who peopled these ways at this hour: prostitutes and mill workers, cab drivers and court rakes and hungry university students rambling home from nights in the taverns or the stews.

In time she satisfied herself that she was not being pursued. From there she hurried, straight as a bee to water, to the Cheevy Street Baths.

Though Kyra had lived in Angelshand until the age of eighteen, she had never before visited one of the city's public baths. The experience, particularly at this hour of the morning, was an instructive one, since the half hour before sunup was the favored time for prostitutes coming off work. Evidently the young Court rakes were aware of this fact, too, and Kyra had a number of offers as she edged her way through the brightly dressed groups among the massive red pillars of the portico.

Once inside, she was interested to notice that two or three of the women who shared the deep, marble-sided tub with her were wreathed in faint clouds of illusion, a cheap but intriguing spell designed to remind a male beholder of someone unattainable but deeply desired. Somewhere in the city some dog wizard was putting his powers to unexpected use, and had Kyra not been intent on the task she needed to accomplish—and on remaining unnoticed herself—she would have immediately asked the women about it from sheer academic curiosity.

So there *was* a dog wizard operating in the neighborhood, she thought, drawing her cloak more closely around her shoulders to shield her wet hair from the cold as she left the place nearly an hour later. After the official purges two years ago, he—or she—would be difficult to track, but it would have to be done, and done soon. It would be easier, she thought, than combing through every room in the house in search of an Eye of Evil through which to track first the wizard and then the man or woman who had paid to have the curse placed.

Besides, she thought, even if there was no connection with her sister at all, the other juniors would kill her if she didn't further her inquires about those spells.

"Miss Peldyrin!"

She turned sharply, startled. Almost eerily quiet an hour ago, Fennel Street was now moderately sprinkled with clerks hurrying to the countinghouses of the harbor and servants making their way to market while the vegetables were still fresh from the fields. With the coming of the sun and the thinning of the mists, even these grimed brown tenements and gray granite paving blocks had taken on color and life. The blind hurdy-gurdy player had established himself on a yellow blanket at the corner of Proggin Alley, and a woman selling straw charms and Hands of God was crying her wares in a faint aura of tobacco smoke and sesame oil.

Behind her Kyra saw Blore Spenson at the reins of his light one-horse chaise. He had called out to her, so it was too late to make him think she was a scarf seller or somebody's maid.

"Thank you." She strode back to him and climbed in, hanging up the flounce of her petticoat on the step. "I was afraid I'd miss breakfast."

Spenson laughed and flicked the reins; he might, she realized a few moments later, have had some other destination in mind than her father's house, but if so, he let it go gracefully and concentrated on steering around a cab driver who'd pulled up in the middle of Bent Hill Lane to buy breakfast from a woman selling muffins from a cart.

"I hope you riding with me means you forgive me. For setting your father at you," he added, glancing briefly at the baffled expression on her face and then turning his attention back to avoiding a butcher's wagon and two court sedan chairs complete with bodyguards— not needed in daylight but a necessity if one were setting out for the gambling hells of Algoswive district at two in the morning. "I never meant to do that."

"Oh, don't take credit for anything extraordinary," Kyra said lightly, feeling the back of her hood where the damp had soaked through from her hair. "Father's been set against me from the day I took vows not to meddle in mundane affairs. I think he'd have been perfectly happy for me to be a dog wizard and put good words on his account books." He drove well, she observed, his touch on the reins as light as it had been on her hand yesterday, and such unexpected hazards as small dogs and two urchins rolling a hoop along the pavement did not seem to take him by surprise. But presumably neither had pirates, Oriental potentates, or irate sea-island natives.

"Would he?" Her prospective brother-in-law glanced sidelong at her, and she saw his fair, level brows bunch. "It didn't sound like he had much use for dog wizards. I know he's run them out of this neighborhood. As you know," he added awkwardly.

"Ah." Kyra's smile was tight. "You're thinking of Tibbeth of Hale."

"He was burned, wasn't he?" The deliberate neutrality of his tone—the setting of the event at a distance— surprised her. He was the only person besides Alix who seemed to realize that mention of the scandal might still cause her pain. And, she thought, he'd seen through her airy lie about her father's attitude toward her magic— not a piece of perception she'd have credited to the stiff and silent man who'd had so little to say at dinner. "I'd shipped as supercargo on the *Inzibar Queen*," he went on. "Her maiden voyage, out through the Tarand Straits; she's still one of our best merchantmen. It was all over by the time I returned."

It occurred to Kyra that if she had had Lord Mayor Spenson for a father, she'd have gone to sea as well.

"Well," she remarked lightly, "the trial did have something to do with my decision to embrace the Academic variety of wizardry, which at least protects its adherents from the vagaries of public opinion."

"Wasn't he your teacher?"

She shrugged. "For a time."

She was aware of his glance touching her profile again and had the uneasy feeling that he saw through her flippancy to the scars beneath. Her eyes were scanning the streets around them, looking for places that her attention persistently skipped—so far, nothing seemed to be pushing away her gaze. On the balconies of the houses of rose and golden brick, maidservants were airing bed linen; a religious procession passed down the pavement on the opposite side, the monks in the blue robes of the Hilatian Order walking in a chanting chain, each man's hand on the shoulder of the man before him, all blindfolded while the flute player who led them piped shrilly to drown out unholy sounds and unholy thoughts. Spenson's horse flung up her head and snorted in disgust at the incense.

"I owe you two apologies, really," Spenson said after a straitened silence, "and thanks. Because you were right. I was having—dreams . . ." He could barely get the word out, and his face had gone rufous again. ". . . about the Earthwygg girl." His blue eyes met hers squarely, as if daring her to speak of the matter, and Kyra, who was about to observe that there was nothing to be embarrassed about except perhaps the implication that he might find Esmin Earthwygg attractive *without* the aid of magic, realized that he was highly embarrassed.

So she said instead, and in a quieter voice than her usual half-ironic tone, "Well, considering the state of that family's finances, it's hardly surprising her mother would try something of the kind on you. She must have been spitting blood when the betrothal was announced."

Spenson looked startled. "I hardly know the girl!"

"Good heavens, you don't think that had anything to do with it, do you? You hardly know my sister."

He turned his attention back to his driving, and for some time he seemed to be intently studying the mare's ears. His mouth settled into the hard line it sometimes had in Alix's presence, and the color was long in fading from his cheeks.

Kyra wondered how vivid the dreams had been.

After a time he said, "I know the difference between a woman who'll make a man a good wife and one who won't."

Hearing the world of discomfit in his voice, she picked her words carefully. "Believe me, you're no more to blame than if—than if someone had put a Get-Lost spell on your carriage and you'd been four hours late for dinner. Spells like that have absolutely nothing to do with their subject's real desires."

"Have they not?" He looked back to her, interest driving the flush from his face. Then he chuckled ruefully. "Well, I suppose their strength lies in how thoroughly they make you think that *is* your real desire, at the time, at least. And being about to marry your sister . . ."

Kyra regarded him for a moment, her brows tugging down over her tawny eyes. "That must have been quite appalling for you," she said. For the first time she reflected that his irrational lust for Esmin Earthwygg had put him through some masculine version of Alix's division of soul, complicated by his genuine dislike of the girl and his precise knowledge of how much of a legal tangle it would take to get out of the contracted match. No wonder he'd had precious little to say, hiding his doubts behind a countenance of weathered oak.

"On the other hand," she added judiciously, "that was no reason to shout at *me* for removing them."

One corner of his mouth turned down, and his blue eyes twinkled. "My girl, *no* man likes to be told that he's been led around by his ... er ... nose."

"Well," Kyra said, "if you say so."

He laughed at her doubtful tone and drew rein to let a cartful of fresh ivy and trailing chains of smilax turn into Upper Tollam Street ahead of them. As he followed the slowly jogging vehicle, Kyra realized that it must contain supplies for the new garlands all the servants would weave and hang tonight. *Poor Father,* she thought with regret. *With smilax ten coppers the basket, and ivy three ...* Spenson's hands on the reins were brown from the sun, heavy with muscle that made their skill all the more surprising. She realized, gazing absently at them, that she had momentarily forgotten her anxiety, and renewed awareness of the shortness of the time left rushed back on her.

Casually, she inquired, "You say he's run off other dog wizards from this neighborhood?"

Spenson nodded. "According to Father. Three years ago there was a woman over on Lesser Queen Street; your father took against her as soon as he heard she was there. He and some of the other guildsmen warned her to find other quarters. And there was a man who worked out of the attic of the Feathered Snake. Quiet and inoffensive, but I heard it was your father who set the Witchfinders on him. So I'll admit I was surprised when I saw you back in his house."

He was quiet for a time, and the wheels of the gig, crushing dropped ivy leaves on the gray paving stones, sent up frail traces of their sappy green smell to contend with the waft of the flowers in the cart ahead and the odors of wash water thrown in the gutters and horse piss from the cab stand on the corner of Upper Tollam Street.

Then his glance returned to her again.

"It doesn't sound like a man angry because you wouldn't turn dog wizard to help his business."

"Well, having quite spectacularly denounced one wizard and thrown another one out of his house, he could scarcely go about hiring a third or a fourth to make up the deficit, could he? I daresay it got to be a habit with him. Do you know what became of them? The woman from Queen Street, I mean, and the wizard who worked out of the Feathered Snake."

Spenson shook his head. "Why do you ask?"

"I'd hate to think my decision seriously inconvenienced a couple of perfectly innocent bystanders, particularly if the Witchfinders really were called in." Kyra spoke lightly, but she remembered Nandiharrow's oddly shaped black gloves and what was—and wasn't—inside them. Half the novices at the Citadel called him Nandiharrow the Nine Fingered as a matter of course, not remembering that up until eighteen months ago he'd gone by a different nickname.

His smile was wry. "I don't think your father feels any wizard is innocent."

"Well, he's quite right, you know." Kyra stepped down from the gig before the open gate of the kitchen yard, through which the flower cart was rumbling. "Will you come in and join us for breakfast, Master Spenson? My sister should be awake by this time."

Her mind was already racing ahead, probing at alleys, leads, inquiries, raging at the constant petty turmoil that kept her from systematically searching the house, but she knew also that she needed food. Besides, she thought, looking up at the man in the gig above her, she found Spenson surprisingly good company.

The mention of Alix's name made him glance away, and his easiness vanished like dew in the sun. "Another time, Miss Peldyrin," he said with the old dinner-party stiffness. "I'm late to the countinghouse as it is. God knows, with all these delays, it's all I can do to keep things together there. We're trying to work in a new factor to send to the Sykerst fur traders, and the man's turned out a fool. I only wanted to apologize for . . . for speaking on matters I should have known better than to bring up." He raised his whipstock to touch the brim of his high-crowned hat and, with a flick of the reins, was gone across the square.

Not an easy apology for a hot-tempered man, Kyra thought, standing for a time on the flagway, watching the broad, brown back disappearing between the shoulders of the buildings that guarded Upper Tollam Street. She remembered that the Spenson countinghouse was down on Salt Hill Lane, and Prandhauer Street was only a short way north of it. Baynorth Square lay nowhere between. He'd gone out of his way rather than let her walk.

She made her way, swift and unnoticed, to her room and concealed Lily's frock in the armoire, hoping Spenson hadn't noticed what she'd been wearing under her cloak. Then she hooked herself into one of her own outlandish dresses, a brilliant yellow garment draped back over a skirt of white and yellow ribbonwork and strange old-fashioned hoops. Part of her teenage desire to revolutionize fashion—at least the fashions she wore—had involved efficiency and a desire to get into her clothes without the aid of servants, so in addition to suiting her jagged looks and strong coloring, most of the gowns she had designed for herself fastened up the front.

She viewed herself critically in the mirror as she put up her hair, which was still damp at the ends, threading it with an old necklace of raw amber instead of the flowers dictated by current fashion. Even at the age of ten she had known she could never compete with the fashionable girls, the girls who studied each sleeve flounce and pleat worn by the leading Court beauties, who could tell by the cut of the stomacher or the number of its bows whether a gown was truly new or last season's made over.

Rather than lose to them in their game, she had made her own rules, and she wondered for a moment, throw-

ing a chain of turquoises over her head and surveying
the colorful result, where that would have taken her had
she not been what she was.

With a shake of her head, she descended to the breakfast room, where her mother and Alix were finishing
toast and cocoa.

From the gallery she caught the whiff of it, and the
sweetness of the chocolate made her stomach grip with
the old craving for sugar. Her mother's light babble
drifted on the scented steam, but Alix, when Kyra entered the room, was silent, though putting up a good appearance of interest. Despite the careful application of
rice powder and rouge, Kyra could see that her sister
had been crying.

"Kyra, darling!" Her mother half rose in a drift of
patchouli. "We were just ... That is, there's a little
problem—a question, really—that we need ...
Well ..." She took a sip of her cocoa to buy herself
time while Kyra reached over to the bellpull to summon Briory.

"The fact is, darling, your father brought up the question of the wedding procession tomorrow morning.
Now, under ordinary circumstances, of course you
would have a place in Alix's carriage ..."

"Under ordinary circumstances," Kyra remarked,
"yes. Briory, could you get me some of Joblin's blintzes
and jam? And coffee, please. Under ordinary circumstances, I'd be carrying a corner of Alix's veil as ma-
tron of honor, assuming that anybody would have
married *me* in the intervening years. Is there cocoa in
that pot still?"

"It'll have skin on it like a lizard," Alix warned.

"At the moment I'd drink it if it *was* lizard skin. I
take it," she added, turning a limpid gaze upon her
parent, "that circumstances have been rendered too extraordinary for me to be invited to go along?"

"Oh, of course not, darling," Binnie Peldyrin hastened to say, reaching over to lay a small, moist hand on

her elder daughter's bony wrist. Kyra had never liked her mother's habit of fingering her daughters and husband and gently extracted her arm from the grip; Binnie noticed no more than she ever had, but her wide blue eyes blinked nervously. "The thing is, you see, since you're not a member of Alix's train at the church, you wouldn't be riding in *her* carriage, and I'd already asked Lord and Lady Earthwygg—I mean, before you came back—to ride with your father and me in ours, and . . . well . . ."

"Hmmn," Kyra said. "And I don't expect either Aunt Murdwym or Cousin Wyrdlees would want me in the carriage with them. Perhaps Father could rent me a closed sedan chair to follow immediately after."

"That was my idea," Alix said, pushing a finger of toast around her plate and apparently thinking better of eating it. Briory appeared silently, bearing a plate of blintzes, which Kyra proceeded first to bury in blueberry preserves and then to demolish with starved speed.

"Aye," came her father's voice from the doorway behind the butler's stolid back. "And a banner to carry behind it saying 'Here's the other daughter' perhaps?"

" 'Here's the witch,' you mean, Father?" Kyra dropped three chunks of white sugar into her coffee cup and turned to regard him blandly. "You're quite right. I'll just walk, with the servants and clients, in the rear. Now, I wonder which of my dresses I should wear. This one is nice, but I've always been fond of the red silk."

Her father shuddered, perhaps at the sheer magnitude of the yellow dress, perhaps at the thought of how it would stand out in any crowd, let alone one composed of soberly dressed servants. "You'll ride in a sedan chair and keep quiet about it," he ordered. "Immediately after your Aunt Sethwit's coach. And belike we'll have the Witchfinders trailing along behind," he added, his mouth setting grimly.

"Well, I'm quite sure the Bishop won't let them into

the church without an invitation." Kyra judiciously poured the remains of her cocoa into the coffee cup and stirred.

"Pah!" her father said in disgust. "You can count yourself lucky you'll not be left outside the door with them!"

While he was speaking, Kyra could hear from downstairs the sounds of the door opening, of voices in the great hall, and so was not surprised when Briory reentered the room a few moments later to announce, "Lady Earthwygg and her daughter are in the drawing room, madame."

"Oh!" Binnie threw up her hands in exasperation. "That horrid woman! Yearning for a gossip, I suppose, or else going to complain about having to rebuy flowers for Esmin, as if the rest of us weren't in the same situation, only a *hundred* times worse. And that reminds me, darling, I've sent next door for Heckson and Fairbody again to help with weaving the garlands, since they have to go up tonight. Oh, and I'll have to tell Merrivale to arrange to have another sedan chair . . ." Fluttering details behind her like colored ribbons, she got to her feet and bustled past her husband and out onto the gallery. "Come *along*, Alix my dearest."

Alix had risen to her feet, and Kyra, looking up from a second blintz, saw the white look on her face as if she were about to visit a bonesetter. Her cosmetics stood out harshly against the pallor of exhaustion and stress, and she hesitated for a moment, tearing unconsciously at her cuticles and looking at Kyra as if she would speak.

But their father stood in the doorway, waiting, and only after Alix departed did he, too, leave, following her along the gallery to the drawing room whence Lady Earthwygg's deep, commanding tones could already be heard, complaining about the cost of irises in the market.

Kyra sighed and leaned her forehead on her hands.

She felt a little better for having eaten but knew that she had a full day's work ahead of her tracing the two dog wizards whom her father had wronged. And the house, she thought with weary frustration, still to search.

The wedding tomorrow . . .

The terrace of the House of Roses came back to her, last summer's heavy heat that made the Sykerst summers such a burden even without the mosquitoes that plagued the pond-riddled landscape. The smell of the roses had been sweet in the air, the slanting sunlight a nearly palpable golden haze. It had been close to eight at night—in the far north summer days were long. "I thought talismans of ill worked only if they were placed where the victim would come in contact with them daily," Kyra had said, looking across the pitted oak worktable to where Nandiharrow the Nine Fingered had been patiently instructing one of the slower students—a hulking, kindly young man named Brunus—in the imbuing-spells that would charge powdered silver and bird bone to glow in the presence of certain types of magic.

"These talismans I've taught you this week, yes," the elderly mage had replied, turning on his perch on the terrace's pink sandstone railing. "But like all magic, the magic of ill changes with the strength of its maker. For instance, even the simple eyes I've taught you to draw today—if you drew one in a house, it would be a matter of dropped stitches, losses at cards, the good china breaking, and a cat throwing up on your sister's bed. If Zake drew the same sign . . ." He nodded toward Zake Brighthand, who was sitting cross-legged on the pavement in the midst of a chalked Circle of Protection, and the solemn, quiet boy raised his head from the sigil he was practicing, startled at the sound of his name.

Nandiharrow smiled. "If Zake drew it, very likely the house would burn down."

"But can you, like, draw them heavy or light?" the boy asked in the slurry drawl of the Angelshand slums.

"I mean, if I didn't much care about hurtin' the folks in the house, could I just make the cat throw up?"

"Of course. And if you drew the signs in a house of strangers whom you were being paid to ill-wish, even with your greater strength, the signs would be weaker and cause less grief, than, for instance, if Cylin—" His gloved left hand gestured toward the solemn, nervous-looking young man at the far end of the table. "—were to draw those selfsame signs in the house of those who had wronged him, those who had hurt him, those whom he hated with all his soul."

The sunlight slipped over the black leather of the glove, making odd creases where two fingers had been sewn back to accommodate the twisted stumps within. Kyra felt a strange, sick catch in her stomach, hearing in the mild voice none of the hatred of which he spoke.

"There are many ways of accomplishing this," he went on, as if speaking of cures for conjunctivitis or alternative means of summoning birds. "One can use the blood of rabbits and chickens, or the moon's dark, or the conjunctions of certain stars. Some wizards will conjure a ghost to be bound to the spell, to hold to it the cold power of death. And an eye marked with a sufficiency of hatred, a talisman wrought in pain and anger, can poison all the atmosphere of a house, even if it be hidden in the bottommost cellar. The tendrils of its power will reach out through the very fabric of the stones until they can kill those who never go into the portions of the house where the ill is situated . . . Which makes tracking them down an extremely lengthy and tedious process."

Was it that, Kyra wondered, which had communicated itself to her unconsciously in the paper of Alix's letter? Had some talisman hidden deep within the house sent its poisoned aura forth so strongly that her fingers had picked it up from the very paper, like the lingering smell of musk, which only in sleep had her mind finally interpreted?

An extremely lengthy and tedious process. It meant each wall of cellar and room would have to be gone over, every floor, every dish in the kitchen and shelf in the library, as she had already gone over Alix's room and the old schoolroom where Tibbeth of Hale had taught her magic. It would take hours ... And meanwhile the whole house was alive with servants weaving garlands in the drying room and making tarts in the kitchen, guests coming agog for gossip in the drawing rooms and musicians tumbling the maids in the attics, Merrivale counting plates for tomorrow's wedding banquet, and the laundry maid ironing Alix's chemises in preparation for the night.

Kyra whispered "Damn" and then was washed with an expensive wave of ambergis perfume.

Looking up, she saw—as she knew she would, mages being trained to recognize and remember scents—Lady Earthwygg standing in the breakfast-room door.

Impeccable in eggplant taffeta over an undergown of lilac silk, a spray of silk pansies in her powdered hair, her ladyship regarded Kyra's brilliant and unfashionable garment with a slight, startled compression of her full lips and, after a moment of fishily silent politeness, averted her eyes from it as from a beggar's verminous rags.

"Your turquoises are perhaps a bit bright for that gown," the Lady said in her smoky voice.

"Are they?" Kyra lifted the string of them around her neck, huge chucks of the brilliant stone alternating with filigreed silver beads. "Well, perhaps, but at least they're real. What might I do for you?"

Lady Earthwygg's hand moved to cover the splendid necklace of diamonds that glittered at her throat, but she stopped herself before completing the gesture. Wizards worked with gems a great deal, and Kyra had spent nearly two years learning to distinguish true crystal from even the most expert fakes. The knowledge was in her eyes as they met the noblewoman's gaze.

"I understand that you're a wizard, Miss Peldyrin." She was a slender woman of medium height and widely famed bosom whose beauty had a rigidly preserved look under a heavy coating of rice powder and rouge, and her air of effortless command and the assurance in her deep voice gave observers the impression that she was both taller and heavier than was in fact the case. "Given your father's attitudes about magic and its practitioners, I don't imagine you've had a chance to see much of real jewelry these last six years." The black eyes narrowed, and she raised her lorgnette on its violet ribbon to study the young woman through it. "Or has that been a sham?"

"If it has, it's certainly one he's practiced on me." Kyra poured herself another cup of coffee and a moment later poured one out for her guest. "I repeat, Lady Earthwygg: What might I do for you?"

"It's what you might do for yourself, child." She settled herself at the table and accepted the fragile porcelain cup, drinking the liquid black, in the fashionable manner. "Oh, I realize wizards aren't supposed to crave such things as jewelry and decent dresses, but you're a woman, after all. I could see to it that you never lack for them again."

"That's very altruistic of you, Lady Earthwygg. Should I ring for more blitzes? Some truly excellent day-old cake? No? Considered in the light of my Council vows, which make it impossible for me to return the favor by slipping Blore Spenson a love-philter to make him jilt my sister in favor of your daughter, your generosity borders on true kindliness."

Her ladyship reddened and set her coffee cup quickly aside. "Don't be ridiculous."

"The cook assures me he used fifteen eggs in the cake."

The older woman's eyes narrowed again. "Or am I behind the fair?" she asked softly. "Was that your father's price for taking you back into his graces? That you'd work your spells on Spenson and make him cast his eyes on that sister of yours?"

Through the door, Kyra could catch Esmin Earthwygg's rather shrill voice from the drawing room at the other end of the gallery: "Well, of course Daddy's going to get me a diamond parure for my Court presentation . . . I suppose yours is, too? Not that you'll ever be presented at Court, which you should be thankful for—it's such a nuisance!—but surely the guilds have something of the kind."

"If you really think so," Kyra said, "I suppose we could ask the Witchfinders in to thaumaturgically examine the Spenson house for marks. On the other hand, mine might not be the marks they'd find, and think how embarrassing that would be."

Lady Earthwygg's eyes shifted quickly. "Well, I certainly didn't mean to imply . . . It's just that these are suspicious times." Her gesture was eloquent of seven centuries of breeding and years of deportment lessons. "Your father has a reputation among the—" She barely bit back the word "vulgar." "—businessmen of the city as a 'warm man.' And I'm told that before you fell from his graces you were quite an acute businesswoman yourself. Surely you can see the advantages in patronage. Indeed, if you are on the outs with your father, my husband may help you with that situation as well."

"Always provided Father doesn't learn that I've scuppered the match he's been working for years to bring about."

"Oh, my dear." She smiled silkily. "I'm sure you're cleverer than that. What would you say to a thousand crowns?"

Kyra sighed and pushed her empty coffee cup from her. "I would say no."

"And four hundred a year."

"Was that what you offered what's his name? The one you bought the passion philters from that you've been slipping Spenson?"

The recollection of his face as he'd spoken of them in the gig—the recollection of what he'd gone through—made her voice flare with sudden anger. She forced it steady again. "It does, as I say, border on kindliness, especially considering that they don't seem to have worked. But then, you can scarcely sue your supplier, can you?"

The noblewoman gave a deep and wholly faked chuckle and brought from her capacious pannier pocket a painted lavender fan. "My dear girl, what are you talking about? And considering the size of your sister's dowry, not to speak of the inheritance, you can't pretend she'd go begging long. Think about it. I know wizardry is an expensive proposition. They're always seeking good-quality gems, proper incense, pure silver and gold. For four hundred a year you'd be able to purchase a house in town and have enough left over to pursue your studies in peace."

"Unless the Witchfinders decide to come after me." Kyra rose from her chair. "Or someone tries to kidnap me in a cab. I'm afraid the answer is still no."

"Five hundred a year."

"Is that your final offer?"

The Lady snapped her fan shut and got to her feet. "Don't be a fool, girl. If you're cast out by your father, what choice have you? To starve and beg your bread like those raggedy mumblers over in the Mages' Yard? To sell weeds and abortions like that wretched man they burned a few years ago? If he'd had friends in high places—what was his name?"

"Tibbeth," Kyra said quietly.

"Tibbeth. If he'd had friends in high places, they'd never have been able to touch him."

"No," Kyra said softly. "No, he did have friends in high places, as it happens."

"Then why won't you accept my offer?"

Kyra regarded her for a moment in silence. Then she said, quite simply, "Because I'm not a whore."

Lady Earthwygg's nostrils flared. With slow deliberation she lifted her lorgnette again and surveyed Kyra's dress. "No," she said. "Only a frump."

Kyra curtsied. "But quite a well-jeweled one, you must admit. And one other thing—"

Her ladyship, the feathers of that last verbal arrow sticking almost visibly from her rib cage, paused on the threshold.

"Should my sister become ... ill ... after the tea you've had with her," Kyra said softly, "believe me, the Witchfinders are going to know about that, too."

Lady Earthwygg's mouth tightened, and she stared for a long moment into Kyra's eyes. Then she said, "Evil to him who evil thinks. It's an idea, my girl."

Turning, she strode off down the gallery with her high, gilded heels clicking indignantly and all her paste diamonds flashing like the sun.

CHAPTER IX

KYRA SANK BACK INTO THE CHAIR IN WHICH LADY Earthwygg had found her and lowered her head once again to her hands. Her sense of triumph evaporated into a gut-deep revulsion.

"I am not a whore," she repeated in a whisper, the unvoiced shadow of words in her mind.

And everyone seemed to expect her to behave like one, she thought—to peddle the core and nature of her being for his or her passing convenience. It wasn't just the Inquisition that made the Academic mages seek their isolated city enclaves like the Mages' Yard here and the House of Wizards in Kymil, not just their sense of futility before the injustices of the world that drove them to the Citadel in the empty Sykerst. It was the desire to avoid being pestered by those members of the mundane world who, while agreeing in principle that such powers should indeed be limited, felt that the wizards should make an exception just for them.

* * *

She had been three months short of her fifteenth birthday when she'd walked into Tibbeth of Hale's shop again.

The jingle of the bell over the door had made her smile. It had brought a sweet-faced girl only a year or so older than herself from the back room, flaxen hair wound in braids around her head. "I'm here to see Master Tibbeth," Kyra had said, and the girl had hesitated, blushing a little.

"My husband is meditating right now." Her voice had been low and rather dreamy. "Perhaps I can help you."

It had taken all Kyra's nerve to walk through the door, to turn her steps south from the Springwell Road instead of continuing on her usual route to the river esplanade and its bookstalls and junk dealers. As she'd wound her way down Ditch Street and Pie Lane and all those nameless, narrowing courts of small shops and soot-blackened Gothic churches, she had been tugged and pestered by the sense that she was taking an action from which there was no turning back, entering a door that would close behind her all those other doors: to her father's business, to marriage—even on her own terms and to the most docile of men—to friendship with the bankers and brokers and money-clever merchants whom she had met and liked in her father's house.

And she wasn't even sure why she wanted to enter that door. *Just go back . . . it still isn't too late . . . You don't even know what it will be like . . .*

But she knew what it was like without whatever lay on the other side: the growing pain, the half-guessed wanting of something unimaginable, something she dimly sensed she would crave beyond reason once she knew what it was.

She wondered how it was possible to yearn for joy of which she had no experience, save in dreams.

Save in dreams.

And now she'd have to get up her nerve and do it all

again tomorrow, or next week . . . or next month . . . Or some other time.

"No, I'm afraid it must be Master Tibbeth," Kyra had said in her most businesslike voice. She had grown six or seven inches since last she had entered the shop, and with her deep voice and harsh cheekbones, she already had the appearance of a woman. "When would be a good time to find him available?"

"Now, my dear."

She turned at the sound of the light, soft voice from the inner doorway. He was standing on the stair with the light falling from the top of the stairwell on the bald curve of his head.

"Now."

When his eyes met hers, they were the eyes of an old acquaintance, eyes she had known, it seemed, for half her life.

He held out his hand as he came toward her, a tall man with the soft bulkiness to him like one of the long-furred, short-faced cats bred in the east. She'd seen him on and off for years, but now she saw him as if for the first time: the brown age spots on the high curve of his brow, the wisps of gray-blond hair that floated like rinsed-out socks around some invisible clothesline strung behind his skull from ear to ear. He was clean-shaven, his mouth and face good-natured, flexible like a rubber doll's, his eyes a light, clear blue. As before, he wore a scholar's long robe. Probably the same robe, with shabby fur at its collar and patches let into its hem.

"Kyra." When he looked down into her eyes, she knew that he knew. "Come upstairs—tell me about your dreams."

That first day he took her through two or three simple tests and taught her spells, spells that even on their first repeating seemed like something she had always known, like a word forgotten on the tip of the tongue. It felt entirely natural to light a candle only with the touch of her mind, summoning the flame to the braided wick, entirely natural to will into being a seed of blue-burning light, heatless as marsh fire, flickering in her cupped palm. Natural to see images in the heart of a crystal or in the colored core of flame. The words he taught her came to her as the logical extension of images already in her mind, the answers to riddles that, once told, were laughably obvious, things she had done once already in dreams. The time she spent learning them over an earthenware teapot by the old-fashioned brick hearth of his cramped study upstairs felt no longer than tea with one of her aunts. She was astonished when she looked over to see the window black with night and running with the autumn rain, as if she had fallen asleep in her chair and awakened suddenly to find it far later than she had thought.

She had a headache, too, a crushing sense of exhaustion that melted with the gentle touch of his fingers on her brow.

"You've done a great deal today."

"I must go," she stammered, collecting her cloak and running down the narrow steps, almost breaking her neck when she tripped at the bottom. He lent her an umbrella, and she had to turn back at the end of Little Potticary Lane when she realized she hadn't made any arrangements about when she next would come.

Already she could hardly wait.

The walk home through rain and darkness was as clear in her mind as if it had been yesterday: the mossy smell rising from the wet paving stones and the stink of the gutters, the way the raindrops caught the gold of candlelit windows high overhead, like dust motes swirling in slanted sun. Exaltation filled her, made her feel that she could hurl aside her borrowed umbrella, spread her arms, and throw herself like a hawk into the pouring sky. And like a helix of snakes, that core of joy had been wound around with ghastly foreboding, a recurring horror that came and went, and the stomach-sinking conviction that she had done something the repercussions of which would change forever the life she had known and planned.

Light and darkness alternated in her like a turning carnival lamp.

She wasn't mad. She wasn't wrong. The power existed; the power was hers . . .

And her father would be horrified. If it came to be known, she would be forbidden to marry, and young as she was, she knew he had been negotiating her marriage with Larmos Droon, son of one of the most powerful merchants in the city. Alix was barely nine. It would be five years at least until he was able to negotiate from such strength again.

He had confided in her, asked her opinion of this boy or that among the families he considered good alliances; Larmos had been mostly her own choice. He was pleasant and malleable and smelled nice, if it had to be someone.

And now that would never be. Lukewarm as she'd been about the whole idea of marriage, that still stung.

Even worse, she could never be her father's business partner, never sit in his countinghouse calculating corn futures, never be his heir. For a flashing moment she felt as if those images—those lemon-colored afternoons of dust and ink and the bright, clipped, precise conversation with her father, his dry cleverness and the obvious pride he held in her—had been an object, a carven box or a lacquered bottle holding both past and possible future, something with heft and actuality in her hands, something snatched away from her. Or something she had accidentally dropped or deliberately given to someone else in a flash of impulse, instantly to be regretted.

Half the time, as she walked among the ring-pocked puddles of the granite flagway, she wondered if there was yet time to pretend this afternoon had never happened. *Oh, I fell down and broke the heel from my shoe, and I've spent all this time in the cobbler's waiting for it to be repaired. I'm terribly sorry I've worried you . . .*

But the thought of never going back to that upstairs room on Little Potticary Lane, of never feeling again this shouting joy, this rush as if she'd drunk sunlight, brought tears of grief and horrible loss to her eyes.

Damn it, she thought despairingly. *Can't I do both? Can't I be both? Can't I have both?*

But she already knew that no one who had training in wizardry could be a merchant. There were too many tales of rival ships wrecked by contrary winds or delayed by sprung planks, while ships in which wizards had invested sailed on past to skim the cream of the market.

And more than that, she knew that her father would be heartbroken.

The house had been lighted like a Yule feast when she'd reached it; her father had come down the high steps, right behind Briory, in the rain. "We've had old Sam and the footmen out looking for you for hours. Where on earth . . . ?"

"I'm terribly sorry, Father," she'd said, handing Briory the umbrella in the shelter of the hall once more and shaking out the soaked hem of her skirts. "I tripped on the steps down by the quays and broke the heel off my shoe. It took the cobbler forever to repair it."

Alix had wakened when Kyra had cried in the night, and though Kyra wouldn't tell her the reason, the little girl had held her close in the shelter of the curtained bed until they'd both gone to sleep again in the whispering of the rain.

Kyra had sent one of the footmen to return Tibbeth of Hale's umbrella, with a polite note canceling their meeting, and for two days succeeded in convincing herself that she really would be more comfortable doing the sensible thing and opting for a life as her father's amanuensis, aide-de-camp, and heir. She'd gone to her long-suffering dressmaker and ordered a glorious scarlet silk; she'd attended a rout party given by the banker Fyster Nyven in his mansion out in Parsley Hill and had danced three dances with boys whose fathers had ordered them to pay court to Gordam Peldyrin's daughter.

Then she went back.

"Tibbeth, I can't stand it!" It had been years since she'd wept in front of her father, in front of any adult member of her family or any of the servants. Pacing back and forth in that small study above the apothecary shop, the black and white brocade of her skirts hissing like the passage of wind through grass, she felt the tears pouring down her face without shame, without defensiveness, as if that tall, gentle elderly man had been her friend from tiniest childhood. "I know I shouldn't give up what I have; I know I shouldn't throw it all to the winds for something I don't even know if I'll like to do!"

"Do you mean you know you shouldn't want to?"

"Yes!" she'd sobbed, furious with herself for such stupidity. "I do want to—about half the time! And the other half . . ." She slapped angrily at the streams of water running down her chin and jaw, and Tibbeth leaned across to her—he was sitting on the raised bricks of the hearth—and handed her another handkerchief, as her own two had been reduced to soggy rags.

"My dear, I'm so sorry," he said gently. Taking her hands, he looked up into her white face, which already bore the marks of strain and exhaustion. "I wish I could give you some grounds upon which to make a choice, wish I could tell you that you *have* a choice. But wizardry . . ." He hesitated, and she saw the echoes of his own ancient unhappinesses, his own struggles to decide which side of a divided heart to follow.

"Wizardry has a way of hurting those who are born with it who do not develop their talents." In the corner the green parrot he kept caged scratched its yellow poll and muttered half a dozen words from a love-spell. "Some do it, especially those whose inborn powers are not all that great. But more often than not they are wretched. I know. I was nearly twenty before I admitted to myself that the yearnings, the thoughts, that came and went in alternation with my more sensible moments were not going to go away."

Kyra turned from him, staring out the distorting panes of the bull's-eye glass window at the row of houses opposite—tall, narrow-fronted, the soot that blackened their brick or half-timbering broken here and there by the vivid pink of window-box geraniums or by white bed linen hung out to air. She whispered, "Damn."

"Would you like to think about it and come back?" There was a gentleness to him, a deep patience; Kyra felt that if she'd thrown herself into the armchair near the window and announced her intention of staying there until she'd thought the matter through, he would simply have remained by the hearth, toasting muffins and making tea for however many hours it took her.

She shook her head and pushed tiredly at the hairpins that had come undone from her auburn mane. "I don't know how often I'll be able to come," she said, her deep voice steady now, though rather subdued. She wiped the last of the tears from her cheeks. "It's sometimes hard to get away."

"Would you like me to teach you a spell for that?" And his eyes twinkled at her look of astonished enlightenment.

She'd gone to him two or three times a week after that. Sometimes she told her parents she was going shopping or browsing through the old-book stalls along the river. Sometimes she merely left a spell behind her that caused everyone in the house to think that they'd seen her minutes ago and she was just in another room. He sent books home with her so that she could study and memorize the movements of the moon and stars; Angelshand in autumn was seldom clear enough for direct study, though when he'd taught her sufficient weather-witching to help, they summoned a light wind that swept the clouds aside one midnight, while they sat

at the window of his pepper-pot roof turret with a tele-
scope. He taught her the properties of the healing herbs
that grew in the tiny yard behind his house and how to
use them for medicines, poisons, and love-philters; how
to witch them so their properties were strengthened;
how to summon to them constellations of chance and
happenstance, the slight tilting of the balances of the
universe in favor of one event over another. In his little
workroom behind the study she learned to use a cruci-
ble and a gem cutter's wheel and to tan leather for ritual
use—learned what metals and crystals were best for
which sorts of talismans and how to write words in silver on leather to summon anger, or docility, or sleep in
those who passed near.

He taught her how to draw power up from the core of
her being, from blood heat and breath, how to drink it
in from the air around her, from sunlight and starlight
and the motion of the tides.

He taught her the words to speak to control this
power, the movements of her hands to concentrate her
mind, the paths of power that ran through every human
body, every leaf, every feather, every rock and river.

"A wizard's greatest power lies in illusion," he said
to her once. "Simple things, mostly. Most people's lives
are lived half in illusion, anyway, so turning it a little
here and there is no difficult feat."

She frowned. "I don't live in illusion."

"Don't you?" He smiled. "What an exceptional
young lady. What color are your housekeeper's eyes?"

Kyra was silent, taken aback. She'd known Merrivale
all her life, but though she could conjure the woman's
warm lap and the slow, sweet drawl of her voice, she
found herself unable to visualize that detail of
Merrivale's face.

"If you were to be walking along the quays buying
books and one of your footmen, on his day off, not
wearing his livery, were at the same stall beside you,
would you recognize him? Or would you simply slip

your mind past him, as you slip it past him from day to day in your house, he being a footman, not a real man. And I know that you, Kyra, are more observant than most."

"Brown," Kyra said at last. "Her eyes are brown. Though to tell you the truth, I couldn't say whether the cook's are brown or blue." Nor, unless she thought about it, what the names of the scullions were; she thought one of them was something like Pib or Tib, but maybe that was the stable boy.

"Very good." Tibbeth smiled, a warm lifting of all the lines of his face. "But how many of the people you know could answer the question even after a little thought?"

Kyra thought about the young men who danced with her, the cluster of girls, all half-afraid of her, half-awed, in gales of giggles at her dry comments, which she now realized suddenly were always barbed and cruel.

"And from that," Tibbeth went on gently, "it is easy to move the mind of—say—some boy you danced with last night, to think that instead of you walking through a room, it's someone he doesn't need to take any notice of, a footman or a chambermaid. Though it's an illusion that won't hold if he's on the lookout for a shapely chambermaid or—although surely no young gentlemen of good family would indulge in such interests—a handsome little page." And his eyes twinkled mischievously again as Kyra sniffed.

"And once those spells are mastered," he went on after a moment, "a very good mage can put the illusion into the mind of the subject and make him or her see what *he* most expects, whatever it is—a cat, or the cook's helper, or whatever, though quite frankly I'm not good enough to do that every time, and it's far safer for me to pick what the subject will see. But as you will find, it's also quite easy to keep the subject from seeing anything at all. A noise at the other end of the room . . . a violent sneeze . . . a sudden itch on the bottom of the foot or the abrupt and overwhelming conviction that there's something in the other room that has to be done *that moment* . . ."

He smiled and spread his big hands, his delight in the small turns and maneuverings of happenstance beaming from his face. "It's all very simple."

And so it was. Everything was that first winter of wonder, discovery, and joy.

Kyra sighed and got to her feet. Time was pressing; she had wasted too much already. Later, she promised herself wearily, she could rest. Later, when she knew Alix was safe.

From down the gallery she could hear Esmin Earthwygg's voice, which had formed a kind of brassy tinkling behind all her ruminations: ". . . darling, don't you know *anything*? His mother slept with the Duke of Spinnaky; that explains how *his* family got the contracts for the Bureau of Pleasures! They say that his sister is the living image of the old duke, in more ways than one. She picks her footmen for their looks." Esmin giggled. "*Just* like the old duke did!"

"Esmin, that's the awfulest thing I ever heard!"

"Goose! It's the truth, and it's all over the Court."

As she strolled down the gallery, Kyra glanced into the drawing room, where Esmin, thin and fox-faced in extremely becoming oyster-colored silk, shared a love seat with Alix. The mothers of the two girls sat some distance off, doing fancy needlework by the small fireplace. Most of the rooms in the house had the more modern stoves, but the drawing room, as a fashionable showplace, retained the older—and more tonnish—means of heating. Binnie Peldyrin had her embroidery frame before her and was working deftly with her silks, chatting effortlessly with her guest about so-called garden wall–style panniers as opposed to the hooped style, but Kyra could see by her occasional glances at the ormolu clock that she was thinking about all the preparations for the wedding—garlands to be braided through the banisters, tables to be set in the hall—that could go forward the moment Lady Earthwygg took herself out the front door.

The house would be topsy-turvy for the day.

Casually, Kyra strolled into the drawing room, where a tea tray had been placed before each pair of ladies. "Alix, darling," she said, "I'm just off to do some shopping in town. Can I get you anything?"

Esmin giggled furiously; Alix glanced up at her with a smile of genuine warmth and pleasure at the sight of her. "No, I'm fine, thank you."

With every appearance of unconcern, Kyra picked up in turn each of the pale blue and white teacups on the tray, feeling through their tepid sides for the taint of something besides the finest leaf obtainable from the wilds of Saarieque.

But the pale liquid felt normal. The reading of tea leaves was considered by the Academics the crassest of dog-wizard tricks—even Tibbeth had looked down on it—so Kyra could only wonder what the delicate patterns strewed wetly on the bottom of the cup might have meant.

"Not flowers?" she inquired innocently, as if the basement weren't chockablock with them, and as she'd hoped, Alix's eyes twinkled with more genuine amusement at the jest.

"Maybe one or two."

"Oh, how can you say that, Alix? You know you have all the flowers you want down in the servants' quarters!"

Around Esmin's uncomprehending chatter, the sisters exchanged a grin, and Kyra strolled out again. As she descended the stair, she thought about the Sigils of Protection. She could lay spells upon a ring that would cause it to heat if it touched any vessel that contained poison.

But the drawing of such a sigil would be detectable

if the Inquisition had an even moderately strong wizard monitoring the house. And if she were arrested, even jailed for a night ...

Kyra wondered how close Lady Earthwygg would sit to Alix during the wedding feast. Probably close, considering her position as the patron's wife.

Briory appeared in the doorway of the kitchen quarters, saw it was only Kyra, and shook her head. "Is that woman never getting out of here?" she whispered, and Kyra shrugged.

"You could always have one of the maids start screaming 'fire,' " she suggested, and Briory gave her a harried look.

"That's all we'd need."

"Yes, and like as not Father would blame me for it and have me driven out of town before he realized it wasn't a genuine blaze." She sighed. Curious, she thought as the butler went to fetch her cloak, that Lady Earthwygg had chosen today to come over and waste her mother's time. Although it was the sort of thing Lady Earthwygg *would* do.

But if Lady Earthwygg plans to poison Alix at the wedding feast, she thought with a grim smile as she descended the high front steps, *she's going to have a surprise in the morning.*

As, for that matter, will they all.

It took her a few minutes and two changes of cabs to lose the Witchfinder following her; after stepping immediately out the door of the second and watching it rattle off with her pursuer in tow, she turned her steps back through the crowded streets near the harbor, in the direction of Little Queen Street.

But habit, she found, was strong. Though circumstance had not taken her there for six years, she found herself turning, almost without thinking, down the alleys that led to Little Potticary Lane.

Even after all these years the route was as familiar to her as the hallways of her father's house. Every pothole

on the pavement, every quirk and gambrel of the crowding houses that grew darker and shabbier as she walked
eastward, the steely gleam of the river at the end of the
streets to her right. Had she really strode along this
granite flagway in the rain, clutching the cane handle of
a borrowed umbrella, seriously thinking about not
studying wizardry, after all? And then the next moment
nearly bursting into tears with the joy of having it, feeling it, knowing that it was alive and glowing like daylight within her breast?

For no particular reason, she wondered if Blore
Spenson had ever experienced that kind of wild vacilla-
tion of emotion, that joy so deep that it was almost pain.

And then wondered why on earth she'd wondered
that.

When first she had met him, she had assumed that he
hadn't, that he was only a merchant with a face like a
meat pie and a soul to match. But though without a
doubt he fought pirates and passed through the spice
markets of the east as phlegmatically as he drove
around cabs and circumvented boys rolling hoops, there
was a good deal more to him than met the eye.

Kindness behind the stiff silence, and uncertainty behind the strength.

It would serve Lady Earthwygg right if he *did* marry
her precious daughter instead of Alix. He wasn't the
man to take kindly to a mother-in-law's airs, and his
horrendous old father certainly wouldn't put up with her
ladyship's gambling, much less an unexplained four-
hundred-crown pension to a wizard. She smiled a little.
If she were a dog wizard, she thought maliciously, she'd
almost be tempted to do as her ladyship asked, just for
the sake of the frustration and rage it would cause her
the first time she tried to put something over on that de-
ceptively quiet man.

But over the satisfaction she felt in contemplating the
poetic rightness of the situation came the awareness of

the spreading lake of pain it would cause. Quite simply, she wouldn't do a thing like that to Spens.

As she had hoped, no one had bought the long, narrow lot halfway down Little Potticary Lane.

The cellar, and the subcellar where Tibbeth had fermented his potions and his colorless little wife had stored her jams, yawned to the sky, half-filled with rubble and overgrown with the feral remains of the back garden. Automatically Kyra identified aloes and boneset, the brightly colored buttons of tansy and anemone like blood-sprinkled coins. Nettle grew everywhere: *to avert danger and ward off ghosts*. She could almost hear Tibbeth saying it as they walked in that vest-pocket walled garden, hemmed in by rickety tenements on all sides so that it was like being at the bottom of a well.

What ghosts, she wondered, haunted that weedy ruin?

She looked down into the cellar. Puddles at the bottom reflected a steely sky. The houses on either side were just the same, their garish, primitive murals a little more effaced with time and soot but their shabby window-box flowers still as bright. On the redder bricks of the adjoining house walls she could see the raggedy outlines of where the floors and stairway had been.

Beggar children raced down the lane behind her, shrieking like birds. One of them, a girl no more than eight, dashed ahead of the others almost to the edge of the gaping cellar pit, laughing and clutching a broken toy horse in one hand. In the cool spring sunlight her dirty face was framed by a tousle of raven curls, and for one moment Kyra looked down into eyes that were huge and blue as the sea: a beautiful child.

Then the girl veered from the empty ruin where Tibbeth's house had been and fled. As Kyra's friends had fled when the walls of the shop had still stood. *A witch lives there . . .*

They had used his books, Kyra recalled wearily, to kindle the pyre they had burned him on.

Closing her eyes, she turned away.

CHAPTER X

"OLD MAN PELDYRIN, PTUI!" THE WOMAN THEY CALLED Hestie Pinktrees turned from the tiled stove of her little parlor with the almost processional grace sometimes acquired by the obese; it was like watching a willow tree pirouette upon its roots, sweeping furlongs of ruffled green skirts and petticoats festooned with lace. "I've never ill-wished a man yet, sweeting, but that crabbed old sourpuss made me wish that I could become the black witch you read about in fairy tales, just for five minutes! Will you take brown sugar, darling, or white, and do try these scones."

She crossed the small, cluttered room with dainty steps, two flat-faced, butter-colored cats fawning around her beaded slippers. Kyra, seated in the old-fashioned upholstered chair with a third cat purring on her lap, looked at the flowered lace curtains, the carefully tended potted plants on every windowsill, the mottled golden sunlight shawling a breakfront crowded with cards, magic mirrors, astrolabes, a *famille rose* pitcher containing dowsing rods, and dozens of porcelain and cut-glass perfume pots—at a guess containing the ingredients of the more common philters and spells—and mentally scratched her hostess off the list of threats to her sister's life.

Considering the relative shabbiness of the neighborhood—a dreary gray street of brick shotgun houses in the factory district south of the river, full of mud, pigs, and children—the place's cozy, jewel-like prettiness was even more surprising.

"Do you not ill-wish, then?" She put a very small note of disappointment in her voice as she picked up the tea and looked sidelong at the woman who'd been driven so unceremoniously out of the third-floor flat in Lesser Queen Street.

Hestie Pinktrees shook her head. "My dear child . . . May I call you Snow-Tear?"

"Snow-Tear?" Kyra said, startled.

"Well, of course you know my customers never do tell me their real names." Laugh dimples puckered the dog wizard's apple cheeks. "And the snow-tear is a flower of the far edge of the northern ice, a place where you wouldn't think flowers would grow at all. But every now and then, when they've had enough sunlight— and it has to be a great deal for them, as for so many who masquerade as tough-leaved shrubs—and enough protection from the bitterness of the winds, almost as if they're unwilling to admit to it, they put out those beautiful pink-edged blossoms, which no one sees except those who venture up to the rocks and ice."

Kyra looked away quickly. "My name is Rosamund," she said. She hadn't counted on a dog wizard having the kind of perceptions that occasionally made conversations with the real Lady Rosamund such uncomfortable affairs.

Pinktrees smiled. "Of course, sweeting. I'm sorry if I embarrassed you." She sat down, her two cats springing gracefully—though they were almost as fat as she—to her lap.

"I never ill-wish anyone," she went on, and her delicate soprano voice grew grave, "because I've never wanted to do that kind of thing to myself. The magic of ill, though it is bounded about with spells to completely protect the mage who uses it, is, when you strip everything away that makes it almost automatic in its effects, a magic of hatred, of rage, of dirty, festering inner pain. Now, there are many wizards who can lay such spells without feeling those things toward the object of the curse, indeed, who can lay the spells without even knowing the person they're cursing, except by the scent of them on the glove or pillow slip or whatever they're given by the one who's paying for it. But it still leaves its mark on the wizard's soul."

Her light eyebrows, two dainty half circles like the finest brush strokes, pulled together with distress. The mild afternoon sunlight winked in the jewels of her rings, small and delicate and oddly in scale with her tiny hands, as she nibbled on the confection of dates and sugar she'd brought to the table. Kyra concluded after one exquisite bite that it was no surprise that the little dog wizard resembled nothing so much as a steamed pudding if she was in the habit of making such tidbits regularly.

"In a way," Pinktrees went on, "it's worse to cast such spells for pay, upon people one doesn't even know. If, when Master Peldyrin and those awful men from the Bakers' Guild turned up and told me they'd rented my rooms right out from under me—and would do the same in any rooms I took anywhere in the West Side, though what business it was of theirs I can't imagine!—I'd put an ill word on their businesses, or sent spells to make all their accountants fall in love in the same week so they wouldn't be able to add straight for daydreaming, or given their wives and mistresses and daughters an unslakable craving for diamonds . . . Well, it would have served them right, and I don't think I'd have taken much ill from it myself. But it still would have left a stain on me, a little char where the fire of hate had been fanned up. And I wouldn't have felt right, let alone that it would have gotten their poor accountants and ladies in trouble over it later.

"But if you came to me and said, 'This or that man hurt me; I want you to make him fall down the front steps and break his ankle ... " '

It was all Kyra could do not to start.

"... then to feel that kind of hatred for him, for pay ... Well, it would feel to me a bit like taking a man into my bed for pay rather than because I cared about him. Do you understand me?"

Kyra put a note of bitterness into her voice. "And what of me? What of the hatred *I* feel that I'm not able to do anything about? What of the pain and humiliation that ... that *weasel* put me through for the mere sport of it?"

"I'm sorry, my dear." The dog wizard leaned over and put a plump hand like a tinted silk pincushion without the pins over Kyra's wrist. "I'm truly sorry, and I will give you the names and directions of others who ... who can help if this is really something you want to do. People you can trust, who do have power, and who won't cheat you. But please, go home and think about it first. And if you need help with any other thing or if, when you've hated enough, you want something to ... to ease you ... do come back."

Kyra got to her feet, shaking out her brilliant yellow skirts; Hestie Pinktrees disposed of her cats and hurried in a great flouncing of taffeta to take Kyra's patched black cloak from the hall tree that nearly filled one end of the wall. As she put it on, Kyra reached out quickly to touch the wall, which was papered with a bright imitation of the beautiful eastern silks that were so popular in middle-class homes, and absorbed the sense, the feeling, of the woman and her magic, so that if she found it anywhere in the big stone house on Baynorth Square, she would know it again.

Hesitantly she said, "Mistress Pinktrees, I . . . I'm sorry Master Peldyrin wronged you. It was a shameful thing to have done."

The childlike mouth pinched, and a look of annoyance flickered in the back of those mild hazel eyes. "Well, I think so," she admitted frankly. "And it's not the first time by a long way that he's trumped up charges against the mageborn. Why, six years ago—"

"I heard about that," Kyra said hastily.

There was a little pause. "Well," Pinktrees went on after a moment, "it all did work for the best, though the custom I've been able to get in this neighborhood isn't near what I'd have commanded north of the river. The man has some cankerworm inside him, and I've found—or at least I like to think—that such a thing will give him more hurt than any spell I could find to cast. And as for your trouble, my child—I don't know how badly you were hurt. But at least think on what I've said."

"I will," Kyra promised softly and took her leave.

Seyt the Pilgrim was the name they'd given her at the Feathered Snake when they'd said they didn't know what had become of him after the Witchfinders had taken him away. But as she'd hoped, his was one of the three names on the piece of cream-tinted paper in Hestie Pinktrees' effusive script, names that, she later found, faded away entirely after a week. The direction was at an inn called the Iron Cock in the Algoswive district; from there she was directed to a large, rambling old house on Tupping Lane where girls sat in windows turned jewel-bright in the dusk, talking with one another or with passersby as they waved bright satin fans or combing their own or each other's hair. Watching them, Kyra realized that several of them she had seen already in the Cheevy Street Baths—good heavens, had it only been this morning? They were the ones who had worn the longing-spells like diaphanous gauze cloaks.

She smiled a little.

A boy in jeweled earrings and a coat of embroidered peacock eyes as gorgeous as any of the women's dresses showed her around to the kitchen in back. Kyra waited in the smoky glare of cheap grease lamps and an overwhelming odor of sausages, and a few minutes later the Pilgrim came down the endless flight of the old back stairs, leaning carefully on a stick.

"Depends on what kind of magic you want," he said cheerfully in answer to her first question. His voice was light and husky, like a young boy's. "I'm willing to do anything, up to a point. It wasn't my original intention to be the house mage in charge of barrenness and temporarily earthshaking love." The hand that made the airy gesture at the kitchen around them—and the musk-laden dark yammering of the rooms beyond—had a slight tremor in its fingers. His wrist was thin, and under the colorless, shabby clothing, his body had an unhealthy fragility; the echo of pain haunted the back of those bitter-coffee eyes.

"A death-spell," Kyra said, and watched how the dark eyes shifted.

"On whom?"

She hesitated artfully, then said, "A member of one of the merchant houses."

He looked away. His hands, never steady, shook more, so he casually closed one around the other to still them. Kyra became aware of one of the girls, a busty redhead who'd come into the kitchen to fetch wine, catching the wizard's eye and nodding vigorously. Seyt opened his mouth, closed it, then said, "I don't think so."

"Big Blossom said you're out on the street Tuesday if you don't pay what you owe her," the girl pointed out, hitching her bottom up onto the soapstone counter and dangling her jeweled feet.

"I'll deal with Blossom," Seyt promised, and turned back to Kyra, fear now as well as pain imperfectly concealed in his face. "That's something I can't deal with," he said frankly, like a bootmaker confronted with a request for a baby's slippers.

"I'll make it worth your while." Kyra knew better than to bring out money in a place like this, but she knew that her jewelry—though probably not worth the brouhaha of stealing—announced what her price range would be. She watched the young man's face narrowly but saw no guilt there, no uneasy self-questioning, only fear, and pain, and the memory of still worse pain.

He shook his head. "I . . . had a run-in with some of the great merchants two years ago," he said after a moment. "God knows why—I'm not claiming I've led a blameless life, but I never did the things they said I'd done, I swear it. But they put the Witchfinders on me anyway." Under his white-shot mustache, his mouth flinched, and Kyra felt a sudden rush of rage at her father, that he would have done this, that he would have trumped up a charge so casually to eliminate a man who was inconvenient to him.

And then she blushed, furious, despairing, remembering . . .

But the Pilgrim's gaze was momentarily distracted into some terrible middle distance, and he did not see. In the common room, to judge by both sound and smell, someone was being violently sick, to everyone else's uproarious amusement. Kyra's color was fading again when his attention flicked back to her.

"If anything happens in that neighborhood," he pointed out quietly, "I'm the first one they'll come looking for."

"With the result," chimed in the red-haired girl, still perched on the pitted counter, her ruffled crimson skirts gathered up to show a startling flash of chubby white leg, "that you haven't had the nerve to do a spell worth more than two coppers to anyone since you got out of prison."

The dog wizard flinched a little, as if she'd struck

him, but turned in his chair and remarked, "The point is that I *got* out of prison . . . and that I still have my fingers, and my tongue, and my eyes, and my balls."

"That's debatable," the girl muttered, hopping down and collecting her wine tray. She made her departure as Seyt turned back to Kyra again and took her hand.

"I'm sorry," he said in his light, quiet voice. "I just . . . can't have dealings with that group of people. At all. I can't risk it. I'll be glad to give you the names of others you could trust, as much as you can trust anyone in this business. But don't go to anyone who isn't on the list, because they'll cheat you for sure."

As he wrote—and Kyra knew she'd be able to take a sense of him, enough of a feeling of him and his magic from the paper to identify any sign he might have left in the house—she asked him, "What about Hestie Pinktrees? I see she isn't on your list."

He looked up with a crooked grin. "I thought you wanted ill-wishing. Pinkie wouldn't wish hairballs on a cat who scratched her, but if you're after something like a love-potion, or a scry-ward, or one of those little glass oojahs that'll keep your pet bird from flying away, Pinkie's your girl."

"And you?" she asked.

The dark eyebrows quirked. Then, understanding, he said, "Well, it's true that one of the things they *did* cut out of me was my nerve—if I knew you better, I'd show you the scar—but that'll grow back. A word of warning, though. If you really are talking about a death-word on a member of one of the big houses, don't go sashaying into the mage's parlor unmasked and wearing your own jewelry or your own perfume. The Witchfinders know a lot more than you'd think. If they trace it to the mage who lays it, it's good odds they'll find you, too."

He got carefully to his feet and bent unexpectedly to kiss her hand.

"I'm not saying you shouldn't do it, because I don't

know who you're after or why," he said softly. "But think about it real hard. I can't call to mind offhand a whole lot that's worth what they do to you if you get caught."

And leaning on his stick like a very old man, he made his way to the small door of the back stairs, and thence, Kyra guessed, back up to whatever heatless attic was going to be his until Tuesday, at least.

Dammit, Kyra thought, striding fast through the darkening alleyways. Poison, magic, passion, grief . . . Her nails bit her palms with the clench of her hands. The wedding tomorrow. Night closing in like the shadow of waiting death. There were other dog wizards in the city, and merchants who'd pay them to keep the alliance from going through.

The screaming rage of her heart she forced into curses, measured to the beat of her feet on the muddy cobbles of Algoswiving Street.

Dammit, dammit, dammit . . .

"Ill, she says!" Gordam Peldyrin threw up his hands in disgust.

"I'm sure it's just nerves, dearest." His wife rose from the yellow-striped love seat to try to coax him down to her side; opposite them, Cousin Leppice flicked open her fan to cover her prominent teeth and tried to look helpfully inquiring instead of avid and Uncle Murdwym surged forward to the edge of his chair.

"Ill? Any daughter of mine started playing off her tricks after all you've done for her, and *I'd* have given her something to keep to her room about."

One appalled glance through the drawing-room door was enough for Kyra. She quickened her step along the gallery, gathered her skirts, and hurried up the stair to the floor above, terror of poison filling her mind. In addition to Uncle Murdwym—chunky as his brother Gordam was lean but with the same golden-brown eyes, the same red hair—his crushed-looking wife, a thin-faced and discontented daughter, and her nonentity of a husband, the drawing-room contained Cousin Wyrdlees, a large, strapping, fair man with a hearty way of talking that accorded ill with his finicky refusal to touch any piece of furniture the dogs might have lain upon. He was looking around nervously at the moment and relating a story about a family in Parchasten whose youngest child had complained of a sore throat at tea time but that had died down to the last servant by supper.

Her father snapped impatiently, "Oh, don't be a fool!"

Kyra shuddered. The Mellidane side of the family was there, too: the widowed Aunt Sethwit, her son Plennin and his wife, and two children who, from their fair hair and small, plump stature, had to be Plennin's children, currently engaged in trying to pat Angelmuffin the lapdog. As she ascended the steps, Kyra heard Angelmuffin's warning growl and then Blore Spenson's light, good-natured voice saying, "Oh, I think we've got a cranky princess here, Pinny. Why don't you leave her be and come have a look at these birds' eggs. Did you know your Aunt Binnie collected birds' eggs?"

Oh, the poor man, Kyra thought distractedly, but in the face of the sick dread in her heart that thought, too, blew aside like ash in chilly wind. Faintly from the drying room floated the gay strains of rondes and gavottes, begun, broken off, started again in a different key or, oddly changed but recognizable still, in a different modality or tempo. When she'd slipped quietly into the hall via the garden door, she'd seen Briory supervising the footmen in the hanging of new tapestries and curtains; the hall itself was redolent of fresh flowers, as it had been the night of her arrival.

Alix's wedding.
Alix's wedding night.
And now she was ill . . .

"Who is it?" Her sister's voice was muffled behind

her door. A moment later she appeared, clothed in the pale green undergown she'd had on that morning, creased and flattened as if she'd lain down in it most of the afternoon, her hair a half-untwisted skein of newly wrought gold and fading flowers. Her eyes were a ruin of tears.

"Are you all right?" Kyra stepped quickly into the room and caught her younger sister in her arms.

Alix's breath came in a long intake, a shuddering release; she turned her face aside. "I'll be all right. It's just . . . I'm just very tired."

Kyra stepped around quickly, took the cold hand in hers, and stared intently into her face. "How do you feel?"

Alix blinked at her, puzzled. "I said all right."

"Father said you were ill."

"Well . . ." The rueful echo of an old twinkle danced at the back of her eyes. "If necessary I'll eat soap or something and really *be* ill rather than go down to that drawing room. Did you *see* who appeared this afternoon *just* as Mother *finally* got that poisonous Lady Earthwygg settled in her carriage? And of course nothing will do but that they have to be invited to dinner, the whole pack of them. Aunt Sethwit and Plennin and their children are staying with Murdwym and his wife, so of course Murdwym is feeling put upon and thinks Papa owes him a dinner at *least*."

Kyra's tense body relaxed, and she felt a rush of irritation. At the same time, it was very unlike Alix to malinger in the face of family duties—and even in the dim light from the bedroom, she could see that her sister's face was marked with strain and that she looked far from well. "Did you know Master Spenson is here also?"

Alix turned away, tears flooding her eyes.

Reaction to the fears that had driven her up the stairs at a run made Kyra's annoyance deeper. "So it's just love."

The two candles burning on the dressing table picked out the burnish of her hair; the gleam changed a little as Alix nodded, but she did not look around. "Just," she said.

Footsteps padded in the gallery, nearly soundless. Kyra looked around quickly as the doorway darkened. "Here's for you to wear tomorrow," began the laundry maid's soft voice; then the woman paused, her arms filled with freshly-ironed linen, as she saw Kyra, and with a stammered, "Oh, I'm sorry," she fled.

Kyra sighed. Another one who listened to the tales of what sorcerous masters kept hidden behind locked doors. "Twit," she muttered savagely, and Alix glanced back at her.

"It's not her fault," Alix said, and studied her sister's face for a moment in the doubled, flickering light. "I'm sorry—I shouldn't have told Papa I was ill." She wiped quickly at her eyes. "It's just that—"

"So you're not really sick."

"Kyra, what is it?" Alix picked the last bits of flowers out of her hair, a fumbling gesture that let them fall to the tufted rag rug beneath their feet. "I'll be fine in the morning, I promise you. I just don't want any dinner. What *is* it?" She pulled away from Kyra's testing fingers, which sought first the heat of her forehead, then the movement of the pulse in her wrist.

"It's just that I don't trust Lady Earthwygg," Kyra said dryly. She caught Alix's wrist again; the pulse was normal. The deeper, secondary pulse, more guessed than felt, was normal, too. No trace of the imbalance that poison would bring.

"Lady—"

"Or Esmin. I wouldn't put it past either one of them to dose your tea cakes with something that would . . ." She hesitated fractionally, then went on, "would have you throwing up on your shoe buckles for two days so they could have one last try at getting Spenson away from you." And when Alix stared at her incredulously, she went on. "Alix, Lady Earthwygg would do anything to get him for her daughter. Anything."

Alix made a soft little sound, half a sob, half a chuckle, and sank onto the edge of the bed where her apple-green flowered overdress lay in a softly gleaming pile. At her movement shadow glistened and prickled on the rocaille beadwork of the crimson wedding dress in the corner, making it seem to move. In the candlelight the vivid silk looked black, like old blood. "No," she said quietly. "No, it's . . . 'just love.' I'll get over it. Everybody does."

Nevertheless, Kyra descended two flights of dark and twisting back stairs to the kitchen quarters and found the sky-blue porcelain cups and plates used for "company" teas. They had been washed already and reposed on their usual shelf in the white-painted butler's pantry; even touching them, willing her mind deep into the delicate, fine-grained texture of the ceramic itself, Kyra could feel no trace of either poison or the magic of ill.

There's no help for it, Kyra thought despairingly. *I'll have to search the place from top to bottom.*

In the kitchen behind her the bustle of supper was commencing, the white and gold fish-shaped tureen being loaded with its attendant dishes into the dumbwaiter by Joblin while Algeron assembled new city walls and palace turrets of gingerbread for another wedding cake. He would, Kyra guessed, be most of the night in the construction of this marvel, for Joblin was never a man to duplicate his effort; he would feel his honor impugned if this second cake were not five times more splendid than the first. The long table down the center of the room was three-quarters taken with the shells of tartlets and pies, into which the two trembling scullions and Neb Wishrom's assistant cook were smoothing custards, scents of ginger and vanilla warring with the thicker smells of garlic, beef, and lime in the heavy air.

They'll be all night, Kyra thought, her heart sinking. *And all day tomorrow . . . I'll never get the place searched. Whoever was paid to place a sign of evil in this house could have put it anywhere. And I'll still have to find who did the paying.*

She fingered the papers in her pocket. Even knowing the names of the dog wizards who might have placed death-marks would help when she finally found the thing. *If* she found the thing.

Under the glare of a dozen whale-oil lamps she watched Algeron's profile, bent above the fragile pink fretwork of a turret cap, and thought of Alix weeping in her room two floors above. The golden light gleamed on a tear of his own; he put down the paper icing cone quickly but not quickly enough and had to fetch a sable brush, such as he would later use for the detailing of colors, to remove the drop from among the candy roses into which it had fallen like a bead of unlucky rain.

Kyra shook her head, collected two rolls and some cheese from the pantry, and stole out through the drying room, where only empty wine cups and the remains of stale cake showed where the musicians had been practicing. She tripped over the garlands piled there awaiting the departure of the supper guests, but no one in the kitchen noticed her in any case.

"Miss Peldyrin?"

At the sound of Spenson's voice she stopped on the second-floor gallery. He detached himself from the end of the group proceeding into the dining room and strode back to where she stood at the top of the stair, moving with the sure strength of a man walking the deck of his own ship.

"Is that for your sister?"

Kyra managed a wry grin and shook her head. It was very good to see him after the exhaustion of a frustrating afternoon. "For me, I'm afraid. Alix said she didn't want anything, though I expect Mother will send her up a tray later." In the glow of the gallery lamps Spenson's sandy hair seemed almost golden; from the rough brown tweeds and regrettable catskin waistcoat he'd had on that morning he'd changed into his bottle-green suit again and looked uncomfortable and slightly untidy. Kyra fought the urge to set down her makeshift meal and repair his cravat.

"I think Father will be just as pleased with my absence from the dining room, and personally, I'm ecstatic about it."

His eyes lost their stolidness and began to twinkle. "You didn't happen to bring enough of that for two, did you? We could sit on the back stairs. Would it be against your principles to put spells around us to keep us from being seen by that lot in there?"

Kyra shook her head with a grin. "I'm afraid it's your destiny to suffer. Though I'm sure Uncle Murdwym's advice on how to fit and command a trading fleet will be of inestimable value to you."

"About as much value as your esteemed Cousin Wyrdlees' advice on how he cures his boils, which he gave me, gratis, without my asking him at all."

"Generous of him," Kyra approved with a gracious nod.

"Though Angelmuffin did finally bite your cousin Pinny. I'm pleased to say her mother told her it served her right."

"I always did approve of Plennin's wife, whatever her name is. For one thing, she serves to make him visible, like a red bow tied round a sheep's neck to find him again in a herd. Do you have appalling relatives as well, Master Spenson?"

He laughed, the ruby in his cravat pin—absolutely the wrong thing to wear with that coat even if it *was* the size of a melon seed—glinting in the branched light of the candles nearby. "Battalions. Well, you've met my father. You'll see the rest of them at the church tomorrow morning." He almost seemed to stumble on the words, and the old expression—or lack of expression—returned.

"Spenson," Kyra said hesitantly, and he held up a hand.

"Spens," he said. "We're going to be related."

"Spens . . . this marriage isn't easy on her, you know. I mean, it never is. I mean, she barely knows you." She floundered, feeling suddenly like a complete fool, not knowing what she wanted to say, something that had rarely happened to her in her entire sharp-tongued life. And what, she wondered, *could* she say? That Alix was crying her eyes out upstairs and there was an absolutely penniless and unsuitable young man baking his heart like a carnival coin into the wedding cake down below? That she still harbored, deep in the back of her mind, the fear that her sister would cut her own wrists in a fit of incomprehensible eighteen-year-old despair?

Spenson was silent for some time. Two days earlier Kyra would have thought that that silence betokened either rejection or complete incomprehension of what she had said; now she understood that this man was a man who chose his words carefully to make sure they truly expressed his thoughts. He just used fewer than Algeron did.

"No," he said at last. "She barely knows me. I've been at sea since she learned to walk." He stood for a time, looking aside and down, the lights from the hall below casting upside-down shadows on the sudden harshness of his face.

"We'll both be learning a new thing," he went on slowly. "I can't stay a ship's captain all my life; it's high time I returned to learn the land side of the business, to take an interest in what will be mine. To find a wife and set up a household. To father heirs to follow me. I know that."

His breath came in a hard sigh, and the bright blue eyes returned to hers. "Are you asking if I'll be kind?"

She wasn't but could not phrase into words all that she wanted to ask. For a time she only stood, looking across into his face, her own habitual glibness defeating her. She could say anything and everything, she realized, except what she truly felt. In that, this quiet man seemed to have the better of her.

"Yes," he said. "I'll be kind."

Kyra looked away, fumbled at the bread she carried, and managed to drop one roll; he caught it neatly, one-handed, and the acrobatic deftness seemed to break the tension between them. She smiled. "You're getting very good at that."

"I'm getting plenty of practice." He smiled back. Then, with a sudden resurgence of his old awkwardness, he went on. "If you'll be speaking with Alix . . ."

"She'll not be speaking with Alix."

Kyra's head came up; beyond Spenson's shoulder she could see her father, framed in the lamplit brightness of the dining-room door. The brown velvet coat skirts belled behind him as he strode down the gallery, and his mouth had a grim set to it. "Master Spenson." He inclined his head to his guest in a clear gesture of dismissal. "I'll see you in a few moments in the dining room."

Spenson looked as if he would speak, his temper flaring like blue fire in his eyes. Then he inclined his head in return and strode quickly away. In another man's house there was little he could do.

"And what's that?" Gordam nodded at the rolls and cheese in Kyra's hands. "Don't you dine among your family like a civilized woman?"

"I was simply endeavoring to respect your oft-repeated wish to have people forget me," Kyra replied silkily. "I'm sure you wouldn't wish me to impose myself on dear Uncle Murdwym and Cousin Wyrdlees."

Balked, he hesitated a moment, then went on. "And just as well. Not only do you have the Witchfinders watching this house as if we're harboring a criminal, but now your mother tells me she's heard the rumor running around that I paid you—*paid you* like a dog wizard!—to cast a glamour on Spenson in the first place to get him to consent to this match!"

"Heavens," Kyra murmured, and pushed a stray tendril of hair back into place. "My guess is that rumor is only 'running around' Lady Earthwygg's elegant patrician mouth. Considering that she offered me money only this morning to do exactly that in favor of *her* daughter, the story can't have gotten far."

"Don't you understand?" Shadow outlined with sudden sharpness the bulge of a vein in his temple, just beneath the thinning wisps of his reddish hair. "It doesn't matter how many people are saying it! From that rumor it's a short step to saying that you and I have been in communication for years, that you've been aiding and assisting me in all my business ventures."

"Oh, don't be silly. Any of your business friends will know exactly how long it takes to get a letter as far as Lastower, let alone out to the Citadel, if and when they can find a messenger willing to go. If it's the Witchfinders you're worried about, their own Magic Office could tell them the impossibility of communication by scrying-crystal with a nonmage like you."

"And yet here you are in my house, on the very eve of the wedding!"

He fell momentarily silent as the petite, dark-haired maid emerged squeaking from the back stairs and skidded to a halt at the sight of him, her hair tumbled about her shoulders; she was hastily straightening her bodice when the mandolin player came springing out on her heels. With elaborate casualness the two of them strolled off in opposite directions along the gallery.

Gordam turned back to his elder daughter with a snort. "In my house," he went on, "while my business languishes, a hundred and forty crowns' worth of flowers rots in the midden, my servants gorge themselves on three hundred crowns' worth of cake, sweetmeats, and imported southern raspberries, and those lute strumming Senterwing savages cover every maid in the place!"

Kyra removed a fleck of invisible lint from the caramel satin of her bodice. "Well, under the circumstances, even Lady Earthwygg can scarcely accuse me of having come to lay spells of good fortune on your business. Bid Aunt Sethwit hello for me and tell her I'll see her, Aunt Hoppina, and Leppice at the ritual bath in the morning." She turned and started up the stairs.

"I curse the day when I heeded your demand to be tutored by Tibbeth of Hale!" His harsh, despairing voice echoed in the narrow confines of the ascending stair. "All my troubles stemmed from that demand!"

Kyra stiffened in her tracks, half turning to look at him through the chestnut tangle of her hair. "It wasn't a demand, Father," she said softly. "It was a plea." And she walked up the stair and made her way back to the yellow room.

CHAPTER XI

IT WAS A PLEA.

And her father had said no.

Wrapped in Alix's fluffy robe, Kyra lay for a long time on the yellow room's high, old-fashioned bed, staring once more into the ascending chimney of trompe l'oeil clouds on the ceiling as if she expected to see the Moon Fairy with her handfuls of sleep dust flitting among the painted putti and birds.

Downstairs, she could hear the muted voices of the footmen, the soft scrapings and clunkings as they brought the long trestle tables in from the stable loft and assembled them, ready for tomorrow's feast. Her ride in Blore Spenson's gig over the jolting cobblestones of Upper Tollam Street seemed weeks ago; her visit to the Cheevy Street Baths, loosening her muscles in the antiquated marble tubs with the steam rising about her face, a memory from some previous lifetime. Lady Earthwygg ... poison ... Hestie Pinktrees' comfits and the smell of sausages and cheap perfume ... Algeron shedding tears into the wedding cake ...

And nothing to show . . . nothing learned . . . nothing gained.

All my troubles stemmed from that demand . . .

It had been the last time she'd let her father see her cry.

But having worked up the courage to finally ask, to finally step out of the column of red pain in which she lived, every hour when she was pretending to be what she once had been—her father's clever helper with the books and the business, the designer of increasingly outrageous dresses and jewelry, the caustic arbiter of social nuance for the amusement of her friends—she could no longer have the refuge of his ignorance.

She'd admitted she was mageborn. There was no going back from that.

"I want you to forget this nonsense," he'd stormed at her toward the end of that stomach-twisting, throat-burning interview in the book room. "It won't do, Kyra. You can see that it won't do. People will find out. People always find out things like that. Good God, people may suspect already if they've seen you going to that man's house in the afternoons. How *could* you deceive your mother and me the way you have?"

But he couldn't forget. He hadn't asked her to help him with the bookwork that evening or the next. She'd lain in her room and heard his step hesitate on the gallery, then pass by. And the omission had lodged in her stomach like a lump of uncooked bread, leaden and indigestible, a nausea that remained with her for days, a silence between them that flooded her eyes with heat and her throat with pain but that neither of them could break.

Once he'd opened the door of her room and come in unannounced, saying brusquely, "You have to understand my position. You're a businesswoman, Kyra; you understand that no other businessman in the city, in the Realm, is going to trust us if you become a wizard! Let alone what Lord Earthwygg will do. The Court's absolutely against wizardry, and without his backing, we'd certainly lose the charity hospitals contract and probably the Imperial Ballet School and the barracks as well! I've worked for thirty years to build our reputation. I can't let you destroy it on a whim. It's your future, too."

"I didn't ask for it!" she cried desperately. In the past year she had found that Tibbeth was right: During those times when, knowing all that her father was telling her now, she had tried to put her studies aside, the pain had only grown worse. It was pain such as she'd never known, a pain of desiring, of yearning, of half guessing, half knowing what that unknown life could be, a pain she hadn't even guessed human beings were capable of experiencing.

"Oh, nonsense, girl; you asked for it only the other day! I'm not trying to be hard-hearted," he went on in a more kindly tone. "But you just aren't thinking of what this will mean for you. And what I'm going to say to Dutton Droon about your marriage negotiations . . ."

"I didn't want to be born this way!" she pleaded. "But I am, and I have to follow what I am!"

He sighed. "Kyra," he said gently, "men and women are born with free souls and free minds. We can choose what we will be, choose which paths we wish to follow. Yes, I know it's difficult. I know you want this now, but you're young."

"It isn't being young!" She half raised herself from the bed where she had lain—it sometimes felt—for all of those two days, though she knew objectively that she'd been downstairs for meals and had gone walking with her mother and even done a little shopping, all activities seen, as if through glass, through the feverish, alternating colors of yearning for the unknown new life and a desperate yearning for the cool peace of the old. "It isn't want! It's need, Father."

He said nothing, but in his eyes she could see him thinking in sentences that started *Girls your age* . . .

Sometimes she thought she was going to die of the

pain. Sometimes it was all she could do to keep from taking a fork or a hairpin and stabbing it repeatedly into the flesh of her hands and arms, though she didn't know exactly why she wanted to do that or what she fantasized it might accomplish. Sometimes she was able to talk to Alix, or read books, or design dresses as if it were all two weeks ago and everything was fine.

She hadn't realized she'd stopped eating until her mother began pleading with her to do so. Then she threw most of it up.

Her father shouted at her for being willful while she lay on her bed with her face turned toward the windows, watching the pigeons wheeling over the gray roof tiles against the cloud-piled sky. Later Alix came in and lay down in the bed beside her, wrapping Kyra's bony, growing limbs with her own soft coltish ones, holding her close and crying.

It was only when Tibbeth of Hale came to the house and took her parents aside into the book room and talked to them that her father called her down.

"Now, I want you to understand me," he said, his narrow, square-lipped mouth clipped-looking and grim. "I'm not paying this man—" He'd jerked his thumb at the dog wizard, sitting quietly in the carved blackwood ("company") chair by the tiled stove."—one single copper, and I don't want to find anything missing from this house; not food, not money, not bed sheets, not silverware, not anything."

"*Really*, Father . . ." Her eyes blazed, but Tibbeth only smiled a little and raised one big brown-mottled hand.

"I understand your concerns," the dog wizard said. "I'm a wizard; it would be easier for me than it would be for most teachers to convince your daughter to demand my services as a tutor in order to gain admittance to a rich man's house. I can only hope that in time, when you know me, you'll understand that I could no more refuse to teach a mageborn child to use her powers than she can help seeking out a teacher. But it's something, truly, that only the mageborn can understand."

"What I want *you* to understand," Gordam snapped, "is that I won't have you teaching her charlatanry. And I won't have you teaching her anything that goes against the tenets of the Church. And you, my girl, had better keep up your studies in mathematics, and bookkeeping, and foreign tongues—you're not to let the education I've paid for slip away while you chase a rainbow you may well decide tomorrow you've had enough of."

Kyra opened her mouth to reply, but again she caught Tibbeth's eye and the small movement of his fingers that said *These are things that can be worked out in time.* She held her peace.

"And above all," her father concluded, and his oak-colored gaze cut sharply to the two of them together, the tall, bulky man in his dark robe, so relaxed in the big carved chair, and the girl standing beside him with her outlandish gown of crimson silk bagging about her sunken body, "I don't want one word of this, *not one word*, to get out. My daughter tells me your kind have spells to keep them unseen as they come and go. Use them. And you, miss ... You're not to miss a ball, you're not to absent yourself from visiting our friends, you're not to whisper to one solitary soul of what you're learning until I can find some way to make it acceptable to the other members of the guild. There's no hope it can be covered up forever, but until I've come up with a way to keep our house from being tarred as wizards, you're to be silent about it. And that goes for your sister, too. Understand?"

"I understand," Kyra said, not in the frightened whisper she had thought would come out of her mouth but with the old ironic accents that she immediately saw he had perceived as arrogance. She said, "Father—thank you," but he was already turning away.

Alix was waiting outside the book-room door. "Father said yes!" she trumpeted, flinging herself into Kyra's arms, holding her as tightly as only a ten-year-old champion could do. "He said yes, he said yes, you're going to be a wizard!" And turning in a swirl of white silk and flying golden curls, she threw her arms around Tibbeth's waist, pressing her cheek to his stomach and holding him tight.

"I see we have a partisan." Tibbeth smiled and stroked the sunny aureole of the little girl's hair.

Kyra turned over with a gasp at the sound of horses in the court below. The windows were flat slabs of ash. From somewhere she smelled incense. Olibanum—the Text prescribed this for the bride's ritual bath.

She rolled to her feet and stumbled to the window. For one blinding second she imagined she would see the entire wedding procession assembled, the bright new banners unfurled in the hands of the footmen, the white carriage mares shaking their crimson-tasseled bridles, and her father just handing Alix into the coach in her crimson gown: see all that and know they hadn't even bothered to call her.

But the sound had only been the grooms bringing in the Earthwygg carriage with its silver door mountings and its yellow emblems of salamander and mushrooms. A moment later Kyra heard the faint commotion of guests entering the hall and, at the same time, the renewed strike of hooves and clatter of iron wheels below her window: Frittilaire Nysett and Cira Prouvet. She glanced out the window again in time to see Tellie Wishrom, her white gown fluttering under the enveloping folds of a stylish cloak with a gray fur collar, hurrying across the yard from the little postern gate and pausing to greet Algeron on the kitchen steps.

Two footmen came out of the kitchen door bearing furled banners between them, in tandem like fence rails; they set them upright against the wall with the slowness of men who had had too little sleep. Kyra felt a pang of sympathy. Their voices and the uneasy stirrings of activity in the house below had formed a continuous background to her thoughts the previous night. She remembered neither those sounds ceasing nor falling asleep herself.

The grooms rugged the Earthwygg and Nysett horses but didn't unhitch them; Lord Earthwygg's matched blacks tossed their heads, breathing faint puffs of white steam. Casting her mind down through the floor below her, Kyra heard the laborious chanting of women's voices attempting to read in unison from copied crib sheets:

Let me bow my head to kiss my husband's knee,
Let me still my voice that his singing may be heard;
Let me shear my hair that he may wind of it bowstrings
and take up in his help the sword, the plow, the
*   distaff . . .*

"As if women haven't been serving as warriors, working in factories, and managing businesses on their own for two hundred years," Kyra muttered, who had never had any real intention of participating in the ceremony.

Someone scratched at the door, and Kyra walked over to admit the dark-haired maid with cans of hot water for her own, thankfully nonritual, bath. The maid, too, had faint blue lines of sleeplessness beneath her eyes, but that, of course, might simply have been due to the musicians. Past her, Kyra could see Lily and the blond maid whose name Kyra didn't know carefully bearing the crimson wedding gown down the stairs, the saffron veil trailing behind like a river of sunshine. In their wake the laundrywoman carried a freshly ironed chemise and the saffron stockings prescribed by the rite. She noted also that the gallery rail had been twined with ivy and vines.

Kyra washed and dressed quickly, choosing one of her simplest gowns, a narrow dress of purple and black that made her, in the mirror, seem older, ageless and thin; it gave her the stern, remote wizard face she knew from the masters at the Citadel. In a way it comforted her, as if she had looked ahead into the future and saw herself there, calmly ensconced in her chosen position, like skipping ahead to the end of a book and reassuring herself that yes, she did indeed live happily ever after.

Yet in her heart she felt a streak of uneasiness as the voices of Tellie, Frittilaire, Cira, and Esmin rose, giggling now as the solemn part of the rite was done. She remembered one of the poems Algeron had written, a falconer's love song to a hawk, and the look in Alix's eyes when she spoke his name.

"Don't be silly," she told herself aloud, and applied the brush to the dark, coppery tangle of her hair. "That's why you became a wizard in the first place, to avoid foolishness like that. Pain like that. You'll never have to put up with that kind of nonsense." And she pushed aside a kinesthetic memory of a man's strength lifting her up before she could identify who it had been.

Blore Spenson and his father were in the hall when Kyra descended the long flight of marble steps. On the second-floor gallery she encountered Lady Earthwygg, just leaving the small dining room with the four white-gowned bridesmaids, aunts Sethwit and Hoppina, and their female descendants. As usual, Aunt Sethwit was garishly overdressed for the occasion in the wrong shade of purple and Aunt Hoppina looked as if her gown had been made at home seven or eight years ago and had been worn regularly since. Leppice's panniers were so fashionable, they almost entirely blocked the gallery and she had to turn sideways to let the brides-maids pass.

"A lovely gown, my dear," Lady Earthwygg purred poisonously, surveying Kyra's plain black and violet through her lorgnette; she was impeccably clothed in the pale blues and yellows of her house, just enough diamonds flashing among her predominant pearls to let everyone know that the family could afford them. "And so suitable. Did you make it yourself?"

"Oh, I'm afraid I never learned to set stitches, just design," Kyra replied airily. "After all, that's what Hylette gets paid for—when she *does* get paid, that is." Having observed the Lady and her daughter over a number of days, she was virtually certain that between them they owed that most expensive dressmaker hundreds, if not thousands, of royals.

Footmen and pages filled the hall, clothed in the powder-blue livery of the Earthwyggs or the dark red of the Spensons and moving carefully among the long tables with their snowy cloths. The air was filled with the smells of hair powder, gardenias, and smoking lamps. The light from the windows was growing and through the upper ones Kyra could glimpse blue sky, but the candles still burned in their sconces along the walls and the three porcelain chandeliers overhead cast a chilly, restless glitter over metal buttons, stiffened ruffles, serried ranks of candlesticks and silverware, and buckles polished so that they winked like gems. Garlands swagged every wall, every stair, every pillar of the hall, festooned the Holy Widow Wortle's sacred niche, and ran like petaled green snakes down the centers of every table, and when Briory, clothed in her best yellow and purple, came through from the kitchen, she was followed by a soft whiff of steam irons and cinnamon.

"Not *going*?" Kyra's father kept his voice lowered, isolating himself and Kyra in an island of quiet at the foot of the stairs. "You came all this way to attend the wedding and now you say you're not going to attend?"

"Well, isn't that how you'd prefer it?" Kyra folded her hands over the carven pineapple on the newel post and tilted her head inquiringly.

His face reddened, clashing severely with the purple velvet of the formal gown he wore over his new suit—

purple also, the color of the house—and his yellow waistcoat thick with embroidered violets, pansies, and irises. "You might have told me that before I rented a sedan chair for you."

She shrugged. "If you'd simply arranged for me to ride in the carriage with Mother . . ."

"I couldn't ask Lady Earthwygg to share the carriage with you, and you know it."

"I suppose not, after she'd offered me four hundred crowns a year to put spells upon Master Spenson to cause him to jilt my sister. Still, no harm done, and this way you won't have people pointing at this lone sedan chair among the carriages and whispering, *There goes the witch.* You weren't expecting me to put a cloaking-spell around the sedan chair so nobody would notice it, were you? Because if it went wrong, nobody would notice the entire procession, and considering how much you've spent on the banners and things, that would be a dreadful waste of money."

"Gives me an idea, though." Spenson appeared in the book-room door, laced into a white velvet suit that made him look like a piglet set for roasting. His cravat was extravagant with lace and was tied in a butterfly style far too high for his muscular neck; in one hand he held a small cut-crystal goblet of cordial, and sweat stood out on his brow. Beyond him, Uncle Murdwym's bellowing voice could be heard.

". . . simple enough, you know. I'm not in trade, but I say if a man can master the accounting for a farm, he can master that for a merchant voyage. It's all the same."

"In the future," Spenson went on, "say, for the naming of your eldest niece, I'll hire you to make everyone *think* that our single carriage and two footmen are . . . oh, two coaches-and-four, eight footmen before and four behind, and new banners. Can you do that?"

"You'd have to give me accurate sketches of the banners," Kyra said judiciously, "and describe the sort of

clothing and livery you want everyone to believe you
and Alix are wearing, and whether the footmen are
handsome or ugly. For an extra hundred crowns I'll
make everyone believe that your first daughter is an in-
comparable beauty, when in point of fact she'll probably be as hideous as most babies are."

Spens frowned. "Could you make her passable for
fifty?"

"Depends on how ugly she is to begin with."

"Hmm. I'll book your services in advance for her
when she has her come-out."

In the doorway behind him Lord Mayor Spenson was
looking shocked. Gordam said hastily, "Very well,
Kyra; if you aren't coming to the church, have it as you
will. I'll let your mother and sister know."

"You aren't coming?" Spenson's frown deepened.

"No." She gave him a brilliant smile. "I'm absolutely
crushed to miss it, of course, but I think I feel a touch
of smallpox or something coming on."

She was turning to go. His square, heavy hand
touched her wrist, the fingers warm, and his eyes looking into hers were grave, as they had been the previous
night on the gallery. Very quietly, he said, "If you want
to be there don't let your father keep you away."

The flippancy faded from her face, and her body relaxed a little. "Do you think I would?"

One corner of his mouth tucked up a little. "Not ordinarily. But I know one gets worn down." With his father, she thought, he'd know all about that, and she
remembered again that he'd gone to sea when he was
little more than twenty. "But Alix will miss you."

"Nonsense! She'll be in such a frenzy, she won't
even notice whether I get into that sedan chair or not."

He looked startled. "She will?"

"Of course. All brides are in a frenzy at their weddings. They see nothing of the ceremonies, or who's
there, or what the decorations are like. Why do you
think they keep looking at their wedding dresses before-

hand? Because otherwise they wouldn't remember them, either. Besides, her carriage will leave the court before she even expects me to come out."

The musicians came trooping down the stairs past them, a barbaric welter of pink and gold and green with ribbons fluttering everywhere. Cousin Plennin's two children followed, clothed as pages and scratching furiously, the baskets of rose petals they bore surrounding them in a traveling curtain of scent. *Four crowns per basket,* Kyra thought automatically, *and fresh this morning.* More roses bowered the dais at one end of the room, where the musicians would play for the dancing and the feast.

"I do hope Father sends refreshments out to those poor Witchfinders who're watching the house," Kyra remarked. "Perhaps they should be invited to the feast."

Spenson's eyes sparkled. "Shall I ask him to?"

"The gentlemen's procession is forming!" Lord Earthwygg's stentorian valet called out, deputizing for his soft-voiced master by the great doors. "Gentlemen, your carriages await."

"Will I see you at the banquet?" Spenson's voice lowered under the surging buzz of imminent departure.

Kyra hesitated. She was fairly sure she could get most of the lower floors searched for a wizard's mark while the procession was on its way to St. Creel but didn't know how long it would take to check through the upper.

She didn't let herself think about what she would do if she found nothing.

More softly still, he said again, "Don't let your father keep you from being there to wish your sister well. I know you love her. I'll speak with him if you want."

She raised her brows. "You think I can't deal with my father?"

"I know you can't *seem* to deal with your father without quarreling. At least I've never seen you do it."

Her mouth twisted in a wry grin. "At least I quarrel with mine instead of giving him what he wants."

Spenson opened his mouth to retort, then closed it in silence. She saw his eyes change.

Her own hand raised to her lips as if belatedly trying to cover her mouth against her words. "Oh," she whispered. "Oh, I'm so sorry."

He returned the cordial glass to a servant's tray, not even looking at it, as if it were not there. The expression on his face did not alter, if expression it could be called; there was only a kind of grimness about the mouth, a kind of weariness in the lines at the corners of the sea-blue eyes.

Silence lay between them as if they had stepped into another room away from the crowds of their families, away from those who expected them to be what they were supposed to be and not what they were.

"Just because it's convenient for my father," Spenson said slowly, "doesn't mean it isn't the right thing for me to do. I've ... spent a lot of my life running away. I can't do so forever."

"No." Kyra felt that somehow her lungs had ceased to draw breath. "No, of course not. And I had no business saying that. I suppose, having spent so many years fighting my own father, I see his tyranny everywhere. Please forget ..."

Spenson shook his head. "No," he said gently. "Because in a way you are right."

"Come along, Spens." Lord Mayor Spenson came creaking up to his son, steely eyes darting right and left as he caught the white velvet sleeve in the iron band of his grip. Under an embroidered cap his thin white hair and densely wrinkled face were framed by the black marten fur of the collar of his gown; the rocaille embroidery on his dark red suit would not have disgraced a king. He held out the white velvet groom's cap prescribed by tradition; after a long moment Spenson put it on.

"The whole town's waiting to see the procession,"

the old man said in a satisfied voice. "It's not every day they see the Lord Mayor's son married; it's a show I've looked forward to for a long time now. We mustn't be late."

"Oh, of course not, sir," Cousin Wyrdlees agreed, hovering reverently at the old man's elbow. "I must say, just looking at the carriages is enough to take my breath away." In his hands he clutched the gilded box that contained one of the House Peldyrin's ancestral masks; the House Spenson males carried similar boxes—older, Kyra noted, and far more elaborately jeweled. In a way, Lord Mayor Spenson constituted an ancestral mask himself.

"Come along, Spens," Uncle Murdwym added with an excess of joviality. "They can't bring down the bride while you're here, you know."

His face like carven wood, Spenson started to follow them to the door. Kyra caught his sleeve and resettled the cap at a more becoming angle. For a moment their eyes met.

Then he was gone, the men streaming out in his wake to their waiting carriages. Through the front doors Kyra glimpsed the flash of colored banners and brilliant livery, the glint of morning sunlight on gilding and glass. It would be good, she thought, to have this man as her brother. How Alix could prefer that . . . that pale morsel of unbaked pastry . . .

A dovelike murmur of voices at the top of the stairs made Kyra turn her head. Against the white cloud of bridesmaids, Alix's crimson gown and golden veils stood out like the flame of the rising sun. The traditional jewels—beryl, topaz, tourmaline, and jasper—flashed from tiaras and necklaces, and the bullion stitching along the edges of the lace had a sharp sparkle, almost like glass. Through the saffron gauze it was difficult to see Alix's face, but Kyra did see her turn and say something to Tellie Wishrom, and her movement was light and graceful, as if she had deliberately put sorrow aside.

Kyra glanced quickly at the door that led into the kitchens and drying room. The maids were grouped around it, watching with envy, tears, and whispering delight, but if Algeron was in the kitchen, he was evidently willing to forgo this last sight of the girl he loved so that the ill luck of having her seen by any man would be avoided.

Conscious of how her own dark dress would stand out among the bright colors of the women surrounding Alix, Kyra stepped quietly back through the book-room door and closed it almost to. Her pulses had begun to race again, her mind fleeing ahead in time—shelves, rooms, furniture, knick-knacks . . . All that endless chatter before they'd leave!

Through the heavily curtained book-room windows she could see Baynorth Square, where the entire neighborhood had gathered around the painted carriage with its flower garden of banners and its dangling tassels and charms of gold and brass. Lord Mayor Spenson was quite right. It wasn't every day, or even every year, that a wedding in the strict form took place. As ruled by tradition, the footmen on every carriage bore baskets of candies, flowers, and small coins to be thrown to the crowd—a guarantee, she reflected as she watched Alix move down the steps beneath her canopy of yellow silk, of the slowest possible progress toward the Church of St. Creel in Little Cheevy Street.

She should have two hours at least.

After the procession jolted away across the square, the house was very silent. In the kitchen Imper Joblin still blustered and chided the scullions in the final preparations for the feast. Kyra wrapped herself in spells of averted attention and walked carefully to avoid knocking into any of the banquet tables in the hall or tripping over the kitchen threshold as she ghosted past them and down the cellar steps. In his corner Algeron was working silently, putting the last touches on the varicolored splendor of the cake; none of them so much as glanced at her as she passed.

In the dark, cool quiet of the cellars, she thought again about the magic of ill.

A wizard seeking to plant a talisman or draw a sigil or an Eye of Evil—according to Nandiharrow's lecture on the subject—would naturally seek out the most obscure spot in the house to hide it: the bottom of a wine bottle or the underside of a shelf. A talisman of death inscribed with the victim's name might be thrust into the middle of a sack of grain or a barrel of potatoes or hidden under a loose flagstone or tucked behind Merrivale's jars of jelly. From there its subtle influence, though undetectable save by the strongest and most experienced of wizards, could spread throughout the house.

"There are many forms of death-marks and Ill-Eyes," Nandiharrow had said, "but all contain the victim's name and something of the victim's. Hair or nail parings are the most favored, of course, followed by clothing, bedclothes—especially pillow slips—jewelry . . ."

But I've already looked through her jewelry, felt of her pillow slips! Kyra thought despairingly.

". . . anything the victim wears or touches, and the more frequently, the better. These marks usually contain secondary masking-spells as well, to keep their influence hidden, until a key—a prescribed set of circumstances dictated in the spell—unlocks a surge of power. This key could be a phase of the moon, a day of the week, a word spoken by the wizard himself, passing in the street."

Or the wedding night of the victim, Kyra thought grimly.

"Other spells draw on the power imbued in them by the wizard himself, and their influence depends on how many times a day the victim comes near it. Again, pillow slips are a favored location; so are the threshholds of the rooms the victim frequents."

And yet she had felt . . . something. Some of the malice that surrounded Alix. Closing her eyes, Kyra ran her fingers over the smooth terra-cotta cylinders of the wine racks, seeking the sense, the feel, of either of the two dog wizards her father had wronged. Nothing. Patiently, as quickly as she could, she fingered each bottle in turn, hoping she would find something but hoping also that it wouldn't turn out to be either Pinktrees or the Pilgrim.

It would, she knew, be easier to detect if it were someone she had met. She was strong enough to pick up some vibration from a third wizard, a wizard she had never met—at least she hoped so. Her experience in this kind of thing was limited, and more than ever she felt the need for more training, more time at the Citadel. There was so much that she did not know.

She had to find the mark. It had to be here somewhere.

Cobwebs clung to her fingers, which quickly collected the black dust of the soot that filled Angelshand's air and settled on everything. The procession should be passing through the small plaza before the Guildhall: Lord Mayor Spenson, she thought dourly, would be soaking in the applause like a sponge below the sea. One of the earliest lessons she had learned in the Citadel—from the old Archmage Salteris, now dead— was the accurate subconscious awareness of time, of the position of sun and stars in the sky at any given moment. Moreover, she knew by the hunger headache she was getting that her hasty breakfast of stolen wedding tart had been some while ago. The crowds would be far more dense as the procession passed through the Springwell district. Small children would be clustered on every street corner and fence, thick as pigeons on the bronze statue of the Emperor Pharos II, to watch the red and gold carriages go by. Behind the last carriages of Uncle Murdwym and Cousin Wyrdlees and whatever familial horrors lurked in the House of Spenson, pink and yellow petals would strew the cobblestones like trampled shreds of paper, turning brown in the puddles and sinking into the general muck.

She shook the thought—and the sleepy ache of prolonged concentration—away and moved on to the room where coals and wood and kindling were stored against the long, awful grind of Angelshand winters.

The cellar was damply cold, her search there messy and completely without result.

Kyra knew about when the long string of carriages, footmen, and garlanded flags should reach St. Creel's Church. She was finishing the last of the store cellars, her temples throbbing, her stomach growling, her nose and throat thick with dust, and her eyes itching furiously. She considered again stopping her search long enough to steal some fruit and cheese from the kitchen—and coffee, too, if it could be managed—but she knew her time was running short, and she had the whole upper house yet to search. It crossed her mind, *They should be there,* and, the next second, a cold shock of horror . . . *Oh, my God, what if the wedding really takes place?*

Fumbling in the pocket of her now-filthy dress, she sat on the stairs up to the pantry. A streak of whitish light fell from above, and to that light she angled the scrying-stone she carried with her. It was hard to keep her hands from shaking. Tired as she was, it took her a long time to get an image, and that disconcerted her, too—she hadn't counted on the search draining her so much.

Small and clear, as if she stood in a window with her back to the street outside, she saw reflected in the crystal's central facet the line of assembled liverymen bearing their banners: golden buns on a white and violet field in the center, flanked by the red and gold house design of the Spensons—the hand with its five golden coins—and the yellow lizards of the Earthwyggs. Garlanded with smilax and hyacinth, its corners nodding with the lilies of hope and the roses of fulfillment and trembling with spirit bells and tiny glass balls and Hands of God, the wedding carriage followed behind, the four white mares prescribed by the Texts tossing their heads nervously whenever one of the flower throwers flung a handful of petals too close or a child dived too daringly for the thrown coppers. Beyond, Kyra could make out the shapes of buildings.

Yes. Little Cheevy Street. She recognized the red porphyry columns of the baths, the squat gray toad of the Pantheon Emporium down the way with its brightly painted advertising signs.

The enormous crowd around the steps of the Little Cheevy Street Baths reminded Kyra momentarily of the crowd of rakes and working girls who had gathered there yesterday morning. Probably a number of them *had* been there, then. An even bigger mob surrounded the front of St. Creel's Church, directly next door.

The Bishop's carriage was there, servants in the church's hieratic red holding the bits of the horses. Two acolytes got hastily up from the church steps, clutching the golden censers required by the rite; in the shadows of the church's porch, Kyra could make out the shape of the wedding pavilion, bundled together like a disused white silk tent with its silver finials gleaming softly in the gloom.

The carriage drew rein. Somebody came running from the church as Gordam Peldyrin, purple velvet robe snapping and face fast achieving a color match from sheer rage, climbed down and went storming up the steps of the church.

The image in the crystal faded and was replaced by that of the Bishop—fully robed in crimson and gold like a secondary bride, surrounded by more acolytes and leaning heavily on a crutch—Kyra's father, and the shirtsleeved and uncorseted owner of the Cheevy Street Baths, assembled in the blue gloom of the church nave.

Though spells of scry-ward had been laid on the

building long ago, still Kyra could make out broken glimpses of the scene.

Far over their heads the windows were living gems of stained glass, fragments of the instreaming colors dyeing the faces of the saints—bronze, marble, papier-mâché and plaster, painted and gilded and discolored with age. Most of the garlands required by the Texts were still in place: lilies, roses, hyacinth, and chrysanthemum; the sun canopy flashed in the gloom with the peculiar spooky luster of gold in shadow; the white silk cloths still draped the altars.

The inlaid marble floor, however, was under five inches of water.

The owner of the baths was gesticulating furiously, the Bishop—slightly the worse for a pharmaceutical slug of poppy syrup—straightening his wig and trying to placate Master Peldyrin, a tiny and farcical pantomime in the white fragment of the crystal's heart.

Kyra did not need to hear to know what had happened. She was perfectly well aware and, in fact, quite gratified to have confirmed that a pipe in the baths next door had unaccountably burst in the night.

CHAPTER XII

KYRA HAD CALCULATED THAT IT WOULD TAKE THE CAR-
riages, footmen, and sedan chairs at least an hour to return to Baynorth Square, enough time to search the
drying room and laundry even though they would return
much more quickly than they had gone.

She was not, however, prepared for Blore Spenson
slamming through the drying-room door not fifteen
minutes after she had seen her father discover the
flooded church; Blore Spenson still in his white velvet
wedding suit, minus his cap, with his lace-trimmed
stock awry and his blue eyes flashing with rage.

"All right, miss, what the hell game are you playing!" he bellowed, and Kyra, who only moments before
had heard the clatter of hooves in the kitchen yard and
hadn't associated the sound of a single horse with any
of the wedding party, spun around, dropping the flatiron
she was checking with a crack to the hard slate floor.

"Good heavens, Master Spenson, you really shouldn't
let yourself get into a rage like that when you're wearing
white," she remarked, straightening up and brushing a

197

strand of cobweb from her sleeve. "Your face turns a most unbecoming—"

"You'd better get used to it!" He stormed across the room to her, and she ducked swiftly behind the ironing table, which, after one quick step to his left, he evidently decided not to chase her around. Instead he demanded, "What are you up to?"

"Me?" She looked down at her hands, which had been washed imperfectly, like her face, when she'd come up from the cellar and were still smudgy with dust. Hunger and the fatigue peculiar to long spells of working magic made her fingers shake; she pressed them to the tabletop to still them and said airily, "Oh, well, I was looking for some books my father may have stored in the cellar."

"Don't play innocent with me! The Bishop falling down the stairs—maybe that could have been an accident; it was damp that night, the step was wet. The mice in St. Farinox—well, all churches have mice. But that stupid charade at St. Creel . . ."

"What charade? And shouldn't you be at St. Creel this moment, getting—"

"You know as well as I do there'll be no marriage this morning!" The drying room was, as usual, hot. His big hand fumbled with his lace cravat, loosening it in sloppy folds like creased laundry around his neck. "You knew it yesterday, when I picked you up at the foot of Little Cheevy Street, with your hair still wet from the baths there and a liar's smile on your mouth! You must have been laughing up your sleeve at me all the way—"

"I am not a liar!" Kyra lashed at him, her head giving one tremendous throb of pain and her hands starting to tremble again despite all she could do to stop them.

"Bah! All those questions about other dog wizards to throw me off the track, and me sitting there solemn as an owl, telling you about this and that—"

"I wasn't deceiving you!"

"The hell you weren't! Butter wouldn't melt in your

mouth, you were so cool, getting me to remember the wizards your father offended, wizards who might have put an ill word on his daughter's wedding, when all the while it was you! And me, like a chump, making the world's fool of myself, telling your father not to keep you from the wedding, telling him to seat you at the family table at the banquet, angry at him for your sake for the way he treated you! My God!"

He slapped his forehead furiously with his hand, his face red and blocky-looking with anger in the frame of his sweat-pointed hair. It seemed to Kyra, exhausted by the morning's search and too little sleep, that her whole attention was focused on those swollen blue eyes, that black hole of a mouth flexing and opening at her, spitting out anger, as her father spit it out, and his friends the guildsmen, and the Witchfinders ...

Rage sickened her, at him, at them all.

"And Alix! My God, talk about illusion!"

"Stop it!"

"Talk about making one carriage look like seven and a single bouquet look like a garland ... Was I ever behind the fair! You got her to see you as some kind of loving friend instead of a dried-up stick who's come to disrupt her wedding out of sheer mischief and jealousy that she's been asked to wed at all!"

"Stop it!" she screamed at him. "That's a lie!" And turning, she strode for the door.

Her foot caught on her skirt hem and flung her heavily down; her shoulder struck the door frame with bruising force. For a moment she sat on the stone threshold, her head pressed to the wall, too sickened, too tired to get up.

Behind her Spens raged, "If not jealousy, then what?"

Kyra drew breath to reply, but the words would not come. She sat on the floor for a long time, her cheek to the dampish, mildew-smelling plaster, her hands twisted together in her lap to keep them from shaking, fighting the pain—not the pain of her bruised shoulder but the pain inside, of memory, of fear, of exhaustion, of the sheer brutal weight of going on with it all. *I'll answer him in a moment,* she thought, quite calmly. *As soon as the pain subsides enough that I can do it without crying, I'll answer.*

The quiet lengthened. In the kitchen, two rooms away, Kyra heard Joblin telling Algeron to go lighter on the jelly. "A spot, a spot only, to keep the meringues from floating away into the air."

Spens asked very quietly, "What, Kyra? Why have you been doing this?"

He sounded like he really wanted to know.

Kyra lowered her face to her hand. *In a moment, when I can talk again . . .*

She heard the rustle of the velvet and smelled the orris-root powder in his clothing; his hand on her back, on her arm, was warm and very strong. With a convulsive move, she tried to turn her face away, but somehow it went in the wrong direction and ended up buried in the lace muddle of his cravat and the scratchy braid of his lapel.

Tiredly, hurtingly, she began to cry.

When he kissed her, she cried harder, though not for the same reasons as before.

After a long time she raised her face and saw his eyes; they kissed again, first gently, then fiercer and fiercer, until it seemed to her they would crush the breath out of one another's bodies and break the bones. There was a reason—several reasons—why she shouldn't be doing this, but it was a long time before she remembered what they were, and then they didn't matter.

Faintly, hooves and carriage wheels clattered in the square. The gate to the kitchen yard creaked: voices, tramping, banners, and baskets thumping as they were put down. Oaths, questions, exclamations of amazement—Joblin's overriding groan, "My cake! The finest example of the confectioner's art in fifteen years!"

Spens raised his head, then took Kyra's hand and got her to her feet. "Is there another way out?"

"Through the garden into the alley; I saw the Witchfinders follow the procession out to the church, and with any luck, they haven't taken up their positions again."

"Well, in that dress you look like somebody's chambermaid, so we should be all right."

They were walking hand in hand down Fennel Street before Kyra asked, "Where are we going?" In white velvet, Spenson looked as out of place among the housewives, strawberry hawkers, servants, and shopkeepers as a phoenix in a barnyard, and the bright sunlight of midmorning showed up the filth and dust that clung to her dress. Spenson's estimate that she looked like a chambermaid had been a singularly generous one. Her red hair hung about her shoulders in a tangle; she ran a hand through it and said, "I look like a ragpicker's child."

"You do," he agreed, and put his arm around her waist. "We're going to my countinghouse, down near the harbor on Salt Hill Lane. The clerks all got the day off for the wedding, and it will be the last place anyone will look for us. Is that all right?"

"It will be if you'll buy me something to eat. I—I only cried because I was hungry, you know."

"Good," Spens said cheerfully. "I can't stand a lachrymose woman." He stopped by the cart of an itinerant bun vendor, steam from the little enclosed stove flavoring air that had already begun to smell of salt and tar. "Do you want the kind with bean paste in it or pork?"

"It's a poor trade for Joblin's wedding tarts. Let's get both."

"A woman after my own heart."

"No," Kyra said, licking the sweetened paste off her fingers. "The woman after *your* heart was Esmin Earthwygg."

"Tell me," Spens said as he closed the door of the

countinghouse behind them, shutting out the noise of Salt Hill Lane and the wharves in a sudden quiet of yellow sunlight, whitewash, and bleached pine, "what it is you are trying to do."

Kyra turned away and perched one flank on a clerk's tall stool and concentrated for a time on wiping the last smears of bean paste from her fingers with one of Spenson's handkerchiefs. Beside her, a many-paned window looked out into a brickyard murky with soot from the factories across the river; on top of the tall desk nearby, the cut-glass inkwell sparkled like a jewel of light and darkness. The place smelled of paper, of dust, of spices from the warehouse next door, of the orris powder of Spens' coat. For some reason she felt shy about looking at him, wondering that there had ever been a time when he was a stranger to her. The taste of his mouth still seemed somehow on her lips, the warm print of his hands on her back. He wore his ridiculous white velvet like a disguise, his diamonds glinting like dew in the sun.

"You mustn't think I'm doing this out of hatred for my father," she began.

Spens shook his head. "I know you love your father," he said quietly, and she looked up, surprised.

"He couldn't hurt you this badly if you didn't."

"I suppose." She looked aside again, not quite knowing where to begin or how to talk about magic and the need of magic with someone who had never felt its yearning.

But once she had started, with the cards, and the water, the Summonings and the note, with the dream of which she remembered so little, and her panicked journey to Angelshand, desperate with fear for what she might find, it became easier; she even laughed a little when she described watching him and her father through the scrying-crystal in the mouse-infested Church of St. Farinox. "I wish you could have seen your own face," she said, and, looking up, saw his eyes dance with appreciation. "When that big mouse ran across your foot . . ."

"You, my girl," he said, "are not to be trusted . . . and does this mean I can't pat a tavern wench on the bottom anymore for fear you'll be watching me through that glass of yours?"

"Good heavens, no! I wouldn't impose a punishment like that on the poor tavern wenches. I can even make you a scry-ward to prevent any wizard from watching you that way, if you'd like. They're really quite simple."

"Hm," Spens grumbled. "Like the Witchfinders around your house?"

"Well, yes. Though the Inquisition watches every mage or suspected mage who comes to the city—and they haven't forgotten me from . . . from Tibbeth's trial. Then, too, Lady Earthwygg might have dropped some rumors in their ears, still hoping to get rid of me and snare you for her repellent daughter."

"Her daughter," Spens retorted, "never had a chance even *before* you told me what they were up to. I still blush at the dreams I had of her, but I never for a minute considered marrying the little shrew."

"Well, at one time I thought it might solve the problem of keeping my sister from having a wedding night."

He reached across and took her hand. "Your sister," he said quietly, "is not going to have any wedding night with me." There was silence between them, as there had been that morning at the foot of the stairs while all the wedding party surged around them, as if she had come through a door and now saw him anew and differently. Kyra felt frantically that she must say something but could not tell what: Yes, no, go away . . . Leave me to the life I've chosen and fought for . . . Don't complicate things . . . Be in my life always.

The words seemed to swirl in his silence like bright-hued, brittle leaves dancing, but she could not frame a sentence that did not fill her soul with panic.

"I didn't know it could be different," he said at length. "I didn't know it could be this. I never would have offered for Alix had I known."

And I never would have gone away had I known there was a chance of meeting you.

But that wasn't true, and her panic increased, her sense of being unable to either have him or leave him, her fear that whatever she said would shatter forever her chance of future happiness—whatever happiness was.

"Don't," she breathed, not knowing what it was she wanted or didn't want.

Spenson drew her to him, and they kissed again, a long deep plunge into dark waters. All the despairing logistics, the helpless sense of uncertainty, cleared and resolved into a single thought: *I want this man. I want him as friend, as lover, as companion, every day and every night and every morning. I want this, whatever it's going to be.*

The wizard in her answered, *You want this more than magic?*

She drew away, dizzy, shaken, filled with the conviction that she was probably temporarily insane. Everything that she must say to him and that he must say to her—*Your father will die of apoplexy . . . I can't give up magic . . . Alix's marriage contract*—all these were in the look that went between them as they sat, hands upon one another's shoulders, breaths a soft mingling of sound.

Then, as if by spoken consent, they each looked away, setting aside that silence and those words until another time.

Kyra drew a deep breath to steady herself and said in her most businesslike voice, "Well, we've bought ourselves a little time, though my father is going to have a stroke when you announce that the entire wedding is off."

"I hope you're a good Healer, then."

"But the problem is far from solved. We're still left

with the question of who would want to kill my sister
and why and, most urgently, how."

Spenson settled back into the wide oak chair beside
the desk and folded his hands over his embroidered
waistcoat. His square face was thoughtful. "In other
words, when it's clear she's not to be married because
the groom has other fish to fry, will the killer try
again?"

"Precisely. I've checked the two dog wizards my father wronged, and it doesn't seem to be either of them;
Cousin Wyrdlees *might* try murder to prevent the birth
of an heir to my father's business, but he's just gotten
himself betrothed to Milpott's daughter, which should
keep him in patent medicines for quite a while. Do you
know of any . . . any of the great merchant families who
would want to prevent the match badly enough to do
murder over it?"

Spenson was silent for a time, stroking his chin; like
her, he had heard of such cases before. Finally he said,
"Not with business as good as it's been this year. Whatever else can be said of him, the Regent's an able ruler;
nobody's scrambling for pickings. And if it was me, I'd
try disgracing the girl rather than killing her. It's safer."

"You have a point," Kyra agreed slowly. "With the
Regent's hatred for magic and wizards, I suppose it
would be foolish to try something with a curse that
could just as easily be done with a bribed footman. And
I don't *think* it's a crime of passion. Algeron Brackett
loves her too much to touch a hair of her head."

"Algeron Brackett?"

"The cook's assistant. He's been writing her poems."

Spenson looked slightly ill.

"Oh, they're quite good poems as far as I can make
out, and they're desperately smitten with one another. In
fact, at one time I was afraid—" She caught herself up,
unwilling to reveal the depth of that secret, hopeless
passion to the man whom she was already forgetting to
think of as her sister's groom. Then she shrugged. "But,

well, if the wedding's called off, that takes care of that possibility."

"So all you could do was search the house."

Kyra nodded. "I didn't go to the church this morning because it was the only time I could be sure everyone would be gone. And in three and a half hours all I could cover was the cellars, the laundry, and half of the drying room."

"You'd have picked up another three hours, clear, during the ceremony."

"Except that I knew there wasn't going to *be* a ceremony."

He grinned, a white flash of teeth that turned his brown face boyish. "I wish you could have seen old Wooley's expression—but you did if you used your scrying-glass. And now of course everyone in both families will be all over the house for the rest of the day. How long would you need?"

"Six, maybe seven hours."

"A night's work, then."

"I did consider that," Kyra admitted. She hooked one slender ankle through the rungs of the stool upon which she sat, with the immediate effect of upsetting it and precipitating herself almost onto the floor.

As he sprang to catch her, Spenson laughed. "You didn't happen to have offended some powerful wizard and been cursed with clumsiness, did you?"

"Of course not," Kyra replied with dignity, setting the stool to rights. "And I'm not clumsy, precisely. It's merely that the world is not designed to accommodate women as tall as I am."

"I see."

"I did think of taking one night to search the house," she went on, sitting down on the deep window seat at his side. "But in a house that large someone always wakes up, and I don't think those wretched musicians ever go to sleep. And with the Witchfinders in the alley and the square, I don't see how I could cast a sleep-spell over the place and do it properly."

"I'll take care of the Witchfinders," Spenson said. "Well, I took care of Lady Earthwygg's roughs, didn't I?" he added as she widened her eyes at him.

"All of them? A tall order even for such a doughty sticksman as yourself."

"Sticks, hell." Spenson got to his feet and offered his hand. "There's one thing I learned in the slave and spice ports of the Jingu Straits: if you want serious derring-do . . . hire someone."

"Hi, handsome." The woman's voice was a throaty murmur in the dark of Mouch Lane. Though the shadows of the granite houses and the crowding mansard roofs of Baynorth Square hid her face, fragments of ice-white moonlight fell through the moving clouds to light threads of her hair and show it fair rather than dark, decorated with bunches of freesia whose frail scent vied with the general stinks of sewage and horse droppings. "It's a cold night to be out." And indeed, her breath was the softest puff of white in the inky dark.

Though she was far back in the alley, Kyra had a wizard's hearing. Had she not, the Witchfinder's muttered dismissal would have been completely inaudible to her.

"Is that a way to talk to a poor girl who's only out for a little companionship? Seems to me I've seen you here before."

Another exhortation, longer this time, exasperated, and cut off rather abruptly in the middle.

Kyra smiled.

A carriage passed by in the square, a clatter of harness and hooves and creaking leather springs, the dim yellow beams of its sidelights jarring briefly down Mouch Lane in time to show two men in rough wool jackets bending over the fallen shape of the Witchfinder while the blond woman readjusted her dress. Behind her

in the lane Kyra heard Spenson's unmistakable brisk
stride. He passed her without seeing her—even had the
windows of the small shops that looked onto the narrow
passage been unbarred and lighted, he would not have
seen her—and she was able to watch him, as if watching a stranger, as he paid off the three of them.

"Take him out to Pennyroyal Commons with the
other," she heard him say as silver clinked sweetly from
the bag he held. "Make sure their hands are well tied,
but don't take their clothes or their cloaks if you know
what's good for you. I'll find it out if harm comes to
them from the cold, and I know who to tell them to
look for."

"We'll treat 'em like they was our little brothers," a
jocular bass voice growled, and in the darkness Kyra
could see the glint of Spenson's smile.

"I'm sure you already have. Off you go, then."

The smaller man, who'd been counting what he'd
been given, looked up with a surprised grin and tugged
a greasy forelock. "Good hunting, then, guv'nor."

The three shapes slid into the grimy shadows, making
them, Kyra reflected, probably a little grimier. When
the last of their footfalls had faded, she let the spells
that cloaked her drop away and, taking care not to trip
over the high doorsteps that lined the curving alley or to
slip on the wet cobbles, made her way to where
Spenson stood looking out into the wan moonlight of
the square.

"Unheroic but efficient," she said approvingly, and he
turned around with a start. She saw the bright twinkle
of his eyes within the leather carnival mask he wore.

"Give me efficiency over heroics any day of the
week." He put an arm around her shoulders and kissed
her warmly on the lips, leaving her flustered, startled,
and prey to a flood of unaccustomed delight.

"The man who's been watching the garden gate is on
his way to Pennyroyal Commons as well."

"Is that the usual dumping ground for the victims of footpads?"

Spenson shook his head. "Most bandits just leave them where they lie. Now and then some young sprig who goes whoring in the dives on Buttercup Hill ends up there."

"Did you ever?" she asked curiously as they made their quiet way back down the lane to the alley and thence along the wall of her father's house toward the garden gate.

His eyebrows shot up. "Great heavens, no! I had more money—and better advice from my disreputable Uncle Drake—than to do my drinking in places like that. But I've gone there more than once looking for some of my stupider cousins who feel that the lower a place is, the more fun it's likely to be." His hand on her waist had a light strength to it, as sure and as protective as if he, not she, could see in the dark. High above them a dim glow marked one of the attic windows; below that, the stronger radiance of many candles turned her mother's window and Alix's to squares of molten gold.

A pang of guilt pinched her like a bodice laced too tight. At Spenson's advice she had not gone anywhere near her parents, although, following their interview at the countinghouse, Spens had returned to Baynorth Square and had had what, through the scrying-stone, looked like an extremely stormy and trying talk with her father in the book room. She knew Spens was going to tell Gordam Peldyrin that in the face of such repeated misfortune he thought it better to postpone the wedding to his daughter indefinitely. As she had feared, her father had flown into a towering rage. In the crystal's silence she was unable to hear any of the bitter recriminations about supplies bought and rebought, the venomous blame for four days business utterly lost, the furious accusations of ruined reputation and the threats of lawsuit. She knew her father far too well to need to. She knew Spenson, too, and could only marvel at the tight-lipped silence in which he met all this. His face grew very red, but he didn't lash back with counter-threats and counteraccusations, didn't—clearly—try to throw blame back on his attacker, and in the end quieted his prospective father-in-law enough to make an appointment for the following day, bow, and take his departure.

And as Kyra had known he would, her father then proceeded to storm up the stairs and along the gallery to the yellow guest room, his long purple wedding robe fluttering behind him, and burst into the chamber to stare about him with the blind rage of a thwarted bull looking for something to charge.

What he had charged—and this was why, though the thought of it nauseated her in advance, she had wanted to be there to have the fight with him and get it over with—was Alix. Her mother, downstairs in what appeared to be an amicable chat with Lady Earthwygg, aunts Sethwit and Hoppina, Winetta Wishrom, and several other influential female merchants or merchants' wives, was too busy trying to stem the inevitable tide of gossip to be of any help, and Kyra knew absolutely that between keeping the servants from running about the town with a dozen distorted versions of the tale and remedying the tumult that the second cancellation of the wedding banquet would cause in the kitchen, no help could be expected from that quarter. So Alix was alone when her father came raging into her room.

When Kyra, nearly an hour later, slipped unseen through the Wishroms' cellar and the postern gate and up the back stairs to Alix's room—as she had suspected, her mother's voice could be heard from the direction of the kitchen, frantically trying to mollify a despairing Joblin—Alix had been nearly ill with weeping.

"He made it sound as if it were all my fault!" she sobbed. "I don't want this wedding—I never asked for it!—but he's going to be my husband and I'll be happy with him! And it isn't my fault all these things happened! Kyra, he—"

"It's all right." Kyra tried to gather her into her arms, but Alix fought free of her, clutched her pillows again, and buried her face in them, golden hair tangling on the embroidered shams. The wedding dress's gold and ruby glory lay over a chair in a welter of stiffened linen petticoats; Kyra wondered whether it was considered bad luck to put it on a second time after the first, abortive attempt. She knew to the penny how much wedding gowns cost, particularly those designed and constructed by the redoubtable Hylette.

On the other hand, she reflected, Spenson wasn't going to marry her sister, anyway, and given everything that had happened so far and might yet happen, a little more bad luck connected with this particular wedding was laughably superfluous.

"I will marry him," Alix whispered. "I will, and I will be happy, only ... Damn it!" Her hand clenched convulsively and buried itself in the down of the pillows with a soft thump. "I wish it would just get *over* with! I can't stand this."

Again Kyra had tried to hold her, and again she had fought free, as if determined to keep her own sorrow, her own decision, to herself. As if she feared that in surrendering even to that touch, all her other strengths would break down and she would wash away in a flood of emotion that she could no longer control. She curled up on her side, wrapping her arms around herself like someone naked in bitter cold.

After that Kyra had no stomach for confrontation with either her father or her mother. Climbing the back stairs to the attic, she had settled herself in one of the deserted rooms of the servants wing, surrounded its door with spells of There-Isn't-a-Door-Here and Don't-You-Have-Urgent-Business-Elsewhere? had curled up on the floor in her old cloak, and had fallen asleep.

"They'll be up till all hours, won't they?"

Spenson's voice in her ear brought her back, startled, to the present. She nodded. "I suspect Mother's been all day receiving callers, serving up tea and cakes, and trying to act as if everything's all right, and betweentimes trying to sort things out in the kitchen. Joblin must be ready to commit suicide—that cake was his masterpiece. His latest project is *always* his masterpiece. I've seen him in tears over a fallen shrimp soufflé. God knows what Father's been up to, and of course the servants are running around like chickens."

"The whole town must know what happened," Spens remarked, narrowing his eyes as he tried to make out something other than the indistinct shape of the roof against the sky. His cool aplomb seemed worlds distant from the stiff silence of the man in the awful red suit— surely it hadn't been just three days ago!—the night of that disastrous dinner with the Bishop. "Are we going to wait till everyone goes to sleep?"

Kyra shook her head. "I don't know how long this will take." Three streets away, the clock in the tower in front of St. Farinox chimed ten. This close to the equinox of spring, she translated mentally, that was roughly the fourth hour of the night, old-style. She'd slipped out of the house at around sunset to meet Spens in a tavern, where they'd supped. She was surprised to find herself ravenously hungry again. "I only hope that having started out to the wedding, this isn't technically Alix's wedding night."

"Could it be?" Spens asked, startled.

"Depending on how the curse is written, yes." She was silent for a time, struggling with another thought, then said slowly, "Depending on how the curse is written, *I* could be the . . . the curse."

Spenson smiled. "Well, your father would say so."

"*No!* I mean . . . The wedding's been destroyed. Having this kind of scandal break, this kind of pressure put on her, could *be* what drives Alix to . . . to do something foolish." The memory of her sister's tears returned to her, the brittle, desperate note in her voice. *I can't stand this* ... Joblin wasn't the only one in the household who was reacting to pressure. Curses had been used to provoke suicides before this. Nandiharrow had instructed them in several that were designed to do just that.

He put a warm, powerful arm around her shoulder and drew her close. "You mean that what I feel for you—and what I hope you feel for me—is a result of the curse? Like those dreams about Esmin?"

"No," Kyra said, and though a part of her mind had toyed with the idea, the moment he spoke it aloud she knew that what she felt was no illusion. Whatever it was—madness or disaster or some random jest of fate—it was as true and as much a part of her as the bones within her flesh. "No."

"No," Spenson echoed quietly. Turning her face to him, he kissed her again, gently, on the lips. "Come," he said. "The night's going to be long enough."

In the blackness of her mother's table-size rose garden, hemmed by the cliffs of the houses all around them, Kyra wrought her spells.

Spenson stood guard by the door that led to the rear hall of the house, a powerful figure in his coffee-colored leather and concealing mask. She closed her mind off swiftly from all but the most superficial awareness of his presence. It was more distracting than she had thought, and she was novice enough, even after six years of formal training, to fear for the disruption of her magic that such a distraction could cause.

She concentrated instead on the Circle of Protection she sketched about herself in the soft spring earth; on the ritual gateposts outside it, to establish the field of clarity around her; on the Circles of Light, and Earth and Air. Within their wall she closed her eyes, sank into meditation, and built within her mind the house she had known since babyhood: the slate of the roofs and the angles of their slopes, the smell of the moss on the chimneys, the bird droppings, the soot. Stone by dirty stone she formed the outer walls in her mind, differing textures, Angelshand granite and Halite brownstone, ornamental marble, plaster, brick, and glass. Room by warm room she touched it inside: the dust smells and dimness of the attics where the musicians celebrated among flute songs, champagne, and the salty sweetness of sex; each bedroom as she recalled it, down to the pattern of her mother's violet satin comforter and her father's yellow and white china shaving things; the plaster garlands on the ceilings, the flittering painted cherubs and trompe l'oeil fruit. The rugs in the empty parlors, the books in the library, the smells of dried herbs and dust in the schoolroom where Tibbeth of Hale had taught her ... The heat and bustle of the kitchen, smelling of tomorrow's bread and today's staling syrups and creams. The hall with its silent chandeliers and smells of cooling wax, cellars with their musty coals and flowers heaped on ice, browning in the darkness ...

Sleep, she thought.
Sleep fill this house.
Sleep fill this house.

She heard the clock chiming again, unable to believe that an hour had gone by. Settling back on her heels, she listened to the house before her.

Where before her wizard's senses had brought to her the hivelike drone of voices and movement, a blended murmur of anxiety and trivial concerns, she now heard only deep breathing and a snore or two. To her inner perception of magic, the spell felt hard and smooth, like blown glass cooled perfectly to its final shape; if she'd tapped it with her nail, it would have rung like a bell.

It was, she realized, the first great magic she had done in truth, not as an experiment, not under the guidance of some other mage, not in concert with others who had more experience than she. At the Citadel she had done magic under pressure; indeed, during the pre-

vious spring's troubles she had performed spells that
had saved lives, including her own. But there had been
others around her.

This was completely hers.

And completely illegal, too. Nevertheless, the joy of
it swept her, a golden exultation that sponged from her
mind the last daydreams about Blore Spenson's kisses.

This was beauty. This was warmth. This was delight.

This was also, she realized, the beginning of what
could be an extremely long and dangerous night. There
was little chance either the Church wizards or the Council members were listening for her, particularly at this
hour, but the fear added a shaky edge to her emotions,
a sense of danger and risk.

Quickly—though her head was aching and she had a
terrible craving again for sweets—she formed in her
mind and cast out around the house the same spells with
which she had surrounded the attic room where she'd
slept: less an unwillingness to enter than a sort of spir-
itual laziness, the sense that whatever business needed
to be done in that house would be better done tomorrow; the sense that there were more important things to
do. The image she conjured in her mind was that of getting out of bed on a very cold morning—unpleasantness
that could just as easily be put off.

Carefully, so as not to unravel the spell itself, she
took back the circles and the gateposts she had drawn,
ritually confirming their actual existence while erasing
all physical traces. This was magic at a higher level
than she'd ever practiced, but it would make them safer
from discovery. It was, she realized, cold in the garden,
and the moon had vanished for good. Even its silver
stains on the clouds were fading. Spenson was hunkered
on his heels by the door, but he rose in one smooth
movement as she came toward him, the gravel
scrunching softly beneath her feet.

"Done?" he whispered, and she nodded.

"We can whisper all we want, though I shouldn't like

to shout." She took his hand and led the way along the house wall toward the brightly lit windows of the kitchen. "Oh, wait a minute. Do you have two pieces of silver you can loan me?"

A little startled, Spens opened again the wash-leather bag from which he'd paid his bravos. Kyra drew her thoughts about her again and with careful precision drew upon each coin a Limitation, exempting her and Spens from the effects of the spells of sleep that now filled the house like curling, invisible smoke. "There. Put that in your pocket—I'll need it back at the end of the evening. What I *should* like is something sweet. I feel like I've just come out of sword training and having the stuffing whacked out of me by Cylin and Mick."

"Cylin and Mick?"

"Friends of mine at the college." She climbed the high brick steps and pushed open the kitchen doors, the warmth and sweetness of its atmosphere drenching her like a summer afternoon. "Cylin's one of those men who'll stay up till dawn, memorizing his lists and spells and theories, and then spend the rest of the day worrying that he hasn't learned enough, or that they won't work, or that the laws of the universe have changed overnight and nobody told him. Mick's so scatter-brained, he'll start to memorize a list and then go off digging through seven or eight encyclopedias or besti-aries if he finds a reference to something that interests him. Or he'll go hunt for it in the gardens, if it's a flower or an insect, and spend the rest of the day chat-ting to Tom the gardener about caterpillars. Like two big kittens, both of them."

And she smiled at the thought.

"Yet they beat the stuffing out of you?" Spens pushed up his leather mask and raised an eyebrow. By the glow of a dozen oil lamps, the kitchen had the strange, dis-jointed feeling of things seen very late at night. Imper Joblin sat slumped at the big oak table, a plate of half-picked quail bones before him and his head on his folded arms. The remains of what would have been dishes from the wedding feast strewed the table's length, a ruin of elaborately wrought creams and jellies, roulades and molds. Two footmen, still wearing the breeches of their formal livery, were likewise sprawled asleep in chairs; the two scullions were curled up against the wall near the wood box, heads tilted back, breathing heavily with slumber. Wood lay piled around them and near the big copper boiler where water was being heated to wash all the cake plates and goblets.

Kyra took a clean plate, picked a sweet crepe and a fragile little fruit tart from the general ruin, and perched on the edge of the table to eat them. With a shrug, Spens found the pot of coffee keeping warm on the back of the stove and poured out two cups.

"Well, all novices have to go through sword training," Kyra explained. "Thank you—oops! You *are* getting quick."

"Practice makes perfect."

"I was a little horrified myself when I was told that I'd have to train with the Council's sasenna for a couple of years. I couldn't imagine what sword practice and hand-to-hand combat had to do with learning magic. I still can't explain how they're connected, but they are. A warrior's training—or at least the way sasenna are trained to be perfect warriors—borders on meditation. You reach a point where your body thinks, not your mind. Where things flow. And suddenly magic makes sense, too."

She shrugged and licked custard from her fingers. "But, of course, one has to be a fairly competent swordsman to get to that point, and in the meantime there's a great deal of blundering about and getting beaten black and blue and wondering why one didn't just stay home and be an accountant."

"Why didn't one?" He held out his hand to help her get to her feet.

"Well, for one thing, you . . . you just *can't*. Not if

you're born with power." She frowned at the memories of trying to do precisely that and shook them away. Turning, she made a move to begin going through the kitchen as she had gone through the cellars and the drying room a thousand years ago this morning.

But Spens laid a staying hand on her elbow. "And for another thing," he concluded softly, "because your father had your teacher killed. Was that it?"

Kyra's eyes met his, tawny into blue, and she shivered at the recollection of those days. After a moment she looked aside. "No," she said, her voice equally quiet.

Spenson followed her as she began to go over the kitchen, systematically touching, turning over pots, note tablets, daybooks, and canisters, running her hands over shelves and along the edges of stacked plates in cupboards, feeling the gold rims of frail shell goblets and delicate mother-of-pearl trays. The kitchen was a good place for a wizard's mark, easily entered by any mage disguised as a tradesman, busy enough to distract, and a place where Alix could be expected to go—especially, Kyra added to herself, if the caster of the curse was aware that Alix went down several times a day to talk to the cook's assistant.

"That isn't the source of the enmity between you and your father, then?" Spens asked. "As I said, I was away at the time—Father was still head of the guild. He told me your father turned in evidence that Tibbeth of Hale was poisoning wells or casting death-spells, something completely stupid for a man of Hale's reputation. Yes, he said he'd caught Tibbeth red-handed, laying a death-hex on one of his corn warehouses. It was obviously a trumped-up charge."

Gently, he put his hands on Kyra's arms just above the elbow, looking worriedly into her face. "I wondered, since you were Tibbeth's student and a wizard yourself, if he did that so that you wouldn't leave him."

Kyra sighed. Even with the sweets she'd consumed,

she felt very tired. The glare of the kitchen lamps, combined with the sleeping forms around the table—even the cat was asleep in a corner where she'd been watching a mouse hole—deepened the air of unreality; it was as if she and Spens had stumbled into some other world, some enclave of dream. The fact that she knew the kitchen so well increased rather than decreased the sense of disjunction of place and time.

She wondered what she could tell him about the scandal, about Tibbeth's trial—about why she had proclaimed to the city, to her father's friends, to the Witchfinders, that she was what she was. Wondered what he would accept and what he would understand.

Facing him, with the warmth of his hands on her arms and his face concerned for her beneath the pushed-up mask and the feathery tumble of his curls, she decided to tell him the truth.

"No," she sighed. "Having Tibbeth of Hale arrested and . . . and burned . . . wasn't Father's idea, you see. It was mine."

CHAPTER XIII

SHE HADN'T EVEN REALIZED THAT TIBBETH WAS PUTTING sleep-spells on her at first. The awareness came gradually, like shapes seen through fog in the shadowlands just before full wakefulness returned in the mornings or as she was passing over at night into full sleep. Then those strange memories would be swallowed by the images of her dreams or would vanish, like the bloom on a plum, over the breakfast table or the maids' chatter as they brought up wash water and shook out petticoats from the armoire.

But Kyra knew that for a month or two she had been sleeping much more soundly than before. Since her earliest, troubled dreams of magic, she had waked once or twice in the night. Sometimes she'd just use the chamber pot and curl back under the quilts beside Alix, who always slept like a log, and drift into her dreams at once. Other times she'd lie awake for a half hour or more, admiring the familiar beauty of the furniture in her room with her mageborn sight in the darkness or listening with a mage's meditative hearing to the breathing

of every sleeper beneath her father's roof, to the skitter
of the cats in the yard and the flick and whisper of mice
in the attic, to the watchman's tread in the square and
the occasional rattle of a carriage with its outrunners
and link boys, and to the soft chiming of the St. Farinox
clock.

When she realized it had been many weeks since she
had done so—when she remembered, first vaguely, then
more clearly, Tibbeth laying a hand on her head and
saying, *You will not remember my saying this*—it came
to her as something she had already known and then
forgotten.

Had he really said that to her?

She couldn't be sure.

For nearly two years Tibbeth had been coming to the
house on Baynorth Square to teach her the arts of
magic. As her father had commanded, he always came
under cover of a spell that cloaked him from the notice
of the neighbors, always entered through the garden
door so that even the servants in the kitchen would
make no remark. On those few occasions when Kyra
went to the house on Little Potticary Lane, she did the
same. Her secret remained a secret. Meanwhile, her father worked gradually but steadily on making Tibbeth
of Hale known and accepted by the men of standing in
the guilds so that one day the news that Kyra Peldyrin
was his pupil would not come as an offense.

Tibbeth himself made this easy. He never offered to
use magic for her father's benefit, never put him in a
position to examine the relative ethics of magic and
business. But he was weather-wise and skilled in the
lore of plants and farming, and generally his advice on
when there would be gluts or shortages in the markets
of corn and wheat was sound. Likewise, he was widely
traveled and well read, and other corn brokers came to
rely on his advice as well. Gordam Peldyrin might look
askance at this big, easy-mannered man who had trig-
gered such a change in his elder daughter, but he could

not complain that the dog wizard took the least advantage of his position in the household.

For Kyra it was a time of uninterrupted wonder and delight. She felt like a ragged orphan turned loose in a shop of silk dresses and toys, like a starving woman seated unexpectedly at a feast. Learning and spells came easily to her, as easily as mathematics had, and, as with mathematics, she found her thirst for knowledge unslakable. Tibbeth gave her lists of books, for which she would comb not only the barrows of old books on the esplanade of the river quays but the catalogues of the booksellers and antiquarians in the more elegant parts of town, on Queen's Square and the Imperial Prospect, and he would take her through the volumes she bought, spell by spell, explaining, demonstrating, and correcting. She studied the parts and properties of plants and animals, the movements of stars and wind and clouds, the migrations of fish and birds. She memorized the various circles of power, drawn to ingather the energies of the earth and air: circles of light and fire, of blood and water, silver and earth and darkness. She learned how to trace runes and sigils, either in silver or in light, drawing them in plain air with her fingertip, learned how to cast illusions about herself and glamours upon others.

During this time Kyra barely noticed that she was growing from girl to woman or that the boys who had danced with her at those balls she was still obliged to attend decked in her increasingly flamboyant gowns now danced with her less. It was as if they sensed the heat of the fire within her and feared that alien, coruscating joy. Even Larmos Droon, who was officially betrothed to her when she turned seventeen, was frequently absent from the parties she attended. She didn't mind, for it gave her a good excuse to leave early and return to her studies. If he had little to say to her, this was not so very different from his usual reticence in the face of her breezy erudition.

Alix, budding from a coltish schoolgirl into a promise of heartbreaking beauty, was delighted for her happiness. She frequently accompanied Kyra on her rambles along the esplanade and to the strange little shops on Angel's Island where odd flowers or herbs and salts from foreign lands might be bought and occasionally, under the cover of Kyra's spells, to Tibbeth's house afterward. She had at that time a blue velvet cloak lined with swansdown, and her daffodil hair scattered across it was like lamplight sprinkling in the waters of the harbor at the fall of summer night. Tibbeth got into the habit of helping Alix, too, with her studies, though she was occupied with no more than the usual polite education of a well-brought-up girl: poetry and essays, geography and history, enough science so that she would not be an ignoramus and sufficient arithmetic to keep household books. Like Kyra, Alix had a facility for numbers, the only scholarly subject she truly enjoyed, though her arithmetic cleverness never reached into the joys of mathematical logic. Alix's own interests, when she wasn't involved with dancing classes and the harp and spinnet lessons so necessary for girls her age, tended to center on her own sewing and hatmaking—at which she was brilliant—and cooking.

But, mostly to be with Kyra, she took up the study of arithmetic under Tibbeth, bringing her books into the schoolroom and sitting under its broad window, the sunlight making a primrose halo of her hair. Frequently Kyra would look up from her memorization and practice to see her master sitting beside the beautiful child, patiently explaining cosines or theorems, a smile on his face.

Then one night she'd wakened and found Alix gone.

"Alix?" Her hand groped at the hollowed pillow, the comforter drawn carefully up to cover the empty spot. It was spring, and the air was chilly. The smell of the soap Alix used, glycerin and lilies, clung to the embroidered sheets. Kyra sat up and saw that her sister was nowhere in the room.

And immediately a wave of sleepiness washed over her. The image of Alix going down to the kitchen for a piece of fruit came to mind. Surely Alix had said she was going down for that purpose and was due to return at any moment. Anyway, this must be all a dream.

Far off, the clock chime spoke thrice.

Kyra shook her head, pushing aside the stifling warmth of sleep, feeling, in the way it clung just too long, the curling hints of magic in it.

She remembered again—not for the first time, she realized, but this time the memory stayed, clear and sharp—Tibbeth putting his hand on her head, saying, *You will not remember this ...*

Cold touched her. A hundred stupid servants-hall tales returned to her, of wizards who kidnapped children for use in demon sacrifices.

Tibbeth? If he wanted children for such purposes, he could have kidnapped *her* the first time she came into his shop.

And anyway, Tibbeth was extremely fond of Alix.

Nevertheless, something made her get out of bed and find her robe, white wool, long and trailing, like a shroud. Closing her eyes, she listened, questing in her mind through the house, seeking the soft tread of a bare foot on the floor.

And she heard, very quietly, the closing of the garden door.

She knew the sound of it, the peculiar muted creak of its brass hinges. She thought of her scrying-crystal, but that required light, and light, she thought, would be seen from her window. Instead she pulled her enormous, gaudily colored wool shawl over her robe and stole in barefoot silence out into the gallery, down the two long flights of stairs to the hall below. The little passage at the back of the hall was dark, but the air there held a trace of ice and the raw smells of wet earth and compost, as if the doors had been opened. She smelled again, very faint, the odor of glycerin and lilies.

She touched the hinge of the garden door so that it would not creak and wrapped about herself the thickest cloaking of spells she could muster.

But Tibbeth saw her. The only reason he did not see her immediately was that his head was bent down, his tall height stooped, over Alix, who had to stand on tiptoe to get her arms around his neck. It was a rare, clear night for autumn, and the late moonlight bleached her golden hair to ivory where it cascaded down over his hands, one supporting her head, the other stroking her slim waist, which was outlined by the thin linen of the nightgown she wore. For the first moment, seeing them together, the enormously tall man half-doubled-over to press his lips to the child's, Kyra thought only of how grotesque the scene was, framed in the dense shadows of the garden gate.

It was only when Tibbeth bent a little farther to kiss the white stem of Alix's throat, only when she sighed like a woman, though in her twelve-year-old treble, and under his hand the nightgown slipped a little off the delicate point of her pale shoulder, that Kyra felt a wave of sick disgust that almost nauseated her, so that she had to fight not to gag.

Even six years later she did not know what she would have done had Tibbeth not looked up then and seen her. She was so shocked, so nonplussed, at the scene that she doubted she could have said a word. Every look Tibbeth had ever given Alix as the girl began to ripen, every time his hand had touched hers during their arithmetic lessons . . . all these were flooding into her protesting mind. All she could think was *No . . . No . . .*

But he did look up. And being a wizard, and her master, he saw through the clouds of illusion that concealed her as easily as he saw through the chancy dark of the quarter moon.

He must have known that as a wizard, too, she would be able to hear him. Still, he lowered his voice to barely the whisper of a cricket as he laid his palm along Alix's cheek. "Return to bed now, my darling," he murmured. "You will remember none of this."

For one instant Kyra saw her sister's face, the half-slitted eyes swimming with a woman's passion, the loose mouth shining with moisture in a filthy and incongruous caricature. Then the features changed, relaxing into the slack expressionlessness of dreams. Obedient, Alix came back toward the door where Kyra stood, her eyes still open but with the glazed look of a sleepwalker, the hem of her thin nightdress trailing over the pebbles of the path.

She passed Kyra without a look, ascended the stairs like a ghost, and vanished into the darkness. Tibbeth was coming down the path toward her, explanations almost visible upon his lips. Kyra turned and closed the door and, as she barred it, wrote the strongest spells of ward she knew upon the latch. She retreated down the hallway almost to the arch that led into the lightless gulfs of the entry hall, not quite sure why she didn't want to be anywhere near the door when Tibbeth touched it but knowing that she could not bear his sight, or his smell, or the sound of his voice ever again.

She waited in the dark hallway for nearly an hour, watching the door, but saw nothing. She had heard, through the door, his footsteps retreat along the pebbles of the path, and they did not return.

"Kyra, I'm sorry."

She raised her hand a little, as if to touch Spens' lips in the half-light of the pantry—to stop whatever words he had to say. For a moment she couldn't look at his face. Indeed, as she told him the story, she'd been going through every cupboard and shelf of the little room where the crocks of flour and sugar, the good dishes and the gold- and silverware were kept, her eyes on what she was doing, speaking as if it had all happened to someone else.

Turning to stop his words, she expected to see appalled disgust on his face, loathing and horror that—would they have? she wondered—covered a little puddle of relief that he hadn't actually gone through with it and married the girl.

But in his blue eyes she saw nothing but pity and concern.

"It happened to one of my cousins," he said slowly, at long last. "An uncle of mine ... Nothing was ever done to him, of course, because she had to remain marriageable ..." His lip twisted with distaste at the word. "Father sent him away—made him factor of a fur station in the Sykerst—but poor Nilla blamed herself for it for years. If Alix has been holding that inside herself ..."

Kyra shook her head. "Alix remembers nothing of it," she said softly. "He saw to that ... and I made jolly damn sure of it." There was a sudden ragged viciousness to her voice, like a flint knife skinning a beast.

She shook her head and moved on through the drying room—which she had already searched—and out into the hall. The tables there had already been taken down, moved discreetly back to storage in the stable loft. *No wonder the footmen looked tired.* The new banners still hung on the walls, to annoy and infuriate her father whenever he looked at them, but the garlands had all been removed from the railings of the gallery, the balustrades of the stair. The tubbed gardenias clustered around the book-room door, sweetening the air with their scent, and the Holy Widow within her niche seemed to wear a miffed expression on her round porcelain face.

Kyra's hands roved almost automatically over the usual occasional tables in their niches and corners, the panels and thresholds of the great outer doors, the ancestral masks in their curtained niche, and the marble steps of the single long, straight flight that ran up the north wall. Though it was not impossible that some dog wizard had come this way—with a good cloaking-spell it was astounding what one could do, as Kyra had learned—it was doubtful, and she could feel no trace of either the magic of Hestie Pinktrees or that of the Pilgrim in the somber flagstoned room.

As she searched, touching each of the hexagonal stones underfoot in turn, probing for the queer psychic heat of a talisman, she continued, "When I got back up to our room, I searched for a wizard's mark by which he could have laid the spells of love on her and summoned her." Her hands trembled with remembered rage as she fingered in turn the masks' vigil lamps. "He'd written them on every one of her nightdresses. Sigils of yearning, of illusion ... the kind of sigil Lady Earthwygg might have paid a tame wizard to put on your pillows, the kind a lover puts on the garments of his beloved. And he came to me the next day."

"My dear Kyra, I would have thought that you, of all people, would understand."

For a moment all Kyra could do was stare at Tibbeth. In a way his words shocked her, off-balanced her, as much as had the sight she had seen in the moonlit garden the previous night. "*I* would understand?"

"Kyra ... " He reached out a broad, brown-spotted hand to guide her into the chair opposite his. Around them, above them, the great house was quiet save for the small stirrings in her parents' rooms, where Foodret was shaving her father and the footmen were bringing hot water and towels for her mother's morning toilette. In the kitchen Kyra was aware of Joblin supervising the preparation of breakfast kidneys and muffins, of Merrivale giving orders to the maids for the day, and footmen stocking the dumbwaiter that supplied the breakfast room on the floor above. The book room in which she and her master sat still held the chill of the night, and outside its window only vague shapes could be seen, stirring about the square. The maids had laid the fire in the stove but had not lit it, and the faint odors of cold ash mingled with the fusty nose itch of dampness, old paper, and dust.

Kyra yanked her hand from Tibbeth's as if there had been a roach in his palm.

"Kyra . . ." He looked hurt. "I haven't harmed her, you know. I wouldn't—you must know I wouldn't. One doesn't eat green fruit—"

"Only rolls it around in his mouth to savor the taste?" she demanded, her voice shaking.

"It was she who savored." He folded his hands and looked at her with those wise, gentle light blue eyes. "And why not? A man—a grown man—who cares for her, who will handle her gently, kindly . . . Not those callow bumpkins you put up with at balls, those smutty, giggling boys she deals with in her dancing classes. And she's more sensitive than you are, Kyra. She hasn't your defenses. That ripening sensuality, mingled with the wonder of a child . . ."

His hand made a small gesture, as if in his thoughts he was tracing the curve of her hip. Kyra had to close her hand around the arm of her chair to keep from striking him. The heat that went through her shocked her, the blind rage and the will to do murder.

As if unaware of her thoughts, as if unaware of the slightest incongruity in his words, he went on. "I couldn't let that budding femininity be bruised out of existence by silly boys who see only her golden hair and doelike eyes . . . or, worse, who see only your father's moneybags."

"Is that why you put spells of Summoning on her nightgowns?" She almost spit the words at him, lurching to her feet, trembling all over with fury that he would have dared to come here, that he would have stood in the hall and sent Briory up to fetch her.

Tibbeth sighed and shook her head, as at a child's willful rage. "Kyra, you don't seem to want to believe that I would never hurt Alix. Or that I would ever do anything to cause her—or you—grief. But—like you, I see now—she was raised with all the prejudices of your parents' class. She wanted me. Don't pretend she didn't come around asking for 'help,' just as if she didn't have a tutor of her own. She wanted love, and she wanted the kindness, the gentleness she sensed that I could give. But even at her age she has been blinded into believing that 'love' is proper only to a boy of twenty who is pretty in the fashion she has been taught to think of as pretty and of whose family her father approves." He clicked his tongue against his teeth. "What do boys of twenty know about a soul like Alix's?"

"They know," Kyra said slowly, "better than to use spells to bring her to their arms when she's only twelve years old!"

A look of infinite patience crossed his face. "Kyra," he sighed, "a girl is a woman at twelve, and you know it."

"Get out of this house," was all she said.

Tibbeth rose, his long, dark robe—almost new these days and of the finest-quality wool—straightening about him with a kind of grandeur. His face was sad and kind. "I will," he said quietly. "And I promise I will make no further attempts to see her. I have said I would not for the world hurt Alix. I can only ask that you not hurt her, either. And you know as well as I do the way of the world, my child, and what would happen to her should any word of this get about either to your father or to anyone else. I presume you will tell him yourself that you have decided, after all, to give up your studies in magic."

Shaking now as if she stood naked in a snowstorm, Kyra could only repeat, in a voice she scarcely recognized as her own, "Get out of this house." She walked to the book-room door to make sure that he did so, but after he was gone, she stood there for a long time, staring straight ahead of her into the shadowy hall, sick with rage at him and with guilt at the overwhelming grief she felt, the sudden shock of the loss of the learning that she now would never have.

Chapter XIV

There was something eerily reminiscent of a fairy tale, Kyra reflected, in walking like her own ghost through the house while others slept. A sense of possession and of power, such as she had had when a small girl, waking in the very early morning to the first creakings of the servants coming down the back stairs to start the kitchen fires. As a teenager she had been lazy, seeking, as many teenagers did, the comfort of her pillows in the morning to make up for the private world of late-night reading, but as a child she had liked to rise in the predawn darkness, wrap herself in a shawl, and tiptoe through the house for the strange enjoyment of seeing it gray and empty, without fires in the stoves, or daylight in the windows, or people chattering in the rooms. She remembered standing beside her parents' bed, reaching out—very gently—to touch the saffron hawser of her mother's hair where it coiled across the snowfield of the pillows, stealing across to the cradle where Alix slumbered and looking down wonderingly at that tiny, exquisite angel wrought of pink pearl, alabaster, and gold.

231

She seldom went around to her father's side of the bed, for the sight of him asleep disturbed her. It was not right that he should be so vulnerable, that he should show her, even unknowingly, the worried frown he wore in dreams.

The sight disturbed her still. She and Spens found him sleeping with his head on his desk in the book room, half-written arrangements for yet another church—Sun-on-the-Hill—spread out all around him and the pen, sticky with drying ink, still in his hand. He was unshaven and looked very tired. By the glow of the candles beside the standish, she could see how his red hair had almost completely faded to gray and how prominent the blue veins in his hands were. She had not remembered his wrists being so thin. A wave of sadness passed over her, drowning the anger she had felt at him while she'd watched him shouting at Alix in the crystal. He was, she thought, only doing the best he could. She searched the room as quickly as possible, avoiding looking at him, for something in the way he lay, with his hand curled around the quill, made her want to weep; when she left, she felt somehow dirty, as if she had spied upon him in his bath.

Spenson, too, was quiet, as if, like her, he felt an intruder's unlawful power. "It's like those old legends of death visiting the house," he murmured, standing in the doorway while Kyra moved about in the shadows of her parents' bedroom, her fingers flickering guiltily over her father's shaving things, pushing through her mother's pastel clothing to touch the back of the armoire. "Each taken where he stood, in the midst of what he did. Or like those stories where everyone is turned to stone."

"They're only sleeping," Kyra said rather too quickly. "And Foodret's going to be ready to slit his wrists when he wakes up and realizes he actually fell asleep on his master's bed." She looked indulgently down at the dapper, elderly valet, lying across the foot of the bed whose sheets he had been turning down when the spell had taken effect.

In the drawing room next door her mother and Briory sat on either side of the dying fire, snoring gently, each with a lapdog curled like a golden muff upon her knees. On the tea table between them lay plates of half-eaten wedding sweets and a couple of glasses of wine. Both women looked exhausted. In the small dining room they found Merrivale and another footman lying like slain soldiers upon the piles of now-useless garlands in front of the ritually consecrated tub. It seemed incredible to Kyra that she had listened only that morning to her mother, aunts, and cousins stumbling through soft-voiced chants on Alix's behalf. The handwritten notes of the appropriate Texts still lay on the sideboard with the required linen towels and consecrated—and extremely expensive—herbal soap.

At the foot of the back stairs the laundry maid, her head back and her mouth open in nearly soundless snores, sat on the floor with her lap full of newly ironed napkins.

"Will they all wake at once?"

Kyra shook her head, passing her hand over the panels of the door to the back stairs, though she suspected that if the Ill-Eye had been drawn there, she would have felt it before. "A few at a time, I think. The servants first, to spare Father getting angry at them."

In the attic they found the musicians in a sleepy tangle of wine goblets and maids. Kyra picked up one of the empty clay bottles from the table and shook her head over it. "Father's best Chablis."

Spens frowned. "You don't think the threat came into the house with the musicians, do you?" He viewed the still-life orgy before them doubtfully. "They're new-comers to the household for the wedding."

Kyra laughed. *"Them?"* Still, she checked over the room carefully, then touched, each in turn, those four disparate young faces and probed gently into their dreams. She found there innocent lust and startling poetry, longings, odd fears, old pain . . . but neither magic nor malice.

In the next attic room, which was scarcely larger than a closet, she found Algeron Brackett, slumped fully clothed upon his bed, with Alix, her face wet with tears, sleeping in his arms. There was something heartbreakingly childlike about them, like playmates taking shelter from the rain together; Kyra pressed her fingers quickly to her lips.

"Her poet?" Spenson asked softly, standing with fists on hips in the doorway, and she nodded. The candle—a leftover from the family's use, like all the candles in the servants' rooms—needed to be trimmed, and the ragged band of smoking flame threw a shuddering limmerance over the two young faces; the boy's fair hair was unbound from its ribbon and lying over his shoulders, and the girl's was a kinked swatch like the rapids of some sun-colored river, pouring in half a dozen channels over the protective circle of his arm.

"Poor things," Kyra said softly. "Even with the wedding called off, it won't help them, you know. He hasn't a bean—well, neither has Alix, when it comes to that, only what Father will settle on her for her marriage portion. I'll have them waken first to give her time to get back to her room. After the day she's had, the last thing she needs is another fight with Father."

Quietly they descended the stairs.

Though she had already searched Alix's room and the schoolroom where Tibbeth of Hale had taught her, Kyra went through them again, touching wall panels, thresholds, furniture, the undersides of the stoves, running her hand among the pillows and comforters on the bed. She found nothing, though whether this was because there was truly nothing to find or whether she was now so weary that she would have been unable to detect a very subtle sign or some unknown form of magic, she did not know. Her temples throbbed with exhaustion as she dumped the wedding dress onto the floor and sat on the end of the bed, bowing her head almost to her knees, her disheveled red hair hanging over her face. Distantly, she heard the clock strike two.

Warm hands closed over her shoulders. She flinched, startled, at the touch, but Spens ordered, "Hold still," and his fingers kneaded gently at the big muscles of her nape. He didn't, like Cylin when he gave neck rubs, work at killing his victim; there was a gentleness to his touch as well as strength, as if he knew how sore the muscles were from the tension of all that had happened that day. Kyra groaned profoundly and then was silent for some time.

"Better?"

"Yes, thank you." She straightened up gingerly and felt at the back of her neck. The candles had been lit on Alix's dressing table but, like those in the mean attic rooms upstairs, were burning badly, the wicks trailing down the sides in ragged pennons of guttering flame. She looked around, wearily, helplessly, at the familiar room, the milky silks of the counterpane and curtains, the familiar loom of the armoire with its decorative scrollwork along the top and its beautiful porcelain handles, the low, squat shape of the blue-tiled stove.

"We should have found something. Once we find a mark, you see, we can trace it back to the wizard and then to the one who paid him to place it—whether it's Fyster Nyven or Dutton Droon or one of the other great merchants."

"Except neither Nyven nor Droon believes in magic." Spenson moved over to the dressing table, his shadow reeling along the ceiling behind him like a drunken giant. Picking up the pincers and candle scissors, he began to trim the wicks. "Most people don't unless they've had contact with it. I've heard both of them going on about how the Inquisition should be disbanded as useless. Your father probably didn't until you came to him and told him you'd been born a witch."

Kyra was silent, remembering things her father had said when she was a child. "He didn't exactly disbelieve, but ... like a lot of people, he didn't think it was anything that had to be taken seriously."

"Maybe it's some other sort of threat," he said. "You said you felt her to be on the edge of despair in her love for Algeron." He glanced back at her, his blue eyes grave.

"Well, initially it occurred to me *you* might murder her."

"I only seriously considered it for fifteen minutes while she and the Wishrom girl were talking about styling their hair."

The grin that passed between them faded. "Somehow I can't see Alix ... harming herself. She's always been too ... happy in her heart."

He raised his brows a little. "You don't think girls who are happy one week take their own lives the next when that happiness is shattered?"

"No ... But for another thing, Alix has always been too sensible. I mean, the sensible thing to do is marry you—or whomever it's going to be now—and take Algeron as her lover."

"Can you seriously see Alix doing that?"

She was silent, thinking about her sister, about Algeron. "No," she said at last. "No, I can't. At least, not going into marriage with that in mind."

"Is it what you'd do?"

"Great heavens, no." Kyra straightened her back, startled at the suggestion. "But then, I wouldn't put myself in that position to begin with. If I didn't want to marry a man, I wouldn't convince myself that I did. And I don't see what you're smiling at," she added a little indignantly.

He obediently grew serious and returned to trimming wicks. The smell of beeswax filled the room above the all-pervasive scents of potpourri and dying wedding flowers.

"The thing is," she went on, "Alix is stronger than that. There's a life in her, a strength that wouldn't break like that."

"I admit I've only seen her when she'd been nattering on." Spenson turned back toward her, folded his arms, and leaned his shoulders against the carved bedpost with its inlay of nacre and glass.

"Oh, Alix is always nattering," Kyra said. "Neither she nor Mother ever shuts up. I can't imagine how Father's kept his sanity all these years. But don't let that lead you to think she's featherbrained. I know she talks even more when she's nervous, which she must have been, knowing you were to marry her, and she tries to cover up the other person's silences."

The erstwhile groom smiled. "When I'm nervous, I go quiet. And believe me, I was, getting ready to wed the one girl and having the most astoundingly erotic dreams about some little cat I'd met twice in my life. It's not that I've never dreamed of ladies before, but never like that. When I met your sister, I could barely look her in the face."

"She'd have made you a good wife, you know," Kyra said after a moment. "Better than me if you're going to settle into running the business and the guild. She's far from silly. She has a positive talent for dressmaking—I know she even altered the fit on her wedding dress, which, given the way Hylette designs, is a miracle to do without destroying the appearance of the thing. But you'd never know it."

She bent down and picked up the gorgeous blood-colored overdress, turning the jeweled bodice over in her hands.

And for a moment she felt it, as surely as she would have felt dampness, as surely as she would have smelled wood smoke trapped in the folds of the silk— the taint of dark magic. It jolted her, though it was barely a whisper, certainly not strong enough to harm anyone no matter how long it was in the room with them.

But the whisper was there. It was a stain of ill left by the curse.

Swiftly she turned the bodice inside out, tangling her fingers in the lacings, snagging bullion embroidery with shaking fingernails. Seeing her expression change, Spens came swiftly over. He watched with a grave face while she ran first her fingertips and palms, then her cheek and lips over the white muslin that lined and gave shape to the silk.

"There was something." She touched her lips to the place again but felt nothing now. "It's been near the curse, picked it up."

It just stands there watching me, Alix had said of the gown on its stand.

"Here? In this room?"

"I don't know." She put the dress down, walked to the wicker stand itself, and ran her fingers slowly, carefully over the varnished willow. No trace, no taint of what she had felt on the dress.

Turning around, she saw Spens holding out to her handfuls of fragile saffron veils. The scent, the taint, on them was so dim that it took her twenty minutes to find it, and then it might only have been her overkeyed imagination. She checked the wedding jewelry over stone by stone, but beryl and tourmaline were stones that held strong vibrations of their own, and any slight vibration of another spell would have been lost beneath them like a single narcissus in a roomful of jasmine.

"I don't know how it could be," she said uncertainly, and stood, her impulse to search the room a third time halting before the thoroughness of her earlier hunts. "I would have felt it. Something that . . . that definite. I know I would have."

She touched the bodice again, trying to deepen her awareness of the curse, to tell at least if it was Pinktrees or the Pilgrim who had drawn the signs of evil there.

But the stain of malignancy was no stronger than the faintest breath, like music too distant to make out even the tune, let alone the voice of the singer. She laid it aside and prowled the room again, running her hands through the sheets of the bed, touching the white curtains, the backs of the lace window shams, every jewel in Alix's open case.

"Damn," she whispered. "Damn, damn, damn."

"Could the talisman be elsewhere, not in the house at all?" Spenson asked, kneeling suddenly beside her when she came to a stop to stoop and feel underneath the armoire. "Someplace she goes all the time—Wishrom's house next door or Hylette's shop? It seems like every time I talked to her, she'd been back to that woman's place for another fitting. You said the talisman might have been under a threshold she had to cross."

"Dear God, you're right." She sat back amid a dusty lake of skirts and ran an unsteady hand through her hair. Her head had begun to throb again, more painfully than ever. "She's been shopping like a lunatic for weeks. She must have been in and out of every boutique and bazaar in the city."

"It makes more sense in a way," Spenson pointed out, settling cross-legged beside her. "Not to have it in the house, I mean. My guess would be either this Hylette woman's shop . . . or Lady Earthwygg's."

Kyra stared at him, startled that the idea hadn't occurred to her. "Of course."

"For that matter," he added suddenly, "what about the wedding carriage itself? If whoever put the curse knew the marriage was going to be in the strict form, the carriage itself would be a guaranteed trigger for the night of the wedding."

"Let's go!"

Kyra felt light-headed and brittle with exhaustion as she and Spens ran down the stairs, her skirts streaming behind her. It was the first time she had worked this many different spells of this intensity consecutively;

even examinations didn't drain the student like this. The only time she recalled feeling this bone-shaking exhaustion had been a year ago, during the magic troubles at the Citadel. And then she had had her masters to back her up.

The carriage proved to contain no trace of magic at all. "Hylette's," Spenson said, standing with his arms folded, one foot propped on the wheel. "Or Lady Earthwygg's, though how you're going to search *her* house . . ."

"It would only have to be the drawing room and the front hall." Kyra scrambled awkwardly down from the high footman's perch. "Those are the only rooms Alix would have entered." She sighed again, weary beyond measure. "Come on. Let's get these spells lifted so I can get some sleep myself."

She raised the spells of sleep a few at a time, picturing in her mind what she had seen: first Alix and Algeron so that her sister could return to bed in her own room; then, with time limitations set by the chiming of the St. Farinox clock so that they would come to wakefulness half an hour later and a few at a time, from servants and parents, musicians and maids, cats and mice, and all that dwelled beneath the slanted, pigeon-smeared tiles of the roof.

Last of all she took back the silver coin from Spenson and removed the sigils from it and the one she carried. Being caught by the Inquisition with such things on them was enough to get her in genuine trouble. What she had done tonight was hideously illegal by anybody's standards; she only hoped that the Inquisition was relying on its on-site watchers rather than the exhausting and energy-consuming process of "listening" to the magic in the world at large. The chance was slim, she knew, but she had risked, literally, everything that meant anything to her in her life on it: her education as a wizard, her future in her art, perhaps her liberty. Her hands were shaking by the time she finished dispersing the last traces of the invisible circles that had powered the spell.

"We'll give them an hour or so to get to bed properly," Spenson said, unexpectedly taking her elbow as she stood up and brushed away the last of her tracks in the soft earth of the garden bed.

"What?" She only blinked at him, too shaky to think.

"I think we deserve breakfast, don't you?"

"At this hour?"

"We'll take a cab to Algoswiving Street." He shrugged. "Where do you think the rakes and gamblers dine when they're done for the night? There's a tavern there that's the best in town if you're not particular about your company."

If Tibbeth of Hale had stayed away from Alix, Kyra wasn't sure what she would eventually have done. He was her teacher, her friend. Between scorching fits of shame and rage she missed him with a growing intensity and missed the practice of magic even more. Her own practice, studying by herself the books she had bought, was not the same without his instruction and guidance. When she read new spells and tried them out unsuccessfully, she had no idea what she was doing wrong. When she found new books, she could not tell whether information that seemed contradictory was true or claptrap, and there was a great deal of claptrap magic being written and sold. Other spells, other writings, simply made no sense.

Yet she shrank from seeking another teacher. She knew by that time that Tibbeth was one of the best dog wizards in the city; she knew also that to seek out the Council wizards in their little enclave in the Mages' Yard would be to announce to the world at large that she was mageborn.

Her father, negotiating with colleagues still deeply suspicious—or completely unbelieving—of wizardry in general, would never have forgiven her. He would have

asked, too, why she wanted to exchange a very powerful teacher for a lesser one.

So she kept silent, as Tibbeth had known she would.
At times she found it impossible to believe that she had
seen what she had seen. Not *Tibbeth*. Not *Alix*. She
must have been mistaken or dreaming.

And in time, the hurt of not seeing him, not practicing, not having his instruction, grew so great that she
considered going back to him in spite of the fact that
she knew that she had made no mistake.

Her father crowed at her, too, over her abandonment
of Tibbeth's teaching. "I always said you'd get over it,
girl." That was like an ant bite, with the ant's head still
stuck under the skin.

But still she would have kept her silence—or, looking
back on it, she thought she would have—had not
Tibbeth summoned Alix to him again.

Just why Kyra had made herself a talisman to counter
spells of sleep and wore it around her neck, she didn't
consciously explain to herself. If asked, she would have
professed her wholehearted belief in Tibbeth's honor, at
least in his given word. It was the first time, too, that
her spells had proved stronger than the spells of another
wizard, the first time her power had gone up success-
fully against another power, though she didn't think of
that at the time.

She wasn't clear what she thought at first, waking to
see the moonlight in a hard, clear bar across the foot of
her bed, so vivid that she felt she could have plucked it
up and wound it around her like a veil. And in that
moonlight, only the thrown-back coverlet and dented
pillow where Alix had lain.

Then anger rushed through her, a wave of killing
heat, like throwing open the door of a stove. It was as
if she knew, absolutely and at once, what had happened
and where her sister had gone.

She rose soundlessly, pulled on her robe, and inter-
cepted Alix at the foot of the long stair down into the

hall. Her sister's eyes were open but filled with a dreamy, wanton glassiness; they did not focus on Kyra as she stopped her and put her hands to the alabaster temples beneath the cascades of moon-bleached hair.

The dream of Tibbeth was there, and it was foul. It fled away before Kyra's touch like roaches before light, but not before she had read in it reveries that the most unclean of prostitutes would not have entertained: a man's reveries, not a woman's. Even at the age of eighteen Kyra was aware of the difference between men's dreams and women's, on that subject at least.

She had sat awake through the night in the chair beside the bed, watching Alix sleep, while anger coursed through her veins like a poison that burned and nauseated so that she felt that she would never sleep again.

In the morning she had gone to her father.

"Tibbeth?" He stared at her, more startled at first than anything else, over the big ledgers in his book room. "That's nonsense. Alix is only twelve years old."

Kyra said nothing, only looked at him, her own face rigid and white with anger; his expression slowly darkened with suffusing blood as what she told him sank in, and his topaz eyes grew pale. It took him a few moments, sitting there, staring at her dark-circled eyes and white mouth, but he began to believe.

"Sweet saints of God, I will kill him."

"Yes," Kyra said softly, savagely.

Something changed in his eyes. "But I won't have her name brought into it. Dear God, it will ruin her chances of any kind of decent marriage! Nor will I have yours come up."

"Don't be ridiculous," Kyra snapped, feeling her anger heat in return: anger at Tibbeth and anger at her father, sitting there and thinking about his precious alliances, his reputation among his peers. "Who else are the Witchfinders going to believe?"

"The Witchfinders?" He was aghast.

"Who else would have the power to arrest him?" she

demanded. "He's powerful, Father. He could escape the regular constables; they'd never catch him. What are you going to charge him with, if not a crime of magic? Stealing your silverware?"

And she saw by the shift of his eyes that he'd been thinking exactly of that, of some charge that did not touch upon magic, that would not reveal to the other members of the guilds that the dog wizard had been free in his house, teaching his daughter.

Bitterly, she said, "Whatever you charge him with, you know my name is going to come up at his trial."

They had argued about it long and viciously. She was eighteen, with an eighteen-year-old's intolerant righteousness; he was her father, with the swollen resentful boil of three years of her rebelliousness bursting in his soul. What was said in the book room that morning on both sides would never be forgiven. In the end Kyra had manufactured talismans of death and plague, marking them with Tibbeth's mark, and had set them about her father's warehouse, and he then went to the Witchfinders and claimed that he had seen the dog wizard lurking there.

At the hearing before Sergius Peelbone, the cold-eyed man who at that time was Witchfinder Extraordinary of the Angelshand Inquisition, Kyra testified that Tibbeth had been turned away from his position as her teacher when she had decided she would no longer endanger her immortal soul by tampering with such an evil thing as magic.

The scandal had been tremendous.

Most of it she had pushed from her mind. Her memory of those days consisted largely of fight after fight with her father, who shouted new recriminations at her every time he returned from the meetings with guild members demanding explanations of how he had happened to be training a dog wizard in his house, interspersed with the razor-suave questions of the Witchfinder at endless sessions in the dark, round

chamber of the Inquisition on Angel's Island. At some
of them Tibbeth had been present, his wrists manacled
with chains overwritten in runes of na-aar—thaumatur-
gical silence, deadness, immunity to all spells—and
bound with the scarlet threads of spell-cord, staring at
her with hatred as she answered the same questions
over and over, told the same seamless, plausible lies.
The summer's heat was beginning—under ordinary circumstances the family would have been making plans
to retreat to their country place. The clammy heat and
the smell of men's sweat gummed her memories of
those days like filthy glue. Sometimes, coming in and
out of the hearing room, she would pass Tibbeth's
childlike, colorless wife, who was sitting on a bench in
the hall with her head bowed down to her hands. Kyra
wondered how young that girl had been when the dog
wizard had first taken her to his bed, and the thought
made her stomach turn.

Very clearly indeed, she remembered standing in the
square before the Cathedral of St. Cyr, when they'd led
him, shaven-headed and wearing a long white shirt of
cotton so thin that the summer sunlight had showed his
body through, to the stake. His books were heaped
among the huge piles of twigs beneath his feet, though
later Lady Rosamund had told her that the Magic Office
of the Church had probably been through them and
taken anything of interest. Mostly what she felt then
was a kind of surprise that the pile of wood was so
huge—more than five feet high—that Tibbeth had to be
helped up it with a ladder and stood like a man atop a
haystack. The spell-cord twisting the ropes that bound
him to the stake looked like long trails of blood.

She made herself watch and listen to his screams.
Having betrayed him, she felt obscurely that this was
something she had to do. The day was grillingly hot, the
air thick with the sewage smell of the river and, here
where the old black slums crowded close around the ancient city fortress, buzzing with flies. They swarmed

around the pyre, crawling on the sweaty faces of the watching crowds. Though she was some distance away, she could see them crawling on Tibbeth's bald scalp as the executioners bound him, and he twitched as the insects bit and rolled his head like a drunkard, trying desperately to shake them off. It was summer, and the wood was dry. She'd heard somewhere that for wizards, the Inquisition picked fast-burning wood that gave little smoke so that the victim would not suffocate before the fire began to blister and then consume his ankles.

Tibbeth had not suffocated. Thanks to the Inquisition's care, there was very little smoke, so Kyra saw everything clearly. She had given little thought to what it actually meant for a man's body to burn from the feet up. She tried to call to her mind the picture of him bending over Alix's bare shoulders in the moonlight, the fleeting images of that filthy dream, while she watched. The stink of charring flesh, the smells of the people around her, the roar of the fire, and the crawling feet of the flies never afterward left her dreams.

It took a lot longer than she'd thought it would. Long before it was over, she slipped away from the crowd—and there was a huge crowd in the square, packed so tightly that she was afraid she wouldn't make it to the shelter of a side street in time—to vomit until she thought she'd faint.

When she had gone back home, light-headed and shaky, her belly muscles aching—and they'd ached for days—Briory told her that she'd been given orders no longer to admit Kyra to the house. "I'm sorry, miss," she said, staring stonily into middle distance beyond Kyra's left shoulder. "Master Peldyrin has taken your mother and your sister out to the summer place at Meadowford until St. Ploo's Day."

"Nonsense," Kyra managed to say, though she felt her face and hands grow even colder than they already were. "If he didn't want me being a witch, it isn't ter-

ribly intelligent of him to force me into being a prosti-
tute, either."

"That's as may be, miss," Briory said, still carefully
avoiding her eye.

"Don't be an ass, Briory—open this door."

But it closed in her face.

"Briory . . ."

She beat the panels with her open hand.

"What about my things? What about my jewelry,
damn you? Briory!"

Turning, she caught a glimpse of a man loitering in
the square, picking his teeth with a straw and carefully
not looking at her. She recognized him vaguely. She
thought he'd been in the outer offices of the Inquisition
one day during the trial. The Witchfinders were watching the house, watching her.

Waiting for—what? Her to use magic against her
family? To show signs that she had lied, that she intended to set up as a dog wizard for herself?

Remembering Tibbeth's screams—the fire wouldn't
even have burned out yet—she felt a cold, sinking sense
of terror she had never known, the terror of being truly
alone and utterly without help.

"Damn him," she whispered, anger flooding in to re-
place the fear. "Damn him, damn him, damn him . . ."

The beauty of her magic, like some enchanted glass
goblet, seemed to shatter in her hands, cutting them to
the bone. Standing on the high steps, she was conscious
of the Wishroms' scullery maid and a couple of chair
carriers down in the square staring curiously at her, a
tall red-haired stick of a girl in a gaudy pink and white
dress, pounding on the shut door of the big stone house.

It came to her that she had no idea where she was going to spend the night.

Head high and pearls jiggling, she'd stridden down
the steps, across the square, and away into the city
again.

CHAPTER XV

STRANGE, KYRA THOUGHT, LYING WITH THE LIGHTWEIGHT quilt drawn up over her chin. After all that, to be back in her parents' house again.

She blinked drowsily up at the painted ceiling of the yellow guest room. Idly, she identified the various birds the painter had depicted: a pigeon there, a dove there, a couple of well-executed sparrows, a cloud of finches like gray and white sunflower seeds scattered over the top of a salad, a startlingly pink parrot. Then she closed her eyes again, shutting out the pale slant of the morning sun.

Not a very welcome guest, perhaps. But here.

Six years.

It had been nightfall that summer afternoon six years ago when she reached the Mages' Yard. It was situated in the quarter of the Old Believers, a shabby slum on the east side of town in the shadow of the old walls, where tightly packed half-timbered houses leaned wearily against one another, their jutting upper stories nearly meeting over the narrow streets. Every third shop seemed to sell old clothes or the bizarre icons of their religion. Men in faded black robes stared at her as she passed, men with long hair hanging in elaborate braids to their shoulders, or waists, or sometimes longer, their beards similarly dressed and tied with ribbons of all colors, to the glory and honor of their twenty-one half-forgotten gods. An old woman, filthy beyond description in a yellow gown that looked as if it had been stolen from a duchess a century previously, caught her arm and muttered at her toothlessly; Kyra pulled free and hurried on her way. Instead of the familiar images of leaden saints in street-corner shrines, the garish, stylized seals of the Old Gods were sometimes visible, painted on the brick walls under decades worth of filth. Strange odors drifted from doorways, and children darted around her like flights of half-naked swallows, vanishing into alleyways too narrow for a cart to have passed. The street was paved with cobblestones the size and shape of cannonballs; green water lay between them, buzzing with gnats and stinking.

She knew where the Mages' Yard was. She had passed it occasionally on her solitary rambles, had once visited Tibbeth's house to find him in conversation over tea with the Archmage. In the gathering gloom she could see that four or five of the dozen houses that bordered the narrow cobbled court were dark. Tibbeth, she recalled, had frequently read in his study without lights. In other houses orange lamplight flickered where men and women crossed the torn sacking of the curtains; not all the houses there were occupied by wizards. Windows and doors were open everywhere to the warm night, and though the rest of the streets in this riverside quarter hummed with mosquitoes, there were none here. Cat eyes gleamed at her from windowsills and broken brick steps. A fat woman in the peculiar five-pointed head scarf of the Old Religion came out of one house, shaking a dishcloth, and Kyra walked over to her, feeling horribly conspicuous in her pink taffeta, her flower-like collar and cuffs.

"I'm looking for the wizards," she'd said, and immediately had felt completely foolish.

The fat woman smiled. "Well, you come to the right place, dearie."

And behind her a voice said, "Can we help you?"

She turned to see a tall woman standing at her elbow, nearly as tall as herself. The open door of the fat woman's little house let fall a bar of grubby light; by it, Kyra saw that this new arrival wore a plain black robe, uncorseted and belted simply, over an equally plain shift. But her eyes—pale green like pearly jade—were the eyes of a queen, and her black hair was pinned back with small gold clasps whose workmanship Kyra identified at once as coming from the most expensive jeweler in the city.

Tired, empty, and queasy from her long walk and the terrible shocks of the afternoon, Kyra held out her hand and said, "My name is Kyra Peldryin. I—"

"I saw you this afternoon in the square," the woman said quietly as the stout Old Believer housewife retreated to her own house like a turtle's head withdrawing into a shell. She left the door open, however. Its light and the light from the single tall window downstairs threw irregular shadows over Kyra and the dark-haired mage. "And we have followed the trial. Was the man truly your master?"

Kyra nodded wearily. Of course, she thought, the Council wizards would take an intent interest in the judicial slaying of even a dog wizard. In her years with Tibbeth she had acquired an acute interest in the slightest shifts of public opinion regarding the mageborn. For them, even with the protection of the Council, it would have been the same. And thus they would know her as what she had spent the last two weeks swearing she was: a girl who had seen the light, gone over to the Inquisition, and sold her teacher's life out of spite.

Bitterness and exhaustion flooded her. There would be no welcome for her here, either. She was astonished she hadn't thought of that before and saved herself the walk.

But the woman asked, "Did he try to have you? Is that why you did it? You look a little old for what we know of his tastes."

Kyra's jaw tightened so that she could not speak; she felt that she'd never be able to speak again. She only felt tired, unable to come or go, and so dirty inside that it surprised her, looking down at her dress and her hands, that she wasn't black with filth. Surely, she thought, what she had done had to show somehow on the outside.

She didn't cry, but she felt herself begin to shake all over and could not meet those sea-colored eyes.

The woman stepped forward and put a strong, slim arm around her waist. "I am Lady Rosamund," she said in a voice like molten gold and sunrise. "Come in and tell me about it."

Below and around her the house murmured with talk. Uneasy talk, sharp and jabbing, not the usual chatter of the maids at their work or the footmen gossiping in the servants hall. The clatter of breakfast dishes was missing. Frowning, Kyra sharpened her concentration, listening down through the house, and picked up, three floors below, her father's angry voice.

"By God, this wedding was cursed from the start!"

"You mean the day was cursed when you hired on those drunken dockside reprobates!" the voice of their neighbor, Neb Wishrom, retorted. "Best musicians in the city—faugh! Best wenchers! Best troublemakers! Let my daughter tell you what they're best at!"

From the attic above Kyra head the scuffle of feet and an opening door, then the voice of—she thought— the harpsichord player asking, "And what's the delegation for, then?" while somewhere below she heard—thought she heard—light, rapid feet springing down the back stairs and the flute player's voice whispering, "Get out through the postern gate and down the cellar next door. She said she'd have it open for me and make sure none are down the cellar. The rest of you cover for me and meet me at the Bountiful Peaches tavern tonight."

Kyra closed her eyes and sighed as Master Wishrom stormed on. "I'll have the magistrates on those worthless tosspots!"

"And you'll have my word behind yours!" She could almost see as well as hear her father smite the top of his desk with his fist. "All they've done since I hired them has been drink my wine and debauch my servants—and now, I find, my neighbors' daughters as well!"

Only a few days ago, Kyra thought, she would have sniffed with wry amusement at the thought of the good-looking young flute player stealing kisses from Tellie Wishrom and would have said to herself, *Silly little goose.*

As she had said, and thought, about Alix.

Now . . .

The Cherry Orchard on Algoswiving Street, as Spens had promised, catered a very good meal indeed to the wealthy rakes who frequented it after small-hours gambling bouts. The place had been almost full when she and Spens entered, the bright coats and lace-edged ruffles of the men and the overly tawdry finery of the local girls and pretty boys half obscured by veils of blue tobacco smoke. The air had been thick with the smells of coffee, ambergris, and beer, but the roast duck and braided breads brought to their table by a black-clothed servant girl had been excellent, and Kyra had been surprised at how hungry she was.

She and Spens had meant to stay only the hour or so that it would take for the household to stir and stumble blinking into bed, but in fact it was only an hour short of dawn when they finally left. At the Cherry Orchard

Spenson pointed out to her various of their fellow customers, young courtiers or older rakes, identifying their
families and political factions and talking with ease of
the true business of the Court: trade balances, the pro-
posed national bank, and the colonies in Dhareen. She
spoke of her training at the college, and he of the voy-
ages he'd made: "I'm sorry now I never studied the
wizardry there, for I'd like to see how it compared with
what you've told me."

Though he said more than once that it was high time
he gave up the sea and learned to manage the responsibilities that one day would be his alone, when he spoke
of the Jingu Straits under the rising sun, or fog on the
wild coasts of the spice lands, or the marketplace in-
trigues of Saarieque, all the stiffness vanished from him
and his blue eyes grew bright. They talked all the way
back to Baynorth Square.

It was only when they reached the garden door and
Spens whispered, "I'll see you tomorrow at the countinghouse," that silence fell between them. For what
seemed a long time she stood in the doorway, looking
across into his eyes, visible to her in the darkness
though she herself must have been no more than a pale
blur and a gleam in shadow, feeling that the night had
been too short. That something more was needed.

Then, as if at some unspoken signal, they stepped together, clenching one another tightly. The part of her
that from time to time during the day had raised the
question of whether she really loved this man—after all,
she had to get back to her studies at the Citadel; she
couldn't *really* fall in love with her sister's betrothed—
made one faint, protesting sound and perished. All that
existed was his mouth, sweet with beer and duck sauce,
and the breadth of his back beneath her gripping
hands, and the warmth of his arms around her waist,
pressing her close against him. Those, and the desperate
surge of heat that seemed to rise through her from the
soles of her feet to her hair, which she would have

sworn lifted like fire from her scalp, a heat unexpected and completely unknown that shook her to her marrow.

It was what Alix felt for Algeron, she thought dimly, with what portion of her mind was capable of forming thought at all. It was what all those songs were about. All this time it hadn't been maudlin hyperbole, after all.

Dear God, I didn't know it would be so strong . . .

They were both shaking, panting, when they drew apart, staring into one another's eyes; then they closed again, more violently, as if they would devour one another there in the darkness, leaving only a hot glitter of ash.

She had been trembling when she ascended the stairs, and it was a long, long time before she slept.

Alix, she thought, remembering her sister's tears. If it was anything like that for them . . .

The memory of Spenson's arms, of his mouth against hers, wrung her like a soaked cloth.

Dear God.

She wondered what on earth she was going to do. She couldn't simply abandon her studies. After all she had gone through for them, after six of the happiest years of her life . . . He certainly couldn't marry a wizard or even take one as a mistress without losing his place in the guild. *And what on earth are you thinking about, anyway? You can't leave your studies to stay here and become Spenson's mistress!*

Some deep, complex shudder within her whispered, *Don't bet on that,* and she shook herself with indignant impatience. No wonder people acted like lunatics when they fell in love. If love was as common as people seemed to think, it was a wonder anybody got anything done.

And in any case, she thought, now was scarcely the time to think of that. With the furor in the house over the flute player—she could hear the troop of footmen her father had sent to the attic descending, with the harpsichord player talking nineteen to the dozen in their midst—it was good odds she could slip away unnoticed and avoid a confrontation with her father herself.

Spenson was waiting for her, as he'd said, at his countinghouse on Salt Hill Lane. She felt a flare of annoyance at the completely unaccustomed softening she felt within herself at the sight of him—*Good heavens, girl, he's only a stocky bull of a man in a dreadful striped waistcoat sitting at a desk!*—until she saw the smile that broke across his face like sunlight when he looked up and saw her, standing in the doorway between the desks of two of his clerks.

She stepped forward and tripped on the threshold, and he caught her hand.

"So what are we going to do?" he asked when they were striding down the street toward the fashionable purlieux of the Imperial Prospect. "Send Hylette's shop to sleep?"

Kyra grinned at him. "Oh, I don't think that will be necessary. You're just going to go in and engage Hylette in conversation while I look for talismans under the doorsills."

His eyes widened with alarm. "I'll do nothing of the kind!"

"Come now, Hylette hasn't bitten anyone in months, and the rumor that her last victim died was horribly exaggerated. I'm sure any of those nice young men who had breakfast at the next table over from us in the tavern this morning could go in and have a perfectly decent conversation with her."

"Then get one of them," Spens said promptly, and they quibbled about it all the way down to Hylette's shop.

Hylette Zharran's dressmaking premises were located in the most fashionable block of the Imperial Prospect, whose unbroken lines of colonnaded shops stretched from the curlicued iron elegancies of Prince DiHony Circle as far as the pseudo-classical marble facings of the Emperor's Gate. Beyond that it was a tree-lined boulevard to the gates of the palace grounds, lined with fashionable shops and blocks of expensive flats, but the truly prohibitive real estate was between the circle and the Emperor's Gate. In the winter the buildings looked like a line of dirty gray cliffs, looming above wheel-cut snow and slushy ice, but the brightness of the spring day mellowed the heavy granite facades and made the dresses of the women—even the servants in their plain dark blues and greens—into flower beds of moving color. The street was one of the widest in the city, and carriages moved easily up and down without the crowding of the sections nearer the river. Doormen in scarlet coats hurried from the bigger shops to help ladies down from the fashionable barouches and landaulets; flower sellers called out to Kyra and Spenson as they passed, comfortably arm in arm, on the wide flagway beneath the arcades. Somewhere a bearded man in the painted leather coat of the Sykerst was playing an accordion; the smell of a fudge vendor's cart vied with the flowers and the perfume of the ladies that they passed.

"For the last time, I'm not going to go in and talk to that woman about furbelows . . ."

Kyra gestured extravagantly, knocking the hat off a passing gentleman in a pink plush coat. "*That* from a man who only last night was telling me how he fought off Jingu pirates."

"Fighting the Jingu-teks was easy compared to having that woman figuring how much I'm worth."

"Well, I'd better not hear any more brave stories the next time you take me into a tavern, then." They stopped before the scrolled bronze doors of the shop. "Watch."

"From a safe distance."

"Nonsense. You have to take me inside, at least. My dear Hylette!" She disengaged her arm from Spenson's the moment they walked through the door and she descried Hylette, exquisitely gowned in pale yellow that matched the rosebuds in her high-piled black hair, sitting at her white-lacquered willow desk in the back of the shop.

"Ah! It is the farouche Miss Kyra Peldyrin!" The dressmaker rose with the languid grace of a much taller woman. Though she barely came up to Kyra's shoulder, Hylette had queenly posture and a commanding presence; the mirrors that punctuated the snowy paneling, and incidentally made the narrow shop look three times wider than it was, repeated and emphasized her fragile beauty as she came over and extended to Kyra the two fingers deemed the height of politeness.

She then raised a quizzing glass on a foot-long golden stalk. "But what is this? This dress . . . you were wearing it the year before you went away from us! Those amazing green ribbons . . . Surely you have come for something new? Something to celebrate your so-beautiful sister's nuptials to this excellent gentleman?" And she smiled her famous tight-lipped smile that covered her prominent teeth.

Amid effusions of delight—Kyra knew Hylette hated her designs but had made them up for her for years because of the prices she paid—and innumerable tiny cups of black coffee, Kyra tried on a walking robe of pink mulled muslin in one fitting room and a polonaise of blue and yellow printed silk in the other. "Ah! These new hemlines—so exquisite if one has, like yourself, the ankles to show off."

Spenson, used to seeing Kyra in her darker, stiffer, and more outlandish personal style, blinked in surprise at the sight of her in the fashionable and decidedly girlish pastel garments that were the highest kick of current fashion.

In the end Kyra bought a pair of lilac-tinted kid gloves, which she managed to drop on the threshold, bump her shoulder when she stooped to get them, and drop again.

"Ah!" Hylette's laugh sounded like the shaking of silver bells. "Still my same precious Kyra!"

"No talisman under the threshold," Kyra reported as she and Spenson strolled off down the colonnade again, Spenson morosely stuffing sweet-scented tobacco into the short clay pipe he'd taken from one capacious coat pocket. "Nor in either of the fitting rooms. I wonder if this is one of the days when Lady Earthwygg receives guests."

It was, judging by the number of carriages present along the curb in Ripinggarth Square. Kyra drew on the lilac gloves—startling against the apple green of her taffeta gown with its dark green silk ribbonwork—and adjusted the spiky ruffles of silk that adorned her hair. "You'll have to do a little work this time, Spens; d' you want to rehearse?"

"I want to go have a beer in the nearest tavern."

"Don't be difficult."

The attack was a two-pronged one and, from Kyra's standpoint, quite successful. She entered first, presented her card—there had been a packet of them in the back of Alix's dressing table, yellow with age—and was conducted to the crimson-walled drawing room, where half the fashionable ladies of the Court were gathered to discuss the extraordinary events of the previous morning. There was a little silence, for though Kyra's father was one of the wealthiest men in the town, he was, when all was said, a tradesman—though not, of course, as vulgar as Neb Wishrom. Lady Earthwygg greeted her silkily—"My dear child, how absolutely barbaric of your father not to permit you to take part in the wedding, had there *been* a wedding, of course." —and promptly ignored her, which suited Kyra just fine. Ten minutes later Blore Spenson was shown in.

Even had Kyra not summoned a spell of misdirection about herself, she doubted that any of the ladies present would have noticed her moving quietly around the drawing room, touching the crimson silk wallpaper here, the polished porphyry of the gilt-edged mantelpiece there. Lady Earthwygg, Esmin, and all their guests closed around the central figure of yesterday's debacle like sharks around a castaway, listening and exclaiming over Spenson's stiff apologies and awkward manufactured accounts of just what was being done about it and how the pipes at the Cheevy Street Baths had come to rupture. Kyra found no talisman of ill, but she did find, rather to her surprise, a small packet of herbs, like a sachet, on the marquetry table next to Lady Earthwygg's chair, herbs whose smell identified them as one of the commoner love-philters and that had been imbued with spells and runes written by Hestie Pinktrees.

"Wonderful!" Spenson sighed when, after a retreat in good order, he and Kyra met again around the corner in Lesser Queen Street. "Does this mean I'm in for another week of passionate dreams?"

"After being kissed by you last night, do you think I'd leave those things where they were without putting counterspells all over them?" Kyra retorted.

Spenson laughed and took her hand. "I can see I'm in for an interesting life."

"Spenson . . ." Kyra stopped in the flagway, forcing him to a halt beside her. There was brief surprise in his eyes before something changed in them, a wariness, an unwillingness to hear or think about what they both knew had to be said. She stepped back from him, all the play, all the easiness, wiped from her face, leaving it harsh-boned and old. "Spens, what kind of life would you have, would we have? What kind of life were you thinking about?"

He said nothing. Like her, he had not been thinking ahead at all.

"Spens, this is . . . impossible. I can't remain in my parents' house; you know that. I certainly can't live with you in yours."

He began to speak, then was silent. His father's harsh voice and cold, demanding eyes seemed for a moment visibly reflected in the doubt that flashed across his face.

"I said Alix would make you a better wife than I would," Kyra said slowly. She raised her hand to still his protest. "No, hear me out. You're the only son, the one who is to take over your father's business; that's what you came back here to do." Once she had begun to speak, the bitter block against even the thought of turning away from his love dissolved, and to her surprise the words came out steadily, without tremor.

"You can't do that if you have a wizard for a mistress, even if I could remain in Angelshand, which I can't."

His blue eyes were somber, struggling with the knowledge that he was the newly elected President of the Merchants' Guild, with the awareness of what his friends would say, his neighbors, his family, and his fellow members of the guild.

"It doesn't have to be known," he said. "And there are places in the city where wizards dwell."

"The Mages' Yard? Since the purge the summer before last, there are few of them there anymore. Their houses were looted; even the few who returned no longer keep the kinds of books and charts I'd need for my education. I won't give that up, Spens. I fought too hard for it."

Even as she spoke, across her heart leapt the memory of the triumph she'd felt in the garden last night, when she knew her sleep-spell to be perfect, that lightning flash of delight that had shaken her to the bones. Magic . . . power running like a river up from the earth and in from the stars, channeled through her hands, her mind, and her will.

The key to that power lay in the Citadel. But through that memory, as through a blazing sunburst, she saw the face of the man across from her, his blue eyes stormy with anger.

"And you can't study that as well here as there?" he

asked. "The town's full of wizards, powerful ones.
Among them you could find a teacher."

"Dog wizards!" Kyra said scornfully. "The most they
could teach me is to *be* a dog wizard."

"It isn't as if you'd have to earn your living at it."

"And you'd support me, I suppose?"

He hesitated a moment, then said, "To keep you, yes.
And what's wrong with that?" he demanded as she
flung up her hands and turned away.

"You wouldn't understand!" She broke from the hand
he reached to seize her wrist and strode quickly away
down the narrow street. Spenson started to dash after
her, ducked around a dolefully singing chair mender
who emerged from an alley bearing a startling array of
his wares on back and shoulders, and overtook her at
the corner.

"Then explain it to me!" His square face was flushed,
his sandy hair tumbled across his brow, and his grip on
her arm crushed the stiff taffeta of her sleeve. "Kyra, I
love you. I want to be with you, to have you near me,
a part of my life."

The dark of the garden returned to her, the taste of
his lips on hers. The craziness, Kyra thought, went two
ways, and she became aware that behind the anger in
his eyes lay fear. The awareness struck her hard; her
body relaxed, and slowly, as the silence lengthened between them, his color and his temper faded.

"Kyra," he said. "After all this is done, I don't want
you to go."

Kyra sighed. All her defenses of glibness, of certainty, seemed to have developed unexpected edges in
her hands, edges that would tear her own flesh if she
wielded them. She found herself struggling for words,
trying desperately to get them right, filled with a terrible fear of saying the wrong thing, of making some ir-
reparable mistake. "Spens," she said slowly, all the
more hesitant because of her distrust of the madness
that had plagued her through the night. "Think about it.

If I remained in Angelshand, how long would it be before scandal broke? Before some matchmaking harridan like Lady Earthwygg discovered that you preferred a wizard to her daughter and had me up before the Inquisition on charges of putting love-spells on you? It would certainly cost you your presidency of the guild."

"Let it," Spens retorted hotly. "My ships still carry cargoes, and the people in the market don't ask about who brings them in."

"And it would cost you your pride," Kyra said, her voice soft. "It would cost you many of your friends, not to mention the business it would lose you, and then you'd be in the position of having to choose between me and what you've always had. And even if you chose me," she went on, raising her hand as he opened his mouth to speak, "it wouldn't be the same between us."

His hand closed around her uplifted fingers. "Let me be the judge of the risks I'll run," he said. "Or are you just saying that because, at heart, you want to return to your Citadel more than you want to remain with me?"

"I don't know." Kyra pulled her hand from his and stepped back when he reached for her, fighting to keep her voice from breaking. "I honestly don't know." And she plunged into the street, crossing it blindly, her eyes stinging with tears, while he stood behind her, mute, his hand outstretched. She didn't know exactly where she was going, though her steps turned automatically toward the river quays; a raw ache of grief clutched at her throat, a terrible helplessness, wanting him and knowing it would never work. Absurdly, she thought, *All those silly songs are right,* as a thread of melody curled through her mind: *An empty pillow, the empty hope . . .*

And transmuted itself, as it had at supper last night, into another modality, another key, a transposition . . .

With it came the sense of having encountered another transposition recently, something else familiar but changed . . . recognizable only if one knew what it had been changed from . . .

Then she knew it. She stopped dead in the middle of Faggot Lane as if she had been struck, and behind her a maid selling milk door to door snapped, " 'Ere, lady, watch where you're goin'!"

"Of course," Kyra whispered, memory dropping into place. And then, flicking the spilled milk from her sleeve, "Damn. Tastes spoiled, too." Turning, she ducked across the street under the nose of a plunging butcher's van and, gathering up her skirts, headed back toward Baynorth Square as quickly as she could go.

Her heart was pounding, her mind filled with the memory of the ugliness she'd felt on the wedding gown's muslin lining—weirdly familiar for all its faintness, teasing at her mind like a song transposed.

As the song had, the memory unwound itself and dropped into place.

There was something in that trace of magic that had reminded her—impossibly—of Tibbeth of Hale.

CHAPTER XVI

WHEN KYRA RETURNED TO THE HOUSE IN THE FINAL FADing of afternoon to darkness, the tension there was as present, as nerve-racking as the persistent, metallic scrape of some monstrous machine. She had gone out openly, only shaking off the Witchfinder with some rather time-consuming jiggery-pokery in a hat shop in Fennel Street; she waved airily across the square at the disgruntled young man as she ducked through the yard gate upon her return. As she passed unnoticed through the kitchen and slipped up the back stairs, she wondered how that young man's colleagues had fared, explaining to their superiors how they happened to wake up bound hand and foot in the middle of Pennyroyal Common.

The unnatural hush in the house—the kitchen was deserted, which at that time of the day was unheard of—made her wonder if the flute player's peccadilloes with Tellie Wishrom had gone farther than a few kisses by the postern gate. Her first impulse was to think, *The silly chit can't POSSIBLY know if she's gotten pregnant yet* ... Then she recalled her own feelings for Spenson, the terrifying heat of his kisses the previous night, and her own feverish response. *I'll skin him alive if he's done anything to her.*

The poor girl was only sixteen, after all.

And what, she wondered obliquely as she turned the sharp corners of the pitch-black well of the stair, was she going to do about herself? The thought of not returning to the Citadel when this was all over was unthinkable; the thought of her not being with Spens, more unthinkable still.

Alix's room was empty when she scratched at the door. The wedding dress and its attendant petticoats and veils had been hung in the armoire, out of sight for the first time since Kyra had returned to the house. The wicker dress form was gone. The room looked curiously pale without that flaming watcher of crimson and gold.

She crossed the room swiftly and pulled out the gown and its veils, like billowing armfuls of fire in what dim light remained in the east-facing window.

Now that she was thinking in terms of Tibbeth of Hale, the touch of him on the inside of the bodice, though not strong, was very recognizable.

It shook her to her bones, as if she had seen the man suddenly standing in the room beside her. In a sense, she thought, she had. She felt her breath quicken and a cold shakiness seize her belly; there had to be some explanation for this.

She touched the gown again, trying to quell her fear in analysis.

The sign was definitely his. The magic was ... the same but different. Shifted, as she had sensed, into some other modality, some other key that she did not understand. She pressed her lips to the place, trying to further shut out her own confused thoughts and let her magic think for her; frequently, if one's mind was clear or concentrated on something else, images would arise to help, as hers had earlier of the change of key. But all

that her mind's eye would see was that final glimpse of
his face through the clear, running distortion of the heat
dance, mouth impossibly stretched in the single scream
that seemed to go on for minutes, eyes bulging with agony and horror and disbelief as the flesh of his thighs
fried and swelled and burst . . .

"Excuse me, miss."

Kyra whirled. But it was only the laundry maid, who
gathered up Alix's discarded shift from the bottom of
the armoire and departed, dreamy and colorless as ever.

Kyra sat down on the end of the bed, her hands trembling now. Tibbeth was dead. Yet somehow his magic
had reached across the years . . .

She pushed the gown off her lap, wanting obscurely
to wash her hands for having touched the place where
the magic had been picked up . . . Picked up from what?
Alix's flesh? She fumbled in the pocket of her gown,
drew forth the scrying-crystal, and angled it toward the
panes of the window. But too little light remained above
the black loom of neighboring roofs and the slate blue
of the shadows; she turned her body a little toward the
dressing table and gestured a single candle into flame.

"Rosamund," she breathed, and called to her mind
the Lady's coldly beautiful face. "Rosamund, I need
you."

The long disciplines of her training let her sink
quickly into the crystal's heart, down past the aureate
pinpoint of the candle's reflected light. The familiar
flicker of the colors appeared in the fine-grained lattices
of its facets, colors that sank and changed into a kind of
gray veil. Then the veil cleared, and to her relief she
saw her ladyship, seated in the small study of the Porcelain House on the Citadel's wooded northwestern
side. Past her mentor's shoulder she could see the glow
of the hearth, the golden gleam of cat eyes where Imp
curled on a footstool beside an open book.

"Kyra, what is it?" The peridot-green eyes looked
anxiously into hers from that tiny, distant image. "Are

you well? Have you learned what threatened your sister?"

Somehow the mere sound of Rosamund's voice in her mind had a steadying effect, the reassurance that she wasn't alone. "I've learned it," she said. "But I don't understand what I've learned."

As the room darkened around her, she told, as well as she could, of the ghost of magic that still clung to the wedding dress, her unshakable feeling that it was Tibbeth's, though it was in fact not only somehow changed but so faint as to be almost unidentifiable. "I don't see how it *could* be his," she said at length, having sidestepped the subjects of Blore Spenson and the two abortive attempts at the wedding itself. "He's dead, Rosamund. I *saw* him die six years ago. He was ... He ..." She could not bring herself to speak of the sight of Tibbeth's abdomen rupturing with the heat, of his screams as his intentines dropped down into the blaze. "He couldn't have survived the fire."

Rosamund was silent for a time, running a lock of her heavy hair thoughtfully through her fingers. In spite of the plain black woolen robe of wizardry, the simple red cotton of her shift, she had all the queenly grace of the daughter of a long line of earls; her green eyes, with their dark rings around the irises, were troubled in the gloom.

"Not himself," she said musingly. "But under certain conditions, if the Inquisition didn't have a very powerful mage attending the death—and as I've said, the Inquisition's wizards aren't first-class as a rule—a wizard's ghost can linger if it has something, some place or person, to cling to. Death by violence ..." She shook her head.

"I checked the schoolroom," Kyra said numbly. "I took special pains with it. Most of his things had been thrown out, but even so, I sensed nothing there." True, she thought, she had not been thinking of or looking for traces of Tibbeth when she had done so. Not Tibbeth alive, Tibbeth active, Tibbeth twisted with malice.

But even so, that kind of hate must have left its mark.

She thought about reentering that room now, in the darkness, fingering once more through the few remaining crocks and bowls. Even playing through that scene in her mind made her shiver.

"Did Tibbeth have a wife, or a son, or a brother or sister?" Rosamund asked. "Someone close to him? The ghosts of wizards can possess those who loved them if those loved ones let them in."

Kyra said, "He had a wife."

A wife who was little more than a child herself. That colorless, dreamy face, that flaxen hair, pale blurs in the dark vestibule of the Inquisition's courtroom . . . Kyra couldn't even recall what she looked like.

But quite suddenly she saw herself sitting in this very room, on the end of the bed as she was sitting now, on a spring afternoon six years earlier, with a pile of her sister's nightgowns on her lap. On each of those fragile cotton garments the mark of Tibbeth's Summoning had been traced, invisible, undetectable to any but a fairly strong mage. He probably hadn't realized that she had the power to read a mark that subtle.

When she had recalled the scene before, she had remembered only her own rage at the taste of the foul dreams with which those marks had been imbued, the dirty sensuality, the unclean Summons that Alix had been sleeping with every night, the marks pressed against her skin. Only now it came to her that the marks were placed so that when the garment was on, they would fall just below the breast . . .

. . . in the precise place where the faint touch of evil lingered on the red bodice's muslin lining.

And she remembered, too, the colorless, dreamy-faced laundry maid who only minutes before had come in to gather up Alix's discarded shift.

"Dear God!"

She dropped the crystal, and her concentration snapped with horror and alarm; Lady Rosamund's image vanished. She scrabbled for it, then sprang to her feet, tripping over the wedding gown and nearly colliding with her mother in the bedroom doorway.

"Kyra!" Binnie Peldyrin caught her older daughter in her arms. "Oh, thank God you're here!"

Kyra stared at her blankly for a moment. Her mother's pleasant oval face was puckered with worry, and the relief that sprang into her dark eyes at the sight of this less successful daughter frightened Kyra a little. "What is it?" Kyra asked. "I've been out; I didn't think Father would be all that eager to see me around."

"Oh, Kyra, your father's fit to have a stroke!" Binnie gasped, clutching her daughter's hand. "He'd never ask this of you; he seems to think all you've brought on the house is ill fortune, which is quite ridiculous, since these things *will* happen . . . I mean the pipes breaking and all those poor little mice . . ."

"Ask *what* of me?" Like her father, Kyra had long ago learned that ruthless interruption was the only way of carrying on a conversation with her mother.

"Oh, is that your magic crystal? I'm so glad you thought to bring one, though I thought they were supposed to be round balls."

"No, they aren't. What *is* it? If you want me to find that wretched flute player . . ."

"What flute player?" Binnie, deflected from her train of thought, stared up at her tall offspring with distracted surprise. "Oh . . . Oh, that dreadful young man! Though I must say he played beautifully," she added, "and he was *very* handsome. I'm sure I can't blame Tellie at all for kissing him, even if he isn't her class and it did make her father furious, but after all, there's been no harm done, and he *has* played at Court . . ."

"Mother . . . !" Kyra pulled away from the soft little fingers and restrained herself from shaking her parent.

"If kissing him was all she did, I'm certainly not going to spend my time tracking him with a scrying-crystal."

"Not *him*!" Her brow wrinkled tragically, and her eyes glistened with sudden tears. "Your sister!"

"My . . ." Her voice trailed to silence.

"Oh, Kyra, Alix has . . . has run away with Algeron Brackett!"

Kyra swore. And yet an instant later the image returned to her . . . like two children sheltering from the rain, asleep in one another's arms in the guttering light of the candles, gold hair mingling with gold. Alix had gone to him for comfort after her father's bawled threats and recriminations, had cried herself to sleep in his arms . . .

And had wakened, warm and locked together, in the deep of the night, nearly an hour before anyone else in the house.

Kyra swore again, mightily.

"Dearest, your language! Though you always did pick up things from the stable boys." Binnie wrung her dainty hands, her face twisted with concern in its frame of lace cap and blond curls. "Oh, I *know* she says she's going to marry him immediately . . ."

"*Marry* him . . . !" Her heart turned cold.

". . . but think of the *scandal*! And your father says—"

"Wait a minute, she *says* . . ."

"In her note." With a prolonged sniffle, Binnie Peldyrin produced it, and only many, many years of proper raising kept Kyra from simply snatching it out of her glycerin-softened grip:

Mother,
   Please, please forgive me for what I do, and please beg Father's forgiveness as well. I know how dreadfully I wrong him, and still more am I conscious of the wrong I am doing to Master Spenson and to all of his house. Please do not think Algeron and I are sim-

*ply running away together. We will be married as
soon as may be, and we will enter into respectable
trades.*

*Never do either of us wish to bring shame upon
you. But I have realized that for me to marry Master
Spenson would be to do him an even greater wrong
than this. I love Algeron far more than words can
ever say and cannot now exist without him at my
side. I know it is too much to ask your blessings, but
I pray that at least we may take with us some understanding.*

*Give all of my love to Kyra, and I beg of you, do
not seek us.*

Your wretched daughter,

Alix

"You have to find her!" Binnie raised her eyes once
more to her daughter's face, which had grown still, like
blanched bone, in the last glimmerings of the window's
fading light. "Your father sent footmen to all the gates
of the city, but nobody remembers seeing them, which
in itself is a little strange, since Algeron is so very
handsome. But if you can use your magic crystal . . ."

Kyra swept her hand in the direction of the dressing
table, and all the candles there burst into simultaneous
flame as she flung herself down upon Alix's little stool
before it.

"Really, dearest," her mother went on, her chirping
voice calmer now, "it amazes me how you do that! But
I do remember when you were quite a little girl, you
used to—"

"Mother, *please*! I need quiet for this."

Her mother clapped both hands over her mouth in a
curiously childlike gesture and sank to a sitting position
on the end of the bed. Kyra found it difficult to concentrate with those doelike eyes gazing at her in awed

wonder and realized that she had never worked even the smallest magic in the presence of either of her parents.

"Perhaps you'd better leave the room for a little bit," she said when no image would appear in the crystal's central facet.

Binnie paled. "You haven't seen something . . . Oh, Kyra, tell me!" Impulsively she clutched at Kyra's wrist. "I'm her mother . . ."

"I haven't seen anything," Kyra said patiently, extricating herself and wondering how her single-minded and efficient father had made it through almost thirty years of marriage to this woman. "I just think I need to be alone."

"Oh, yes, of course, of course . . . Just let me hang up Alix's wedding dress . . . I can't think how it came to be dumped like this across the end of the bed, but the silk crushes so easily, and it cost *ten crowns a yard*! And that Hylette charges absolutely scandalous prices. I can't *believe* Lady Earthwygg has all her gowns made by that woman, because I *know* the Earthwyggs are all to pieces and it's only your father's money—"

"*Mother!*"

"Oh, yes! Yes, of course . . ." She scampered from the room, still clutching yards of saffron veil.

They can't be getting married tonight, Kyra thought desperately, turning her attention back to the crystal. *Tonight can't be her wedding night.*

She angled the crystal to the candles' light.

Still no image would come.

Panic mounted in her for a moment. *Don't tell me Mother unnerved me that much.* Quickly she searched the crystal for images of her father and saw him at once, talking to—*thank God!*—Spenson in the book room. She called Alix's image to her mind again, seeking her, seeking Algeron . . .

But the only thing she saw reflected in the crystal's depth was the dozen points of the candlelight, like golden stars sunk in the fog-white rock. She concentrated on those points, channeling all her thoughts, all her attention, trying to shut out the sudden rise of voices in the hall below. *This is ridiculous; I've found both of them in the crystal before. It isn't as if either of them is mageborn.*

So intent was her concentration that she neither heard nor felt the jar of footfalls in the back stairs until the door was thrown open and Spenson grabbed her by the wrist. "Come on!"

"What . . . ?"

She found herself dragged to her feet and down the hall in a tangle of long legs and petticoats, still clutching her scrying-crystal in one hand. The sudden breaking of her almost meditative state left her disoriented. She could hear her father's voice downstairs and the shouting of other men but couldn't piece together words. Lily the maid sprang out of their way as Spenson hauled her to the back stairs and shoved her through the narrow door.

"Spens . . ."

"Run for it!" he panted as he hauled her down the dark hairpin switchbacks of the narrow stairwell. "The Witchfinders!"

"What?"

"They're here. They have a warrant for your arrest; they came in while I was talking to your father. Lily showed me the back stairs. They say they have a witness who swears she saw you turn a beggar into a dog."

"What?"

Kyra was still cursing with great vividness as they burst through into the kitchen, fled past the startled Joblin and his scullions, and pelted on through into the hall leading to the garden door. As they swept through the pantry, Spens caught up a broom and a three-foot metal candle snuffer, tossing the latter to Kyra; she had recovered sufficiently not to need dragging in his wake and strode at his heels, her voluminous skirts gathered up in her free hand.

"Alix and Algeron have eloped," she gasped as they plunged into the darkness of the garden. "Spens, they're getting married!"

"Halt, in the Regent's name!" The voice came from the corner of the house, where the cobbled kitchen yard ran back toward the street, but Kyra's mage-sighted eyes picked up dark forms by the black slit of the garden gate. "Two by the gate," Kyra said softly as she guided Spens along the grass verge of the path at a run. Their feet made little sound, and the night, typically of Angelshand in the spring, was thickly overcast. "I can't use magic ..."

"Don't—you'll never clear yourself if you do."

Footsteps crunched the gravel, then there was a dry, thrashing tangle of feet snaring in low hedges and rose-bushes. Kyra heard a man swear; evidently the Inquisition's sasenna lacked the mageborn vision in darkness. Spens swung the broom, and there was a satisfying crack, followed by gasps and curses; he grappled and scuffled with someone, first on gravel, then on grass, then in the thorns. Though not only common sense but every impulse inculcated by her training made the use of magic against another human being nearly impossible, Kyra had no qualms about using her mageborn senses against a man nearly blind in the pitch-black shadows. She bent the candle snuffer over the skull of one warrior when he lunged, clutching at her, and shoved the other, stumbling, off Spens with the broom. Spens finished the operation with an elbow across the man's face, a boot in his groin, and a hard shove that sent him reeling into his advancing fellows while Spens and Kyra dove through the postern and into the stinking gloom of the alley beyond.

"This way!" She caught Spenson's sleeve and dragged him three steps right and through the gate to the Wishroms' kitchen yard, which thankfully was still unlatched from the flute player's earlier retreat. Instants later they heard the Witchfinders thunder up the alley.

"And to think I threatened to skin that nice young man," she muttered, leading Spens quickly to the cellar door, down the steps, through the drying room there, and up on the other side to the pantry. All the Wishroms' servants were, of course, in Baynorth Square watching the excitement. No one opposed them as they passed through the downstairs offices and out a side door into Mouch Lane.

"What now?" Spens asked as they calmly hailed a cab at the corner of Upper Tollam Road and rattled away from the scene of the crime.

Looking across at him in the dim flashes of light through the cab windows from the oil lamps in these more elegant streets, Kyra saw that his eyes sparkled as they had in the Cherry Orchard when he'd spoken of pirate fights over breakfast. His face, sweat-streaked with exertion, had turned suddenly young.

The cab was an old one, badly sprung and stinking of wine and tobacco; the jolting of its iron wheels over the cobblestones jarred Kyra breathless, so that she could barely speak.

"We have to find Alix! Spens, they've eloped!"

He blinked at her for a moment, nonplussed; then his eyebrows dove. "Eloped . . ."

"The marks—the evil eyes—were on her shifts, probably the one she's wearing and whatever she took with her. The laundry maid . . ."

"How could they get there? Who . . . How do you know?"

"I found them," Kyra said, trying to call to mind what Tibbeth's wife had looked like. In addition to glimpses in the vestibule of the court, Kyra recalled seeing her half a dozen times during the year she was going to Tibbeth's shop to study but could call to mind nothing of her face—only the impression of extreme youth.

Tibbeth had been right about the power of illusion in her own life. It had never occurred to her to regard that

flaxen nonentity as a person in her own right any more
than it had ever occurred to her to note the color of
Merrivale's eyes or the names of the footmen and maids.

She did remember that Tibbeth's wife had been no
more than a few years older than herself. She had assumed that the laundry maid was much older, but that,
she knew, could be the result of the poverty that lined
a woman's face, thickened her figure, and robbed her of
teeth when she was no more than twenty-seven or
twenty-eight.

She had never inquired. Her face heated with shame.

"I think my mother's laundry maid was Tibbeth's
wife," she said after a time. "I don't really remember;
she wasn't someone I took any notice of in those days.
Lady Rosamund says it's possible for a wizard's ghost
to occupy part of the mind of someone whom the wizard knew well, if that person lets him."

"I see," Spens said quietly. "Then it was she who
called the Witchfinders."

"She saw me with the wedding dress," Kyra said.
"She knew then I'd guess and didn't want me tracking
Alix."

"And where is Alix?"

"That's just it!" Kyra cried helplessly. "I don't know!
I can't get an image of her in the crystal! It's as if she
were mageborn herself—or had a counterspell."

"Could she?"

"Well," Kyra said, calmed a little by his reasonable-
ness, "scry-wards do cost a good bit of money, though
I suppose Alix could have traded her jewelry. As young
as she is, she doesn't have much—" She broke off
again, thinking, remembering the note. Then, abruptly,
she half stood and leaned out the window of the cab.
"Driver! Yoo-hoo . . . !"

The man half turned in his seat, bright green eyes
peering over a thick muffler. "Yes, miss?"

"Never mind Salt Hill Lane; take us to Pea Street
south of the river!"

CHAPTER XVII

"Good heavens, child, you know I can't give you that kind of information, even if I knew it!" Hestie Pinktrees looked from Kyra to Spens and back, then paused suddenly and turned to consider Spenson again.

"Yes," Kyra said. "Him. The one Lady Earthwygg wanted the philters for. I wrote counterspells all over the latest one you sold her this afternoon, by the way."

Pinktrees chuckled richly, her whole rosy face dimpling with delight at the joke, then rose to her feet like the ascent of the harvest moon. "So you were mageborn all the time! Shame on you, coming in here telling me stories about ill-wishing a man who'd wronged you! Little slyboots." In deep settings of flesh and kohl her eyes twinkled good-humoredly. "But you might have saved yourself the risk of discovery, Snow-Tear, my child. That one looks too stubborn for a philter to give him anything more than itchy dreams. Would you care for some tea, either of you? It's so chilly out tonight." And she bustled from the room in a foam of flowered skirts, as if the Emperor's gardens had suddenly decided to uproot themselves and take a walk.

"Snow-Tear?" Spenson asked, and Kyra shook her head. "Itchy dreams, indeed."

"I realize it's nearly suppertime." The plump dog wizard rustled her way back in with an enormous silver tray between round white hands like bejeweled puddings. "I made these this morning; you do look famished."

Kyra realized she hadn't eaten anything since the tea sandwiches at Lady Earthwygg's. She'd meant to get something from the kitchens and avoid dining with the family—without the musicians to fill it, the silence in the dining room would have been unbearable even if Alix had not eloped—but her mother, and then the Inquisition, had forestalled that plan. Spens was looking askance at the white and yellow china plates of powdered tea balls, date bars, and lemon tarts, but Kyra ran her fingers lightly above them and sensed no magic in them beyond the magic of a skilled cook, no ill save those inherent in such a quantity of butter and sugar.

"Did you make a talisman of scry-ward for my sister?" She handed a comfit to the still-doubtful Spenson. "It's important that I know," she added, seeing Pinktrees hesitate. "I know she's eloped with that boy of hers."

"As who wouldn't?" the mage giggled.

"Who indeed? But I have reason to believe that a death-curse has been laid on her, a death-curse that will fall on her wedding night."

The fat woman sat up straighter, her rosy mouth suddenly losing its laughter, a lemon tart hanging unnoticed in her pudgy hand. In the tiled stove the fire hissed softly on the coals; the two butter-colored cats lay in the pool of the russet light that came through its barred grate, curled in on themselves like enormous slippers. Behind the swagged lace and velvet ribbons that decorated the windows, Kyra was ever more conscious of the denseness of the night.

"Pinktrees, we have to overtake them! We have to find them, and find them soon!"

"They won't be in danger tonight," Spenson said, and both women turned to look at him in surprise.

"Well, think. Even if they stop at the first big village outside of town—Underhythe to the south, or Mintrebbit to the north, or Glidden up along the river—by the time they get there, it'll be too late to find a priest. Whatever they're doing tonight—and they may be romantic enough to sleep apart at whatever inn they've sheltered at—they won't be married at least until tomorrow afternoon."

"Unless they've taken ship," Kyra said, her eyes dark with fear in the soft reflections of the candles. "If they were going to Senterwing or the colonies, the ship's priest could have wed them."

"In that case there is nothing we can do," Spens said quietly. "Not tonight, not tomorrow ... Never." He looked across at the dog wizard in her lilac clouds of ruffles and lace. "*Have* they taken ship?"

"I don't know." She set her lemon tart on the tiny plate before her, regarding him with deep concern in those oddly wise hazel eyes. A cart went by on the road, filled with laborers on their way back from Little Harbor, drunk and singing in the darkness. The cats rolled luxuriantly over into undignified positions and settled themselves to serious slumber. The steam of the teapot sent soft whispers of chamomile and lemon grass into the still air.

"One of Lady Earthwygg's footmen came here about noon, asking me to go to her house immediately and telling me it would be well worth my while, which indeed it was. Your sister, my dear—and my! but she's a beautiful girl, and so sweet—was there, and that nice young man."

Pinktrees sighed reminiscently and helped herself to

what remained of her tart and another one as well. "Her ladyship said that Alix, as she called her, and Algeron were going away and were afraid that Alix's sister, who was a wizard, was going to try to stop them, and would I give them a scry-ward so that the sister couldn't find them? I should have known there was something afoot, for I charge twenty crowns for a scry-ward, and Perdita Earthwygg has yet in her life to lay out twenty *coppers* for something that doesn't benefit *her*. Alix looked as if she'd been crying her eyes out, poor lamb, with the end of her nose all red under the powder, and holding onto Algeron's hand, though I noticed it was she who did all the talking. Such a handsome young man, but he didn't have two words to say for himself and was obviously terrified of Lady Earthwygg."

Kyra smiled, recalling Algeron's account of his brief career as Janson Milpott's secretary. Whatever volcanic outburst of passion and love had drawn Alix into realizing she couldn't live without Algeron, she had a fairly clear idea of who was in charge of the logistics of the flight.

The dog wizard sighed again. "She said her parents would never forgive her and that her father would send his men after them and would get you—although of course I didn't associate it with *you*, my dear Snow-Tear—to scry for them in your crystal so that they could be dragged back."

"Had Lady Earthwygg given them money?" Kyra asked.

Spens looked startled for a moment at the very idea. Then, as he thought about it, his homely face broke into a grin. "That little vixen . . ."

Pinktrees nodded. "After I'd given them the talisman—a very nice bit of silver and rabbit skin, with two chips of opal worked in . . ." She ticked the ingredients off on her fingers around the comfit she held. "Lady Earthwygg even provided the opal, which was tremendously good of her, since, gimcrack as the stones

were, they were far better than anything I can afford,
and the footman brought them their cloaks; Alix clasped
her ladyship's hand and said how she'd always thank
her for giving them the money to take a proper start of
their life together."

"Of course." Spenson chuckled with pure delight.
"Lady Earthwygg would give her whatever money she
asked for just to get her out of town."

"Well, her ladyship certainly did look like Saffron
does when he thinks I haven't noticed him licking out
of the butter icing spoon. Isn't that right, my tiny cream
cake?"

One of the cats on the hearth—twenty pounds of
"tiny cream cake" at the lowest possible computation—
twitched a fluffy tail in sleepy response.

"I thought she might have," Kyra said slowly, "from
what Alix said in her letter about starting in respectable
trades. The only thing preventing her from marrying
Algeron was money to get them set up in business."

"Well, it isn't surprising, considering the amount
Lady Earthwygg has paid me for love-philters and to
put marks on your house, Master Spenson, to make you
desire that rat-faced daughter of hers." Pinktrees poured
out another cup of tea for herself and judiciously se-
lected a date bar. "Not that the poor girl's looks have
anything to do with it, because actually the girl's quite
pretty, and my own niece has a face like a door scraper
and it didn't stop the kindest young man in the world
from taking to her—but that Earthwygg girl has eyes
like a shrike. But as to where they were bound, truly, I
don't know. Her ladyship kept me afterward to make up
another love-philter—'now that troublesome chit is out
of the way,' I believe she put it. But she did serve me
some truly excellent raspberry tartlets, and with the cost
of raspberries at this time of year, that was generous of
her."

"How did she pay you?" Kyra broke in, leaning forward.

The dog wizard looked startled. "Well, in flimsies, naturally."

"I mean, did she send a servant out of the room for the money, or was it there in the room with her when you entered?"

"Ah!" Pinktrees rose and rustled her way to the exquisite cherrywood sideboard near the window. She withdrew a small purse of stamped leather from whose top protruded the edges of a substantial roll of yellow bank notes. "How extremely clever of you, my dear."

"What?" Spenson looked from one wizard to the other, completely lost, as Kyra moved her chair closer to the stove and bowed her head over the purse, which she held cradled between her hands. Their hostess dimpled and came back to the table to hand him another tart.

"Now, this is just a little wizardry, dear," she said in a motherly voice. "Sit quiet and have some more tea."

He retreated, discomfited, to the depths of his overstuffed chair, and the fluffier of the two cats, having risen and stretched from claw tip to the last ostrich-feather curl of her tail, sprang into his lap and confidently made herself at home.

Kyra closed her eyes and sank her perceptions into the soft fabric of the leather and the money.

For some time she was aware only of its touch and its smell: the faint camphory perfume of the bag, the scents of the leather mingling with the dim portpourri that had been in the sideboard's secret compartment, the ambergris that clung to Lady Earthwygg's clothing and hands, the gray filthy smell that any money would pick up in handling. She was conscious of the warmth of the stove against her knuckles, her cheeks, and her knees through her gown, conscious of Pinktrees' jasmine perfume and the slightly rotted scent of the paper-whites in the swirled vase of Kymil glass on the sideboard, of the lemony scent of the tarts and the resinous fragrance of

the fire, of the leather and orris root and the smell of
Spenson's flesh.

Then, deeper, pictures began to form in her thoughts.
The vision of Lady Earthwygg's drawing room came
easily, for she had been there herself that day. It was
earlier than she had seen it, the sunlight lying strong
against the red silk of the wallpapers, gleaming on the
variously colored marbles of hearth and window seat
and floor. Her ladyship was dressed not in the stiff
white and rose gown she had worn that afternoon but in
a wrapper of bronze-green silk frothing with lace and a
lace cap on her storm-colored hair. Alix and Algeron
sat, looking stiff and anxious and a little embarrassed,
on the curly-legged love seat where Esmin had been
seated that afternoon. Alix wore the plain dark gown of
one of the maids, Lily, perhaps, quite possibly the one
Kyra had borrowed for her expedition to the Cheevy
Street Baths. Had that only been the day before yesterday?

Alix was saying, "I've computed what we'll need to
set myself up in a good shop in a good street in Kymil.
Algeron can easily find employment as a pastry chef either with one of the established pastry shops or in a private mansion. Five hundred crowns would keep us well
until business starts coming my way."

"Five hundred," Lady Earthwygg began, aghast either at the sum or at Alix's temerity in asking it.

"How much did you offer my sister to make Master
Spenson fall in love with Esmin?" The doelike brown
eyes, red-rimmed though they were with spent tears,
met the bulging black ones with cold steadiness.
"That's got to be easier once I'm out of the way."

"I always said you were an outrageous hussy, girl!"

"As long as I'm an outrageous hussy in Kymil, you
shouldn't have complaints," returned Alix. Algeron
gazed at his beloved with awe at such courage. "Besides . . ." And here Alix smiled and looked for a moment like her usual teasing self. "I'm not, really. Kyra's

the outrageous one. Though I suppose I am a hussy now. I just ... want to be happy. I want to be free." And her hand closed around the slim, muscular ink-stained one that it held.

"My pearls didn't bring very much," she went on after a moment. "You know girls my age don't get real jewelry, and besides, the best of them were given to me by my mother, and I wouldn't sell them were I starving. You're our only chance, my lady."

Kyra opened her eyes, slowly drawing her mind back from the images that clung to the pouch, the pouch that throughout the interview had been on that little table at her ladyship's side where Kyra had later found the packet of Hestie Pinktrees' herbs. Pinktrees was nibbling yet another tartlet and talking quietly to Spenson, who was stroking the cat.

"I must say I was rather proud of myself, getting into your house to mark it for the love-spells. At my size, you must admit it's quite a trick to go unseen." The dog wizard sighed regretfully. "I suppose your lady's going to go through now and take all the marks away."

She looked around quickly, though Kyra had made no sound, and Spenson followed the direction of her eyes.

Kyra set the pouch down, feeling a vast tiredness within her. "Kymil," she said. "They're headed for Kymil."

Spenson guessed that the lovers had made for the village of Underhythe, on the main Kymil road. But to Kyra's urgent demands for immediate pursuit he responded, incontrovertibly, that not only would all the city gates be closed at this hour, they would certainly be watched by the Witchfinders. Anyone attempting to leave before the gates opened at dawn for the market carts would be stopped and questioned at the very least, and there were enough Church dogs in the Magic Office to make Kyra put the thought of cloaking-spells out of her mind.

"I'll be back here before sunup with a couple of horses and some clothes for you." Spens latched the door of the countinghouse on Salt Hill Lane behind them and led the way through to the inner storeroom whence the ladder ascended to the loft. He moved with calm and efficient briskness, a man long used to getting out of tight places. "I'll bring breeches and a jacket—you can put your hair up under a hat."

"Nonsense, there's nothing more obvious than a girl with her hair pinned up to look like a boy." Kyra flipped open the coal box beside the little iron stove; her voice and Spens's footfalls echoed hollowly in the long, bare-walled attic room where in times past the clerks had slept. "You must have a pair of scissors here somewhere. Thank God you're not one of those stingy employers who ration the coal." She emptied what little kindling was left in the box onto the grate and arranged two or three chunks of coal over it. The room was large, but if she took the bed nearest the stove, she thought, she would be warm enough through the night. The blankets Spenson took out of the cupboard were fusty-smelling but clean and fairly thick; even her best These-Blankets-Stink spells failed to bring a single flea to the surface.

"I never thought to be thankful for my face, but life is full of surprises; it looks far more like a boy's, anyway."

"No." Spenson eased down to his knees behind her, where she sat before the open hatch of the stove's black belly; half turning, she saw the coin-bright gold of the new flames glint on the buttons of his garishly striped gold and crimson waistcoat. "That mouth could never be mistaken for a boy's." His hands slid under the rufous chaos of her hair; very gently, his lips sought hers.

"Spens . . ."

Slowly, like a collapsing silk pavilion settling over

the air trapped within it, they sank to the floor, mouths taking warmth from one another, hands buried in each other's hair. As the firelight flared, it threw their shadows over rafter and wall; the smell of burnt dust from the rarely used stove filled Kyra's nostrils, and the reminiscence of Hestie Pinktrees' lemon tarts on Spenson's breath.

"We should be—"

"There's nothing further we can do for them tonight," he murmured. "There's nothing further *you* can do."

She raised her head, her hair hanging down over the lace of her collar. "They could be dying."

He only looked up at her, not contradicting; his eyes were somber. He was right, she knew. There was nothing further she could do, not even search for them in her crystal to see if they were dying or not. For the first time the sense of her own complete helplessness washed over her, the sense that even had they somehow gotten out of the city without being seen, they would still not have made it to Underhythe before morning. The helplessness was followed almost immediately by rage, by the desire to spring to her feet, to pace, to kick, to curse, to smash her fists against the lathe of the walls; and that rage, by a wave of trembling and the inchoate, infuriating, nearly overwhelming desire to cry.

She dropped back down on him, clinging to him for a long time in a kind of fever, while his arm closed around her, and through the rustling stiffness of her skirts and petticoats she felt against her legs and thighs the unfamiliar strength and bulk of him. In time her trembling stopped, as if the solid calm of him had come slowly to be absorbed into her flesh.

When the clock on some nearby chapel chimed midnight, Spenson stirred a little; Kyra whispered, "Don't go." The fire had sunk, though the smoldering coals gave forth a nearly lightless heat. For the first time since she could remember—perhaps, she thought, for the first time in her life—the thought of lying alone in the darkness filled her with dread. By his breathing, by the occasional movements of his hands over the stiff fabric of her back and sides, she knew that he had slept no more than she. He settled again and drew her close. She wasn't sure what she feared in the darkness, the thought of Alix or that last vision of Tibbeth of Hale, eyes popping out, mouth stretched, screams drowned out by the roaring of the fire as the flesh of his legs and feet sizzled and fell away. She pressed her face to the smooth satin of the waistcoat beneath her cheek, breathing its smoky odor and trying to will herself to sleep without dreams.

When the clock chimed three, Spenson rose quietly and departed. Kyra occupied herself with cutting her hair until she heard the muffled clunk of the latch that announced his return.

"There." She ruffled the coarse brush of what was left. "How's that?"

"Absolutely horrible." He dropped the bundle of clothes he was carrying and picked his way across the room to her, moving with the clumsy caution of a nonmage in the dark. "It *looks* like it was cut without the aid of a lamp."

"Well, I couldn't see around the back with the mirror."

"Here." He found a couple of candle ends in a drawer, flipped open the stove to kindle them, and took the scissors. It surprised her how conscious she was of his hand when he touched the side of her face to steady her head, how every finger movement in her hair and the thin flick and whine of the blades seemed to have a tremendous significance.

It's ridiculous, she thought, *that all those silly songs those musicians sang and all Algeron's absurd poems should be so true.* If everything in the world did not precisely speak his name, all things seemed to relate to him in some fashion or other, an effect that, when she had read of it in novels, had previously seemed affected and ridiculous. She supposed she would be saner again presently.

"I didn't hear any horses," she remarked, turning her head a little to glance back at him.

"Hold still or I'll take your ear off. I sent one of my clerks to leave them at the Pelican Inn on the Kymil road; I thought we'd be less conspicuous getting out of the city without them. There." He handed her the scissors back and gathered the cuttings from the floor. "You'll look like a respectable footman out for a day's errands in the country."

He crossed to the bundle of clothing and drew out a shirt, a pair of breeches and a coat of the dark, severe cut common to servants, and a pair of stout shoes. He himself had changed out of the bottle-green suit he'd worn the previous day into a countrified short tweed jacket and top boots. Kyra retreated out of the candlelight to the farther end of the attic, shivering a little in the cold as she stripped off her heavy taffeta gown and layers of petticoats, and pulled on the masculine attire. It was only when she had transferred the contents of her dress's pockets to her coat pockets and turned back for the mirror's assistance in tying her neck cloth that she saw Spenson struggling gamely into a voluminous black dress he had to have borrowed from his cook or housekeeper and barely stopped herself from bursting into laughter.

"Here, it goes on over the head." She strode over to help him; he gave her a wry grin as his head emerged from the tangle of bombazine. "Drawstrings cross over, then tie in the front; to be really fashionable you should have another petticoat, but I doubt the guards will notice. You'll need a good deal of stuffing."

He shook out a lace cap and a muslin mobcap to put over it as she made the necessary adjustments to his attire. "I thought they might be looking for a red-haired youth in company with a man," he said as he arranged the caps over his curly hair. "How do I look?"

"Like the ugliest woman in Angelshand."

"Good." He produced his short-stemmed clay pipe from the satchel and proceeded to cram his jacket and breeches into the now-empty sack. "They should be opening the gates for the first of the market carts in a few minutes. By the time we get there, the square should be a bear garden. Ready?"

Kyra glanced nervously at her reflection in the mirror. In spite of the unfamiliar jut of her ears and cheekbones and the faint film of dirt that darkened her jaw in imitation of beard stubble, she thought she still looked absolutely like herself, and Spenson's disguise, in her opinion, wouldn't fool a nearsighted drunkard.

"You'd be surprised what people don't see," Spenson told her, gesturing with his pipe as they crossed the worn stone paving of the Great Bridge under the beetling brows of the St. Cyr fortress. The bridge was empty of its usual daytime crowd of flower sellers, old-clothes barrows, and street-corner entertainers. Kyra found it curious to have an unobstructed view of the harbor downriver, the dark masts of the ships pricking up through the floating white seethe of low-lying fog, the riding lights like embers in cinder-gray gloom. The world smelled of morning and low tide. "Just because it isn't done with magic doesn't mean it won't work."

It was just under a mile from the Great Bridge to the city's southern gate, through soot-blackened slums and jostling crowds of factory workers bound dull-eyed for their day's endless labor. Among them, however, rattled brightly painted farm carts on the way to the city's great markets, costermongers' barrows, donkeys laden with new lettuces and asparagus, poultrymen bearing cages of spring chickens, young girls driving small flocks of lambs in from the sprawling, muddy suburbs to the south. When they reached the square before the massive stone towers of the city gate, Kyra saw that Spenson was probably right. The broad, brick-paved space was a riot of farmers, produce, and animals; the air was thick with the drawl of country patois and the smells of dew and dung. The cavernous old city gate was choked with wagons, donkeys, and countryfolk; the two Church sasenna standing in the shadow of its heavy portcullis and the red-robed hasu beside them couldn't possibly see everything in that milling crowd.

Sucking on the stem of his pipe, Spenson hung back inconspicuously until a rumble of iron wheels and ponderous hooves behind them in Bridge Street signaled the advent of the Kymil stage. Farmers, pigs, and henwives swirled and surged out of the coach's way, forming eddies of barking dogs or women cursing as their fish baskets were upset; Spens ambled through them, nodding greetings and apologies here and there with the lace edge of his mobcap down over his eyes, and edged himself past the coach and into the gate passage while the sasenna and the hasu were stopping the vehicle and peering through its windows at the bleary-eyed and resentful passengers.

"A pity we can't simply take the stage," Kyra remarked when the coach passed them some time later on the broad street that led down from the gate through the sprawl of small shops and filthy, unpaved lanes that made up the first of the city's suburbs. Dawn was already bright in the sky; the birds were singing in the scrubby trees and backyard gardens, mingling with the bleat of goats and the grunting of pigs.

"You can bet they have someone on it." Spenson gestured with his pipe after the huge red and yellow vehicle vanishing down the wide, rutted street. Then he pulled a penknife from his skirt pocket and began digging out the bowl. "Thank God we're past the gates, anyway. I thought they'd smell it if I smoked my usual blend and wonder what an old servant was doing puffing on Gentleman's Special at half a crown an ounce."

Kyra laughed and shoved her hands in her jacket

pockets. "They'd assume you'd been pilfering your master's tobacco, of course. It's what all my father's footmen do."

"Come to think of it, probably mine do as well." He grinned, shoved his mobcap back a little from his forehead, and gestured at the straggling brick houses and gaudily painted taverns lining the road. Farm carts still passed them, jolting heavily where the pavement was broken into mud-filled potholes; the air smelled of brewing beer, young grass, and cows. "These houses go all to hedges once we're outside the town; if you'll keep guard, I can change clothes behind one before we get to the Pelican. If we ride fast, we can probably make Underhythe by midafternoon."

"Will they get in touch with your teachers at the Citadel?"

They had slowed the horses to a walk after the first long gallop. The sun had risen, its slanting rays salting the tops of the hedges on either side of the road and making the clumps of elder and rowan visible beyond them glitter as if every fifth leaf had been dipped in gold. The night's damp coolness was passing off, new grass and turned earth thick as perfume in the air, laden with the weight of the coming summer. The sharp *pink-pink* of the chaffinch and the warbling of robins filled the hedges; now and then, from the farmlands beyond the hedges, men's voices and the lowing of plow oxen could be heard.

"Of course." Kyra reached for the dozenth time to adjust the thongs in which she habitually bound up her hair on journeys, only to have her fingers encounter nothing but shorn ends. "Officially, they have to notify the Council, usually by scrying-crystal, if a Council wizard is detected in malfeasance, no matter how absurd the charge. I don't think Rosamund will believe for a moment that I actually turned a beggar into a dog because he was bothering me—for one thing, I haven't the faintest idea how to go about it—but the Council and the Inquisition both will be listening for me."

"Listening?" Spens frowned, squinting as they passed from leaf dapple into a patch of sharp morning sun.

"They can . . . can sense if I use powerful magic, can trace me through it—can feel where I am and what I have done. It takes a tremendous amount of energy and several high-level wizards working in concert, so it isn't done as a general rule—I mean, not just to check up on people. And if I *do* use magic for any purpose whatsoever connected with other human beings, the least that will happen will be that they'll disown me, cast me out of the Citadel and refuse to teach me, or protect me, anymore."

She looked straight ahead as she said it, over the horse's ears to the green and gold tunnel of the roadway, trying not to show the tight curling of dread that seemed to close around her lungs and heart. Even as Tibbeth's student she had prided herself on her strength and adeptness. Once Lady Rosamund had spoken for her to the Council and sponsored her admission to the Citadel and its teachings, she had striven hard to be the best, to learn all that she could of the riches so suddenly poured into her hands. It had never crossed her mind— even while she was ill-wishing the front steps in the terrified desperation of that first evening—that she would ever be caught in wrongdoing, much less accused of a wrong she had not done. That she would be ejected at this late date from the world she had struggled so doggedly to win.

I can't let it happen, she thought grimly. *I CAN'T.*

And some alien voice in her whispered, *But if you did, you wouldn't have to make the choice about staying with Spens or not.*

The thought went through her like lightning that, striking from the sky, burned in seconds on its way through to the ground: heat, enlightenment, agony . . .

And then, in its wake, rage at herself for even considering the surrender of her education as an option.

For a moment she saw the yellow moonlight shine in Alix's open eyes, bleaching them of any human color, she saw the wanton smile of the lust-spells that robbed her of all rationality in the dreamy drug of passion for a man. And superimposed on that, like a doubled image in a flawed glass, herself clutching at Spens like a desperate teenager, frenzied only for the touch of his hands.

It crossed her mind to wonder if Spenson was thinking that, too.

She glanced sidelong at him, for a moment imagining his wishes: *If she couldn't go back to that wretched Citadel, I'd have her for myself,* and her own furious reply, *How dare you?*

They had not spoken of what had passed between them in Lesser Queen Street: the urgency of his grasp, the stormy anger in his face. *Can't you learn as well here as there?*

But when she looked at him, she saw only his puzzlement and concern, and that, too, irritated her. *Dammit,* she thought wildly, *he has no right to do that to me. No right to make himself this important to me this quickly.*

If the Inquisition caught him with her, he'd be punished, too.

She shifted her weight forward and kicked her startled mount into a trot.

By midmorning her annoyance had been swallowed up in the awareness that they were being followed.

Twice she halted, standing in her stirrups to strain with all her mageborn senses, her mind teased by the suspicion that all was not right on the road behind them. Twice she only heard the distant voices of farmers, the whistle of magpies, and the murmur of trees. Still, uneasiness plagued her. When they drew near the modest posting inn called the Bear and Pig, she remained behind the sheltering trees of an elder copse and sent Spenson, well disguised by a spell so that no one would later identify him as the President of the Guild of Merchant Adventurers, to inquire after a young blond couple who had passed that way the day before.

Only as she sat waiting for him in the dense, insect-humming shade, listening down the road behind, did she realize that she still heard the voices of those same distant plowmen, though they had not passed a tilled field for some miles, and the magpies whistling in the selfsame way. Closing her eyes, she listened more deeply, probing with her mind at the illusion. And as illusions did, the voices dislimned and changed so that she wondered how she had mistaken for voices the swift, muffled thudding of many hooves and why the clink of harness buckles and the metallic rattle of crossbow bolts in their quivers had sounded so much like harmless bird cries.

"They've been by here, all right."

She jerked about, startled. Spens put a hand on her calf to steady her.

"What's wrong?"

"I think the Witchfinders are on our trail. They're still three or four miles off—didn't we pass a crossroad back around that bend?" She nodded toward the shady rise of elms behind them.

He nodded, gathering the reins to mount. "It goes to Byrnefelling Farm and past that to Utter Plunket. Won't the High Council sense it if you use a spell?" He reined around after her as she retraced their steps at a trot.

"They would if I used anything very violent or very high-level. If I threw a ward across the road, for instance, that the horses refused to pass. But Daurannon the Handsome—one of my instructors—always says that a spell that's too subtle to be detected is just as effective as one that's too strong to be resisted and works better if it's other mages you're trying to fool. They don't have very many high-level wizards in the Magic Office; I doubt they'd send one after me." She sprang down and tossed Spenson the reins, then fished in her pockets for one of the hairpins she'd worn the previous day, an old one wrought of amber and silver.

She had to write the talismans of light with extreme care, seven or eight of them, very tiny and none containing much power in itself, on stones and the undersides of leaves for some distance down the road before it reached the crossings; small spells of drowsiness, of inattention, of distraction mingled with tiny and unthought convictions that someone had said something about Utter Plunket . . . The sense that left and downhill was the best way to go—wider, clearer, better. After that she took a makeshift broom of elder twigs and dusted away the tracks on the main road, thankful that no rain had fallen lately to make the path muddy.

"Now come," she said, and Spenson rode down the farm path, leading her horse, while she followed afoot on the grassy verges, now and then leaving small signs of inattention and illusion so that the pursuers, unless they were quite powerful mages indeed or were looking very hard, would not be sure where exactly the hoofprints left the road.

It cost them nearly a half hour, and toward the end she had to fight panic at the thought of how near the Witchfinders were coming. But when they finally cut cross-country back to the Kymil road and proceeded through the thin woodlands at a rapid trot, she heard the sounds of pursuit fade and turn eastward. She did not hear them again for nearly two hours.

CHAPTER XVIII

"DAMN. THEY'RE BEHIND US AGAIN." KYRA DREW REIN TO
listen, the noon sun hot on her shorn head and unpro-
tected nape. "Coming fast, with no effort to conceal it."

"They know you've seen through their illusions,
then." Spenson leaned forward and felt his horse's
sweaty neck. They'd ridden at a hard trot, trying to
make up time, since the crossroad. "We can't outrun
them on these beasts, anyway. They must have gotten
remounts at the Bear and Pig. Can you tell the horses
where to go if we're not on them?"

"Do you know the way to Underhythe from here?"
She regarded him in some surprise as he stepped from
the saddle and untied the leather satchel that contained
their lunch of bread and cheese.

"Of course. One of my uncles has a farm at Utter
Plunket. I spent my summers tramping this part of the
country. Down you get." He reached up to catch her as
she dismounted, her legs nearly giving way with the
weakness of hours of unaccustomed riding. "There's another crossroads a mile and a half from here, leading

out to Far Peddley. Can you get our friends—" He patted his big roan's neck, "—to go as far as they can hellbent for leather down that road?"

"I'll do my best." Kyra caught her tall bay's bit, drew its head down close to hers, and whispered the words of command appropriate to the beast's small, skittish brain. From her pocket she took her scrying-crystal, conjured in its depths the sleepy crossroad among the willow trees, and, from that image, sent the vision of the place into the horse's mind, as well as the urge to run to the brink of exhaustion. "Go!" she cried, and stepped back. The bay flung up its head and pounded off at a run, the roan plunging at its heels with the aroused instincts of a herd animal in a stampede. Spens caught her elbow and guided her along the weedy verge of the road to a gap in the hedge—they were in farming country once again—that had been incompletely repaired with a few elm boughs woven into the thick masses of privet. These he pulled free to allow her through and replaced, inexpertly and at the cost of severely scratched fingers, behind them.

Then, hand in hand, they set off along the rough ground of the hedgerow, avoiding the plowed land that lay, upturned and breathing its thick peaty scents, below.

"So you spent your summers tramping this part of the country, did you?"

"Yes!" Spenson said defensively, and leaned against an apple tree to wipe his sweaty forehead with his sleeve.

Kyra, sitting slumped at the tree's roots, raised her head a little and gave him a dour look. "I can only assume you had either written directions or a competent guide." The back of her neck and the tips of her ears were smarting with sunburn. Though hardened by sword practice and used to walking miles in the cold sprucewoods around the Citadel, she had rarely ridden a

horse in the past seven years, and the points of bone at
the bottom of her pelvis ached from jarring contact with
the saddle. Even lunch had failed to cheer her. She was
tired and, as the sun hovered nearer the beech woods
away to their right, becoming concerned. Moreover, her
shoes, though Spenson had been careful to get a size to
fit her feet, had originally belonged to someone else, a
matter of less concern while riding than it had become
during the past five hours afoot.

Spenson took his pipe from his pocket, tamped tobacco into it from a small leather pouch, thankfully,
Kyra thought, his half-a-crown Gentleman's Blend and
not the cheap, stinking variety with which he had cam-
ouflaged himself against the guards at the city gates. "I
suppose you'd rather we continued on the road and got
ourselves arrested by the Witchfinders?"

Kyra didn't deign to give him a reply. With their
wanderings through the woods and hedgerows, turning
now east at a swamp that Spenson swore surrounded a
pond he had once known, now south to follow a spring
that didn't lead at all where it had (he assured her)
twenty years ago, her feeling of helplessness had returned, insistent and terrifying. Last night she had
known there was nothing she could do. This afternoon
it seemed to her that all this green, smiling countryside,
with its mossy pools, its chuckling streams in their ivy-
shawled clefts, its lichened oaks and pale stands of
birch and beech, had become her enemy. Or, if not her
enemy in the sense that Tibbeth of Hale and the Witchfinders were her enemies, at least insofar as her parents,
and her playmates, and the boys at the dances had always been her enemies: turning her aside from her
goals not out of malice but out of a kind of well-
meaning stupidity that did not and could not understand
the hideous urgency of her quest.

And Spenson, who had insisted that they stop for
food and rest out of a maddening conviction that she

was more tired than she thought she was, was no help at all.

"That pond we passed *has* to be Mickle's Pond," Spens said reasonably, drawing on his pipe. He'd taken off his jacket and neck cloth in the heat and looked far more at ease, like some bullnecked gentleman farmer or huntsman, a totally spurious impression, she thought bitterly, considering his navigational ineptitude. "That means if we go south from here, we should strike the road that runs from the rectory to Podding's Farm. My guess is that Alix and Algeron went to the rectory."

"They'll have married by this time," Kyra said softly. Her eyes went to the sun, touching the tips of the trees; within an hour, the land would be washed in shadow. Within three, it would be dark. Night. Alix's wedding night.

Her heart quickened in her ribs again, a terrible, anxious pounding as the recollection of the evil she'd felt upon the silk returned to her like the backtaste of poison. She got to her feet, pulling away from his help.

"Kyra, I'm sorry," Spenson said quietly. And then, when she didn't look at him, he added, "It's not far."

It was well after dark when they stumbled, quite by accident, upon the rectory of Underhythe. "Dear me, yes, they were married this afternoon." The local priest made a move toward the low doorway that had to, Kyra guessed by the smells of cooking and the faint rattle of cleaning up, be the kitchen; she shook her head vigorously and caught his gray sleeve.

"Did they say where they were going?" she asked. "Where they would spend the night?" The concern in his blue eyes—he was an elderly man with a bachelor's trembly fussiness—irritated her; he looked at her like a kindly father viewing a lost urchin out past her bedtime. With reason, she supposed impatiently. Her clothes were muddied, her face and hands were scratched from a hedge they'd scrambled through, and she'd begun to walk with a decided limp from a blister on her toe. But that was still no reason for him to peer at her as if debating whether to send her around to the kitchen for leftovers handed through the back door.

Behind her, Spenson stood with folded arms, wrapped in the illusory darkness of her protective spells; the elderly priest barely glanced at him and, unless Spens spoke, would not afterward remember that she had had a man with her at all, much less what he looked like.

"The young lady said they would be seeking a good inn, but I suggested instead that they rent Hythe Cottage. The widow Summerhay owns it; it stands out on the far field of Summerhay Farm, and it is much nicer for a young couple on their honeymoon than an inn. It used to be a farm cottage, but there's nothing of the farm left but the orchard. Very pleasant it is, apples and a few pear trees; the cottage itself is just the four rooms, but the barn's still in fair condition for their team and gig."

Alix must have reckoned transportation costs into the amount she braced Lady E. for, Kyra thought. Such practicality certainly didn't sound like Algeron.

"They did seem a most respectable young couple or else, of course, I would have had nothing to do with such a scrambling affair."

"Where is it?" demanded Kyra. "How far? It's important," she added as the man looked miffed at her interruption of his rambling encomium of the virtues of Hythe Cottage. "It's desperately important that I reach them tonight. Alix is my sister; there has been terrible news."

"Ah!" He relaxed a little, and Kyra breathed a sigh of relief. Alix must have given him her right first name at any rate. "You continue down the road to the first crossroad—that leads out through Summerhay Farm. There's a gate, but it's easily climbed. You'll pass a hay barn about a mile in from the gate; Hythe Cottage lies about five miles beyond that, on the other side of the spinney." He peered at her over the tiny oval lenses of his spectacles. "It will be quite late by the time you arrive, you know."

Kyra, already groaning inwardly at the thought of another six or seven miles on her smarting right foot, was burningly aware of that fact. "Is there any chance you can rent us horses?" she asked. "Or a horse and gig of some kind?"

Spens leaned forward and breathed in her ear, "Since when do you have any money?"

"Don't make difficulties." She turned back to the priest, who was clasping and unclasping his pale blue-veined hands by the dim glow of the oil lamps on the parlor's little table. "My companion would be glad to pay you, of course."

So much, she thought, for keeping Spens invisible—at least the priest wouldn't be able to describe him later.

Spenson, for whom she hadn't had a civil word since shortly after sundown, merely raised his eyebrows at her and got a furious, urgent look in return.

"My dear child," the priest said, earnestly, "of course if I could do so, I'd be glad to . . ."

Kyra had to close her hand sharply to prevent herself from slapping the man out of sheer irritation. Of *course* there was some problem.

". . . but my sister, who keeps house for me, has taken the gig to visit our mother over at Mickle's Farm. Mother is nearly eighty and has severe rheumatics in her joints. Clariss should be back at any time." He glanced at the heavy blackwood clock, nearly invisible in the shadows that covered the far end of the room like a grimy arras; its ticking had made a thick, subconscious background to their conversation, like the frantic thudding of Kyra's heart. She followed his eyes. It was eight-thirty. *Damn it, damn it, damn it . . .* "I could offer you some supper until she arrives," he added hospitably, and his thin, pale face acquired a little life at the prospect of a good gossip with people he didn't see every day in his village rounds.

"I'm afraid we can't wait," Kyra said. "Thank you very kindly all the same. Come along ... Bill," she added, remembering that above all else she must neither speak Spenson's name where anyone could hear it nor allow to waver the spells that turned people's eyes from his features. "Stupid old fuddy-duddy," she added as soon as they were past the rectory's low hedge and on the road again. "I hope his fool of a sister falls out of the gig and breaks her leg. The least she could have done was put off her visit till another night." In spite of her ability to see in darkness—and the night was moonless, the shadows that overlaid the road intense—she stepped on a round stone that caused a stab of pain like a knife wound in her blistered foot.

Spens caught her elbow and held on to it this time in spite of her effort to wrench free. "We'll get there," he said.

"If you hadn't—" She broke off and limped along in silence for a moment, glad for the touch of his hand on her arm.

"I'm sorry," she said at length. "I couldn't have done any better. And you were good to come with me at all. I've been a harridan all afternoon, haven't I?"

"Unspeakable," he replied imperturbably.

She sighed. "And to think I held your temper against you."

"Oh, when it's something I think is important—a business deal, or my breakfast muffins, or getting you to stay in Angelshand—I get livid if I'm crossed. But I know you're frightened for Alix, as I am. I never loved her, but she's a sweet girl if you can put up with her chatter."

"I told you she only chatters when she's nervous."

"If I made her that nervous, it's well we *didn't* marry." He shifted the empty satchel on his shoulder and looked across at her, peering a little in the cricketshrilling darkness. Though she could see his features clearly, she knew hers were only a moving blur of white to him, and maybe not that much. "When we find them . . . Will you be *able* to fight the death-curse that's on her?"

They walked in silence, leaning a little now on the stout sticks Spenson had cut for them from beech saplings in the course of the afternoon. Kyra's whole body shrank from that thought, the dread of it almost smothering the pain in her foot and the gnawing of hunger in her belly. Above the trees a barn owl shrieked like a madwoman's ghost; fox eyes glinted briefly in the sedgy tangle of the roadside ditch, then vanished. The night air, thick with loam and apple blossoms, seemed to twist with danger, like black silk drawn cuttingly tight around her throat.

"I don't know," Kyra said softly. "Tibbeth was only a dog wizard, but he was one of the most powerful in the city. I've had six years of training at the Citadel, but . . . All the omens, all the readings I was getting before I came here—weak magic would never have caused disruptions like that. And from everything I've studied, the spells of the dead are very strong."

They reached the crossroads and the gate that notched the dark, cold-smelling loom of the surrounding hedge. The splintery bars creaked alarmingly as Spenson helped her over, and she had to summon a tiny seed of blue light, floating in the air above his head, to guide him as he worked the sticks and the satchel through the gate, then clambered after them. To their left lay rough pasturage dotted with trees—Kyra thought she could see a couple of shaggy-coated horses sleeping near the hedge at the top—to their right, behind a fence of withes, there was a meadow where young hay grew rank and thick in the low ground. A nightjar whistled one or two notes, then fell silent. The track between pasture and meadow was rougher than the road had been, potholed and rimmed with stagnant water, and Kyra was glad of the walking stick and the strength of her companion's arm.

"You've studied them. You've come across one?"

She shook her head. "One—one doesn't, you see." She was silent a moment, thinking again about the Citadel's academic isolation, apart from businessmen and matchmakers and families . . . and the clamorings of the heart.

"It's ironic that the Academic wizards, the ones who have the real power, frequently get very little experience, because our vows forbid us to meddle in human affairs. We learn, we study, but . . . apart. Alone. Against each other, in test situations—sometimes in quite dangerous test situations, but very few mages are actually killed in training. Last spring was the only time there's been actual danger at the Citadel in years. I'm told it's the same with the sasenna, the sworn warriors, in times of peace. It's the dog wizards who encounter the . . . the randomness, the peril, of actual events."

"And it's the dog wizards who cause all the trouble," Spenson said quietly.

There was a dry anger in his voice, and Kyra glanced quickly over at him. Of course, she thought. His ships had been in port eighteen months earlier, when an unscrupulous wizard had summoned a storm that had wrecked three-quarters of the Saarieque trading fleet so his patron's ships might scoop the market when they finally came in. Merrivale had written her that her father had lost thousands of crowns' worth of investments; Spenson would have lost not only money but crewmen whom he knew in that all-encompassing ruin. It was scarcely surprising that her father had been able to find other businessmen ready to follow his lead in persecuting Pinktrees and the Pilgrim. Little wonder that her father had worked so hard to get his friends—and the family of his prospective son-in-law—to forget Kyra's very existence. That Spenson had not shunned her on sight, as her father did, was a testimony in itself to his tolerance that made her ashamed of her own first judgment of him.

"It isn't ... it isn't magic itself, you know." Anyone else, she thought, and she would have sprung hotly to the defense of her art—or she would have a few weeks ago. "Most of the wizards I know are good people," she went on hesitantly, "powerful and dedicated to their art. It isn't even the dog wizards, really. I mean, Hestie Pinktrees is the sweetest woman you could meet."

"Who'll sell a total stranger the means to cause another total stranger to pledge marriage to a girl who'll make him miserable for the rest of his life?" Spenson cocked an eyebrow at her. Kyra sighed and scratched uncomfortably at her cropped hair.

"Anything can be turned to evil," Spenson continued after a moment, speaking slowly, as if framing his thoughts with difficulty. "Wealth, law, magic—the longing to please God ..."

"Love," Kyra said softly, remembering the yellow moonlight in Alix's open, dreaming eyes.

"Love is the worst." Spenson's hand reached out to hers, thick fingers closing around thin, cold bone. "Because it's so difficult to tell whether one is doing evil or good."

"There's the barn." Kyra stopped and pointed to the ramshackle structure, barely to be seen among the trees on the rising ground above the meadow. "That means the house can't be—"

She froze in her tracks as a drift of magic came to her, a waft of the strange, vibrant knowledge of illusion being worked ... and under the illusion, suddenly, the jingle of bridle bits and the rattle of crossbow bolts, the smell of horses and of men. An instant later, from the dark behind the barn, a mounted shape appeared, and a man's voice called out, "Halt in the name of the Inquisition and the Witchfinder of Angelshand!"

Kyra looked around desperately. From the concealing trees a line of riders filed, black-clothed Church sasenna and gray-coated Witchfinders, and with them, one red-robed young man with a shaven head whose gaze, she knew, penetrated both darkness and any illusion she cared to fling. "Cover your face!" she gasped, and Spenson pulled up his loosened neck cloth, wrapping the lower part of his face so that only his eyes were visible. "Tibbeth's wife must have ridden with them. If Tibbeth is in her, he can track his own curse."

"How many hasur?" he asked, catching her arm again and drawing so close to her that their shoulders touched. His eyes were as used to darkness as ordinary eyes ever got; she could see him peering in the direction of the oncoming riders.

"Just one—in the robe. Can you see him?"

"No, just shapes. Can you put an illusion on me so that I look like you?"

"What? He'll see through that."

"The others won't. Make yourself look like me, and when the fighting starts, dive for the bushes." They were retreating already in the direction of a stand of laurel on the other side of the pasture ditch. "Can you summon a horse if I free one of theirs? Some of them will have to dismount to arrest us."

"If not, I can summon one of those at the top of the pasture. Spens," she whispered, even as she began the spell of illusion.

"Put some distance between us." He hefted his stick, his craggy face grim but his eyes, in the overcast darkness, bright with the peculiar glee of a born fighter.

"Spenson, no; they're armed."

"Use magic if you have to, to get free and save Alix, but not till it's desperate. Now do what I say and get ready to dive." A sudden, ghostly glare of witchlight flared into being over their heads, half blinding them and illuminating them for the advancing sasenna. The warriors dismounted: three men and two women, middle-aged but lean as wolves, with the oddly youthful faces of those who had been without responsibility for years, since they had made the final decision of their lives and had sworn their vows to be the weapons of the Church. Their black clothing was marked with the many-handed red sun of the Sole God. Two of them carried crossbows; the other three, swords. All wore pistols in their belts.

Spenson hesitated visibly, then tossed his stick to the ground some three feet away from him.

The sasenna came forward, the hasu at their heels.

He waited until they were close enough to touch him before he swung at the nearest with the satchel he'd carried in his other hand, almost concealed against his side. The flying mass of leather and buckles caught the man across the face, staggering him back for a fraction of a second; Spenson wrenched the pistol from the man's belt and shoved past him to smash the butt across the hasu's temple with all the force of his arm. Kyra dove for the laurel bushes, her heart frozen with terror. She heard someone cry out and smelled blood but dared not raise her face from the leaves on the thicket floor. The noise of the struggle seemed to go on forever—he couldn't *possibly* break away from five of them!—and it was all she could do to keep her mind on the spells of illusion that surrounded him, the spells that would fade and break once he was out of her vicinity.

A horse whinnied furiously. There was a clatter of hooves, a woman swearing, the slapping wallop of a crossbow firing, and a moment later the hollow boom of a pistol, sulfur mingling with the blood. Other horses thundered away; she whispered the words of illusion and kept her face buried, for she heard the scuffle of clothing and the creak of a sword belt's leather, and then a man's voice said, "Your honor? Your honor?" Flesh patted softly, hesitantly, upon flesh.

Wrapping herself in illusion, Kyra snaked out of the thicket. One of the sasenna still knelt over the hasu's body. The Church wizard's crimson robe looked black in the starlight, as Alix's gown had in the dark of her room. So did the blood trickling sluggishly from the man's face. Silently, as she had been trained among the High Council's own sasenna, Kyra moved away, thirty, forty feet, not daring to send any but the smallest of illusions to the mind of the kneeling man for fear that the touch of magic would waken the hasu back to consciousness. The hoofbeats had faded into distance, but they could catch Spens and be back at any time.

She thought of the crowsbows and the smell of the blood. There was no trace of Spenson or his pursuers. He had put his life at risk, she thought, to leave open her path back to the Citadel, her path away from him.

Dear God, she thought, don't let him die.

When she was fifty feet away, she reached out with her mind, and the lone sasennan's horse, patiently cropping the roadside grass, flung up its head and wheeled. The sasennan looked up with a cry, but Kyra had already seized the beast's bridle, her heart hammering in panic; she missed the stirrup twice, between native clumsiness and the stiffness from her earlier ride. The man shouted at her, leveling his pistol.

The roar of it was like the clap of doom, but in the moonless dark of the night the ball didn't come anywhere near her. The horse sprang nervously to the side, jerking on the bit; panic alone gave Kyra the agility to spring up, belly over saddle, her feet groping for the stirrups, and she dragged herself upright even as the horse moved off. The sasennan put on a burst of speed and got a divot of sod from the flying hooves in his face for his trouble. Kyra wheeled her mount, put it in the direction of the tiny farmhouse the priest had assured them lay at the end of the road, and galloped for all she was worth.

CHAPTER XIX

DARKNESS LAY UPON HYTHE FARM LIKE THE SHADOW OF the plague. Riding hell-bent for leather up the overgrown cart ruts, Kyra felt the stirring of evil in the air before she ever saw the house: a hot wind swirled briefly around her, causing the horse to shy with such suddenness that Kyra was nearly hurled over its head. As she fought for balance and shortened a rein to keep the beast from bolting, she thought she heard from somewhere, quite close by, the fading sea whisper of a crowd.

She knew better than to try dragging her terrified mount any closer to the house. Her legs gave way again as she sprang down, though their strength came back in less time than before. The horse tried to jerk away, and she pulled the big head down close to hers and stroked the velvet nose. "Stay as close as you may," she whispered, weaving the words with understanding, with a Summons, with the beast's true name. "Come to me when I call."

Released, the horse trotted back down the road a few

yards, but—running already toward the house—Kyra heard it stop and begin to graze.

Please don't let me be too late. Please . . .

Her shoes jarred the uneven roadbed, the blister biting her foot as if she'd trodden on broken glass. In the cold her breath left a feather trail of whiteness, and the sharp air sawed her lungs. But now and then on her cheeks she felt a sticky warmth, as if she had stumbled through a patch of summer noon, and that brought the sweat to her face and lifted the hair of her nape. Somewhere quite close to her she caught a whiff of the rankness of sweaty wool, dirty hair, unwashed humanity—mobbed, packed, thick in some hot open daylight space.

Before her the house crouched lightless, eyeless, and the nightjars and owls that had cried in the manse woods were silent. Only the buzzing of flies sawed at the darkness, and though, looking up, Kyra saw no smoke from the cottage chimneys, still she smelled burning.

The door was locked. "Alix!" Kyra pounded desperately on the thick oak of the planks. "Algeron!" The smoke stench was stronger close to the house, but there was a quality to it of strange distance, as if it came to her from far down a corridor whose end was lost in darkness. Panting, she ran the cottage's length, ducking through a rickety gate to the kitchen yard, but the door, too, was latched fast. It was a tiny place, perhaps four rooms in all, ivy blanketing two walls and invading the braided thatch that overhung the eaves. When she rattled the door handle, she felt for an instant that the brass was burning hot to the touch, so she jerked her hand back in pain; a moment later, as she tested it with the backs of her fingers, it was cold.

Stumbling into the woodpiles and rain barrels and stray pieces of scrap lumber that country houses collected about their walls, she ran back toward the front of the place, testing the heavy windows, wondering if she might drive some piece of wood through the tiny diamonded panes.

Had the image of Tibbeth of Hale not been so branded into her mind, she would never have heard the footfall behind her. Her pounding on the window drowned everything, it seemed to her, but the hammering of her own heart. Later she wasn't sure that it had actually happened, but for one paralyzing second she smelled the acrid pungence of burned, half-rotted flesh—close, almost on top of her—and veered around in time to take four feet of swung plank across her left shoulder instead of on the back of her skull.

For that first second, through a stabbing shock of pain, she could have sworn that the colorless, wild-haired woman attacking her had Tibbeth's face.

Kyra ducked, catching a second blow on her upflung left arm. The wood was being threshed at her with almost superhuman strength; the pain was incredible, taking her breath away. As her instructors in the arts of war had taught her at the Citadel, she dove straight in at the woman—Gyvinna, Merrivale had called her, she thought distractedly; of course it was Gyvinna, she remembered Tibbeth speaking that name now—smothering her next attack and robbing her of the advantage of the plank's length. Gyvinna kicked at her stomach, hard and straight, like a man. Kyra blocked it and twisted aside, her left arm barely responding to the shock of impact, and Gyvinna grabbed with insane strength at her throat.

Kyra's mind had been responding slowly, still balking over the fact that she barely recognized this woman, that she had no quarrel with her. But when those harpy nails dug into the skin of her throat, when the distorted mouth, the eyes bulging with mad hatred, hovered inches from her face, her training took over. She swung her arm up and over Gyvinna's wrists and dropped her full weight like a hammer on top of them, shoulder and body behind the blow. She felt flesh tear from her neck as the other woman's grip broke. The next instant, left hand pushing her right fist for force, she smashed her elbow straight into Gyvinna's nose, slamming her backward. Blood poured down the blond woman's face as she grabbed, snarling, again, but Kyra was taller and in far better training. She caught Gyvinna by the neck and slammed the back of her head as hard as she could into the wall beside them, once, twice, until she heard the plaster crack.

Gyvinna sagged in her grip. Kyra dropped her and ran once more for the front door.

It was open. The woman must have been in the house, heard her, and come out.

Smoke filled the house, so thick that Kyra's mageborn eyes could not pierce it, and she stumbled over a footstool and banged her shins on some unknowable article of furniture on her way through the dark front room, her lungs burning with heat. Flies swarmed, huge, stable flies as long as her thumb, snagging in her hair and crawling on her eyelids; the voices of the crowd were very clear in here, the smell of their filthy clothing, the chanting of the Inquisitors ... even the rank, sewery stink of the river.

She heard no flames, but she knew where the evil was centered and called around her the strongest spells of protection she knew as she groped her way with streaming eyes to the door that had to lead into the bedroom. *Don't let me be too late* ...

Tibbeth was in the room. She knew it.

Moaning, a thin sob; then, desperate, Algeron's voice. "Alix, stay with me! Don't fall asleep ... Don't leave me ... Hold on, Alix ..."

"... hurts ..." Almost unrecognizable, slurred with pain and fever. "Oh, God, hurts ..."

From somewhere Kyra heard a noise that could have been the buzz of a monstrous fly or a whisper of laughter.

"Alix!" she cried. "Algeron! It's me, Kyra."

She summoned light.

It sputtered, fuming and sulfurous, above the bed where they lay, a yellowish glare that died almost instantly, then wavered into being again. Light slithered over Alix's apricot hair, which was hanging disordered nearly to the floor; Algeron's beautiful, sensitive face was twisted with agony as he released one of the ivory shoulders he was holding to clutch, sobbing, at the calf of his leg. White showed all around the gray of his pupil, itself only the thinnest of lines rimming an iris swollen like that of a man drugged. He barely seemed to recognize Kyra as she strode across the little bedroom.

"Fever," he whispered desperately. "Pain. Alix . . ."

He swung around with a gasp, staring into the room's darkest corner, where the armoire loomed. Kyra felt her own eyes dragged there. There wasn't—not quite— anything there.

"Hold on to her!"

He managed to nod, tears of pain streaming from his eyes. Kyra reached across him and ripped Alix's shift open down the front, dragging it over the girl's head. From the darkness in the corner she thought she heard another buzzing, another sound that could have been a thick indrawn breath, a satisfied giggle.

She couldn't be angry, she thought. Anger was the foe of magic, the ruin of concentration.

Her hands were quite steady as she drew chalk from her pocket. She laid the shift on the floor and around it drew the broken Circle of Ingathering, the inside-out star that imprisoned, the long grounding lines and the runes of lightning and water. She felt, as she summoned the essences of those elements, nothing except a cold perfection, a triumphant exactness, precisely as when she had driven her training sword straight through Cylin's guard to the red circle marked above his heart, and knew she had forgotten nothing.

"Hold her, Algeron," she said again, the calm of her own voice astonishing her. "Don't let her slip away."

He whispered, "My legs . . . burning. We're burning up."

She glanced back, making herself not feel anything, half expecting to see genuine flames. Alix, naked among the tangled sheets save for the gold ring on her hand, moved and whispered something neither of them could hear.

"Hold her."

She turned back, facing into the darkness in the corner. Behind her she could hear Algeron's voice murmuring:

"If my love be a song, then you are the harpist's strings,
Were I a purling river, they would find you at the
     springs . . ."

The yellowish witchlight flared again, then dimmed away, and it seemed to Kyra that the armoire was casting a shadow like the shape of a man's shoulders and head.

Hestie Pinktrees had spoken of the magic of hatred, the magic woven of ill. For six years Kyra had been aware of the hatred buried deep in her, a nameless thing dwelling in a well whose cover was secured with chains. Deliberately, chain by chain, Kyra unloosed it, opened the cover, called it forth, and gave it a name, her own name. Like the ancient witches who wove spells with their own hair, their own tears, their own breath, she wove of that hatred a rune of power, surrounding herself in it as in a cloud: the rage of her betrayal, the fury of learning that the hunger of her soul to him had been no more than a blind, a means to an end.

She could see Tibbeth very clearly now, standing in the corner. He looked as he had looked that night in the garden, douce and reasonable in his dark robe, even to the moonlight that seemed to shine out of nowhere on his high, age-spotted forehead.

"My dear Kyra," he said softly. "Aren't you getting just a trifle hysterical about this?"

"You murder my sister and you ask me that?"

He made a little tutting noise through his teeth. "It's her choice, Kyra." Even the soft, high voice was the same. "You weren't there; you wouldn't have understood if you had been. But she said to me one night in the garden . . . She said, 'Before I would have another, I will love you until I die.' She did say that."

"Under your spells!"

He moved a little. She could see, under the hem of his robe, his bare foot, the red and black flesh glistening with charring, the burned bones sticking through. "What are spells, Kyra? I knew you wouldn't understand, not the deeper secrets. Not the love a man can bear for a ripe and innocent girl, not that girl's first, undying love for the man who could lead her, could show her—"

"I know what you wanted to show her!" Kyra nearly spit the words at him. "And I know where you wanted to lead her! I looked into her dreams."

"Oh, tut. A fearful virgin's judgment on something she doesn't even comprehend. How were they different from the dreams that I see now in your eyes that you've dreamed? It's all the same hunger, you know."

"They were different," Kyra said thickly, "because I am twenty-four and she was twelve. Because I chose and you had to put runes of lust and filth all over her nightdresses to get her dreams to reflect your longings."

"Kyra, Kyra," he chided, and stirred again in the shadows. The stench of his burned flesh came off his robes. A fuzzy black fly crawled along the curve of his head; another one struck Kyra from behind, tangling in her cropped hair, but she did not take her eyes from the man before her.

"That's your family's prejudices speaking, you know,"

he said. "Your father's morbid respectability, his terror of what others might think of the slightest deviation from what they consider normal, your mother's fear of her own body. When a man finds gold, of course he sponges the dirt off it so that it will shine. But if you will have it so, if you will take it upon yourself, like all your family, to dictate even the thoughts of those around you, I will let her free. I had thought better of you, but I bear you no ill will."

"But I bear it to you!" Kyra raised her arm and summoned to herself all the power of the lines she had drawn, all the strength of the lightning that burned unseen in the air, all the deep serenity of the earth and the passion of the sea. "And I will not let you go, to return to her again when I'm far away. Thus I conjure you to enter this circle, to be one with the runes you have drawn on that cloth. I bind you to them, that they compass you about, so that you cannot stir from them ever again."

In the darkness of his corner the ghost began to laugh. It was a thin, flickering sound like the squeaking of wind, through which Tibbeth's real voice appeared only in flashes, as color appeared in changeable silk. It was echoed behind her by a thick, guttural bubbling from the door.

As Kyra swung around, pain arrowed through her legs, the searing burn of fire, though when she struck at them, there was no fire to be seen. This only came glancing through her mind, for at the same instant Algeron cried out, leaping to his feet as the woman Gyvinna rushed through the door, a rusted scythe upraised in her hands and broad ribbons of blood flowing down her mouth and chin.

Kyra fell back, clamping her mind down on the spells of protection that guarded her and Alix from the worst of the dead man's malice; on the bed Alix sobbed with agony, clutching at her calves and thighs among the tangled sheets, and the pain of flameless fire seared again through Kyra's legs as well. In the doorway Algeron seized the haft of the scythe, struggling to wrest it from Gyvinna's grip. But the woman was strong. She thrust him aside and slashed at Kyra, the filthy metal missing her neck but opening a gash in her forearm and hand as she dodged, and with the heat of the blood and the shock of the pain came another blaze of anguish in her legs as her concentration cracked. The smell of smoke was thick in the room: the heat of a summer afternoon, the stench and fevered mutter of the crowd. Algeron caught the madwoman from behind, gasping as she writhed in his grip to knee at his groin and, when that failed, bite at his hands and arms. Her face was barely human, running with blood out of which two pale eyes stared like an animal's; perhaps it was that which allowed him, when he wrenched the scythe from her grip, to strike her with all his force across the side of the head.

He would never, Kyra thought obliquely, with the detached part of her mind not given entirely over to the spells she held about them, have struck something that he considered a woman.

Gyvinna collapsed to the floor. For a moment the only sound in the room was her sobbing breath.

Then Alix moaned. Standing above Gyvinna, the scythe in his hands, Algeron threw an anguished look back at the bed but held his ground.

When Tibbeth spoke again, his voice came out of Gyvinna's dripping mouth. "I am your master, Kyra. The magic in your mind is my magic. You can't fight me."

"My magic is my own," Kyra said softly. "I am my own. I cast you out. You are none of me, and I none of you." She turned back to face the corner and saw that Tibbeth's dark robe was gone, his legs and thighs a charred and blackening mess, dripping yellowish fluid that seemed to puddle about him on the scrubbed oak planking of the floor. Flies swarmed about it as they whined through the darkness over Alix's bed.

Shakily, Kyra repeated the words of the conjuration, bending her will upon Tibbeth, drawing him toward the rune-written shift that lay in the magic circle's center. She heard Alix cry out, striking with feeble agony at the flies that crawled over her naked flesh, felt renewed pain flash through her own legs, charring sinew and muscle while her mind was still alive to feel. The smell of smoke filled her throat, burned her eyes; she was certain that beneath her borrowed breeches the skin was blackening, blistering, sloughing away. He had felt that, she thought, and had kept his mind focused on the magic of his hate. She could do no less.

For the first time she felt Tibbeth's will give, felt it writhe and twist like a monstrous fish when it felt the hook.

Alix screamed. Behind her Kyra heard a faint sob, and a woman's voice, thick with blood and hurt, whispered, "Tibbeth?"

By his breathing she could tell that Algeron was still there as well; by his breathing also, she knew he was in terrible pain. "He's using you, Gyvinna," Kyra said softly, her voice stammering slowly over the words, forcing them out around the strain of concentration. "He's using your mind to channel his own. As he used your hands, your body, as a tool of his revenge."

There was silence, then another thick, broken sob. The pain grew less, and she felt Tibbeth's spirit jerk against her will. Glancing behind her, she saw the laundrywoman's face ghastly in the yellowish blear of the witchlight, the pale eyes blinking rapidly, trying to remember, or fighting the overwhelming urge to sleep again.

"I don't . . ." Gyvinna whispered. "I'd just close my eyes, and he'd be with me again."

"To use you."

"No . . . Yes." The woman sat up a little, her head

rolling, the bloodied hair leaving stripes on the lead-hued cheeks beneath. From the tail of her eye Kyra saw Algeron, still standing between Gyvinna and the bed, his eyes staring, fighting to keep from doubling over with pain.

Gyvinna sniffled and wiped her bleeding nose with the back of her wrist. "And why not? It wasn't true, what they said of him. About Miss Alix. It was me he loved, so why ... why shouldn't I be with him, whatever way he wants? He loved me ..." Her eyes slid closed.

Algeron's breath scaled into a short, shallow sob, and his knees buckled; Alix whispered something about fire, and her hands threshed helplessly at the swarming flies. The pain in Kyra's legs redoubled, sweat pouring down her face, her body shaking as part of her mind drew back from the spells of conjuration to fight the physical shock that would soon render her unconscious. She was aware of the blood running down her gashed arm, of the flies swarming over the raw, ragged flesh.

"He loved you when you were a little girl," she said quietly. "*Because* you were a little girl. He loved you because you were helpless, and pretty, and in his power. As he loved Alix ... and probably others besides."

Gyvinna's china-blue eyes flared open again. The worn face, prematurely lined, showed suddenly how young she really was. "That's a lie!" she sobbed. "A dirty lie! A man's first true love ... What does age matter? A girl can be a woman ..."

"How old were you," Kyra pressed, "when first he came to you?" Her lungs were burning, as if the air she breathed were nothing but scalding smoke. She felt the skin of her face, her hands, sear and crinkle, felt fire lancing through the cut on her arm, the blistering weakness of her legs. "Did he call you in dreams as he called my sister?"

"You're making that up!"

The pain lessened. Kyra gasped, her chest hurting as

if a sword blade had been driven through her lungs; she had to fight for the breath to speak. "Then why is he taking revenge on Alix? Why is it *her* wedding night that woke his ghost to murder, and nothing to do with me? Why did he call you to write the death-marks on *her* wedding clothes?"

The woman only stared at her with huge, protesting eyes, panic and pain turning her face blank. A renewed spasm of torment swept Kyra's flesh; Algeron tried to get to his knees, tried to lift the scythe but collapsed, clutching his legs and weeping. Furious, Kyra drove her words like a spear into Gyvinna's consciousness, willing her to understand before they were all consumed. "It wasn't me he hated, Gyvinna, it was Alix! Think about it!" she shouted as Gyvinna turned her face away, her eyes closing again, seeking the comfort of her dream. "Think about it, damn you! Remember what you did! Remember why you came *here*, why you followed the draw of the spells to this place, how you knew to lead the Witchfinders to ambush us. Because he couldn't have her, and he couldn't stand to see her in another man's arms!"

"No . . ." Her voice was barely a whisper. And then, in a scream that ripped the night like a murderer's knife, *"Nooo!"*

"I conjure you!" Kyra screamed in the same instant, swinging back to the darkness of the corner, the darkness of pain and rage, the darkness whose magic was shredding her flesh and mind. "I conjure you to the sigils you have wrought; I bind you and charge you to hold to them."

Gyvinna's screaming scaled upward, louder and louder, as if with the sound she was vomiting forth all the memories of what she had willed herself not to suspect about the man she had loved. And with those screams Kyra saw the shadow in the corner shrink and change, dwindling in size as the pain in her own flesh became transparent, revealed as illusion and not reality.

The pain in her heart remained, a core of blackness intensifying, seeming to shrink in upon itself and to grow at the same time—rage, grief, and torture, hurting her as she had tried to forget that she could be hurt.

She was barely conscious when she saw the thing come crawling out of the shadows at last, a thing like a twisted insect the size of her hand. Her will drew it to the broken Circle of Ingathering; when she saw it crawl over her sister's torn chemise, the sight set her teeth on edge, as if it were groping at her own flesh with its dirty, fingerlike feet. But her teachers in the Citadel had taught her well. She kept her mind focused on the spells of power and mastery as she closed the circle with fingers trembling so badly that they could barely hold the chalk.

Behind her, Gyvinna was moaning brokenly. No sound at all came from the bed. The flies had gone. The darkness in the room cleared slowly, yielding to the witchlight that gradually brightened from yellow to white, like a softly shining candle. There was nothing in Kyra's consciousness but the building core of pain in her breast: no triumph, no joy, no relief.

Within the circle the shift burst into flame. The filthy clot of shadow that had crawled upon it wriggled a little in the fire, then was gone. A few minutes later Kyra began to cry, the black core within her cracking open, the pain running away, first thick as ebony syrup, then thinning, until at last it seemed to her that it was only the water of her tears.

Chapter XX

THE SMELL OF BACON WOKE KYRA, AND THAT OF COFFEE. By the slant and color of the light, it was early afternoon.

She lay on an old-fashioned wooden settee by a cold fireplace in a completely unfamiliar room. Quilts were piled beneath and around her in an inadequate attempt to mitigate the settee's hardness. Her body ached as if she'd been beaten with a plank.

She *had*, now that she recalled it, been beaten with a plank. When she moved, huge bruises made themselves felt on her back and arms beneath her ragged and soiled linen shirt. Her right arm was bound with rough bandages, the flesh beneath shrieking with pain. Her back and legs ached ... Burns ... She recalled the pain of fire.

Her hand flew to the back of her neck to encounter the angry flame of sunburn. Hesitantly, she brought her hands down to touch her calves and thighs beneath the quilts. The sunburn was the only burn on her body, though she felt stripped and scorched inside.

322

Slowly she looked around. The room where she lay was a large one, sparely and simply furnished: two settees by a wide brick hearth, a big table beneath the windows, spread with a cloth of tatted lace. The walls were plaster the color of clotted cream, mottled with old leaks and discolorations. The ceiling beams were black with decades of soot. Around the small panes of the half-open casement windows, ivy hung like a street urchin's untrimmed hair, the light shining through the new leaves so that they seemed to glow of themselves. The smell of trees drifted in, and the clucking of a nearby stream. A robin warbled in the hedge.

A lot of quilts, blankets, and pillows were heaped along the walls. She remembered, as out of the depths of a half-obscured dream, helping Algeron carry Alix from the bedroom.

Shaken, exhausted, and broken as she had been last night, she had still had that much sense. She half raised herself on her left elbow—it hurt excruciatingly, but her bandaged right arm was worse—and saw that the door that led into the bedroom was shut. That chamber would probably be unfit for anyone to sleep in ever again.

She wondered if poor widow Summerhay would charge them for damages.

In the kitchen a cup clinked on a saucer, a tin pan rattled against a metal stove top, and she heard Spenson say, "Even without cinnamon to put on them, I'd say these are the best I've ever eaten."

Algeron was explaining how honey and cider could be used in the making of sweet rolls when Kyra, wrapped in a faded quilt, limped through the kitchen door. Happiness and relief flooded his face like spring sunlight when the clouds rolled away, replaced immediately by such shocked concern that Kyra wondered what the hell she looked like. Spens, who'd been sitting with his back to the door, a plateful of bacon and rolls before him, was turning even as he rose to his feet. He caught her, quilt and all, in the arm that didn't have a sling on it and drew her into a hard, coffee-flavored kiss.

In spite of the care both of them took for their own and each other's bruises, the ensuing embrace was quite painful. Neither cared.

"God, I thought I'd never see you alive again!"

"I was terrified for you; did they hurt you badly?" She drew off a little, touched the sling, and began reviewing spells of healing in her mind. Not, she thought, that she'd have the strength to so much as charm warts for days.

Spens grinned. The kitchen had broad windows in its planked walls and a divided door whose open top half afforded a view of the overgrown farmyard and the vine-covered well. Sunlight flooded the room, making his eyes bright as blue tourmaline.

"The crossbow bolt just nicked my thigh, which was damned good shooting in the dark. It did more harm to the horse, and not much of that. I got this—" He indicated his disabled right arm with his left. "—in the woods when the stupid beast blundered into a tree. But you . . ."

He cupped her cheek with his hand and looked worriedly into her face.

She whispered, "You risked your life."

"Without you I wouldn't have wanted it."

She shook her head. "You risked it so I wouldn't be caught. So I could go back to the Citadel."

He grinned a little. "I never said I was a good businessman. When I last saw them, the Inquisitors were following a false trail south like somebody in Kymil was selling tea at a penny a pound; I sent that hasu and his guard after them about an hour ago."

"Kyra!" A pale and haggard-looking Alix appeared in the open half of the divided kitchen door. She pushed open the lower half and hurried in, in passing setting on the table the small basket of eggs she carried and the tin pail of milk. "Oh, Kyra, are you all right? I dreamed . . ." After a swift embrace she drew back, looking at her sister with the same worried expression Spens had. "Your hair! Why did you—"

"It's a long story," Kyra said.

Alix was wearing a simple brown dress over a coarse chemise clearly obtained from some old linen chest in the cottage's attic. Her fair hair was braided and wound coronetwise about her head, and her eyes were blue-smudged with fatigue. Algeron guided her gently to one of the several bent beechwood chairs that surrounded the kitchen's painted table; even the short walk to the neighboring farm for milk and eggs seemed to have exhausted her.

"Kyra, what happened?" she asked softly, putting her hands over her older sister's as Kyra, too, sat. "I dreamed . . . ugly things. Evil things. There was something about Tibbeth, your old teacher . . . I felt frightened. I kept wanting to run away, down the road into the dark, but Algeron held on to me and kept telling me I shouldn't run, that he'd protect me."

"And he did protect you," Kyra said softly, glancing up at the fair young man who stood behind her chair. The cook blushed hotly and looked away, but Alix's hand stole up to where his rested on her shoulder.

"I think I must have had a fever," Alix said after a moment, her brows drawing down into a frown. "I felt so tired this morning, drained. And then . . ." She looked across at Spenson, who had just returned from the stove with two enameled tin cups of coffee, and color flooded to her pale cheeks.

"Oh, Master Spenson, I'm so sorry," she whispered. She rose, taking half a step toward him and extending her hand. "So terribly, terribly sorry . . ."

He put one of the coffee mugs into her grip, something she clearly did not expect. As she stared blankly at it, he asked, "Sorry you didn't saddle me with the pain of eternally wondering why my wife doesn't love me?"

She colored even more deeply; he raised a warning finger and said, "Now, don't burst into tears. I've already been through this with Algeron ... who makes better sweet rolls than my cook, I might add. If you weren't going to go make your fortunes in Kymil, I'd think about hiring him myself."

Kyra dug a chunk of butter wrapped in oak leaves from the egg basket and smeared a lavish quantity on one of the aforesaid rolls. "I'm afraid that now he's married to Alix, you couldn't do that without raising a tremendous scandal. But you're quite right."

"As a matter of fact," Spens said, guiding Alix back into her chair, "I'd begun to think about other plans myself."

Kyra didn't see Alix's startled glance pass from her sister to her former affianced groom; she was far too busy pouring honey over a second roll.

Alix carefully ladled a little milk off the top of the pail to put in her coffee, then took a sip. "What I really don't understand is what 'Vinna the laundry maid was doing here. And what happened to her? The poor thing looks like she was set on by robbers."

Kyra set down her roll. She remembered thinking, when she'd risen from the settee in the other room, that the figure half-invisible under the quilts on the other settee had been Alix. "I'll see to her," she said softly.

Gyvinna was standing in the outer doorway when Kyra entered the sitting room, starting out into the ivy-dappled sun of the porch. She didn't look around, only held the quilt closer about her shoulders, and bowed her head with the resignation of one who had all her life submitted to the will of others. Someone had wiped her face, though her nose was swollen grotesquely and both her eyes were blackened. Brown blood still streaked her colorless hair.

Kyra said softly, "I am so sorry."

Gyvinna only shook her head.

"What will you do now?" Kyra came around to stand beside her in the sunlight of the door. Try as she would, she could remember very little of what the woman had looked like six years ago. She was like Cousin Plennin, ordinary to the point of invisibility, especially, Kyra reflected bitterly, to one who habitually ignored servants and paid scent attention to those who had no immediate bearing on whatever matter lay at hand.

"I realize I should have sought you out and asked you that six years ago," she continued quietly. "I'm humiliated to say I never thought of it."

"No." The laundrywoman's voice was a gluey, nasal drone. She turned to look at her, and there was no malice, no anger, only resigned and hopeless weariness in the blackened, tear-reddened eyes. "No. Nobody did. Not my family, neither. They'd been scandalized, Tibbeth marrying me so young. Thirteen, I was. And even before that he'd . . . Well, I knew he was fond of little girls. But he said I was special, you see. His only one." She raised one broken-nailed, work-worn hand to pick at the blood in her hair, concentrating on it as if it were far more important than what she said or the woman who, last night, she had tried to kill.

"In a way I did know. But I didn't want to. And if I just closed my eyes and . . . and let my mind sort of drift, I didn't have to know."

How easy it would have been, Kyra thought with a sudden rush of disgust, for him to mark her garments, her bed sheets, the doorsills of the kitchen over which she daily passed, with the sigils that would make her love him, believe him, and turn a blind eye to all that he did. The full foulness of the magic the man used came to her like the taste of bile, the perversion of the art, the joy, the splendor of the magic that was her own life. No wonder there were laws against it.

On the other hand, she thought with a sudden rush of

sympathetic pain, it was equally possible that he had needed no magic to make this poor woman love him.

"It's hard to explain how it was with Tibbeth." Gyvinna's voice was barely audible, and she did not raise her eyes, or cease picking at her hair. "He made me *feel* I was special. Not just . . . not just then, when I was little, but even after we was married, every day of my life."

The clotted voice was wistful. Kyra closed her eyes. Now even that was gone from her. To take from her the memory of that love's specialness had been an act of cruelty, no matter how desperately required. As for Kyra, she no longer felt the swollen core of rage inside her, but it had left an empty space, a hollow where the echo of the pain drifted now and then like wind down an alleyway vacant of life.

Gyvinna raised her head, looking sidelong at the woman beside her—her husband's prize pupil, the rich daughter of rich parents, the woman who had consigned to the flames the only thing she had loved in her life. "I was jealous of you, you know," she said simply. "Of the time he spent teaching you. But I knew even then he . . . there was things in his life that I wasn't a part of. But as long as he'd come home to me at night, that was all I cared for. And after he was gone, when his voice came whispering at me in dreams . . ."

She shook her head warily, wiping a cautious hand under her swollen nose. In her voice was the resignation of a woman who had finally faced what she had known in her dreams to be long true. "I know he was magic. I knew when he formed up beside me in the bed that . . . that there was some ill being done. I know he shouldn't have done what he did. I truly do. I knew it last night. I think maybe I knowed all along he wasn't . . . wasn't good. But I'll miss him. Like I've missed him every day of my life."

"What did happen?"

"You don't remember any of it?"

Alix shook her head and picked a daisy from the grass of the stream bank where Kyra had found her, in the dappled shade of one of the old farm's apple trees. The priest had been right. Even half in desolation, the little cottage with its thatched roof and ivied walls was beautiful, restful beside its clucking stream. A pity, Kyra thought, that it would be haunted now. She would have to warn the widow Summerhay lest others try to spend the night in that room.

From the direction of the house came the soft noises of packing, Spenson and Algeron assembling the young couple's few effects preparatory to their departure for Kymil immediately after lunch. The bedroom had proved to contain no signs of last night's events save a burned spot on the floor within the chalked Circle of Ingathering and hundreds of dead flies.

"Only that I was afraid," the girl said softly. "And that Algeron was there." She regarded her sister with grave, apologetic eyes. "He really is competent with pastries and cream, you know; I don't think there will be any problem of him finding work. I mean, I know he made a botch of Master Milpott's accounts, but I'm certainly not going to let him run his own business, so we should do well."

Kyra laughed at Alix's matter-of-factness. "I daresay, and he may even make a name for himself with his poems one day. That was a stroke of genius, by the way, getting the money from Lady Earthwygg."

Alix giggled, which drove the wanness from her face and made her look more like herself. "I did feel guilty about asking for so much, but the way she'd been pushing that hateful Esmin at Master Spenson, I felt she deserved it."

"More than you know." Kyra grinned. "You do know, by the way, that if you open a dressmaker's shop, you're going to have to deal with a steady parade of the Esmins of the world."

"Oh, yes." Alix nodded. "But I'll just do as Hylette

does and charge them an annoyance tariff. Hylette also charges what she calls the surcharge of horror if some girl comes to her with a design she thinks is dreadful, but I think that's unfair."

"Ah," Kyra said. "So that's why she always charged so much to make up my dresses."

"She was just jealous," Alix said quickly. "Because your designs were so much more original than hers. And in any case," the younger girl went on, lowering her eyes and gently stroking the daisy's white petals, "if I'd ... done what Father wanted ... I'd have had to deal with all the Esmins of the world anyway, you know, and not gotten paid for it." She raised her eyes, and Kyra saw that they were filled with tears again. "Is Father very angry?" Her voice was barely a whisper.

"Have you ever known him not to be when his will was thwarted?"

The trembling of Alix's mouth tweaked into a hasty attempt to cover a grin, but a tear slipped down her cheek nevertheless. "It's just that ... well, Master Spenson is right." She glanced back in the direction of the barn. Algeron was hitching a nice-looking pair of gray ponies to a two-wheeled red gig. "You see, after that awful scene in the church, I went to ... to talk to Algeron. And it was *just* to talk. We must have fallen asleep. And when we woke up ..."

"I know what happened," Kyra said softly, and Alix blushed. More quietly still, Kyra added, "And I understand, God help me," causing her sister to look up with a quick, inquiring look of surprise.

Alix opened her mouth to ask, but Kyra shook her head, and after a moment the younger girl said, "How did you find us?"

Kyra's grin returned. "What do you think I've been doing for six years in wizards school? Learning to pull doves out of my sleeves?"

"Will you be going back to your school now?" She was looking past Kyra's shoulder, and without turning,

Kyra knew that Spenson must be helping Algeron, one-handed, strap up the baggage. Spenson in his rough brown jacket and appalling red waistcoat, his high boots and shirt open to show the surprisingly soft skin of his neck . . .

She pushed the thought from her mind, though it was some moments before she could speak.

"I have to," she said when at length she could trust her voice to sound casual again. And when Alix opened her mouth to protest, she went on. "With you it was a choice of following your heart, Alix, a choice between something that meant nothing to you and something that meant everything. Magic . . . *is* my heart. Real magic, properly taught. Having started learning what it is, why it is . . . having seen its power last night when I—" She hesitated. "—when I saved you—I couldn't possibly go back to dog wizardry. And besides," she added a little bitterly, "the Inquisition is looking for me in Angelshand. In fact, considering the magic done here last night, I assume they're on their way. So I can't return in any case."

Her throat tightened again, and she fell silent lest her voice shake so that Alix could hear it. Fitting, she thought, that after she had robbed Gyvinna first of her husband, then of the ability to cherish his memory, Gyvinna, by forcing a confrontation with the Witchfinders, had been responsible for cutting off any possibility of Kyra returning to Angelshand with Spenson. Too many images went through her mind: the weight and bulk of his shoulders as she clung to him in the loft above the countinghouse, the surprising softness of his mouth against hers, the splash of heatless sunlight on his sandy hair as they walked through the arcades along the Imperial Prospect to breach Hylette's sacred precincts. But like everything in Kyra's life, these were interspersed with other images: the servants whispering impossible tales of the doings of mages and old Lord Mayor Spenson's tirades against dog wizards over dinner, Gyvinna's blind devotion to the man who'd used her, and the drugged, wanton gleam in the child Alix's eyes. And behind everything else, the cool shape of the Citadel's glimmering towers, silhouetted against the pale northern sky.

"And it's just as well," Kyra said. "It's just as well."

Alix looked surprised. "I thought you loved him. I mean . . . Well, it seems to me . . ."

"I do," Kyra said softly. Spenson was coming toward the stream bank where the two sisters sat, and Kyra got quickly to her feet. "And that's the reason I have to leave. Before I destroy myself and everything I've worked for to take hold of that love."

She turned and headed back to the house, leaving him standing, his hand held out in the brightness of the spring sun.

" 'Don't think too harshly of her.' " Gordam Peldyrin repeated the words as if they had been dipped in tanning liquor before he put them into his mouth. " 'Don't think . . .' She has cost me, first and last, over three thousand crowns, what with the veils, and the jewels, and the garlands—the cost alone of two wedding cakes . . ."

"Gordam," his wife murmured, reaching to touch his rust-colored velvet sleeve. Outside the closed doors of the Red Hare's private parlor, muted voices sounded in the inn's common room as porters came downstairs bearing luggage and guests shared final cups of the inn's famous coffee before the arrival of the Sykerst mail coach from Angelshand.

Peldyrin shook her off as he might have shaken a moth. "She has made a laughingstock of me in front of the town council. She has done *something*—God knows what, for Earthwygg won't tell me—to offend the wife of my patron at Court."

"Now, Gordam, you don't know that for certain. Perdita was perfectly polite when she spoke to me."

"And if Spenson hadn't been so obliging as to ante-date his repudiation of the contract, we might easily have been sued by the Lord Mayor himself! He was certainly threatening it. And you say don't think too harshly of her."

Binnie turned to her silent daughter. "Is she all right? Did she look well?"

Kyra nodded. She suspected that at least a part of her father's irritation had to do with her own appearance, robed once more in the faded black of a Council mage. It was a reminder not only of her own betrayal and desertion but of the insult that whatever current explanations he had to make to the Inquisition regarding his elder daughter added to the injury of the younger's defection.

She bit back the sarcasm of her reply to him. He had lost a daughter he cherished and all the hope of an alliance with some powerful merchant house. His anger, she realized, stemmed from considerable pain.

To her mother she said, "She looked radiant." It was a politic lie, avoiding the whole topic of the curse, which, she knew, would only hurt and enrage her father more and make her mother anxious. Besides, she knew from the Underhythe priest that when Alix and Algeron had taken hands before the shabby little altar of St. Ploo, Alix *had* looked radiant, filled with the dizzy joy of allowing herself at last to follow her heart.

Which was fine, Kyra reflected wryly, if one was that certain about which way one's heart was going.

She swatted the image of Spenson as if it had been a bug on the wall and swept it under some mental rug. An entire night's practice at this exercise—on the average of once every five minutes throughout the sleepless course of the darkness—hadn't made it any easier. When Spenson had taken the inbound mail coach back to Angelshand yesterday, she had wanted simply to take the outbound one to the Sykerst, to the village of Lastower whence she could walk to the Valley of Shadows herself, to get away from the crowds and stenches and unclear issues of Angelshand, away from this small green countryside, from all reminder of what she was leaving.

She had to return to college. In the scurying-stone the previous night Lady Rosamund had told her of furious interviews with the Witchfinders, of arguments concerning just what sort of magic *had* been worked at Summerhay Cottage. It was more than clear to her that she could not go back to Angelshand. Spenson had his father, stubborn, bitter, and masterful, had the business of which he was sole heir, had the responsibilities for which he'd given up the sea. It was he, indeed, who had reminded her of hers. "I'll send them out to you here," he'd said yesterday afternoon, in this same parlor after a strained interview that had taken all her willpower. "What they have to hear, they can't very well hear from me, you know."

No, she agreed silently. They couldn't very well hear of Alix's marriage and the final ruin of the House Spenson alliance from the rejected bridegroom. But the thought of confronting her father again had made her jaws ache in the dark interstices of last night when she hadn't been thinking about Spens.

With a slight tremor in her voice she went on. "Mother, you know Alix. She told me in confidence where she got the money to start up a dressmaker's shop in Kymil, so I can't tell you—"

"A dressmaker!" her father groaned.

"—but I can say it wasn't anything shameful, and it was, in fact, very clever."

"Wasn't shameful!" Peldyrin's thin mouth tightened to a line like a black string. "The mere fact that after her upbringing she's gone to fetching and carrying for women who should be her social equals is shameful!"

"Oh, nonsense, Gordam." To Kyra's unending astonishment, her mother rounded briskly on the fulminating paterfamilias. "You know Alix always loved to design her dresses, and she did a far nicer job of embroidery than Hylette ever did. Personally," she said, turning back to Kyra, "I think it's a great shame that she couldn't open a shop in Angelshand, because I think she'd beat that overbearing Hylette all hollow. But I can see," she added hastily, seeing her husband begin to exhibit signs of imminent seizure, "that it wouldn't do."

Movement in the courtyard outside made her glance out the window. The huge mail coach, bright red paint and brass fixtures gleaming under a liberal coating of mud, had come clattering into the inn yard. Hostlers hurried from the stables to take the bridles of the six sweating horses. Ordinarily, Kyra would have made the journey to Lastower—and the Citadel beyond—as she had made it that first time, afoot. But after the conference with Lady Rosamund, it had been agreed that speed was the safer course. Once Kyra was safe in the Citadel, negotiations with the Inquisition could proceed more calmly over the fact that, however much she had used her magic last night, she hadn't used it against another human being.

In the bright sun of the inn yard the blue-coated coachman clambered down from his high seat, while passengers climbed stiffly out and inn servants began tossing down and sorting luggage from the roof and the basket behind.

"And there's your coach." Binnie Peldyrin stepped forward and embraced her tall daughter; for the first time, Kyra felt no awkwardness in returning the embrace. If nothing else, she thought in the moment before she shoved the memory aside, Spens had taught her how to hug.

"Father?"

She turned to him. Sullen anger still gleamed in his eyes. He was a man, she realized, who would see all that he had striven to attain destined to pass to a mere nephew—and one whom he despised, at that—a man who had been cheated of his dreams of dynasty. Though he hadn't realized yet that he'd been asking his daughters to give up their dreams for the fulfillment of his—it might be years before that thought occurred to him, if it ever did—he was still furious and hurt.

Grudgingly, he held out his hand to her. "A safe journey to you."

She brushed the hand aside and took him in her arms. For one moment he stiffened as if she'd been one of the ladies at the Cheevy Street Baths. Then, with a strange little movement of his shoulders and back, he seemed to put aside his anger, remembering not the outrageous and outraging teenager who had so wantonly disrupted his plans but the bright-gowned, bright-eyed little girl he'd used to hug.

They embraced with the elbow-bumping awkwardness of two scarecrows kissing. Then he pulled on his fur-collared mantle as if it had personally affronted him and strode imperiously from the room.

Binnie smiled up at her daughter. "Brittany Nemors will know where Alix sets up her shop; Brittany went to school with me. She knows all the new dressmakers." They passed through the common room, where a very stout man and a thin woman were gathering several noisy and uncomfortably dressed offspring around a fortress of baggage. The largest of the girls was singing tunelessly about the personal habits of her next-younger sibling; the smallest boy was crying. Kyra shut her eyes in horrified anticipation, realizing that these were to be her fellow passengers for perhaps as much as ten days and nights of constant company.

At her elbow, her mother's voice pattered cheerfully on. "Mark my words, dearest. Before Alix bears her first son, your father will be so sick of Cousin Wyrdlees that he'll take that nice boy Algeron into the family business; corn factoring can't be so very different from baking."

Kyra rolled her eyes.

"And in any case, you know that he'll want to raise

up his grandson to inherit. It'll all work out. These things do."

Kyra looked down at her as they stepped into the muddy yard. It had rained last night—she could have told to the minute when it had begun and when it had ceased—and the wheels of the coach were clotted thick with mud, the morning air filled with the high, damp warmth of the coming summer. The coach itself looked very gay; all the government mail coaches had been newly painted the previous summer to celebrate the birth of the Regent's heir.

Hostlers were leading out her parents' gig and team, with Sam sitting up already on the coachman's seat. Her father climbed impatiently in and settled the lap robe about his bony knees, for all the world like an affronted tomcat washing itself in a corner. Other grooms were hitching the fresh team to the mail coach, massive horses shining like new coppers, twitching their haunches and flicking their docked tails at the flies.

"Do write me. I know your father will take a little time to come around to that, too . . . But it was good to see you again."

Binnie stood on tiptoe to kiss her one last time; Kyra hugged her again, pushing aside the start of fresh tears, and picked up the carpetbag she'd left by the inn's door. As she watched her mother pick her way across the muddy yard, her mind was already occupied with the journey ahead: ten ghastly days through the deeper and ever-deeper mud of the Sykerst's abominable roads, two nights at most of decent inns followed by a succession of straw-covered plank beds in post houses—thank God most people refused to share beds with wizards! Black bread and hard cheese and smoke-flavored tea with honey and listening to endless chatter about childbirth and illnesses and love affairs from the women on the coach, interspersed with inaccurate and maddening questions about magic.

The coachman was calling, "Board up! Board up!"

It occurred to her belatedly that she should have written a note for her parents to take to Spens. But, her throat tightening again, she knew there was nothing she could have said.

He had his life. She had hers. The mere fact that the Inquisition would make it impossible for her to return to Angelshand for months, perhaps years, told her how futile was any thought of being with him.

She'd have to ask Lady Rosamund if there was some kind of unlove potion, some counterspell for the heart. She certainly couldn't continue to go through the kind of pain she'd been in last night. "I suppose I should have done all that when I was sixteen, as Alix did," she sighed to herself. "Measles are worse when you get them as an adult, too."

She swung her carpetbag up to the footman on top of the coach, missed her distance, stepped back to avoid having the heavy bag come crashing down on her head, stepped on the hem of her robe, and would have collapsed back into the mud if someone hadn't come around the side of the coach at that moment and caught her in one strong arm.

"I thought it was just because of all those silly petticoats women wear," Spenson said, righting her and taking the bag. His right arm was still in a sling—sprained rather than broken, she had ascertained—but he moved with all his old buoyant lightness. His neck cloth certainly looked as if he'd tied it with one hand.

Behind them, the stout man in the red coat handed child after child up into the coach. Kyra replied, "Nonsense, you should have seen me before I learned to manage petticoats," but her heart was hammering so painfully in her ribs that she could barely think. The part of her not singing with delight at the sight of him throbbed with a bitter ache, wondering why he had come to renew the pain yet again. More awkwardly, she said, "I didn't know you'd come out with Father."

"I didn't." He tossed her satchel to the waiting hands

on top of the coach and handed her in, climbing up after her and wedging himself between her and the two oldest girls, who had already embarked on what promised to be a week of pinches and hair pulling. "And believe me, the only thing that I can think of worse than riding half a day from Angelshand with the parents of my erstwhile bride is what *did* greet me in the courtyard of my house when I returned there last night."

Kyra stared at him blankly. The hasu who had ridden with the Witchfinders returned to her mind, the ability of a mage to see through darkness and illusion. Good God, he wasn't a fugitive himself because of her . . . ! "Not the Witchfinders?"

"Worse," Spens said darkly, but there was a sparkle in his eyes. The coachman cracked his long whip. The Sykerst mail jolted forward, nearly pitching Kyra, Spens, and their two squabbling seat mates into the welter of red coat, striped skirt, and diapers opposite them. As Kyra groped, completely breathless, for something to think, let alone say, he went on. "Though the Inquisition may have been watching the house. That's certainly the excuse I made to Father when I told him I was leaving Angelshand for two years to be our house's factor to the Sykerst fur traders at Lastower."

Kyra stared at him. "Lastower . . . Two *years*?"

Lastower. A day's ride from the Citadel . . .

"What did he say?"

"Nothing I'll repeat in front of those little girls across from us," he replied cheerfully. " 'Traitor' was the mildest. 'Ingrate,' 'dilettante' . . . I'm inclined to think you were right."

"About what?"

"About him being the one who put my responsibilities into my head when he became eligible for Mayor. A post he'll have to quit now. And finding me a wife to keep me from running off to sea again. I sent that poor Gyvinna woman a hundred crowns, just on the strength of her calling down the Inquisition and giving me a reason to get out of Angelshand."

Kyra was shocked. "You're the heir! You can't just walk out!"

"You did."

"That was different!"

His blue eyes twinkled as he took her hand. "Not as different as you think."

She recalled the look on his face during the fight in the garden, the wild brightness of his eyes in the field of Hythe Farm. Remembered his silence as he faced his duty to family in Angelshand, a stocky man in a red suit with nothing to say.

"Spens," she said, her eyes glinting, "I do believe you're a fraud."

"I do believe you're right."

The shadow of the inn-yard gate darkened them for a moment, then vanished in the warm dappled light of the country sun.

"Are you a witch?"

Kyra raised her head a little from Spenson's good shoulder to look past his back at the small, pinch-faced girl tugging her sleeve.

"Luce . . ." the girl's mother hissed reprovingly.

The child refused to be deterred. "Are you going to turn him into a toad 'cause he kissed you?"

Spens looked around at the girl with a grin; Kyra said, "Good heavens, what good would that do me? I'm trying to come up with spells to make him handsomer than he is." She drew back her head and looked into his smiling eyes. "Not that it would be necessary," she added, and frowned. "Two years? You've obviously never visited Lastower. It's the most deadly place imaginable."

"Well," Spenson said, "with luck I'll get out to the Citadel now and then. And there are worse fates."

"Such as?"

"Well," he said quietly, "not seeing you again was

one of them. And after a day's drive thinking of you—and of Father and my duties—the still worse fate, as I said, was waiting for me in the courtyard of my house."

"For heaven's sake, what?" Kyra asked.

Spens shuddered and drew her more closely into the circle of his arm, as if for protection. "Lady Earthwygg and her daughter Esmin," he said. "So you see, there was nothing for it but flight."

"Spenson," Kyra sighed in exasperation, dropping her head once more to the broad tweed shoulder, "one of these days I really *will* turn you into a toad."

The little girl asked, with glowing eyes, "Will you teach me how?"

About the Author

At various times in her life Barbara Hambly has been a high school teacher, a model, a waitress, a technical editor, a professional graduate student, an all-night clerk at a liquor store, and a karate instructor. Born in San Diego, she grew up in southern California, with the exception of one high-school semester spent in New South Wales, Australia. Her interest in fantasy began with reading *The Wizard of Oz* at an early age, and it has continued ever since.

She attended the University of California, Riverside, specializing in medieval history. In connection with this, she spent a year at the University of Bordeaux in the south of France and worked as a teaching and research assistant at UC Riverside, eventually earning a master's degree in that subject. At the university she also became involved in karate, making black belt in 1978 and competing in several national-level tournaments. She now lives in Los Angeles.